KITTY HAWK AND THE MYSTERY OF THE MASTERPIECES

Book Five of the Kitty Hawk Flying Detective Agency Series

Iain Reading

Copyright © 2015 Iain Reading

All rights reserved.

ISBN-10: 150848886X
ISBN-13: 978-1508488866

This book is dedicated to the victims of MH17
and Kristiana Coignard.

Other books by this author:

Kitty Hawk and the Curse of the Yukon Gold
Kitty Hawk and the Hunt for Hemingway's Ghost
Kitty Hawk and the Icelandic Intrigue
Kitty Hawk and the Tragedy of the RMS Titanic
Kitty Hawk and the Mystery of the Masterpieces
The Guild of the Wizards of Waterfire
The Dragon of the Month Club
The Hemingway Complex (non-fiction)

www.kittyhawkworld.com
www.wizardsofwaterfire.com
www.dragonofthemonthclub.com
www.iainreading.com
www.secretworldonline.com

TABLE OF CONTENTS

Prologue — 1
There Has To Be A Rationale Explanation...

Chapter Zero — 3
All Roads Lead To Rome

Chapter One — 4
The Return Of Charlie

Chapter Two — 7
A Wheelbarrow Full Of Walnuts

Chapter Three — 13
The View Of The Sea At Scheveningen

Chapter Four — 21
I'm Far More Curious About The Other Two

Chapter Five — 25
It Just Feels Right

Chapter Six — 28
Well, That Kind Of Sucked

Chapter Seven — 31
We'd Like To Hire You

Chapter Eight — 35
The Creepiest Sound I Have Ever Heard

Chapter Nine — 39
FFAGFFEE

Chapter Ten — 42
That Must Be The Police

Chapter Eleven — 45
I Think You Just Gave It To The Bad Guys

Chapter Twelve — 49
I Don't Know If I Can Actually Solve This

Chapter Thirteen — 53
Good Old Richard

Chapter Fourteen — 56
The Unbreakable Kind

Chapter Fifteen — 61
Better Than A Computer

Chapter Sixteen — 65
Hello Kitty

Chapter Seventeen — 71
So What Do We Do Now?

Chapter Eighteen — 74
Unbelievably, Extraordinarily, Ridiculously Mind-Bogglingly Difficult

Chapter Nineteen — 80
No More Math For Me For At Least A Week

Chapter Twenty — 84
Urgent We Meet

Chapter Twenty-One — 87
The More Eyes, The Better

Chapter Twenty-Two — 91
That Guy

Chapter Twenty-Three Do You Really Not Know Me By Now?	94
Chapter Twenty-Four I Told You It Was A Crazy Thing To Do	97
Chapter Twenty-Five We're In A Bit Of A Situation Here	101
Chapter Twenty-Six Staring Me Right In The Face The Whole Time	105
Chapter Twenty-Seven Sixteen Point Six Six Two Megahertz	108
Chapter Twenty-Eight Urgent We Meet	112
Chapter Twenty-Nine I Know It's A Long Shot, But...	116
Chapter Thirty The Cathedral Of Fight?!?	120
Chapter Thirty-One Exciting Modern Miracles	124
Chapter Thirty-Two Die Reichsparteitagsgeländetennisspielmauer	127
Chapter Thirty-Three Why Don't We Take The Train?	132
Chapter Thirty-Four Are You Sure You Want To Do This?	135
Chapter Thirty-Five I'll Bet Your Jaw Hits The Floor	139
Chapter Thirty-Six Da Da Da Duh, Da Da Da Duh	144
Chapter Thirty-Seven And While We're On The Topic...	148
Chapter Thirty-Eight There's A Fine Line...	151
Chapter Thirty-Nine There's More After The Wedding?!?	155
Chapter Forty What Do You Think The Odds Are?	158
Chapter Forty-One Like The Plot Of A Bad Movie	161
Chapter Forty-Two Wait A Minute... Do You Smell That?	164
Chapter Forty-Three Were All These Things Connected Somehow?	168
Chapter Forty-Four The Real Surprise Was Yet To Come	171
Chapter Forty-Five That's Good Enough For Me	175
Chapter Forty-Six What Do You Mean By 'Our People'?	178
Chapter Forty-Seven Maybe Even Thousands	181
Chapter Forty-Eight Right Into The Heart Of Darkness	185

Chapter Forty-Nine — 190
Where In The World Does He Think He's Going?

Chapter Fifty — 193
Startling And Dizzying Beauty

Chapter Fifty-One — 196
Why Don't You Put The Gun Away?

Chapter Fifty-Two — 199
Into Thin Air

Chapter Fifty-Three — 203
Not All Puzzles Have Solutions

Chapter Fifty-Four — 208
All Part Of The Adventure

Epilogue — 212
Three Coins In A Fountain

Some Further Reading (Spoiler Alert) — 215
Sample Chapter from The Dragon of the Month Club — 223
A Message from the Author — 212

Kitty Hawk and the Mystery of the Masterpieces

PROLOGUE

There Has To Be A Rationale Explanation...

It was the creepiest thing I've ever heard in my entire life.

With my skin crawling with goose bumps, I listened as the psychopathic tinkling song of a child's music box quickly faded into the high-pitch hiss of static and was quickly replaced by a sound that brought new meaning to the phrase of having one's blood run cold. My knees literally went weak at just the sound of it, threatening to collapse under me like watery rubber.

Oh my God, oh my God, oh my God, I thought to myself over and over again as my mind raced to find some explanation for the completely bizarre and otherworldly sounds that I was hearing. *There has to be a rational explanation for this. This is real life, not a horror movie. There has to be something that somehow explains this!*

These were all reasonable assumptions, of course, but what I was hearing was so completely fantastical that it seemed to defy all attempts at finding a sensible or logical explanation.

I closed my eyes for an instant as the room began to swim dizzily out of focus around me. My heart was beating so fast that my brain was simply overwhelmed by sensory input and it took me a second or two to recover from the wave of sudden lightheaded vertigo that had washed over me.

This can't be happening, I told myself. Of course it *was* happening, but my brain simply refused to accept that it was real and the resulting disorientation made me feel like my entire world had suddenly been turned upside down, leaving me confused and struggling to find solid ground.

But I was determined to find my feet again.

Just breathe, I told myself as I took a very deep breath, which instantly began to make me feel a little bit more in control. I slowly exhaled and opened my eyes again, repeating this thought over and over like a mantra until I finally began to get a hold of myself.

Already feeling much better, I forced myself to take another breath and concentrate on exactly what it was that I was hearing. It was a voice–a woman's voice that was supposed to sound human but there was actually nothing human about it. The voice was also speaking English, but what it was saying made absolutely no sense whatsoever and the effect of it was fiendishly unnerving.

There has to be a rational explanation for this, I told myself again as I glanced over at the others and forced myself to stand my ground. Of course, in the end there *was* a completely rational explanation for all of it. But little did I know how far I would have to go to try and find it or how many answers would still be left unsolved once I did.

CHAPTER ZERO
All Roads Lead To Rome

From: Kitty Hawk <kittyhawk@kittyhawkworld.com>
To: Charlie Lewis <chlewis@alaska.net>
Subject: All Roads Lead To Rome

Dear Charlie,

I can't believe it!!! You're coming to Rome!!

You are absolutely right. We have to meet up!

I am leaving Ireland tomorrow morning and slowly making my way sightseeing across Europe. But as you know, all roads lead to Rome. I will see you there in a few weeks.

It seems like forever since we saw each other. I can't wait to see you.

Talk to you soon.

k.

CHAPTER ONE
The Return Of Charlie

Despite the fact that I'd only just arrived, I'd already found my favorite spot in the city of Rome. After flying in a few days earlier in my trusty De Havilland Beaver seaplane, I left it tied up at a small marina in a tiny fishing village on the coast and traveled inland to the capital city of the ancient Roman Empire.

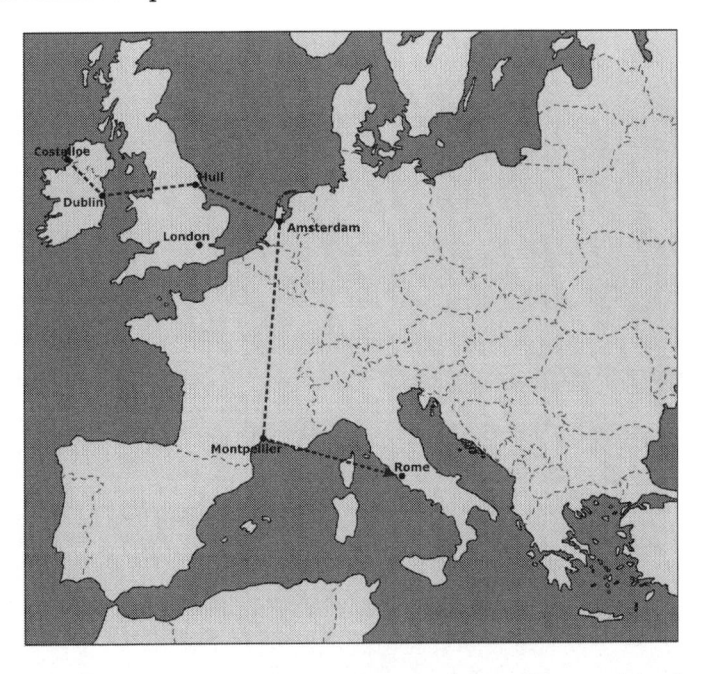

After quickly settling into the small apartment I'd rented in the heart of the city, I didn't waste any time putting some walking shoes on and heading out to explore. There were so many things to do and see, after all, and I didn't want to waste a single second.

The first afternoon was a complete blur, I have to admit. I must have walked about ten miles through the narrow and busy streets of the city, past beautiful churches and ancient ruins, dramatic statues and soaring fountains. I really wanted to see everything, and by the end of the day I think I'd come pretty close, but in truth I'd seen nothing. In my rush to experience the entire city in one go, I'd only begun to scratch at the surface of the immense wonders of what the frenetic and serene city had to offer.

I didn't mind at all that I'd zipped through everything so fast and nearly broken my feet on just that very first day. I had two more weeks ahead of me to go back and revisit everything at a more realistic pace, after all, and my hurried grand tour after I'd first arrived was more of an orientation tour than anything else.

But despite being overwhelmed with sights and sensations on that first day, I'd already found my favorite spot. I knew it from the first second I saw it. The *Circus Maximus*.

I know what you're thinking. Why not something famous like the Trevi Fountain or St Peter's basilica? Why not the Pantheon or the Roman Forum?

Those places are all amazing, don't get me wrong. But just down the street from the famous façade of the Colosseum, nestled between two of the seven ancient hills of Rome, there stands a wide open space more than two thousand feet long–an elliptical dip in the ground covered with grass that looks suspiciously man-made. And there's good reason for it to look that way since it *was* built by the hands of men (and women too, presumably). It is the *Circo Massimo*, the ancient Roman stadium where a hundred and fifty thousand spectators had once witnessed the spectacle of the chariot races.

Standing along the edges of the stadium, it's difficult to imagine the splendor of the ancient stadium that had once stood there. Unfortunately, there's not much left of it except a long depression in the ground surrounded by a few ruins here and there. But even those simple things are enough to allow you to close your eyes and picture the stands full of people, the cheers deafening as the thundering horses and clanking chariots pursued each other around the long oval track in search of glory and victory.

That same track is used nowadays by early-morning joggers or people out for a leisurely walk on a summer evening. But with the faint afterimage of such a colossal structure all around them, one cannot escape the quiet and unassuming history of the place. All in all, a perfect place to call my favorite spot, not to mention the perfect place for me to meet with Charlie for the first time in Rome.

Charlie was in town for a convention on the development of the fishing industry in third world countries hosted by the World Food Program and the UN Food and Agriculture Organization. The latter of these two organizations had their headquarters just kitty corner from the *Circus Maximus* so it was a convenient place for him and me to meet to go out for dinner together.

"I can't believe it," I heard a reassuringly familiar voice say from behind me as I sat on the grass at the edge of the *Circus* and watched the joggers circling around. "Kitty Hawk."

I turned to look and saw a face that I hadn't seen since the last time I'd visited Alaska many months before.

"Charlie!" I cried, jumping to my feet and running along the top of the edge to wrap my arms around him in a friendly hug. "It's so great to see you!"

Charlie put his strong arms around me and held me close for a few moments while I closed my eyes and remembered all the golden memories we'd shared together with his brothers on the Chilkoot Trail and up in Canada's Yukon. He smelled so different than before. The Charlie in my memories always smelled like an intoxicating combination of campfire smoke, sweat and aftershave, with perhaps a hint of fish thrown in. But there in Rome, far away from the campfires and fishing trawlers of Alaska, only the smell of his aftershave remained.

"How are you, darlin'?" Charlie asked, his infectious grin exactly as I remembered it except for a new growth of long, scruffy facial hair that now covered his chiseled jaw.

"What's this?" I asked, grating the backs of my fingers across his unruly stubble. "Are ya trying to grow a beard?"

"You don't like it?" he asked, stroking his beard thoughtfully.

"A bit of stubble is good," I replied, teasing. "But this is... like you've been living in the back woods for the last six months."

"How do you know I wasn't?" Charlie asked, still grinning.

"Did they install some WiFi for the bears out on Admiralty Island since the last time I was there?" I replied, laughing. "Because you've been e-mailing me quite regularly since I left Canada. That'd be pretty hard to do out in the back country, don't ya think?"

Charlie tilted his head back and laughed. An amazing and beautiful laugh that I hadn't heard in so long that it made my heart ache to be sitting by a campfire with him and his brothers, back by the shores of Lake Tagish under a sky filled with the ghostly green fire of the aurora borealis.

"It's so good to see you, Kitty," Charlie said, his voice quiet and sincere.

"It's good to see you too, darlin'," I replied, smiling and staring up into his hazel-green eyes. "It's been a long time."

CHAPTER TWO
A Wheelbarrow Full Of Walnuts

A few hours later, Charlie and I were wandering together through the tapered and busy backstreets of Rome after a wonderfully mouth-watering display of food. One thing I had quickly learned upon my arrival in Italy was that the food was absolutely amazing. There were simply no words to describe the sublimely robust and genuine flavors and textures of every dish I'd tried thus far. Back in Canada I'd thought I'd known what Italian food was, but once I got to Rome, I quickly learned that I simply had no idea how good food could be.

"The Italian food is *sooo* good here," I said blissfully, my mouth half full of spaghetti carbonara.

I immediately felt stupid for making such a ridiculous observation from the moment the words left my mouth. I looked up and expected Charlie to laugh at me, but he simply smiled warmly and nodded understandingly.

"Here in Italy, you mean," he said, still nodding as he reached over to grab a narrow wedge of deliciously crispy bread from the basket on the table. "I couldn't agree more."

I couldn't help but smile. Charlie had a way of always understanding.

"Let me try some of your ravioli," I said, reaching over to steal some food off his plate. I prepared myself to evade him swatting at me with his fork to try and stop me like my mother would have done, but instead he slid his plate forward and let me take whatever I wanted.

Sinking my teeth into one of the tiny packets of beef and pasta was a divine experience. The taste of it was meaty and gritty and absolutely heavenly.

"That may be the best ravioli I've ever had," I observed reverentially as I reached over to grab another stolen sample from Charlie's plate.

"I have to agree," Charlie said. "Although I'm not sure the Italians consider pasta to be a main course like we do in North America. I get a feeling it's meant to be more like a starter."

I nodded in reply as I continued chewing and savoring every bite.

After we finished, Charlie insisted on paying the bill, despite my protestations, and we pushed back our chairs from the table of the outdoor restaurant on one of Rome's many delightful piazzas and strolled across the open space, silently soaking up the charm and atmosphere.

"How about some ice cream for dessert?" Charlie asked.

"Like McDonald's?" I said, grinning as I spotted the familiar golden arches in one of the old buildings across the open square. "Count me in!"

"Sounds good," Charlie replied and then pointed to a colorfully painted pushcart at the edge of the square selling ice cream. "Or maybe some Italian ice cream?"

I blushed in embarrassment for a moment, feeling stupid for suggesting McDonald's, but as I glanced over at Charlie, I could tell from the look on his face that he would actually be interested in either option.

"You choose," I said.

Charlie smiled. "It's a tough call," he said, taking a moment to decide before finally settling on the Italian ice cream from the man with the pushcart. "But you know what they say: *When in Rome...*"

"Sounds perfect," I replied, laughing. "Although it looks to me like the Romans are going to McDonald's and only tourists are going to the guy with the ice-cream cart."

Charlie laughed too and we strolled leisurely over to get some authentic Italian dessert.

"What flavor for the beautiful lady?" the mustachioed man in a white apron behind the pushcart asked me when it was our turn to order.

"Ummmmm," I replied, scanning the list of flavors. "Pistachio."

"Very good, one pistakio," the man replied, pronouncing the word correctly with a hard 'ch' sound. "And for the handsome gentleman?"

"Chocolate," Charlie replied, reaching for his wallet to pay.

"No no," I insisted. "This time I pay."

Charlie nodded in acquiescence and held the ice cream while I unzipped the inner pocket of my jacket and pulled out a few Euros to pay the man.

"I love this pistachio ice cream," I said after paying, and Charlie and I continued our stroll through the crowded square toward a beautiful sparkling fountain. "Sorry, I mean pistakio. I never heard of such a flavor before but I've been getting it constantly since I got here, it's so good."

"The Italians sure know about ice cream," Charlie said, nodding. "This chocolate is out of this world as well. You wanna try?"

Charlie held out his ice-cream cup for me to steal a sample of it with my tiny plastic spoon.

"They sure do know about food and ice cream," I agreed as I relished the deep chocolate flavor swirling down my throat. "Although the organization of the train system could use a bit of work."

Charlie stopped in his tracks and looked at me with an amused smile. "You think so too, huh?" he asked. "Because I have to tell you, I was in Switzerland for a couple of days before I came here and the difference was like night and day. In Zürich it was neat and clean and organized and everything worked. Then I hop on a flight to Rome and we land at the airport and get off the plane onto a bus to take us to the terminal. Everyone gets on the bus, and the driver asks the flight attendants, '*Is that everyone from the plane?*'–'*Yes it is.*'–'*Are you sure?*'–'*Yes, I'm* sure.'–'*Okay, see you later.*' Off the bus drives and we're almost at the terminal when someone calls on the radio saying '*You forgot someone on the plane.*' So we drive all the way back to pick them up then back to the terminal again. And then when we get inside, I go to the bathroom to wash my hands and there's no soap and the towel roll dispenser looks like it hasn't been changed in a month with the linen hanging limp and spotted with dirt from the machine. And when I pull down on it to get a clean towel and the whole thing falls off the wall."

Charlie was really on a roll now, ranting about his first impressions of Italy.

"So I just wiped my hands on my pants," Charlie continued, "then went to the train station to get a ticket into the city. I got a ticket then stuck it in the machine to stamp and validate it, and the machine wouldn't let go of it, no matter how hard I pulled to get it back. I asked the train conductor standing nearby for some help, in case maybe I was doing something wrong. He shook his head and said, '*Don't worry, I wasn't going to check anyone's tickets anyway,*' then waved me onto the train."

I was laughing so hard by this point that I couldn't eat any more ice cream. All I could do was stand and laugh at Charlie's crazy story.

"So then I got to my hotel," Charlie said, "and tried to take a shower, but the drain in the shower was clogged and I could only shower for fifteen seconds or so before the water started spilling onto the floor. So I went to the reception desk to ask the man in the Armani suit if they could please fix it. They said no problem, they would do it right away. The next day I tried to have a shower again, but again the same problem, only fifteen seconds to quickly get everything clean. I went to the desk again to tell them about it, and again they said they would definitely fix it. When I came back later at the end of the day, I stopped in again and asked the guy in the Armani suit whether they'd fixed it yet or not. '*Oh yes yes, it's fixed now,*' he assured me, but then, the next day I went to have a shower and still the drain wasn't working. So I packed my bags, put them safely up high ground on the bed and then took a nice long, leisurely shower. By the time I was done, there was an inch of water on the floor of the entire room and it was even running down the corridor outside and I had to splash through it on my way out to check into a different hotel."

"You're making this up," I replied, still laughing uproariously. "This can't be true."

"Every word is true, I swear it," Charlie said, grinning as he stood with his arms outstretched in a gesture of greeting. "Welcome to Italy!"

Charlie was smiling and enjoying making me laugh when his eyes narrowed suddenly and a look of concern flashed across his face as he stared past me to the corner of the square where some kind of commotion was arising.

I quickly turned my head toward the sound of the disturbance and saw a young woman in a bright red gypsy shirt dashing through the crowd, weaving and ducking as people tried to grab onto her. Off to the left in the opposite direction from which she was running, a man in a cream-colored sports coat was waving his arms and shouting after the girl.

"My wallet!" he shouted. "Grab her! She stole my wallet!"

My eyes flicked back to the girl in the red shirt who was now securely in the tight grip of some quick-thinking people in the crowd.

"Give it back!" one of the men holding her by the arm cried out.

"Who? Me?!? I don't have any wallet," the young woman replied, pulling her shirt up over her head to expose her naked chest underneath. "See? No wallet."

All eyes in the square, including mine, stared fixated at the naked young woman, our mouths open in astonishment at the crazy scene unfolding so quickly before us.

"Come on, Kitty," Charlie said, his voice serious. "Forget about her. That one there has the wallet."

I spun around and saw Charlie staring intently across toward the completely opposite side of the crowd where a young girl in black had just ducked into a side street. I could see by the keen look in Charlie's eyes that he hadn't been fooled for one second by the young woman's revealing antics and had seen through the confusion of the moment that she'd surreptitiously handed the stolen wallet to her young cohort waiting in the crowd.

"Oh my God, that's sneaky," I muttered under my breath as I sprinted across the square after Charlie who was already disappearing around the corner and up the side street in hot pursuit.

Rounding the corner I could see Charlie up ahead, threading his way gracefully through the throng of people, close on the heels of the young girl in black. I could hardly believe how fast and agile Charlie was for someone as tall as he was. With the young girl zigzagging fast through the swarms of people in front of her, Charlie was still closing the distance between them quite quickly. I myself, on the other hand, was galumphing along like a clumsy Clydesdale compared to the two of them and with every passing second they drew further and further ahead of me.

Suddenly the young girl zipped off to the right and ducked into a narrow alleyway. But Charlie was only an instant behind her and spun around the corner, bracing against the wall as he went so he could reach out with one hand and grab the back of the girl's shirt.

The last thing I saw was the girl just barely slipping out of Charlie's grasp as the two of them disappeared around the corner. I wasn't sure whether he'd got her or not and would have to wait a few more seconds before I could catch up and find out the answer.

Grabbing the corner of the brick wall like Charlie had done, I spun myself into the alleyway and nearly had a heart attack when I was suddenly confronted with a chaotic pile of arms and legs and walnuts standing directly in my path.

I tried to stop myself, but it was too late. Before I knew it, I was tumbling through the air after having tripped over someone's outstretched leg, falling face first into Charlie who was lying on the ground and clutching the back of the young girl's shirt. I tried to twist in midair and avoid colliding full-on into Charlie, but I couldn't make it. The two of us smashed together, shoulder to shoulder, with enough force to drive the air from his lungs and jolt his grip loose enough that the young girl was able to wiggle free.

"Dammit!" Charlie swore, twisting in vain to untangle himself as the girl bolted the rest of the way down the alley and disappeared around another corner.

"Sorry, Charlie," I said, pulling my legs free and standing up to dust myself off a bit before helping him to his feet.

"Don't worry," he replied, standing up straight and turning to help untangle the two innocent bystanders who'd been bowled over by the entire incident.

"Oh yes, thank you, thank you," the tall, thin and nervous-looking man said as Charlie helped him to his feet. He brushed the dirt out of his dark, unruly hair and beard before adjusting his eyeglasses and turning his attention to tidying his dusty vest and sweater.

"Help me off the ground, you *ingrato*," the woman on the ground yelled at the tall, thin man.

"Oh yes, sorry sorry," the thin man cried in realization as he tried to reach down and help her up. But he was too late. Charlie was already helping her to her feet.

"I'm terribly sorry, ma'am," Charlie said as the timid-looking woman with dark hair regained her balance and also began to brush herself off.

"Don't worry, it's not your fault," the woman replied with a sweet and flirtatious smile as she gazed into Charlie's eyes for a moment before turning to smack her partner on the arm. "It's his fault. Him and his stupid walnuts!"

The woman had a point. There were a *lot* of walnuts strewn all across the alleyway, apparently from an overturned wheelbarrow but now with many of them squashed and rolling underfoot.

"I'm sorry about your walnuts too," Charlie continued, setting the wheelbarrow upright again and bending down to start gathering the nuts together. The woman and I kneeled down to help Charlie too, pushing the spilled piles of walnuts over toward him so he could put them back where they belonged.

"This sweater is ruined," the thin man observed, standing off to the side as he brushed off the various walnut pieces and dirt stains from his clothes.

"Why don't you help us with your stupid walnuts?" the woman hollered impatiently at the tall man.

"Oh yes, sorry sorry," the man replied as he scurried over and knelt down to help the rest of us.

"Again, I am so sorry about this," Charlie said as the last of the still-intact nuts were loaded into the wheelbarrow, leaving a trail of walnut debris strewn across the alley. "About your walnuts and your sweater."

"Oh, don't worry, please," the thin man replied with a bright smile. "A quick shower and I'll be good as new."

"While you're in the shower, why don't you shave off that beard as well?" the woman commented dryly, chuckling to herself as she gave me a grin. "You'll never find a wife with all that hair on your face!"

I glanced over at Charlie and gave him my best *I told you so* grin.

"What did I tell you, Charlie?" I said under my breath.

Charlie gave me an amused smile and then apologized to the man and woman one last time for disrupting whatever it was they were doing with such a huge wheelbarrow of walnuts.

"Again, I am terribly sorry about all of this," Charlie explained. "I was trying to catch this young girl who had just pickpocketed a tourist back on the *piazza* and was making off with their wallet."

The dark-haired woman laughed cynically. "Typical," she muttered. "It's getting as bad here as down in *Napoli*."

"*Napoli?*" I asked.

"You know, Naples," the woman replied, smiling at me affectionately with her warm brown eyes. "In Naples they would have picked your pocket before you even stepped off the train."

The woman then turned to say something in Italian to the thin man, scolding him for something. I smiled and chuckled as I watched them beak back and forth at each other like a comedy duo.

"You must forgive me," the thin man said as he stepped up and reached out to shake Charlie's hand. "As my sister reminds me, I've been terribly rude and failed to introduce myself. My name is Matteo and this is my sister Vega."

CHAPTER THREE
The View Of The Sea At Scheveningen

"You're bleeding," Vega said, nodding toward Charlie's leg. I turned and looked down at his knee where the pants were ripped and torn and stained dark red.

"Oh my God, Charlie!" I gasped, kneeling down to see how bad the damage was.

"Don't worry," Charlie replied, pulling his pants up so I could see through the hole to the ragged and bleeding skin underneath. "It's a bit scratched up but nothing serious."

"Nonsense!" Vega cried as she also leaned over to take a closer look. "Our house is just down the street. We have to clean that up and put a bandage on it before it gets infected."

Charlie opened his mouth to protest but quickly closed it again when he realized that Vega wasn't going to take no for an answer. She grasped him by the elbow and rushed him up the narrow side street before Matteo and I knew what was happening.

"Clean up the rest of your walnuts and meet us at home!" Vega called back over her shoulder as she and a slightly confused-looking Charlie rounded a corner and disappeared from sight.

"*Mamma mia,*" Matteo said sadly as he glanced over at me and slowly lifted his wheelbarrow to begin pushing it down the street.

"What are all these walnuts for anyway?" I asked.

"*Nocino,*" Matteo replied, his face brightening.

"*Nocino?*" I asked, confused.

"It's a kind of walnut liqueur," Matteo replied proudly. "I make it myself at home from an old family recipe."

As we walked together with his wheelbarrow, Matteo reached into the pocket of his vest and produced a small silver flask. He unscrewed the top and held it toward me so I could smell it.

The aroma of the liqueur was amazing. Sweet and nutty and earthy, it filled your nostrils and made you think of picture-perfect Italian countryside and terracotta tiled houses.

"That smells amazing," I said. "Do you really make it yourself?"

Matteo nodded as he set down his wheelbarrow in front of a set of wooden doors and put away the flask. Pushing open the doors, he continued inside with the walnuts through a narrow tunnel leading into an open courtyard before stopping again in front of a pastel red door at the far end.

"This is us here," Matteo said, setting the wheelbarrow off to one side and opening the red door to usher me inside. "This is our house."

Behind the door, a long flight of stairs with painted wooden railings led to the upper floors. I could hear Vega's voice echoing off the walls from somewhere high above us as I followed Matteo up the stairs. I strained my ears to hear what she was saying, but I couldn't quite make it out.

"Stop being... big baby... such a tough guy..." I heard reverberating throughout the stairwell. "... get those pants off!"

"What in the world is she doing up there?" Matteo asked, chuckling to himself.

"I have no idea," I replied, laughing, "but it sounds like Charlie has his hands full."

Matteo and I continued up the stairs to the top floor where a door stood ajar leading into a beautiful and spacious high-ceilinged apartment beyond. I stepped inside while Matteo closed the door behind us.

"Would you like something to drink?" Matteo offered with a wink. "Some of my homemade *nocino*, perhaps?"

"No, thank you," I replied politely as I ventured further into the open living room area of the apartment, an almost cavernous space underneath a series of enormous wooden roof beams running at regular intervals across the ceiling. Along the far wall, a series of tall shuttered windows opened out to overlook the narrow street below where we'd just been walking. At the left there was a cozy little sitting area with several chairs and a pair of sofas arranged around an unused fireplace where several oil paintings were on prominent display. Off to the right behind that, the opposite wall was covered almost entirely with antique bookshelves of various sizes and vintages, each of them filled to absolute capacity with a haphazard collection of books.

"Someone likes to read," I observed with a wry smile as Matteo continued into a half-open kitchen further beyond.

"Oh yes, my father was an avid reader, no doubt," Matteo called back over his shoulder. "This is his house, actually. But unfortunately he just recently passed away quite unexpectedly."

"I am so sorry," I said, feeling bad for having said anything.

Matteo gave me a smile and dismissed my worries with a wave of his hand. "Oh, don't worry, please," Matteo replied. "We all have our time and this was his. He'd lived a long and good life, but since he died, Vega and I have moved back into our old bedrooms until we can figure out what to do with the house."

"It's really a beautiful home," I said, gazing around the room as the late evening summer sunlight poured through the windows beyond and filled the room with life.

"Oh yes, and that's exactly the problem," Matteo agreed, rubbing his fingers together like he was counting money. "A place like this? In this part of the city? *Caspita!* No one can afford to buy it! And since our mother passed away when we were both still children, Vega and I are living here and sharing the cost of the upkeep until we can sell it."

"I'm sorry to hear that," I replied, feeling bad that I seemed to only be able to bring up sensitive topics of conversation.

"No, no, don't worry," Matteo replied with another wave of his hand. "Now, are you sure I can't get you anything? Coffee? Tea? Pellegrino?"

"Some espresso would be nice," I replied.

"What other coffee is there?" Matteo said with a grin as he scurried off to the kitchen. "In the meantime, please have a look around and make yourself at home."

With Matteo off puttering around in the kitchen, I took his advice and wandered around the room a little bit, casually perusing the titles of some of the many stacks of books on the bookshelf. Most of them were in Italian and looked like antique books by writers I'd never heard of. But one title I easily recognized, even though it was in Italian—*Il Codice da Vinci*. It made me smile to find *The Da Vinci Code* on a shelf with so many other serious-looking books.

As I made my way from the bookshelves to look out the windows, I could hear Vega putting the final touches on Charlie's medical treatment.

"You see?" I heard her voice say from a room somewhere down the long hallway. "That wasn't so bad, was it, Mr. Tough Guy?"

Charlie mumbled something in return that I couldn't make out, and I almost felt sorry for him as I chuckled to myself and strolled past the windows toward the fireplace to take a closer look at the paintings hanging there.

I was interested in one painting in particular that had caught my eye because it was so different from the others. It stood out because instead of using bright and vibrant colors like in the other paintings hanging nearby, this particular one used only dingy grays and browns and looked quite ordinary and simple by comparison.

The painting showed a view from the sand dunes out toward a turbulent scene of high winds and rough seas. Along the shoreline, a scattered group of bystanders watched as a sailing ship was pulled ashore through a violent surf of crashing waves.

I stopped to take a closer look at the boiling whitecaps of the lines of waves pounding the beach. It was interesting to see how much paint the artist had used. Instead of simply painting the scene onto a two-dimensional surface, the artist had piled on astonishingly thick layers of paint, absolute globs of it with every successive brush stroke, sculpting the paint into the form of angry waves and giving the waves a three-dimensional effect that seemed to leap right out of the canvas.

The use of paint in this way fascinated me. Of course, I was nothing more than a complete and total amateur when it came to paintings and art, but I'd taken a stronger interest in it since my adventures a couple of weeks earlier in England and Ireland involving a painting of the *Titanic*. On my way to Rome to meet up with Charlie, I'd made my way across

Europe and visited the great art galleries of Paris and Amsterdam, seeing as much art as I could and learning as much as possible about how it was made and the history behind it.

This use of paint to create a three-dimensional effect was something that I'd seen before. At the Van Gogh Museum in Amsterdam, I'd stood transfixed in front of a wall of paintings showing various fruit trees in bloom. One in particular kept me especially mesmerized–a painting of a tall peach tree with delicate pink-white blossoms carefully sculpted with tiny beads of oil paint on a background of blue sky. The effect was absolutely hypnotizing when viewed from a few steps' distance. The tree was brought completely alive as the blossoms intruded into the space in front of the canvas, crossing the barrier between the world of the painting itself and into the real world beyond.

One of the museum's docents had noticed me standing there, staring in awe at the painting, and came over to talk to me.

"It's remarkable, isn't it?" the stately-looking middle-aged blonde woman said to me with a smile. I glanced down to read her name tag. Petra, it read.

"Breathtaking," I replied in awe. "I've never seen anything like it before."

Petra nodded and stood silently beside me for a few moments, allowing me to enjoy the scene.

"We have these paintings arranged on this wall more or less how Vincent himself might have wanted them displayed," Petra said thoughtfully as she gestured with her hand to the five paintings on the wall in front of us. "In letters to his brother Theo, he would often talk of how he would like to see his paintings framed and arranged if they were ever put on exhibition. Perhaps this was a little presumptuous of him to say, but people often forget that Van Gogh was no mere painter. In fact, long before he ever thought of picking up a brush and trying to paint for himself, he had already worked for many years in his uncle's upscale art gallery in The Hague, learning firsthand the expertise required to most effectively display works of art."

"Really?" I asked, surprised to learn that Van Gogh had held a sort of 'normal job' before taking up painting. "He didn't always want to be an artist?"

"Oh no," Petra replied. "Like most people, he had absolutely no idea what he wanted to be in life, drifting along, living off the generosity of other people, working as an art seller for a while and then deciding that wasn't for him and that he actually wanted to join the Church and be a pastor like his father, but that didn't work out either, and he finally decided that his true calling in life was to be an artist."

"Well, at least he got that one right," I replied with a shrug of my shoulders.

Petra nodded. "When we look around now at this beautiful museum, it does seem like he got it right," she admitted. "But don't forget that during his own lifetime, Vincent barely sold a single painting, which is quite remarkable when you consider that his incredibly supportive brother actually worked as an art dealer. But at the time, no one wanted to buy his work."

"That's crazy," I said, looking around the room at the seemingly endless succession of masterpieces hanging on the walls. "These rooms are *full* of dozens of priceless paintings and you're telling me that in Vincent's time no one wanted to buy them?"

"Exactly!" Petra replied. "And that is precisely the reason *why* our museum here has so many of his works together in one place—because no one wanted to buy them. Only years later, long after Vincent's death, did his work finally get discovered and start to sell. It was selling so well, in fact, that at a certain point the Van Gogh family made a decision to stop selling off his work and tried to keep the remaining pieces within the family. That decision ultimately led to the creation of this entire museum you see around you here today because once the family realized they could no longer afford to pay the taxes on such a valuable collection of art, they made a special deal with the Dutch government to have the works put on display here in this permanent museum."

"Taxes?!?" I asked, surprised.

"Yes, of course," Petra replied. "The family was far from being rich, after all. And yet they owned hundreds of priceless works by the then-famous Vincent van Gogh. The inheritance taxes on such incredibly costly assets were beyond what the family could ever possibly afford."

I had to laugh at this. It seemed ridiculous yet it made perfect sense.

"Well, whatever the reason is, I'm just glad to be able to see so many of his paintings here in one place," I said.

"And that's exactly what Vincent would have wanted," Petra said graciously as she took a few steps back to let me continue making my way through the museum. "He saw himself as a kind of artistic champion for the common man, making art that everyday people could enjoy."

I thanked Petra for her time and continued on through the rest of the museum. But as I sat in the park behind the building later that day, I couldn't help but think back to what she'd said.

As I sat there on a park bench enjoying the sun and drinking a bottle of water, I watched as an endless stream of tourists lined up and made their way into the museum. There was also an equally incessant stream of people leaving the museum with special long, triangular boxes with rolled-up posters of Van Gogh's art inside. Vincent may not have enjoyed much success within his own short lifetime but a hundred years later his dream to have normal people enjoy his art had certainly become a reality.

"You look hypnotized by that painting, my dear," I heard Vega say from beside me, snapping my wandering thoughts back to the present. She and Charlie had apparently finished their medical treatment and were now joining me in the living room.

"And what's the prognosis?" Matteo asked as he breezed into the room with a silver tray containing various coffee-related supplies. "Will our patient survive?"

"I think I'll make it," Charlie replied.

"He wasn't a very good patient," Vega said as she made her way over to help Matteo put everything down on a low table in the middle of some sofas and chairs. "Too much Mr. Tough Guy and too proud to ask for help."

"I know what you mean," I replied with a giggle and Charlie rolled his eyes at me.

"Would you like some coffee as well, Charlie?" Vega asked. "Or tea?"

Charlie looked at his watch and glanced over at me.

"We should actually probably be going," he said. "We don't want to be an imposition."

"Don't talk nonsense!" Vega replied, turning her back on him. "You have time to stay for one cup of tea."

Charlie smiled and surrendered to the inevitable.

"Espresso is fine," Charlie replied as he and I walked over to find a place to sit.

"These paintings on the wall," I asked once everyone settled in with a tiny cup of espresso perched delicately in their hands. "Are they real?"

It occurred to me from looking around the enormous and stylishly decorated apartment that I was sitting in that Vega and Matteo's father clearly had a fair bit of money and that the painting on the wall might actually *be* an authentic Van Gogh instead of something that just sort of looked like one.

"Real?" Vega asked, confused.

"Those old things?" Matteo replied cheerfully with a shrug. "They're just some paintings that belonged to our father. I think a friend of his painted them."

"Oh," I replied, nodding my head.

"What did you *think* they were?" Vega asked.

I shrugged my shoulders and pointed up to the drably-colored seaside painting that I'd been staring at when everyone had come into the room.

"I was in Holland just last week," I replied. "And I thought this one looked an awful lot like something by Vincent van Gogh."

Everyone turned to look at the painting on the wall.

"Van Gogh?" Matteo said, furrowing his brow in bewilderment. "It's so dull and simple. Aren't Van Gogh's paintings all bright and colorful?"

I shook my head. "Not his earlier works," I replied. "I mean, I'm not an art expert, of course, but in the Van Gogh Museum in Amsterdam they have his paintings all arranged chronologically and you can see how his style progressed as he moved from one place to the next. And before he moved to Paris and saw the brightly colored works of the various Impressionist painters of the time, his paintings done in Holland are all very drab and colorless, just like this one."

"Is that so?" Matteo asked in surprised curiosity. "I had no idea."

"Sure," I replied, nodding as I pulled out my iPad Mini and shuffled over on the sofa until I was sitting next to Matteo. "Let me see if I can find some examples."

I flipped open the cover of my iPad and went to the website of the Van Gogh Museum in Amsterdam. They had a really great website where I found a list of online galleries with examples of Van Gogh's work arranged by time period:

The Netherlands, 1880-1885
Paris - 1886-1888
Arles - 1888-1889
Saint Rémy - 1889-1890
Auvers - 1890

I clicked on the link for the gallery of paintings from the Netherlands and began to flip through the various images. Matteo leaned forward and adjusted his round glasses so he could watch carefully as I moved from one dark dull gray-and-brown painting to the next.

"You see?" I said, looking up at him with a smile.

"Yes yes, I see," Matteo replied in fascination as he set down his coffee and took the iPad in his hands so he could continue to flip slowly through the gallery of images.

As Matteo continued to look through the paintings, I took a sip of espresso and glanced over at Charlie and Vega after a moment. I was surprised to see them suddenly staring across in Matteo's direction with mild expressions of concern.

"What is it?" I asked, spinning back toward Matteo who was staring down at the iPad in complete shock, his eyes wide and mouth hanging open. "What's wrong?!?"

Matteo looked up at me in shock and turned the iPad to face me. On the screen was the image of a dull gray painting of the seaside on a blustery and windy day. It was the exact same painting that was hanging on the wall on the other side of the room from us at that very moment.

"Read what it says," Matteo said breathlessly.

View of the Sea at Scheveningen, 1882
Vincent van Gogh (1853-1890)

Oil on Canvas, 34.5 X 51 cm
Van Gogh Museum, Amsterdam
(Vincent van Gogh Stichting)
F 4

Van Gogh painted this small view of the sea using thick gobs of color and a rough brushstroke. The raging, foaming sea, the dark, thundery sky, and the boat's flag whipping in the wind all give a good impression of stormy weather. Van Gogh painted this picture on the spot, at

Scheveningen, a beach resort near The Hague. He had to fight against the elements: the gusting wind and flying sand, which stuck to the wet paint. Most of this was later scraped off, but a few grains can still be found in some of the paint layers. Please note: this painting is no longer on display, having been stolen from the museum on 7 December 2002. For more information, see the press release on the theft.

"What in the world is it?!" Vega asked in growing concern as she saw the same stunned expression slowly come over my face as well.

I looked up at Matteo in utter disbelief after reading the final two sentences of the painting's online description.

"Stolen?!?" I exclaimed as Matteo and I simultaneously spun our heads around to stare across the room at the painting that was hanging on the wall of their father's apartment. "The painting was stolen?!?"

CHAPTER FOUR
I'm Far More Curious About The Other Two

Matteo was up and out of his seat in a flash, hurrying across the room with my iPad in his hands and me not half a step behind him as he made his way over to take a closer look at the painting on the wall. Charlie and Vega sprang out of their seats as well, still confused about what was going on but quickly reading the text that the two of us had just read as Matteo held the iPad up to compare the two paintings side-by-side.

"I don't believe it! They're the same!" Matteo said as his eyes flicked back and forth between the painting on the wall and the image on the screen in front of him. "It's the same painting! Look, there's even bits of sand in the dried paint on this one!"

Matteo handed the iPad off to Charlie and his sister as he leaned in close and adjusted his eyeglasses to examine the brushstrokes of the painting on the wall.

"What is this?!" Vega cried, holding the iPad in her hands and staring up at the wall with a look of complete mystification. "How is this possible?!?"

"Do you have a ruler?" Charlie asked suddenly.

"A ruler?" Vega replied uncertainly.

"To measure it!" I cried, immediately understanding what Charlie was thinking. "To measure the painting and see if it matches."

"Of course!" Matteo exclaimed as he dashed from the room and returned a few moments later with a clear plastic ruler.

"It's in centimeters," Charlie (an American) said in confusion as he stared down at the ruler.

"So are the measurements from the website," I (a Canadian) replied as I grabbed the ruler from him and quickly measured the rough dimensions of the painting.

"*Trentacinque da cinquanta*," Matteo said, his voice barely above a whisper as everyone crowded close around me and carefully watched over my shoulder. "Thirty-five by fifty."

"It matches," Vega said, her voice filled with stunned disbelief.

"But how can this be?" Matteo asked, his voice rising as he took a step back and looked over at his sister. "This must be some mistake. How can this painting be here in father's house? There must be some logical explanation for all this."

"Call Giulia," Vega said suddenly.

"*Si*! Yes, of course!" Matteo replied and dashed across the room to grab his telephone. "Brilliant idea!"

"Giulia?" I asked, not understanding.

"Our sister," Vega explained as Matteo dialed the phone and began a brisk conversation in Italian. "She's a television presenter and a few months ago she did a piece about art in the Vatican and she interviewed several art experts, including a couple who live in her building. I remember that one of them was Dutch so maybe she knows something about this."

I nodded in understanding as Matteo quickly wrapped up his conversation and came back to join us.

"She's on her way over," Matteo said, out of breath from his hurried and excited conversation. "She thinks her neighbor, Marieke, is also at home and will try to bring her as well. They don't live far so it won't be too long, I hope."

"Marieke is the art expert?" I asked.

"Yes, yes," Matteo replied as he paced uneasily in front of the windows.

At Vega's suggestion, the rest of us sat down again to finish our coffee and try to have some nice conversation to pass the time. Matteo continued to pace for a few minutes more, but eventually even he sat down with us and quietly sipped his coffee while he nervously tapped his foot on the floor.

It was difficult to sustain a conversation after the unexpected revelation that an authentic and possibly stolen Van Gogh was hanging on the wall not ten feet from us, but Vega stayed cool and did the best that she could. She asked what Charlie and I were doing in Rome and I tried to explain about my plan to fly around the world, but I couldn't concentrate properly and it didn't take long before our eyes strayed over to the strange dull gray painting hanging on the wall, wondering what its story was. Occasionally I would glance over at Charlie whose eyes seemed to tell me that perhaps he and I should be polite and take our leave.

Not a chance, darlin', my eyes told him in return. *We're not going anywhere. I wanna know what the deal is with this painting just as much as Vega and Matteo do.*

"They're here!" Matteo cried suddenly after ten or fifteen minutes of somewhat nervous and awkward conversation. Hearing a sound outside on the stairs, he sprang out of his chair and rushed over to the door to wait impatiently as the sound of approaching footsteps grew ever louder.

"*Ciao ciao*," I heard a woman's voice echo in greeting from somewhere near the top of the stairs.

Matteo said something back in Italian and then stepped out of the way to allow the newly arrived guests to step inside. The first one through the door was clearly Giulia, tall with long dark hair and eyes that were so dark in color that they were almost black. Following right behind was an older woman in her mid-forties with straight blonde hair and a kind of mousy look to her.

Following Vega's lead, Charlie and I stood up and made our way over to greet the new arrivals.

"We'll have to speak in English," Matteo said, introducing Charlie and me to his sister and her friend. "Our two new friends don't speak any Italian, I'm afraid."

"No problem there," the blonde woman replied as she smiled and held out her hand to me in greeting. "I'm Marieke. It's nice to meet you."

"*Hhhooda ahfond*," I replied, trying the only two words of Dutch that I'd learned during my time in Amsterdam. "I'm Kitty."

"*Goeie avond, mevrouw*," Marieke replied, smiling brightly in response to my painful attempt to speak her language.

"I'm Giulia," the tall, dark-haired woman spoke next as she also reached over to shake my hand.

"I'm Charlie," Charlie said, introducing himself to both of them as well. "Charlie Lewis."

"It's a pleasure," Giulia said, smiling warmly as she reached out to shake Charlie's hand, her cheeks blushing slightly and her eyelashes fluttering almost imperceptibly as she did so.

"Would anyone care for something to drink?" Vega asked politely while Matteo fidgeted nearby. He was clearly eager to get all the social pleasantries over with and find out about the painting. I could hardly blame him. I have to admit that I was barely able to contain my excitement at finding out what Marieke had to say.

"Nothing for me, thank you," Marieke replied. "I'm actually quite keen to have a look at this painting that Giulia's been telling me about."

"It's this one right here," Matteo said with obvious relief as he gestured over toward the first painting on the wall to the left side of the fireplace. "This is the one I called about."

I carefully watched the expression on Marieke's face as she turned and slowly approached the painting. Her initial reaction was one of complete shock and surprise, but as she moved closer to the painting itself, the expression gradually softened into a look of curious confusion.

"Interesting," Marieke said quietly, her brow furrowed in concentration as she carefully inspected the painting. She pulled a rectangular magnifying glass from her purse and leaned in close to painstakingly examine every surface feature and brushstroke.

The rest of us stood by in almost breathless silence while the seemingly endless minutes ticked by and Marieke slowly conducted her meticulous inspection.

"*Mijn God*," Marieke mumbled to herself as she slowly shook her head and took a step back from the painting.

"And?" Matteo asked anxiously. "What do you think? Is it authentic?"

Marieke nodded slightly. "One would have to take the painting out of its frame and inspect it further to be sure," she said. "There would be records back in Holland of what the back of the genuine painting looks like, and so on, but..."

"But...?" Matteo asked expectantly.

Marieke turned to face us and continued nodding her head slowly. "But it does appear to be authentic, yes," she admitted.

Matteo let out an explosive sigh of either relief or desperation, I wasn't sure which.

"But how is that possible?!" Matteo asked. "What would such a painting be doing here in our father's house? How did it get here?"

Marieke furrowed her brow and seemed to think this over for a moment.

"What did your father do for a living?" Marieke asked.

"He worked as an executive for Agip," Giulia replied. "The petroleum company."

Marieke's brow wrinkled further. "It is certainly a mystery," she said finally. "But that's for the police to solve, I suppose. You do realize that we'll have to notify the police, right? Not to mention the Van Gogh Foundation back in Amsterdam."

"Of course, of course!" Matteo replied emphatically. "We must call them straight away, in fact. This very minute, tonight!"

"I doubt they will send an inspector over so urgently tonight," Marieke chuckled. "But tomorrow, certainly."

"Then I will sleep right here on this sofa until they arrive," Matteo said as he rushed across the room to grab the telephone. "And not let this painting out of my sight for an instant."

Matteo dialed the number and the rest of us watched as he carried on a frenzied conversation in Italian with the police to explain the situation.

"The police will send an inspector tomorrow," Vega informed the rest of us as she eavesdropped on Matteo's conversation. "Sometime in the afternoon."

"I will be very interested to hear what they have to say," Marieke said as she watched Matteo continue his energetic conversation on the other side of the room.

"Me too," I muttered under my breath with a cynical chuckle.

"Of course," Giulia replied. "I think we're all curious to find out how this priceless Van Gogh ended up here on the wall of our father's house."

"True," Marieke said, nodding absently. "But to be honest, I'm far more curious to find out how these *other* two paintings ended up here."

Marieke reached out and pointed toward a pair of paintings that were hanging off in the corner on the opposite side of the fireplace.

"What do you mean?" Vega asked, turning her head to look at what she was gesturing to.

"Well, in light of the fact that this Van Gogh over here is almost surely authentic," Marieke replied, "then I can only assume that the Monet and the Pissarro hanging right over there are authentic as well."

CHAPTER FIVE
It Just Feels Right

"Monet?!?" Matteo exclaimed, returning from his phone call with the police with his eyes bursting wide in astonishment.

"And Picasso?!?" I asked, not sure that I'd heard Marieke correctly.

Marieke shook her head and turned toward me as Matteo quickly put down the phone and hurried across the room to inspect the other two paintings. "Not Picasso," she replied as she started to take a few steps after Matteo. "Pissarro. Camille Pissarro. He was also an Impressionist painter like Monet and he's actually a favorite of mine. Part of my master's thesis dealt with aspects of his work, in fact."

I nodded and scurried along after both of them, eager to get a closer look at the two paintings as well.

"Which one is which?" I asked enthusiastically, too curious to worry about revealing my ignorance of all things art related.

"Well, don't forget that I might be wrong about all this," Marieke said as she leaned in close to the first painting, her face hovering barely inches from its surface while Matteo and I watched anxiously over her shoulder. "These may simply be very good copies or perhaps have some other innocent explanation, but..."

"But?" Matteo asked nervously.

"But this one here looks like an authentic Monet to me," Marieke said, leaning back again so all of us could see.

The painting showed the dimly lit interior of a train station, with faceless human figures hustling back and forth underneath a sky formed by the iron skeleton of a peaked glass-paneled roof. At the heart of all this action, a pair of monstrous black locomotives sat like mechanical beasts atop long snaking rail lines while they belched clouds of blue smoke and steam into the air. The whole scene was so vibrant and full of life that I could almost sense the heavy industrial clanking of metal in the pit of my stomach and taste the gritty soot-filled air.

"How do you know it's real?" Charlie asked as he, Giulia and Vega joined the rest of us in crowding around in a tight semi-circle in front of the painting.

"I don't know for certain, of course," Marieke replied. "But as I said, it appears to be genuine. The mixing of color is typically Monet. The brushwork looks right. And Monet did paint a number of very similar scenes to this one of the Saint Lazare train station in Paris."

"But...?" Charlie asked, ever the skeptic.

Marieke shook her head. "No but," she replied. "As incredible as it sounds, I have to say that from first glance it appears to be authentic."

"*Oh mio Dio*," Matteo muttered under his breath in disbelief.

"But it's actually this last one that really interests me," Marieke said, side-stepping over so she could examine the final painting. "Academically speaking, at least."

As Marieke sidled to the right, the rest of us followed suit, barely lifting our feet as we shuffled comically over and watched her every move.

"And...?" Matteo asked, tense and nervous as he watched Marieke lean in to study the painting up close.

I couldn't help myself and also leaned in over Marieke's shoulder for a better look, unable to resist being drawn in by the mesmerizing scene. This painting was different from the other ones hanging on the wall next to it. It felt different. Calmer somehow.

The painting showed a brightly lit street at night with people and lamp-lit carriages lined up along an impossibly long boulevard in an orderly frenzy of activity. As I followed Marieke's lead and leaned in closer, I could see that the brushstrokes were broad and simple, almost crude in execution, so that the closer you got, the less the painting looked like what it was supposed to look like. It was almost as though the artist had intentionally kept the scene devoid of details, preferring instead to leave those to the eye and imagination of the beholder.

Pulling my head back again to a more suitable viewing distance, the boulevard scene took shape again and burst gloriously back into life. From a distance, the pattern of broad and simple brushstrokes seemed to make everything shimmer like a photograph on water, leaving you with the impression of a scene that was alive with light and energy.

Is that why they call it Impressionism? I thought to myself, tilting my head to one side at this sudden realization. I opened my mouth to ask Marieke about it but quickly closed it again when I saw the look of intense concentration on her face as she examined the painting, scanning it from top to bottom and closely scrutinizing every minute detail. It was as though the painting could speak to her across the more than a hundred years that had passed since its creator had first put brush and oil to canvas.

"It certainly *looks* right," Marieke said after a few minutes, standing upright again and taking a few steps back. "And there are a number of very similar paintings to this one that show day and night views from Pissarro's apartment at the *Hôtel de Russie* in Paris."

"So you think this one is authentic as well?" Matteo asked, incredulous.

Marieke slowly nodded as she continued to stare at the lively nighttime scene hanging on the wall across from us. "At first glance, yes," Marieke replied. "As I said, it certainly looks right but more important than that, it *feels* right."

"It feels right?" Vega asked in confusion. "What do you mean?"

Marieke nodded again. "It just *feels* right," Marieke repeated, finally taking her eyes off the painting and turning to face us again. "I can't explain it. It just makes me feel the same way a real Pissarro would."

For a moment everyone was silent as they looked over at the painting and tried to understand what Marieke was trying to say.

"You look disappointed," Charlie remarked, glancing over at Marieke after a few moments and seeing the somewhat tense expression written on her face.

"Or concerned," Vega added with her own look of worry on her own face as well.

"I have to admit that I was hoping for some innocent explanation," Marieke replied as she slowly shook her head in incomprehension. "That maybe these paintings were just clever forgeries or something like that."

"But you think they're real?" Giulia asked breathlessly.

Marieke nodded. "That is what my heart and gut are telling me," she replied. "I have no idea how in the world they ended up on the wall of your father's house, but these paintings are the real thing and they are probably worth millions."

CHAPTER SIX
Well, That Kind Of Sucked

The inexplicable discovery of such priceless works of art hanging right in front of their noses proved to be too stressful for Matteo. He collapsed into the nearest chair, slumped over with his head in his hands while his sisters did their best to comfort him. But, of course, the bizarre turn of events was also quite an emotional drain on them as well. If Marieke was right and the paintings proved to be authentic, there were a lot of questions to be answered as to how exactly they had ended up hanging next to the fireplace of their father's house.

After a couple more cups of coffee and tea it was getting quite late so Charlie, Marieke and I finally bid our new friends goodnight and left them to discuss the matter among themselves as a family. But after all their kindness toward us, and with all the stress they were under, Charlie and I decided to offer to take all of them out to dinner somewhere nice the next evening.

"You pick the restaurant, of course," I said, giving Matteo a bright grin and a reassuring pat on the shoulder. "I am sure you know somewhere amazing."

"Oh yes," Matteo replied, surprising me by returning my grin. "I know the perfect place."

With those plans made, Charlie and I politely took our leave and caught a taxi back across town where he dropped me at my hotel before continuing on to his own.

It was late but I could tell that sleep would be impossible after all the dramatic events of the past few hours, so after changing into some pajamas, I curled up with a blanket on a chaise longue next to my open window.

The view was beautiful. Down below me the brightly lit ruins of the Roman Forum stood watch timelessly under the strange shadows of rows of umbrella pines. Somewhere nearby, a pair of cats were moaning threateningly at each other and in the distance I could hear the faint wail of an ambulance, but other than that the night was quiet and perfect as I sat by the glow of my iPad and exchanged email messages with my mother on the other side of the world.

Eventually I began to yawn and with my eyelids growing heavy, I shut the window and crawled into bed. But even then sleep was still a long time coming. My head was filled with daydreams of priceless works of art and an unending stream of questions. But soon enough those daydreams turned to slumber and the next thing I knew, the light of the sun was streaming in through a gap in the thick curtains covering the windows at the foot of my bed.

Kicking my blankets off, I lay in bed for a long and lazy while, checking my email and playing a few games on my iPad before pulling myself out of bed and getting ready for the day.

To be honest, I was actually anxious for the day to already be over. My mind had skipped hours ahead to our dinner date with Vega and Matteo and I was dying to hear if the police had been able to shed any light on the mystery of the paintings that we'd discovered hiding in plain sight.

But first things first. Long before any of the events of the previous night, I'd already committed myself to visiting the Vatican that day, specifically the Sistine Chapel. The lines to visit the Vatican Museum were notoriously long and I figured it would take me the better part of the day to maneuver my way through them. So, after a quick shower and breakfast I hit the streets and began to wind my way across the city toward the tower dome of St Peter's Basilica. Down past the Roman ruins, across the *Piazza Venezia* and through a maze of streets to the *Pantheon* and *Piazza Navona*, and finally across the Tiber River with *Castel Sant'Angelo* to my right, straight down to the wide open space in front of St Peter's—the *Piazza San Pietro*.

By this time it was already mid-afternoon and my feet were aching and numb from all the walking. And to top it off, despite the fact that I was standing just a few hundred feet from the Sistine Chapel itself, I still had to walk even further to reach the entrance, flanking the long way around the side of Vatican City to join a seemingly endless line of people that snaked along the outer walls, all of us waiting to enter the museum.

I bought myself a bottle of water before joining the line and did my best to isolate myself from the crush of tourists as we slowly shuffled forward a few inches at a time until finally crossing the threshold into the museum itself. Once inside the crowds almost seemed to get worse. A slow-moving mass of humanity zombie'ing along through a labyrinth of rooms and past impressive-looking paintings and sculptures by artists with familiar-sounding names like Caravaggio and Raphael. Not that I was able to take the time to really stop and look at many of these priceless works of art, however. The sluggish river of people seemed to carry me along with it, flowing deliberately and inevitably toward the final destination of the Sistine Chapel.

Through some doors again and I found myself drowning in a crowd of people spilling backward like water behind a dam until finally stepping into the legendary chapel itself. Still shuffling along, I craned my neck to gaze up at the instantly recognizable scenes that were painted on the ceiling by Michelangelo himself more than five hundred years earlier. I knew from researching on the Internet ahead of time that the scenes were from the early books of the Bible starting first with God's creation of the universe, followed by the creation of Adam and Eve, and finally the story of Noah and the great flood.

At least I think that's what they were, anyway. It was difficult to tell since the ceiling was too far away to see clearly and with the Vatican guards constantly barking at the heavy crowd to remind them to keep moving, I didn't really feel welcome enough to stop and take a leisurely look.

But I do remember one of Michelangelo's painted scenes with perfect clarity. Who could miss it, after all? It is one of the most famous works of art in the entire world, after all. God's creation of Adam. A scene depicting the two figures, their arms outstretched and reaching out across the void toward each other, their fingertips almost touching so God can pass the spark of life down to Adam.

It was beautiful and unmistakable, even when seen from all the way down on the floor of the crowded Sistine Chapel. But with the stifling air pressing in on me and the never-ending flow of humanity slowly pushing me along, I found myself swept out the exit at the other end of the chapel before I even realized what was happening. In just a few short minutes it was all over.

Well, that kind of sucked, I thought to myself with a chuckle as I headed for the street to go meet Charlie and the others for dinner.

CHAPTER SEVEN
We'd Like To Hire You

"Oh, *mamma mia*, I hardly slept a wink last night!" Matteo said after we'd all sat down and he'd taken care of ordering drinks and food for everyone.

The five of us were sitting at a corner table near the back of a quiet little *trattoria* just a few blocks from the train station. The place was small but very charming and from what I could tell, it seemed to be run by two handsome young brothers who worked the front of the restaurant while their mother busily prepared all the food in the kitchen beyond.

"It's true," Vega nodded vigorously in agreement with what Matteo was saying. "I could feel the floor shaking for half the night as he paced back and forth in front of the fireplace."

"Well, you can hardly blame me," Matteo protested, his voice rising and his hands doing half his talking for him. "It's not every day that you discover that the dusty old paintings hanging on your wall are actually worth millions of dollars. What if someone had come in to steal them?"

"Who would come and steal them last night?" Vega replied. "They've been hanging there for years and no one even knew they were there!"

"No. Not until this morning, at least," Matteo said accusingly as he turned to glare at Giulia. "When I heard about them in the news!"

Giulia returned the glare and casually took a sip of wine.

"What do you expect?" she replied calmly. "I'm a journalist."

"Anyway, thank God the police finally came and took them away," Matteo continued. "I was finally able to get some sleep."

Vega grinned and reached over to tousle Matteo's hair playfully.

"Yes, we can tell," Vega said. "You look like you just got out of bed."

"I did!" Matteo replied, making everyone laugh as one of the waiters arrived and set down a huge plate of antipasti.

"So what did the police say?" I asked as everyone pulled their chairs forward and started helping themselves to the various selections of cold meat and cheeses.

"Not much," Matteo replied, waving his finger in the air dramatically. "They sent one of their senior investigators as well as an Interpol agent who specializes in art and antiquities trafficking but both were just as baffled as we were as to how those paintings might have fallen into our father's hands."

"So that's it?" I asked, surprised. I have to admit that I was rather disappointed. I'd been anxiously waiting to hear all the juicy details.

Matteo shrugged his shoulders. "Their first step will be to determine whether the paintings are authentic, starting with the Van Gogh," he explained. "They said that they'd already called in some experts from the Van Gogh Foundation in Holland to look at the painting and see if it's the one that was stolen from them. If it is then they'll work with the Dutch police and Interpol to try and see if they can figure out how the painting got from Amsterdam to our father's living room."

"And the other two paintings?" I asked.

Matteo shrugged again. "Those two are even more of a mystery," he replied. "If they turn out to be authentic then not only will they have to figure out how they ended up hanging on our father's wall, but also where they came from in the first place."

I nodded in understanding and thought this over. "And you still have no idea how your father fits into all of this?" I asked.

"We have no idea whatsoever," Vega replied, glancing over at her brother and sister who were both shaking their heads slowly. "Our father worked for a petroleum company. He wasn't some master criminal who could break into the Van Gogh Museum in the dead of night and make off with a priceless work of art."

"It is definitely a mystery," Matteo agreed with a sad nod of his head.

For a moment there was an awkward silence and I found myself feeling rather sorry for Matteo and his sisters. I could hardly imagine the shock that all of this must have been to them.

"Maybe you should hire Kitty to investigate it for you," Charlie suggested with a chuckle.

"What do you mean?" both Matteo and I replied simultaneously.

"Well, you wouldn't know it to look at her," Charlie continued, still grinning and trying to lighten the mood, "but Kitty here is her own one-woman flying detective agency."

"Yah, right," I laughed, finally getting the joke. "*The Kitty Hawk Flying Detective Agency.*"

"I still don't understand," Matteo said looking back and forth between me and his sisters in confusion.

"Charlie is just joking," I said, leaning forward with my elbows on the table. "Don't pay any attention to him."

Charlie leaned forward as well, still chuckling but with a serious expression on his face.

"Kitty is just being modest," Charlie said reassuringly. "But don't be fooled. She is actually quite a formidable solver-of-mysteries. In fact, that's how the two of us met, isn't that right, Kitty?"

My face flushed red with embarrassment, thinking back to that night almost a year earlier when Charlie had snuck up on me in the Alaskan wilderness. (Although, to be fair, at the time I was in the process of doing some sneaking and spying of my own—on his brothers and their stash of stolen gold.)

Charlie grinned at me for a second before launching into the story of our Alaskan and Yukon adventures while I sat there helplessly listening to him and blushing every time he overexaggerated my contributions to the whole crazy adventure. The way he told the story it was definitely a good old Alaskan tall tale, and by the time he finished Matteo and the others were sitting there with stunned expressions on their faces.

"And that's not all," Charlie continued, leaning back in his chair and patting me on the shoulder. "Tell them about what happened in the Florida Keys. And Iceland. And Ireland."

All eyes were on me and I found myself blushing again, my face burning bright red.

"I... I don't know..." I said, stuttering over what to say as the waiters cleared the table and brought out our main courses.

I had no idea what to say but Charlie rescued me by leaning forward again and telling the stories for me. He told them all about my underwater exploits down at Fort Jefferson in the Florida Keys, about my run-ins with the forces of man and nature in Iceland, and finally the tale of my Titanic adventures in London and Ireland. His enthusiasm for the stories was infectious and as he told each of them, in turn, I found myself jumping in excitedly here and there to fill in various details.

By the time Charlie finished, the waiters were clearing the last of the dinner plates from in front of us and replacing them with frozen slices of whipped gelato, topped with fresh berries and dripping with raspberry sauce.

"That is unbelievable," Vega said while her brother ordered espressos for everyone. "All of it, I mean. Everything that happened to you is simply unbelievable."

"Every word of it is true," Charlie assured them. "You've even seen it for yourself. In a way, Kitty's the one who figured out that it was a Van Gogh hanging on your wall in the first place. Without her..."

Charlie's voice trailed off and now it was his turn to blush as he realized what he was about to say. Without me, they might never have known about the priceless masterpieces hanging on the walls of their father's house. And as they say, ignorance is bliss. Without me, their lives would be considerably less complicated and difficult.

Biting my lip, I bowed my head uncomfortably and Vega reached across the table to touch me reassuringly on the arm.

"Without Kitty, we probably wouldn't know about any of this," Vega said as she gave me a warm smile. "But I'm glad that we've made all of these discoveries. Our father was a good man, but he was also very *riservato*—very quiet and reserved—and to be honest, in many ways we hardly knew him. All his life he worked very hard and when we were growing up we didn't see as much of him as we would have liked." Vega paused for a moment, her eyes starting to well up with tears.

"What my sister is trying to say," Giulia said, putting her arm around Vega as she spoke, "is that we're glad to learn whatever we can about our father. Even if it's all a bit of a mystery."

Vega looked up at me and smiled, nodding her head in agreement.

"Then it's settled!" Matteo announced brightly. "The three of us would like to hire you to investigate the story behind these mysterious paintings."

I looked across at Matteo in confusion. "What do you mean?" I asked.

"We'd like to hire you," Matteo repeated. "*The Kitty Hawk Flying Detective Agency.*"

I burst out laughing.

"I am so sorry," I explained, still chuckling. "But that was just a joke. Charlie and I didn't really mean that I actually run a flying detective agency."

"Well, maybe you should," Matteo replied with finality. "Because it sounds like you have a nose for it."

And with that I was hired. Of course, I had absolutely no idea what they thought I could possibly do for them, but at that moment I was too stunned to think of anything else to say. And besides, I have to admit that I was quite curious about the paintings myself. I was dying to know where they'd come from in the first place and how they'd ended up where they did.

"Now, you'd better eat your *semifreddo* before it melts," Matteo said with a smile, settling the matter once and for all as he reached for his spoon.

CHAPTER EIGHT
The Creepiest Sound I Have Ever Heard

After dessert Charlie paid the bill for all of us, patiently fending off any and all offers to give him money. From there we caught a taxi across town for a nightcap of Matteo's homemade *nocino* back at their father's apartment.

It was strange to be back there somehow. The blank walls on either side of the fireplace seemed to glare accusingly at me as Matteo took our coats and invited us to make ourselves comfortable in the living room.

"*Nocino* for everyone, then?" Matteo asked as he headed for the kitchen. "Or coffee? Tea?"

"Tea for me," I replied.

"Espresso," Vega said.

"The same," Giulia added.

"What?!? Will no one try my lovely *nocino*?" Matteo asked.

"No!" Vega and Giulia both snapped in reply, laughing.

I smiled and laughed along with them while Matteo turned to talk to Charlie.

"And you, Charlie?" Matteo asked. "Do you want to try my *nocino*?"

I looked over at Charlie and saw that he was still standing at the edge of the living room, his eyes narrowing as he looked down along the long hallway leading to the apartment's bedrooms.

"What is it?" I asked, turning in my chair to get a better look at him. I could tell by the expression on his face that something was wrong. It was the same expression that I'd seen on his face back in the Alaskan wilderness. An intense look of concentration, his senses heightened and alert to potential danger.

"I'm not sure," Charlie replied slowly, frowning slightly as he continued to stare down the hallway.

"Is something wrong?" Vega asked, her face turning to a frown as well as she pulled herself to her feet.

"What is it, Charlie?" I asked, getting to my feet as well and taking a few steps toward where Charlie was standing.

"Do you hear that?" Charlie asked, still staring intently down the darkened hallway.

I immediately stopped in my tracks and listened. I couldn't hear a thing.

"I don't hear anything," Matteo whispered as he and the others slowly gathered around Charlie, straining their ears to hear what he was hearing.

I held my breath and listened again, this time closing my eyes and concentrating as hard as I possibly could. For a moment I still couldn't hear anything but then after a few seconds my ears began to make something out. A sound like high-pitched static, very quiet, muffled and barely audible.

"It sounds like a tea kettle," Vega said. "From the neighbor's apartment maybe?"

Charlie shook his head and took a few steps down the hall with the rest of us following close behind.

"Not that sound," he said, still shaking his head as he crept along with his ear close to the wall. "What I heard was something different."

As we made our way slowly down the hall, I could hear the hissing tea kettle sound getting ever so slightly more perceptible with every step. But it was still so quiet that it barely registered on my ears.

"What was it, then?" I whispered. "What kind of noise did you hear?"

Charlie stopped and ran his fingertips along the wall, leaning his head in close to put his ear directly on the wall.

"It was something else," Charlie replied. "Like voices."

"It could still be the neighbors?" Vega suggested, creeping along behind Charlie and putting her ear on the wall to listen as well. "Or their television?"

Charlie kept shaking his head.

"No, it wasn't like that at all," he said. "This voice wasn't..."

I glanced over at Charlie, examining every line on his frowning face, searching for a clue as to what he was talking about.

"Wasn't what?" Matteo whispered.

"Human," Charlie replied simply as he turned to face us. "The voice I heard wasn't human."

When Charlie said this, I felt like the blood drained completely from my entire body. My skin went cold and an icy shiver raced down my spine.

"What do you mean, Charlie?!?" I asked, my voice tensing with fear.

Charlie didn't have the chance to reply. Before he could even start to open his mouth, the wall behind him suddenly swung outward, moving fast in an abrupt and violent motion that was clearly intended to push him off his feet and send him sprawling to the floor.

But Charlie was too quick and spun out of the way to safety. Unfortunately, I wasn't quick at all and simply stood there with my mouth hanging wide open and staring dumbly as the wall panel swung rapidly toward me.

Seeing my predicament Charlie reacted instantly, lunging forward and blocking the panel with his palms to stop it just inches from my face. He almost certainly saved me from getting my nose broken, but unfortunately for him his sudden defensive move threw me off balance and instinctively I clawed and grabbed at him as I fell backward.

As the two of us toppled to the ground, I saw a black-clothed figure burst out of the wall and start running for the front door. In one swift, fluid motion, the figure hit Charlie in the back and sent him sprawling to the floor on top of me and then jumped over both of us and pushed its way past Vega, Matteo and Giulia, intentionally pulling them off balance and sending them all crashing down on top of Charlie and me.

Everything happened so unbelievably fast that none of us—least of all Charlie, who was on the bottom of the heap of tangled arms and legs—had time to get back up again to give chase. By the time any of us managed to scramble to our feet, the mysterious figure was long gone.

"Check at the windows!" Vega cried as Charlie dashed for the front door of the apartment. "You can see down to the street from there!"

Charlie nodded curtly and turned sharply to head for the front windows. He pulled the closest one quickly open and leaned out to scan the street below.

"Do you see anything?" I asked, dashing down the hall and rushing up behind Charlie to look out the window as well.

Charlie shook his head.

"I think I saw him disappear around the corner up there," he said, pointing in the direction of the crowded piazza just down the street. "But I can't be sure of it."

By now the others had crowded around the window with us as well and were peering down into the dark, narrow streets below.

"He's long gone anyway," I commented as Charlie took a last look around before closing the window once again.

"Who *was* that?" Vega asked, looking at us with scared, wide eyes.

None of us had any idea, of course, and shook our heads one after the other.

"More importantly, where did he come from?" Charlie asked as he turned to head back for the hallway. "Do you have some kind of recessed closet back there or something?"

"There's nothing back there at all, as far as I know," Matteo said, switching on the hall light as we all made our way back to where the mysterious figure had unexpectedly emerged from behind the wall.

I turned the corner and immediately saw that one of the panels about halfway down the hallway was hanging open at an odd angle, revealing a crack in the wall with a dark space beyond.

"Is it some kind of secret room?" I asked.

Charlie motioned at all of us to stay back a safe distance while he approached the hidden door to check things out. Bracing himself for another sudden attack, he cautiously reached forward and forced the wall panel further open, watching carefully as it swung outward.

As the door opened, I immediately saw that I'd been right—there *was* a secret room hidden behind the wall. The room was completely dark but in the dim light I could make out that it was about the size of a small closet with a wooden chair and a small desk off to one side.

Charlie breathed a sigh of relief. The room was so small that we could easily see that there was no one else lurking inside, waiting to spring out at us. But it was also immediately apparent that something in that room was the source of the strange hissing sound that we'd heard earlier. As the door swung open, the previously muffled sound suddenly became clear as day and for the first time I was able to recognize what it was.

It was radio static.

The sizzling, crackly, whining noise like a high-pitched tea kettle was nothing more than simple static from some kind of radio receiver.

"It's white noise," I muttered under my breath.

I saw Charlie glance back at me and nod his head. "It is," he said.

"But what about the voice you heard?" Vega asked as she cautiously took a few steps closer.

"The voice that wasn't human," I added, giving myself the chills all over again even as I said it.

"I don't know," Charlie replied slowly as he took a couple of steps closer as well.

We didn't have to wait long for an answer because at that moment a clock somewhere back in the living room struck the top of the hour and the sound of static from inside the room hissed a bit louder.

And then, suddenly, the creepiest sound I have ever heard filled the air.

From somewhere inside that tiny room, the thin, crackly sound of a child's music box echoed off the walls, playing some unfamiliar melody that floated past us down the hallway.

Oh my God, what IS that?!?? I thought, my body suddenly running cold with terror. In a panic I looked quickly around me and saw that everyone else's eyes were as wide open in horror as mine were. The sound of that tinkling, staticky song playing over the radio sounded like something straight out of a horror movie, and the fact that it was coming from out of that dark and sinister-looking secret closet behind the wall only made it more frightening.

Oh, wait a minute! Did I just say that the sound of the crackly music box was the creepiest sound that I've ever heard? Let me correct that because to be perfectly accurate, it is actually the *next* sound that deserves that particular title. What all of us heard next made my blood run completely cold and turned Matteo as white as a sheet.

After a few seconds, the tinkling melody of the music box stopped abruptly and for a moment there was nothing but the sound of static again. I was about to open my mouth to say something but whatever demonic radio station was playing inside that room, it still had some surprises in store for us. Before I could say a word, there were suddenly three long scratchy beeping sounds like a kind of slow, maniacal alarm clock.

And then came the *really* creepy thing.

"*Attention!*" a dead and lifeless woman's voice suddenly said. "*Foxtrot–foxtrot–alpha–golf–foxtrot–foxtrot–echo–echo.*"

CHAPTER NINE
FFAGFFEE

Fighting back the overwhelming urge to run away screaming, I forced myself to stand my ground and looked over at Charlie with my eyes so far wide open in fear that it actually hurt.

What the hell is this?!?? the expression on my face said.

He started to shrug his shoulders but before he could finish the gesture, the eerie sound of the woman's voice began to speak again.

"*Foxtrot–foxtrot–alpha–golf–foxtrot–foxtrot–echo–echo,*" the emotionless voice recited before pausing again. "*Foxtrot–foxtrot–foxtrot–foxtrot–echo–foxtrot.*"

As the voice continued, I spun my head around to look back down the hall toward the others. A few feet away from me, Vega and Giulia were crouched low against the far wall, clinging to each other in fear. Both of them were deathly pale and frightened but that was nothing compared to Matteo, who was standing behind them looking so scared that he might actually keel over and die at any moment.

But even then the voice still wasn't finished. After repeating its last phrase one more time there was a slightly longer pause and then it started up again, this time reciting an eerie sequence of numbers.

"*One–four–four–seven, three–five, seven–five, two–six–nine–nine,*" the voice droned on and on, pausing slightly after each group of numbers. "*Seven–six–seven–five, four–eight–zero–nine...*"

Looking back at Charlie, I was relieved to see that some color had returned to his face and he was looking a bit more like his old self again. And his looking more in control gave me a much-needed boost of confidence as well.

"Write this down!" he hissed in a tense whisper. "The numbers! Write them down."

Yes! Good idea, I thought and reached for my bag to grab my notebook.

It didn't take me long to realize that I'd left my bag in the other room but thinking quickly on my feet, I pulled out my iPhone and hit the "record" button on the video camera.

My hands were shaking like crazy but somehow I managed to hold up the phone at arm's length and point it toward the door leading into that dark, hidden room.

Just stop it! I scolded myself. *No more being scared! Whatever this is, there's a perfectly rational explanation for it.*

I knew in my heart that this was true, but standing there with the insanity-inducing voice continuing its endless recital of seemingly random numbers, I couldn't even begin to imagine what the explanation could possibly be.

"*Seven–three–two–three...*" the voice continued, and then suddenly it broke the monotonous stream of numbers for a brief second before starting up again. "*I say again... foxtrot–foxtrot–alpha–golf–foxtrot–foxtrot–echo–echo...*"

I say again?!? I thought to myself. *Is that what it just said?*

Out of the corner of my eye, I saw Charlie take two quick steps across the hall toward me.

"It's repeating the same thing all over again," Charlie whispered in my ear as he put his arm protectively around me.

I nodded in reply. It seemed like he was right. The voice seemed to be repeating the same long string of words and numbers that it had just finished reciting just a few seconds earlier.

God only knows why, I thought to myself, feeling slightly nervous about what new and horrible thing would happen once it finished the second time around. But as it turned out, however, there was nothing to worry about.

"*Seven–three–two–three...*" the voice repeated and then paused for a second before finishing with one final word. "*End.*"

And that was it. The voice finally stopped broadcasting its fiendish sequence of numbers and fell silent once again, leaving nothing but the dull crackle of static behind it.

Charlie held up the palm of his hand and waited for a few long moments, tilting his head to one side to listen. We all held our breath and listened along with him but there was nothing else to hear—nothing, that is, except the low sound of static.

"Everyone stay where you are," Charlie commanded as he crept cautiously forward toward the partly opened wall panel for a closer look. "Let me check things out first."

He didn't have to tell me that more than once. The last thing in the world I wanted to do at that particular moment was get any closer to that creepy little room. In fact, I wanted nothing more than to run as fast as I could in the completely opposite direction just in case that dead-sounding voice started to speak again. If that happened, I was afraid that I would completely lose my mind.

Charlie pulled open the door as far as it would go and carefully inspected the inside of the tiny room. Once he was satisfied that there was definitely no one else hiding inside, he turned around and gave me a quick nod to say that it was all clear.

"It's just a radio," Charlie said, leaning forward into the darkness to turn the volume down slightly.

"A radio?" I asked, hesitantly lifting myself to my feet and switching off my phone as I stood up straight again. "What kind of radio?"

Charlie shrugged. "Some kind of old-fashioned radio receiver," he said, stepping off to one side so I could see.

Squinting my eyes I could vaguely see what he was talking about. On the small wooden desk at the right side of the little room there was a square black box with various large dials and dim glowing lights on the front of it.

"But what is it?" I asked, my curiosity getting the better of me as I took a step closer for a better look.

"*La voce*," I heard Matteo say in a quiet whisper from somewhere behind me.

I turned my head to look back at the others. Vega and Giulia were still crouched low against the far wall with Matteo standing just a few feet behind them, nervously stitching his hands together and looking like he'd just seen a ghost.

"La vochay?" I asked, not understanding what he'd said.

"*La voce*," Vega corrected me, unwrapping her arms from Giulia and sliding slowly back to her feet. "It means 'the voice'."

"You got that right," I laughed nervously. "That was really weird."

"No, no, you don't understand," Vega said, looking worriedly back at her brother. "The story of 'the voice' is something our brother used to tell us when we were children. I haven't thought about it for years but I remember that it used to give Matteo the most terrible nightmares."

"Not just Matteo," Giulia added, walking over to give her brother a reassuring hug. "Whenever he told us about it, I was usually too scared to sleep too."

"I'm not sure I understand," I said. "Is it some kind of children's story?"

Matteo took a step toward me, shaking his head. "No, no, nothing like that," he corrected me. "It's something I was absolutely terrified of as a child. A strange, frightening voice that I could sometimes hear as I lay in bed at night trying to fall asleep."

"When we were growing up, Matteo's room was just on the other side of this wall," Vega interjected, reaching over to tap the wall panel next to the hidden room with her knuckles.

"At the time I was very young and had a pretty good imagination so no one ever really believed me," Matteo continued. "And after a while I stopped hearing it so in the end I was not even sure myself whether it was real or not."

"But now..." Vega said, looking back at the hidden room wistfully.

"But now...?" I asked expectantly.

Vega looked at me with an expression of complete bewilderment on her face. "Well, now it seems like maybe it *was* real after all," she said simply. "And it has been going on for a very long time."

CHAPTER TEN
That Must Be The Police

For a moment we all just stood there, dazed and staring silently into the darkness of the hidden room as we struggled to understand what was going on. I felt a shiver run down my spine again as I remembered that dead and lifeless voice rattling off its haphazard string of numbers. Whatever 'the voice' actually was, the thought that something so strange and creepy had been going on for so many years right under the noses of Matteo and his family made my skin crawl.

But what was it? What was this mysterious voice? And did it have anything to do with the person who'd broken into the apartment?

"We have to call the police and report the robbery," Charlie said, rubbing his jaw as he tried along with the rest of us to figure out what in the world was going on.

"A robbery?" I asked, confused.

Charlie looked at me and nodded. "Didn't you see?" he asked. "The person who jumped out of the wall and knocked us all over was carrying something. *Two* somethings, I think, actually."

"But carrying what?" I asked with a frown, angry with myself for being so unobservant.

"I'm not sure," Charlie replied, still rubbing his chin thoughtfully. "It was too dark and quick to see. Maybe some kind of short tube?"

"A rolled-up painting maybe?" Vega suggested, nodding her head in agreement. "I saw it too."

Dammit, I thought. *Am I the only one who didn't notice?*

"Oh God, more paintings?" Giulia asked, looking quite unhappy at the thought of it.

"I'll call the police right away," Matteo said as he rushed off toward the living room to use the telephone.

"I hope there's not more paintings in there," Vega said worriedly, nodding her head toward the opening in the wall.

"I don't think so," Charlie said as he leaned inside to look around into the various dark corners of the hidden room. "Although I can't see much of anything in here, to be honest."

I took a couple of steps closer and peered over Charlie's shoulder. On the wooden desk next to the still-crackling radio I could see that there was a small desk lamp.

Kitty Hawk and the Mystery of the Masterpieces

"Switch on the lamp," I suggested, tapping Charlie on the shoulder and pointing down at the desk.

Charlie shook his head. "I tried that already," he replied. "The bulb must be burned out or something."

"Or just not plugged in," I replied, reaching over him to grab the lamp's electrical cord.

Charlie looked sheepishly at me as I pulled up the loose dangling cord and dropped the plug in the palm of his hand. Chuckling and shaking his head in amusement, he knelt down and ran his hand along the power cord of the radio, following it down to the base of the wall so he could plug the lamp in.

The instant he inserted the plug into the socket, the room burst into light and finally we could see properly. Not that there was that much to see. The room was small, about eight feet wide by four feet deep, with unfinished wood and plaster walls on the inside. The only interesting things in the room were at the right where a wooden chair and desk were set up in a little niche with walls on three sides. On the desk was the clunky radio set that I'd already seen the outline of, plus some blank scraps of paper and scattered pencil stubs.

At the back near the wall a single wire snaked around from behind the radio and was lying loosely on the surface of the desk. Above that, just underneath a small shelf with some small boxes on it, a long piece of crinkly old paper with a list of letters written on it was tacked to the wall.

```
FFAGFFEE
EEECDDDB
FFFFEF
FBFFBB
AGGFEDD
DEFGAFA
EDEBCBCG
FFACCCCAA
CGAEFCFG
FEFEFEGF
CBCDCDEE
GEGEBEG
DBCAAA
CFACDCACDE
FAAAGFC
GCDBCFFFE
CCEEGGE
```

I leaned in for a closer look at the list of letter groups, and as I scanned down the list, it seemed like there was something familiar about it, but as hard as I tried, I couldn't quite put my finger on it.

"Before the voice started reading out numbers it was reading letters in phonetic alphabet," I observed offhandedly. "That must have something to do with this."

Charlie nodded and continued to look around the rest of the small room, but there wasn't much else to it. Other than these few things we'd already seen, the room was dusty and bare. I'd been expecting some kind of crazy chamber of horrors, but now that I could see everything by the light of day (or in this case by the light of an old desk lamp) I was relieved to find that it was just a perfectly normal room.

Okay, sorry, it most definitely was not a *normal* room. But considering how scared I'd been just a few minutes earlier, I was thankful to find such an ordinary-looking space hiding on the other side of that wall instead of God knows what else.

"The police will be here right away," I heard Matteo say and turned to see him poke his head around the corner of the door, out of breath after hurrying back from the other room. "What's all this, then?"

Charlie shook his head in reply to Matteo's question. "I have no idea," he said as he quickly kneeled down to take a look under the desk.

"Is there anything there?" Vega asked.

"Nothing," Charlie replied, shaking his head again as he pushed himself back to his feet.

"But what's all this stuff for?" I asked, leaning forward to take a closer look at the boxy radio and the strange list of letters pinned to the back wall. "Why is this radio in here and what are all these letters?"

Charlie and Vega leaned over the desk next to me to take a closer look as well.

"Strange," Charlie muttered. "But I have no idea."

Standing up straight again I saw that Matteo and Giulia were busy examining the walls and ceiling of the tiny room.

"When I was a kid my bed was just on the other side of this wall," Matteo observed, his voice soft and distant as he measured the walls with his eyes.

"And right on the opposite side of this other wall is the bathroom of the master bedroom," Giulia said, placing her hand on the back wall. "No wonder we never noticed there was a missing space in here. This whole room is designed so no one would ever find it."

"But why?" I said, asking aloud the question that everyone was already thinking.

"And who?" Matteo added.

"And for what purpose?" Vega asked, looking at her brother and sister with a slightly worried expression on her face.

Whatever the answers were to all of these questions, they would have to wait because at that moment our thoughts were interrupted by a sudden knock on the door.

"That must be the police," Matteo said, spinning on his heels to head for the front door. "That was quick."

CHAPTER ELEVEN
I Think You Just Gave It To The Bad Guys

Matteo was right. It was the police who were at the door. Down the hall from us I could hear him speaking quickly in Italian, explaining all the crazy events of the past half hour to the newly arrived policeman.

As they rounded the corner, I saw that our new guest was an enormous man, tall and muscular with incredibly broad shoulders. He was wearing a perfectly tailored black suit that made him look more like a kind of comic book villain than a real-life policeman.

Continuing his explanation, Matteo slowly made his way back down the hall toward us with the policeman following alongside and listening intently.

"...*cinque–cinque–quattro–due–nove–uno*..." Matteo said, mimicking the tone of the strange woman's voice that we'd heard earlier.

Hearing this, the policeman gave Matteo a funny look and raised his eyebrows in disbelief.

"*E 'vero*," Vega said, looking over at the rest of us for confirmation. "It's true."

"I am so sorry, perhaps we can continue in English?" Matteo apologized, gesturing toward Charlie and I. "Our friends here don't speak Italian."

"Of course," the enormous policeman replied with a friendly smile as he extended his hand toward us. "I am Inspector Alighieri."

"Charlie Lewis," Charlie replied, shaking the Inspector's hand firmly.

"Kitty Hawk," I said, also reaching out to shake hands and wondering whether the Inspector's powerful hands might crush my relatively tiny fingers. His grip was strong and firm but not overpowering and as he leaned closer I caught a faint whiff of some strong, pungent-smelling tobacco smoke on his suit jacket.

"My colleagues will be here shortly to join us," the Inspector explained. "I am much faster than them because I was already in the neighborhood. I was just down the street here on the *piazza* having a drink when I heard the call, in fact."

"Of course," Vega replied, nodding.

"Is this the room you were talking about back here?" the Inspector asked, pointing with his notebook to the wall panel that was standing ajar behind us.

"Yes, yes, that's it," Matteo replied and the rest of us stood aside to let the Inspector pass.

Inspector Alighieri's shoulders were so wide that I wasn't sure he would fit through the opening but after examining the swinging wall panel for a moment he somehow ducked his head and turned himself so he could slide easily inside.

The Inspector quickly looked over the room from every possible angle but it didn't take him long to come to the same conclusion that we had come to just a few minutes earlier.

"There's not much here worth stealing," the Inspector commented as he quickly inspected the radio and then picked up one of the small boxes from the shelf to examine it.

"Not anymore, anyway," Vega replied.

The Inspector nodded. "You said that the intruder was carrying something as he ran from the scene?" he asked Matteo.

"That's right," Matteo replied. "Two things, we think, actually."

"A short, fat tube about this long," Vega said, holding her hands up about a foot apart. "A rolled-up painting, maybe."

"Pretty small for a painting," the Inspector observed.

Vega shrugged her shoulders. "I suppose that's true," she said.

"And the other item?" the Inspector continued.

"Some kind of device," Charlie said. "Like a narrow cell phone or..."

Charlie's voice trailed off and he glanced over at the rest of us for help in describing it.

Don't look at me, I thought, still angry with myself for not noticing anything.

Matteo shook his head emphatically. "Not a phone," he said. "It was too thin."

"Did it look like this, by any chance?" the Inspector asked, lifting up the small box he was holding.

On the front of the box there was a picture of a small, narrow electronic device about four inches long and an inch wide. It was all black with various silver buttons on it and a digital display screen. "Digital Voice-Activated Recorder," the box read.

"That's it!" Matteo cried, reaching over to take the box from the Inspector and examine it more closely.

Charlie looked over Matteo's shoulder and nodded. "Yes, that's it," he said. "Definitely."

Tilting my head so I could better see the side of the voice recorder's box, I finally found my chance to contribute something toward solving the mystery.

"They used it to record the radio broadcasts," I said.

I looked up again to find everyone staring blankly at me.

"How do you know?" the Inspector asked with a perplexed look on his face.

"The wire," I replied as I proudly pointed to the wooden desk where the wire connected around the back of the radio set was still hanging loosely. "The connecter plug on the end matches the input jack on the side of the recorder."

Everyone turned their heads simultaneously to see what I was talking about and slowly, one by one, they began to nod their heads.

"Makes sense," Charlie said. "The voice activation function would mean it could be set to switch whenever there was something being broadcast."

"But who's 'they'?" Vega asked.

"They?" I replied, not sure what she meant.

"You said *they* were using it to record the radio broadcasts," Vega explained. "Who is 'they'?"

"Well, that's the big question, isn't it?" Charlie said. "Who's been sneaking around in here, listening to this radio and God knows what else."

"I thought the big question was what the creepy voice was in the first place," I replied, giving Charlie a grin as I jabbed him in the ribs with my elbow.

"Matteo mentioned that you had a recording of this strange voice," Inspector Alighieri asked me as he ducked and turned sideways to maneuver his muscular frame out of the tiny room and back into the hallway. "Is this true?"

"Yes, sir," I replied, quickly pulling my iPhone out of my back pocket and opening the video app. I flipped through until I reached my most recent video and then hit play.

As the sound of that eerie voice again filled the hallway, I found myself shivering uncomfortably. As the movie continued to play back, I handed the phone to Inspector Alighieri so he would see it for himself. Somehow, it was even *more* disturbing to listen to it playing back on the tinny-sounding iPhone speaker, accompanied by my wobbly camera work filming the dark hallway. It was like watching some terrifying home movie in some Hollywood horror movie.

The Inspector flipped his notebook to a new page and began to take notes. The movie played all the way to the end and the Inspector reached down and started it again from the beginning for a moment, taking a few more notes as he did so.

After about thirty more seconds, he glanced up toward the end of the hallway where a pulsing rhythm of blue police lights from the street below was flashing on the walls.

"My colleagues have arrived," Inspector Alighieri said, nodding his head toward the lights of the newly arrived police car. "Please excuse me for a moment while I go downstairs to consult with them."

"Of course," Vega said and we all followed the Inspector down the hall as he made for the front door.

"We'll be back up in a moment to make the official report," the Inspector explained politely as Matteo rushed ahead to open the door for him. "It won't be long."

"Please, take your time," Vega replied as the Inspector disappeared out the door, and we soon heard his heavy footfalls descending the stone steps leading down to the courtyard.

"I'll put on some tea in the meantime," Matteo said, heading for the kitchen while the rest of us mingled around the living room.

"This is unbelievable," Giulia said tiredly as she slumped down onto the sofa in front of the fireplace. "I feel responsible for all of this. I never should have done that news story about the stolen painting."

Vega dropped down next to her and patted her on the arm. "It's not your fault," she said reassuringly. "I have a feeling that whoever broke into the apartment tonight knew exactly what they were looking for."

"And what was that?" Giulia asked. "The voice recorder?"

Vega nodded. "And that rolled-up tube, whatever that was," she replied.

"The rolled-up painting I can understand," Giulia said. "God knows what long-lost masterpiece that might have been, but what's so important about the voice recorder?"

"That recorder might have recordings of past broadcasts on it," I suggested, taking a seat in the chair next to them and joining the conversation.

"Of what?" Giulia asked. "A bunch of numbers?"

"The numbers must have some meaning," I replied. "Although we'll probably never know what that is since they just made off with what are probably the only recordings of them."

Giulia laughed. "Well, if that's the case then at least we're the only ones who have a recording of the most recent broadcast," she said. "On your phone, I mean. Whoever it was that broke in here ran off before that one even started."

That's a good point, I thought to myself. *I hadn't thought of that.*

"That might not be entirely true," Charlie said, clearing his throat.

"What do you mean?" I asked, turning my head to see Charlie standing over by the windows. He was looking down at the street below with a troubled frown on his face.

"If the only copy of that last broadcast was the one on your phone," Charlie replied. "Then I think you just gave it to one of the bad guys."

CHAPTER TWELVE
I Don't Know If I Can Actually Solve This

"What?!??" I cried, jumping out of my chair and rushing over to the windows. I looked down to the street where Charlie was looking and saw nothing at all, just empty narrow streets with a single police car parked at the curb with its blue lights pulsating. "What are you talking about?!?"

"I don't think Inspector Alighieri was a police inspector after all," Charlie replied as Vega and Giulia also joined us by the windows. "I just saw him exit out onto the street and walk straight past that police car like it wasn't even there. I mean, he wasn't acting suspicious or anything, just walking casually, but before I knew it he just strolled up the street and disappeared around the corner without saying a word to anyone."

"What does that mean?!?" I asked, turning to Charlie in disbelief.

Charlie looked at me and tried to smile half-heartedly. "I think it means he wasn't actually a police inspector after all," he replied. "I think he must be working with whoever it was that broke in here."

Vega and Giulia shared a worried look.

"Who was working with who?!?" Matteo asked obliviously as he entered the room with a tray full of tea cups and a pot of hot water.

"Inspector Alighieri," Vega explained. "It seems he wasn't actually a policeman after all."

"What?!?" Matteo cried in disbelief, triggering a complete repetition of the last thirty seconds of conversation that had taken place before he entered the room.

As Charlie began to explain what he'd seen to Matteo, there was a sudden sharp knock at the front door.

"That must be the *real* police," Giulia observed caustically as she excused herself to go answer it.

"I can't believe it!" Matteo cried as Charlie finished the second telling of his story.

"Me neither," I agreed enthusiastically, feeling so stupid for trusting Inspector Alighieri (or whatever his name really was). "No wonder he was so keen on writing down what I'd recorded."

A moment later, Giulia and a pair of genuine-looking uniformed police entered the room. "These fellows are the real thing," she assured us with a cynical smile. "I checked their IDs."

Matteo offered the policemen some tea and for the next hour the five of us each repeated our version of the evening's events and showed them the secret hidden room.

When it came to Charlie and me to tell our version of the story, we had to have Matteo and Vega assist as translators since the two policemen didn't speak very good English.

That should have been my first clue that Inspector Alighieri was a fake, I thought to myself bitterly. *His English was too good.*

The police were polite and professional and took detailed notes of everything we had to say. After we'd finished a technician arrived to take some pictures and try to lift some fingerprints from the crime scene, particularly from the cardboard box that the bogus Inspector Alighieri had handled, but other than that there wasn't really anything that they could do. They explained that an investigation regarding the mysterious paintings from the living room was already underway and obviously the break-in that evening was connected somehow, but until they could figure out what the two things had to do with each other, there was little else for us to do but wait. Even the fact that someone had impersonated a police officer or the possibility that intruders might return again didn't seem to concern the policemen that much. None of the crimes were serious enough to justify placing a man on guard outside of the building to keep an eye on things, they explained.

"Typical," Giulia scoffed after she saw the policemen out again and returned to the living room where the rest of us were still sitting.

"So they really aren't going to stake out your apartment just in case the burglars decide to come back?" I asked.

Giulia shook her head and then turned to her brother and sister. "Maybe the two of you should come sleep at my place until all of this is sorted out?" she suggested.

"I was thinking the same," Vega replied worriedly.

"I'm not going anywhere," Matteo said firmly. "This is our home and someone needs to look after it. We can't just run away and hide our heads in the sand."

"Maybe Charlie could stay here with you?" I suggested. "And me too?"

Charlie nodded in agreement. "I'd be happy to stay, if you'd like me to," he said.

Matteo nodded enthusiastically. "Most definitely," he said.

Vega looked relieved at this suggestion as well. "I would certainly feel much better about staying here if there was a man around," she said. "No offense, Matteo."

"None taken," he replied.

"Then it's settled," I said, smiling brightly. "Charlie and I will spend the night."

"And we'll stay up late drinking tea and *nocino*," Matteo said with a laugh. "Because I don't know about the rest of you, but after all of this I need a drink."

One by one the rest of us all shook our heads. Even after all the excitement of the night still no one wanted to try any of Matteo's *nocino*.

Everyone seemed content with another cup of tea as we sat up for a while sleepily discussing all the crazy things that had happened.

"The only thing I don't understand," I said. "Is why they would break in here to steal the recording device."

"That's the *only* thing you don't understand?" Matteo asked. "I don't understand *ANY* of this."

"You know what I mean," I replied, laughing. "But if it's true that there were previous broadcasts of these crazy number sequences then why wouldn't these burglars just record those themselves. They are being broadcast over the radio, right? Anyone could do it."

"Maybe they didn't even know about any of this until they read about it in the news this morning?" Vega suggested, teasing her sister.

"Or maybe the burglar was just grabbing everything he could get his hands on?" Giulia said, ignoring Vega's comment.

I thought about this for a second and then shook my head.

"I'm not so sure," I said after a moment. "They seemed to have a pretty good idea about *something*. I don't think they just randomly broke in here and accidentally found that secret room behind the wall. They had to have known it was there."

"True," Vega agreed, her voice sounding tired and strained. "And that's what's so frightening about all of this. That there apparently are people out there who knew about that room when those of us who actually lived and grew up in this house had no idea it was there."

For a few long, awkward moments no one said anything. I stared down at my tea for a second and tried to decide whether or not I should ask the question that was burning in my head.

"Did your father know it was there?" I finally blurted out, looking up and locking eyes with Vega.

Vega took a deep breath and slowly looked at both her brother and sister in turn. "I don't know," she said quietly, pausing to take another very deep breath. "But I think he must have known. I think whatever all of this is, it's something he was involved with and none of us in his family even knew about it."

Vega looked over at her brother and sister again, her eyes big and sad.

Giulia was nodding her head slowly. "As much as I don't want to believe it's true, I think Vega is right," she agreed.

"That's why we're hoping you'll be able to help us," Matteo added, looking across at me hopefully.

I looked around the room at those three pairs of dark Italian eyes staring back at me over the coffee table and I suddenly felt the full weight of what I'd so casually agreed to earlier that evening back in the restaurant. All the half-serious joking about hiring me as a one-woman flying detective agency instantly felt a million miles away and I knew that we were actually talking about something deadly serious.

Oh my God, what have I gotten myself into? I screamed to myself as I struggled with the storm of conflicting thoughts that was raging inside of my head. *Am I crazy or something? This isn't a joke anymore. These are real people who are counting on me here.*

I looked over at Charlie and was surprised to find him staring back at me with a look of calm confidence in his eyes. He didn't say a word but simply nodded his head at me almost imperceptibly.

You can do this, his nod said. *I believe in you. And I'm right here with you to help if you need it.*

"Of course, we don't want to put pressure on you," Vega said, smiling apologetically.

Lifting my head I clenched my jaw and confidently looked across at my three newest friends. "I don't know if I can actually solve this thing," I admitted to them. "But I'll certainly try my best."

And I knew exactly where I was going to start.

CHAPTER THIRTEEN
Good Old Richard

"Richard? Richard? Are you there?" I cried in frustration as I tried to fiddle with the various settings on my iPad and make a connection. "Can you hear me?"

Having fully committed myself to solving the mystery of the paintings and the strange hidden room, I realized that the most obvious place to start was with the bizarre and enigmatic number sequence that we'd heard broadcast over the radio just a few hours earlier.

The radio set in the hidden room had been tuned to a shortwave frequency over ten thousand kilohertz, which meant that the broadcast it was receiving could have been coming from just about anywhere, especially since it had been after sunset when such frequencies can easily travel around the entire world. The transmission we'd heard had been pretty staticky, at any rate, so it was unlikely that it had been coming from anywhere nearby.

But what was it? What did all those crazy words and numbers actually mean?

First things first, I grabbed my phone and played back the video recording so I could listen again to exactly what the strange voice had been saying. Thanks to Charlie's quick thinking, I had started recording *before* the voice had said "I say again" and started repeating the whole thing over from the start. That meant that whatever the message was, we had captured the whole thing.

The sound of the creepy inhuman voice still gave me the chills but now that I knew what it really was it no longer completely freaked me out. Listening to it over and over again a few times made it abundantly clear that we were dealing with some kind of coded message. And fortunately for me, I'd had a little bit of experience with codes and ciphers in the not too distant past. Of course, I wasn't a cryptographer or a code-breaker. Not even close. But I knew someone who I hoped might be able to help.

"Yes, Kitty, I can hear you perfectly," I heard Richard's voice come in loud and clear over my iPad speaker. "And I can see you."

Richard was a friend of mine from London who I'd met just a few weeks earlier during my adventure solving *The Tragedy of the RMS Titanic*. He was a professional tour guide who specialized in Jack the Ripper and Sherlock Holmes walking tours, and most relevant of all to my current situation, among his various interests and hobbies he was a pretty good amateur cryptographer. I was hoping that Richard could help decode the mysterious message for us.

"Then why can't I see you?" I asked, still checking settings and options menus for the answer.

"Oh, what a bloody fool I am, I am so sorry," I heard Richard say at the other end and suddenly his face appeared on my iPad screen, clear as day. "I had the camera disconnected. You can never be too sure who's watching you these days."

I laughed and shook my head in relief.

"Thank God," I said. "I thought my iPad was broken or something."

"Afraid not," Richard replied. "Just my own stupidity."

I lifted the iPad up in the air and slowly panned the camera around the room to introduce Richard to everyone.

"Richard, these are my new friends here with me in Rome," I said. "Matteo and Vega and Giulia. And my old friend Charlie."

"It's a pleasure to meet you all," Richard said cheerfully as everyone waved hello.

"How are things in London?" I asked, propping up the iPad so we could all see each other.

"Oh, you know," Richard replied. "Another day, another group of tourists through the streets of the East End in pursuit of the Ripper."

"And how is Ellie?" I asked, continuing the polite chitchat despite my desperate eagerness to get to the point.

"She's fine too," Richard replied. "She's right here with me."

On the video screen I saw Richard reach up to turn the camera at his end for a second so I could see Ellie waving hello. Ellie was the Goth Girl who I'd also met a few weeks earlier when I'd been on my various adventures in England and Ireland. Those adventures had brought all of us strangers together and she and Richard had apparently hit it off because they'd been seeing each other ever since.

"Hi Kitty," Ellie said. "How is Rome? Is it beautiful there?"

"It's amazing, Ellie," I replied, smiling broadly. "You should come visit here sometime. And Richard too."

Ellie laughed. "I'd love to," she replied. "But I'm not so sure about Richard. He's a bit of a shut-in, I'm afraid."

The camera at the other end panned back to Richard's face again.

"Who needs to leave the house with such wonderful technology as this?" Richard asked with a bright smile. "Just look at us communicating with each other from a thousand miles away."

I hesitated for a second but then decided that I couldn't wait any more. I was simply dying of curiosity. "Long-distance communications are actually part of why I am calling you so late," I said apologetically. "I was hoping you could help us with something."

Richard nodded. "I had a feeling this was more than just a simple social call," he said. "Tell me."

I reached over to the coffee table and grabbed my iPhone as Vega and I quickly gave Richard the short version of everything that had happened to us over the past few days.

"Have you ever heard anything like this before?" I asked, lifting my phone to the iPad camera so Richard could see it and hear it.

I pushed play and immediately the creepy sound of the woman's voice filled the room, rattling off her endless series of numbers.

Richard listened for a few seconds, nodding his head thoughtfully.

"Numbers stations," he said simply.

I quickly reached forward and pressed pause on my phone. "I'm sorry, what was that?" I asked anxiously.

"A numbers station," Richard repeated. "That's a numbers station."

Good old Richard, I thought. *I knew he'd have the answer.*

I shuffled eagerly forward onto the edge of my seat and looked back to see that the others were doing the same. "And what in the world is a numbers station?" I asked.

Richard shrugged his shoulders and leaned back a bit in his chair. "Well, to be honest, no one really knows," he said. "But probably they're used by government intelligence agencies to communicate with spies in the field."

I frowned and nervously bit my lip. I wasn't sure what answer I had been expecting, but that certainly wasn't it. "Spies?" I asked. "Like James Bond?"

Richard laughed. "Not quite," he said. "More like the ordinary fellow down the street running the local falafel stand. These communications are for agents who are *really* deeply embedded in whatever country their mission is and who you'd never suspect of being intelligence assets."

This was getting a bit too much for me. *Spies? Falafel stands? Embedded agents? Intelligence assets?*

"Maybe you'd better start from the beginning," I suggested.

CHAPTER FOURTEEN
The Unbreakable Kind

Far away in his living room above Baker Street in London, Richard sat up straight in his chair and leaned toward the camera.

"There's not really that much to tell," he said. "But for several decades now various amateur radio enthusiasts around the world have noticed something very strange as they tuned their radios up and down through the shortwave bands. Surfing the waves of static and legitimate broadcast stations they would occasionally come across something that was completely out of place. Something so utterly bizarre that the instant they heard it the only thing they could do was simply stop cold and sit there listening—exhilarated, mesmerized and terrified all at the same time. What they were hearing was what is now referred to as *numbers stations*—radio broadcasts consisting of strange robotic-sounding voices reading out seemingly random letters and numbers in various languages.

"On various frequencies, for different lengths of time and at different times of the day or night—sometimes predictably, sometimes not—these broadcasts could be picked up by virtually anyone with a decent radio receiver. Each of the different broadcasts seemed to follow their own specific format. Perhaps a little bit of a song is played at first, repeated over and over so that whoever's listening can tune in better. This is then followed by a systematic reading of multiple groups of letters and numbers in various languages like English, German, Russian, Czech, Spanish, even Vietnamese or Chinese, although not all of the so-called *numbers stations* actually use numbers. Some of them transmit using other formats like Morse code or even more recently things like digital data bursts.

"Over the years these stations would continue broadcasting with various degrees of frequency and duration. Some of them have been transmitting regularly for decades while others have come and gone, even going silent for years before coming back again and resuming their regular broadcast schedule."

I could hardly believe my ears. "Transmitting regularly for decades?" I asked. "Decades?!?"

"Absolutely," Richard replied. "Some of these stations have been broadcasting since the days of the Cold War, before you or I or any of us were even born."

"But how is that possible?" I asked. "Don't people hear them? Why don't the authorities do something about it?"

"Kitty," Richard replied, his voice quiet and serious. "The people sending these transmissions *ARE* the 'authorities'."

There was no denying that logic. But I was still so stunned with disbelief that I hardly knew what to say. "And they're still broadcasting even nowadays?" I asked after a moment to get my thoughts together.

"Absolutely," Richard said again. "There are a number of known stations broadcasting regularly. In fact, some of them might even be on the air at this very moment."

Without even realizing it, all five of us sitting in that living room in the heart of Rome simultaneously turned our heads and looked over toward the hallway leading to the hidden room.

"Right at this very moment?" I asked, my voice slightly tinged with uneasiness. "You mean we could switch our radio on right now and hear one of these things?"

"If you're lucky," Richard replied.

'Lucky' isn't exactly the word I would have chosen, I told myself.

"Should we try?" Matteo asked hesitantly.

Vega and Giulia didn't look very convinced but I knew that eventually my morbid curiosity would get the best of me so I just went for it.

"Okay, Richard," I said, grabbing the iPad off its stand and carrying it toward the hallway, gesturing for the others to follow me. "Tell me what to do."

Pushing the wall panel fully open, I stepped into the room and switched on the lamp to take a seat in front of the desk. One by one, Charlie and the others gathered around the door to watch me.

"First show me the radio set you have there," Richard said.

I turned the iPad around obediently and showed Richard what we were working with.

"How's that?" I asked, switching the power switch and watching the various dials glow into life.

"Perfect," Richard replied, typing furiously on his computer at the other end of the video chat as he looked up some information. "Try this first. Go to nine point four five zero megahertz."

"Okay," I replied, reaching up to adjust the frequency dial. "But how do you know what frequencies will be broadcasting?"

"I actually don't know for sure," Richard replied. "But for the past couple of years some groups of dedicated amateurs have organized themselves and have been tracking these numbers stations on the Internet, so we'll just try a few of the currently active frequencies and see if we get lucky."

There was that word again–*lucky*.

I twisted the dial and skimmed across the airwaves with noisy static and faint hints of classical music and interference whining here and there as I went. Slowly I began to zero in on 9.450 MHz and leaned forward to listen carefully.

Right over my shoulder, the others also leaned in from the hallway, perking their ears and bracing themselves for what might come next.

"There's nothing, Richard," I said after a few long seconds of careful listening. "Just static."

"All right then," Richard replied, clicking with his mouse a few times and squinting at his computer monitor with Ellie watching over his shoulder. "Try this one. Eleven point five two three megahertz."

Spinning the dial again I skated over the noisy frequencies up to the eleven thousand hertz range.

"*..is the BBC...*" I heard for an instant, buried among the whistling static somewhere around ten thousand hertz, followed by a snippet from some majestic symphony.

"Here we go," I mumbled to myself as I fine-tuned the dial to 11.523 MHz and listened carefully.

Static. Nothing but static and the distant crackle of cosmic ray interference.

"Nothing there either," Charlie said from behind me as I heard the clock back in the living room begin to strike the top of the hour.

Maybe we won't get lucky after all, I thought. Part of me was disappointed but I have to admit that another part of me was secretly relieved.

"Okay, one more and then we'll give up," Richard said, clicking through another couple of webpages. "Last one. This one was first discovered all the way back in the 1980s. Thirteen point four two seven megahertz."

"Aye, aye, sir," I replied, laughing as I spun the dial up again.

They always say that the third time is the charm and in this case it couldn't have been more true. As I raced up the dial and zeroed in on the exact frequency, a tinny and robotic-sounding middle-aged woman with a strange accent slowly emerged from the fog of static.

"*Fiver–three–four–oblique–zero–zero*," the voice said.

I felt a familiar chill run down the length of my spine and turned my head to look back at Charlie and the others in amazement.

"I can't believe it," Vega said breathlessly as the voice continued to repeat the same six-word phrase over and over several times before falling silent.

"Is that it?" I asked after a few more seconds of dead static.

"It must have been a null message," Richard said.

"What do you mean?" I asked.

Richard thought about this for a second. "Like a message to say '*hello, we're still here, but there's nothing to tell you right now, bye*'," he finally said.

I nodded my head. "Makes sense," I replied.

"Try this one next," Richard said. "It's just past the top of the hour and that's when many of these stations start to broadcast, so maybe we'll get lucky again. Go to eight point four two zero megahertz."

I began to get excited now. My uneasiness and fear had now been replaced with the thrill of the chase, like we were in pursuit of some fleeting and elusive apparition dancing away from us across the radio dial.

As I approached 8.420 MHz, the shifting dunes of static gradually settled down and the chimeric sound of a young woman's voice began to materialize.

"*Dva–shest–chyetirye–shest–vosyem,*" the voice said. "*Tree–dva–shest–chyetirye–vosyem...*"

"What language is that?" I whispered loudly as the voice continued reciting numbers.

"Russian," Richard replied from the other end of the video chat.

I sat there with my mouth hanging open, absolutely hypnotized by the woman's voice. It was flanging and robotic-sounding but also beautiful somehow and I felt like I could almost imagine what she must look like.

"*Chyetirye–shest–vosyem–dva–shest,*" the voice continued. "*Null–null–null–null–null.*"

With that last number (presumably zero) repeated five times, the broadcast went silent.

I waited a few seconds and then turned the iPad so I could see Richard better. "These aren't real people talking, are they?" I asked, still imagining what that Russian girl must look like.

"Heavens no," Richard replied. "At least not live in real time. At best it's a compilation of recordings of some real human being reciting the numbers one to ten which is cut together into whatever series of numbers are required. Like an automated phone message."

I nodded my head. Of course that was what it was. It was too robotic to be anything else. And yet this voice had sounded almost human.

"This is really unbelievable," I heard Matteo say and turned to see that he was actually smiling. He looked as excited as I was.

"Shall we try one more?" Richard asked.

"Definitely," both Matteo and I said at the same time. Charlie was nodding his head too and even Vega and Giulia were smiling a little bit as well.

"Okay, something a bit different this time," Richard replied as he flipped to another webpage. "Eighteen point six six seven megahertz."

"On my way," I replied and cranked the dial up to 18.667 MHz.

This time as I zeroed in I was expecting the sound of another voice but instead it was a slowly alternating electronic tone that emerged from all the staticky hiss and noise.

"*Whee-oooo, whee-oooo, whee-oooo,*" the noise went, over and over again.

"What is this?" I asked in bewilderment.

"Something different," Richard replied. "Just wait."

"*Whee-oooo, whee-oooo,*" the noise continued, over and over until I was about to open my mouth and say something again. Then, suddenly, the tones changed and seemed to go crazy, beeping and booping all over the place like some crazy random ringtone. This continued for about a minute and then there was one, long final tone and then the whole thing went silent.

"What in the world was that?" I cried, laughing out loud by the time the whole thing finished.

"I told you it was something different," Richard said with a grin. "It's called a polytone sequence. Each tone represents a specific number and when you run the whole sequence through a computer decoding program, it spits out a series of numbers in the end."

"So it's still all numbers?" I asked. "That's it?"

"That's it," Richard replied. "But unlike the earlier voice stations, this kind of transmission requires a special computer program to interpret it– and by that I simply mean to convert the tones to numbers. Not to actually decode it."

"How would you decode it, then?" I asked.

Richard shrugged. "The same way you decode the more basic voice transmissions," he said.

"And how do you do that?" I asked. "Because that's actually the reason I contacted you tonight. To help us decode the message I played for you earlier."

"Are you serious?!?" Richard asked in surprise.

"Of course," I replied. "You were so helpful a few weeks ago in figuring out Bruce Ismay's *Titanic* code that I thought you might be able to help us with this new coded message as well."

Richard took a deep breath and leaned back in his chair with his hands over his head.

"I'm afraid that's impossible," he said apologetically.

"What do you mean?" I asked with a frown.

"Bruce Ismay's *Titanic* code was one of the most basic substitution ciphers imaginable," Richard said. "And as you might recall, even that one was impossible to crack until you finally did it for yourself up there at Newgrange in Ireland."

"And this one?" I asked. "What kind of code is this new one?"

Richard leaned forward again and looked at me earnestly through the eye of the video camera.

"The unbreakable kind," Richard said simply.

CHAPTER FIFTEEN
Better Than A Computer

"Are you sure, Richard?" I asked, disappointed and confused. "Are you sure these *numbers station* codes are unbreakable?"

"Absolutely sure," Richard replied emphatically. "Absolutely, one hundred percent unbreakable. That's the reason they use them. Because they can never be broken."

"Who is 'they'?" Charlie asked from behind me.

Richard exhaled deeply and thought this over for a second. "Well, like I said before, spies and government intelligence agencies," he replied. "You know, like the CIA, GRU, MI6, Mossad, and God knows who else. But in truth no one really knows for sure. That's the beauty of using one-way shortwave radio transmissions. They travel long distances and are notoriously difficult to pinpoint. That is precisely why they use them."

"So all these broadcasts we just listened to?" I asked. "No one has any idea where they are coming from?"

"Basically, yes," Richard replied. "Although the ones we just listened to are fairly well known and broadcast regularly so there are some theories as to their sources."

"Theories like what?" I asked.

"Well, the first one we heard," Richard replied, "the one with the woman speaking English. According to the Internet repository of wisdom, that one originates from Polish intelligence."

"Polish intelligence?" I asked. "Speaking English?"

"Why not?" Richard replied. "Apparently the Russians use all sorts of languages, English, French, Russian, etc."

"So the second one was Russian?" I asked. "I mean, according to the Internet repository of wisdom?"

Richard shook his head. "That one is supposedly Ukrainian," he replied. "But the last one we heard–the weird polytone transmission– that one is apparently Russian."

"And what about the one from my phone?" I asked. "The one I played for you earlier? Do you know where that one is from?"

"I have no idea," Richard said. "Of course, I'm not an expert on this stuff but if you send it to me, and also tell me the frequency it was received at, I could take a look and see if it matches any of the known station entries in the online database."

"Okay," I replied, grabbing my phone and quickly attaching the movie file to an email so I could send it to Richard.

"Give me a few minutes," Richard said as soon as he'd received it. "I'll call you back."

"Okay," I replied and we both hit 'end'.

The next ten minutes were extremely nerve-wracking for me. I'd thought, after Richard had instantly recognized the recording of the voice on my phone, that maybe he would really be able to help decipher the message as well. But I guess I'd just let my excitement get me carried away because if Richard was right and this *was* some kind of message cipher used by the most advanced and secretive intelligence organizations in the world, then despite the deceptively simple appearance of those seemingly random sequences of numbers, whatever the underlying message was, it would surely be impossible to break. How could it possibly be otherwise?

With all of this weighing heavily on my mind, the five of us returned to the living room and Matteo made for the kitchen to get us some fresh cups of hot espresso.

Sitting down on the sofa, I turned toward Vega to ask her a question. "You said the other night that this house belonged to your father, right?" I asked.

"Yes," Vega replied, nodding.

I turned to Giulia next. "And you said that Matteo's bedroom was on the other side of the wall of that hidden room, right?" I asked.

"Right," Giulia replied, looking somewhat bewildered.

"So, if Matteo used to hear those strange voices when he was still a child," I continued. "Then that means that someone has been using that hidden room back there for a long time."

"Presumably, yes," Giulia replied.

"And I think we can all agree that that person was probably your father, am I right?" I asked.

Slowly everyone nodded in agreement.

"It only makes sense that it would have been our father, yes," Vega replied.

"Was there anything unusual about the work that your father did?" I asked. "Like did he make a lot of business trips to foreign countries or anything like that?"

"What are you trying to say?" Vega asked suspiciously.

"I think what Kitty is trying to ask is whether it's possible that your father was a spy," Charlie interjected.

Vega and her two siblings burst into laughter.

"A spy?!?" Giulia chuckled. "Not likely."

"Why not?" I asked, not understanding the joke.

Vega grabbed a photo frame off of a side table and flipped it around to show it to me. "Let's just say he was hardly the type," she said.

The picture was of an older man, bald with slight fringes of thin white hair at the sides, overweight with glasses and wearing shorts and sandals with white socks pulled up to the knees. I almost laughed when I saw it. Vega was right. He was hardly the type you would imagine when you thought of someone as being a spy.

"Looks pretty ordinary to me," I said. "But if Richard were here, he would probably tell us that it's the most ordinary people who make the best spies."

"Are you saying that our father may have been working for some kind of intelligence agency?" Matteo asked.

"If what Richard was telling us is true about the origins of these so-called numbers stations," I replied. "Then I think it's definitely a possibility."

Vega laughed. "Well, it seems completely impossible to me that he could have kept such a thing secret for so many years," she said. "But you're right. It's definitely a possibility."

"Then, I think the question we need to be asking ourselves right now isn't how *we* are going to decipher this new message," I said. "But rather how would your *father* have deciphered it?"

"How do we even know that message was intended for my father?" Vega asked. "Just because he was listening in doesn't mean that every message would be for him. And besides, he died almost three months ago. Surely whatever spy agency he might have been working for would know this."

She had a point.

"True," I said. "But even if this particular message wasn't intended for him, there would still have to have been some way for him to decipher any of the other messages he'd received. Did your father have a computer?"

Vega shook her head. "No, sorry," she said. "We bought him a laptop years ago, but he never used it so Matteo just took it home with him and used it instead."

"He must have had something," I replied. "Some kind of decryption machine or device that would have allowed him to decipher those messages. In fact, that's probably one of the things that the burglar was carrying with him when he ran out the door since there's clearly nothing else left in the room anywhere. There's nowhere to hide anything in there."

My train of thought was suddenly interrupted by the chirping of an incoming video chat request on my iPad. It was Richard finally calling us back.

"Hello again, everybody," Richard said cheerily after I connected the call.

"And?" I asked anxiously. "Did you have any luck?"

Richard shook his head. "Sorry, Kitty," he said. "I couldn't find anything. None of the numbers stations that we currently know about match the format and frequency of the message you sent me."

Dammit, I thought.

"How can that be?" I asked. "Surely there were messages before this one. How is it possible that we found something completely new?"

"I don't think you did," Richard said. "Don't forget there's a lot of space out there on the airwaves. Who knows how many stations might be out there that no one knows about. If a particular station doesn't broadcast very often or if the messages are quite short like this one was, then it's quite possible that simply no one ever stumbled across it even after so many years."

It wasn't a very satisfactory answer but it seemed that it was all we were going to get.

"Well, thank you for trying anyway, Richard," I said. "I was hoping that we could at least find out where the messages were coming from, since it seems that the intruders earlier this evening might have made off with the decryption computer."

"Decryption computer?" Richard asked, wrinkling his forehead in confusion.

"You know," I replied. "Like some kind of device to decode these unbreakable number messages."

Richard laughed. "Lord no," he said, chuckling through his nose. "You don't need a computer to do that. You need something *better* than a computer."

Now it was my turn to be confused. "What on Earth is better than a computer at breaking unbreakable codes?" I asked.

Richard disappeared for a moment, ducking down somewhere off screen for a moment before returning to view.

"This," he said, lifting his arm and holding a pencil up to the camera.

CHAPTER SIXTEEN
Hello Kitty

"A pencil?!?" I asked incredulously. "How is that possible? Is it some kind of super secret spy pencil? Like a deluxe James Bond super secret decoding pencil?"

Richard shook his head. "I'm afraid not," he replied. "Just a plain old normal pencil."

I was very confused. "Then how?" I asked. "How could someone solve such an advanced and complex message encryption without some kind of computer or something?"

Richard shuffled forward in his chair with an amused smile on his face. I could tell from his expression that the tour guide part of his personality was delighted at the prospect of giving us all a little lecture on the secret world of advanced spycraft.

"Imagine that some fellow selling falafel on a street corner in Tehran is actually a spy for some foreign intelligence agency," Richard began dramatically. "And then one day the police decide to search his house. They find a radio, but lots of people have radios so it's not that suspicious, but just imagine if they found a decryption program on his computer or some kind of decoding device in his house? That would definitely be the end of his career as a spy—not to mention his end as a falafel maker."

"What's with all this falafel stuff, Richard? Are you hungry or something?" I asked, teasing. "Or do you just have some secret love of falafel?"

"Doesn't everyone like falafel?" Richard replied, grinning.

"But of course, you're right about all that," I continued. "Obviously if they found something like that in his house it would mean a death sentence for him."

"Exactly," Richard agreed. "So whatever system is used to encode these numbered messages not only has to be completely secure, but it also has to be extremely simple to decode."

"Is that even possible?" I asked.

"Most definitely. It's called a *one-time pad* and it works like this," Richard replied, reaching forward to grab some paper off his desk. "There are twenty-six letters in the alphabet, right?"

"Right," I agreed.

"If you assign each of those letters a number, you end up with something like this," Richard said.

```
01 02 03 04 05 06 07 08 09 10 11 12 13 14 15 16 17 18 19 20 21 22 23 24 25 26
A  B  C  D  E  F  G  H  I  J  K  L  M  N  O  P  Q  R  S  T  U  V  W  X  Y  Z
```

Richard finished scribbling furiously and held up a chart matching every letter of the alphabet to a number. A being 1, B being 2, and so on.

"Now let's say I want to send you a secret message to say hello," Richard continued. "Something simple like just *HELLO KITTY*."

All of us laughed at Richard's choice of phrases but he was already on a roll in a world of his own so he didn't even notice.

"If you write out the message using letters instead of numbers, you get something like this," Richard said, holding up another chart, this one with his message written out with a number corresponding to each letter.

```
08 05 12 12 15 11 09 20 20 25
H  E  L  L  O  K  I  T  T  Y
```

"So if you just use the numbers then the message reads like this," Richard said.

08 05 12 12 15 11 09 20 20 25

"Okay, got it so far," I said, nodding my head as I glanced back to see Charlie and Matteo pulling their chairs forward so they could follow Richard's explanation more closely.

"So now we use the *one-time pad* to encode the message," Richard said. "And all that is is a series of random letters or numbers that only two people in the world have a copy of—me and you. And if you check your phone you'll see that I just sent a series of random numbers to you."

I reached for my phone and checked my messages and sure enough there was one.

14 27 63 81 72 19 43 56 44 12

"Okay, I've got it," I said. "Now what?"

"Now grab a pencil because I am about to send you a coded message," Richard replied gleefully.

I reached into my shoulder bag and grabbed a pencil and my notebook.

"Go for it," I said with a grin. "I'm ready."

"Message commencing," Richard said, changing his voice so he could pretend to sound like a robot. "Two–two–three–two–seven–five–nine–

three–eight–seven–three–zero–five–two–six–six–four–three–seven."

Charlie and the others were crowded around me now, watching over my shoulder as I scribbled down the string of numbers.

"...six–four–three–seven," I mumbled to myself as I finished writing. "Okay, I've got it."

22327593873052766437

"And now you're ready to decode," Richard said proudly as he leaned back in his chair. "You have everything you need."

"I don't get it," I replied uncertainly. "What do I do?"

"Well, let me answer that by telling you what I did to my message before I rattled off that series of numbers just now," Richard explained. "I took the number value of each letter in my message and added it to each corresponding number in the random number key. So the first letter H, the eighth letter of the alphabet, gets added to fourteen which is the first number of my decoding key, and the result is twenty-two, which is the first two numbers of my coded message to you."

Finally I understood. It was so simple. All I had to do was subtract each number from the coded message from the corresponding number on the decoding key and then convert those numbers to letters to get the final message.

Flipping to a new page of my notebook, I carefully wrote out the various number sequences as everyone watched over my shoulder. At the top I started by writing out the coded number transmission that Richard had read out. On the next row I wrote the decoding key numbers that he'd sent to me on my phone. Once I finished all that I simply did the math and came up with the final decoded number sequence that I was then able to convert to letters to get the final message.

coded message from Richard		22	32	75	93	87	30	52	76	64	37
minus decoding key	−	14	27	63	81	72	19	43	56	44	12
equals final numbers	=	08	05	12	12	15	11	09	20	20	25
final message		H	E	L	L	O	K	I	T	T	Y

Smiling proudly, I held up my notebook so everyone could see, but there was still something that was bothering me.

"But I'm a bit confused, Richard. How can this possibly be such an unbreakable code?" I asked. "I mean, how is this any different than the kind of secret codes that me and me friends used to send messages when we were kids?"

"It's actually *completely* different than that," he replied. "When you were a kid you probably used the same decoding key over and over again.

But in this case the spies would *never, ever, ever* use the same key more than once. If they did it would compromise the entire code and it would no longer be secure. As long as the decoding key is completely random and is never used twice, the code is completely unbreakable."

"That makes sense, I guess," I mumbled to myself as I tried to wrap my head around everything. All of the math was starting to give me a headache.

"That's why they call it a *one-time pad*," Richard said. "Because you only use it once and then throw it out. Plus they often come in the shape of a pad or big list of random-looking letters or numbers."

"Letters?!?" I said, suddenly sitting up straight in my chair. "What do you mean?"

Richard looked at me for a moment and then shrugged his shoulders. "Well, the key doesn't necessarily have to be numbers," he said. "Letters can have numerical value too so a random sequence of letters can just as easily be used as a decoding key as numbers."

A random sequence of letters?!? I thought to myself, almost jumping out of my chair. I looked up at Charlie who had already read my mind.

"Wait here!" he cried as he dashed down the hallway to the hidden room. He was back in a matter of seconds with the piece of paper that had been tacked up onto the wall above the desk. He quickly handed it to me and I knelt down on the floor in front of the iPad camera so I could show it to Richard.

"A random series of letters like this?" I asked.

```
FFAGFFEE
EFECDDDB
FFFFEF
FBFFBB
AGGFEDD
DEFGAFA
EDEBCBCG
FFACCCCAA
CGAEFCFG
FEFEFEGF
CBCDCDEE
GEGEBEG
DBCAAA
CFACDCACDE
FAAAGFC
GCDBCFFFE
CCEEGGE
```

Richard leaned forward and squinted his eyes as he carefully examined the list. "Where did you find this?" he asked.

"It was pinned to the wall behind the desk in the secret room," Charlie answered.

"Just out in the open?" Richard asked. "Not hidden somewhere?"

I nodded my head in excitement but I could tell from the look on Richard's face that he wasn't convinced.

"What is it, Richard?" I asked. "Don't you think that this is the key?"

Richard sighed and leaned back in his chair, shaking his head slowly. "I suppose it *could* be," he replied. "But I really don't think so. It doesn't look right and there are nowhere near enough characters to be a proper decoding key."

"But what is it, then?" I asked. "Does it look familiar to you?"

"Not really, no," he admitted apologetically.

Frustrated and disappointed I lowered the paper away from the camera and slumped on the floor. "So, if this isn't it," I asked. "Then what *would* one of these so-called *one-time pads* look like?"

"It depends," Richard said. "But probably quite small. Maybe an inch or so across."

"I'm not sure I understand," I replied. I tried to imagine what Richard was talking about but in my disappointment I simply couldn't do it.

"Maybe I have a picture of one somewhere," Richard said, pulling himself out of his chair and disappearing out of sight off camera.

On the speaker we could hear Richard rummaging around in his apartment with Ellie as they tried to find what he was looking for. After a few minutes he returned with a thick hardcover book in his hands and sat down to open it. He flipped through the pages for a moment until he found what he was looking for and then turned the book toward the camera so all of us could see.

"Like this," he said as the five of us in Rome crowded around the iPad screen. "You see? It's a little tiny book with a bunch of pages of nothing but number groups. Even the paper is special because it's a kind that burns instantly but doesn't leave any ashes behind."

I stared at the tiny booklet for a second but it was nothing like anything I'd ever seen before in my life. But to my right I suddenly heard Giulia gasp in surprise, and when I turned toward her I saw her standing there with an absolutely flabbergasted look on her face.

"Oh my God," she said in astonishment. "I've seen one of those before!"

CHAPTER SEVENTEEN
So What Do We Do Now?

"You have?" Vega asked, looking over at Giulia with her eyes wide. "You've seen one of these little books before?"

Giulia nodded briskly. "Yes," she replied. "I think it was when we were sorting through father's things after he died."

"Where?" Vega asked, her voice tense with excitement. "Where did you see it?"

Giulia thought about this for a long moment. "I'm... I'm not sure..." she finally replied, looking anxiously around the room as she struggled to remember. "I think it was here in the living room, but..."

"But...?" Vega asked nervously.

Giulia looked over at the bookshelves and suddenly her eyes lit up.

"The books!" she cried. "It was on one the bookshelves somewhere. Stuck behind a book, I think."

Vega whirled around to face the long wall of bookshelves that lined the opposite side of the room.

"Which book?" I asked. "There are hundreds of them."

"Thousands, actually," Vega corrected me glumly.

"I don't know..." Giulia replied, taking a few hesitant steps toward the imposing wall of books. "I think... no wait, forget it. I simply don't know. I have no idea."

Vega let out a frustrated sigh that sounded a little harsher than she meant it to, but we were all very tired and our nerves were starting to get a bit frayed.

"Well, look on the bright side," I said, trying to sound as cheerful and optimistic as I could. "There are five of us and with everyone looking it shouldn't take too long to find it. Right?"

I looked over at the others hopefully.

"You're right. Of course, you're right," Vega replied after a moment. "Why don't you start at the left shelf? I'll take the second one. Then Matteo, then Giulia, then Charlie, okay?"

"And I'll just wait right here and make a cup of tea," we heard Richard say over the iPad speaker.

"Don't go anywhere," I joked as we all headed for our assigned shelves.

Everyone laughed and quickly got to work pulling books off the shelves and looking behind them. Far off to the left in the A's and B's section I started to do the same, standing on my tiptoes to reach the top shelves and playing a game with myself to try and guess what the books were based on the Italian names that I was reading off the spines as I went.

Miserere mei, Deus
Divina Commedia
La Vita Nuova
De Virtutibus et Vitiis Libellus
De Caelo et Mundo
Orgoglio e Pregiudizio
Ragione e Sentimento
Figuratio Aristotelici Physici Auditus
De l'infinito, Universo e Mondi

Most of the books were quite old and looked like they might be very valuable, but there were also a few relatively newer ones here and there scattered in-between. Clearly Matteo and Vega's father had been an avid collector of books and there seemed to be books about everything–philosophy, music, religion, art, poetry, history, and on and on covering every possible subject imaginable. They were neatly organized alphabetically by author but other than that there seemed to be no discernable common thread tying all of them together. In fact, the only thing that they all seemed to have in common was the fact that not a single one of them had the tiny little book of numbers that we were looking for hiding behind it.

Nearing the end of the B's, I smiled when I saw a title that I'd seen there on the shelves a couple of days earlier–*Il Codice da Vinci*–*The Da Vinci Code*.

Wouldn't it be funny if the decoding pad was behind this one, I thought as I slid the book out from the shelf and peeked behind it.

"Oh my God," I gasped in laughter as I pulled the book the rest of the way off the shelf.

"What's so funny?" Charlie asked me from a few shelves down the wall.

"I found it!" I cried triumphantly as I reached into the gap between the books on the shelf and extracted the tiny little booklet that was hiding there. "Hidden behind *The Da Vinci Code*."

"That's so funny," Vega said, laughing as she slid the books in her hand back into their places on the shelf.

"Your father had a sense of humor, it seems," Charlie said as he and the others gathered around me to see what I'd found.

The little book in my palm was almost identical to the one in the picture that Richard had shown us. It was made from a long strip of thin, delicate paper that was folded accordion-style back and forth to separate the individual pages and on each page there were numbers. Ten rows by ten columns of nothing but numbers.

I flipped to the first page of the booklet and took a closer look. At the loose end of the page there was a slightly jagged edge where previous pages had apparently been torn off. Clearly each page was intended to be used only once before being ripped off and discarded or burned, just like Richard had said.

```
2598 1447 7112 2526 6707 7471 5098 7190 9958 9585
3255 6815 5639 2660 2313 8533 3317 0766 0483 2073
3678 1824 0120 2677 7610 0579 3502 5833 0660 6311
4868 8353 4867 4157 3355 3709 4354 1223 7442 4388
1585 7879 1022 1423 9995 1779 1798 0918 1472 4317
2449 4266 1993 5285 5405 3894 8515 8111 6482 1391
3066 6537 5965 9366 7106 2496 3894 9792 8986 4806
4735 1519 4857 4067 5269 0523 4669 5465 6663 5317
1631 7286 0933 9887 5879 0651 5604 0303 3428 1475
7010 5151 0016 1066 6372 4561 2930 7955 4031 7437
```

"Hello! Don't forget about me!" Richard called from the iPad that was still propped up on a side table in the living room. I turned my head and saw him there on the small screen, grinning and waving his arms above his head.

"Sorry, Richard," I replied, laughing as I brought the little book over to show him as well.

"Yes, yes," he said as he examined the book via the video camera. "That's it. That's most definitely a *one-time pad* type of decoding key."

"So what do we do now?" I asked eagerly.

Richard glanced up at me from the iPad screen and gave me a grin. "Now we decode the message," he said simply.

CHAPTER EIGHTEEN
Unbelievably, Extraordinarily, Ridiculously Mind-Bogglingly Difficult

I wish that I could tell you that decoding the message was relatively simple. In fact, I'd be happy if I could honestly tell you that it was actually an extremely *difficult* thing to do. But the truth is that it was an unbelievably, extraordinarily, ridiculously mind-bogglingly difficult thing to accomplish.

Seriously.

It was *so* incredibly difficult, in fact, that I am dreading even trying to explain it to you here on the pages of this book. And not just for my sake either. I might be the one who has to type the whole explanation out in some hopefully coherent fashion, but you're the one who has to actually read it all.

So, are you ready?

Good luck to both of us.

Deep breath. Here we go.

With my notebook in one hand and my iPhone in the other, I flopped myself into a chair in the living room. "First things first," I said aloud to no one in particular. "I have to write out the entire number sequence from the video."

As I got to work, Charlie and the others returned to their seats and watched as I pulled out a pencil and hit play.

"*Seven–three–two–three... I say again,*" the voice began before pausing for a moment. "*Foxtrot–foxtrot–alpha–golf–foxtrot–foxtrot–echo–echo...*"

"Wait a minute," I said, stopping the playback. "Here is that series of letters in phonetic alphabet again. These *have* to have something to do with that list of letters that was tacked to the wall. That can't possibly be a coincidence."

Charlie grabbed the list off the table and nodded at me. "Play it back again," he said.

I hit play on the video again and the series of phonetic letters started again from the top.

"*Foxtrot–foxtrot–alpha–golf–foxtrot–foxtrot–echo–echo,*" the voice said and then paused before repeating the same thing again. "*Foxtrot–foxtrot–alpha–golf–foxtrot–foxtrot–echo–echo.*"

"That's the top line on the list," Charlie said as he shuffled over on the sofa so the rest of us could see the paper as well. "F–F–A–G–F–F–E–E."

```
FFAGFFEE
EEECDDDB
FFFFEF
FBFFBB
AGGFEDD
DEFGAFA
EDEBCBCG
FFACCCCAA
CGAEFCFG
FEFEFEGF
CBCDCDEE
GEGEBEG
DBCAAA
CFACDCACDE
FAAAGFC
GCDBCFFFE
CCEEGGE
```

Okay, what does that tell us? I thought. *Not much.*

I hit play on the video again and we listened to the second short series of phonetic letters.

"*Foxtrot–foxtrot–foxtrot–foxtrot–echo–foxtrot,*" the voice continued, pausing again and repeating this second sequence as well. "*Foxtrot–foxtrot–foxtrot–foxtrot–echo–foxtrot.*"

"And that's the third one on the list," Charlie said, tapping the page with his finger.

"So, what does that mean?" I asked.

Simultaneously all of us turned toward the iPad screen where Richard was still watching us from his living room a thousand miles away in London.

"What?" Richard asked when he saw us all looking at him. "Don't ask me what it means. I have no idea."

"Is it also some kind of code?" Vega asked.

I shook my head and was about to answer when Richard beat me to it.

"No, not a code. It can't be since the voice message is broadcasting the same text that's on that sheet of yours," Richard said. "There's nothing to decode."

"Then what can it possibly be?" Vega asked.

"Maybe some kind of call sign like airplanes use?" I suggested. "Like, for example, my aircraft call sign is Charlie–Foxtrot–Kilo–Tango–Yankee."

Richard nodded his head. "Yeah, maybe something like that," he agreed. "Or some kind of message identifier or something."

"Keep going," Charlie urged me with a nod of his head. "Let's hear the rest of it."

With the phonetic letter groups out of the way, the voice went straight into the numbers as soon as I hit play.

"*One–four–four–seven, three–five, seven–five, two–six–nine–nine,*" the voice began. "*Seven–six–seven–five, four–eight–zero–nine...*"

On and on the voice went until the end of its transmission and all the while I wrote down every single number group, putting spaces whenever the voice stopped for a short pause.

"*Seven–three–two–three... end,*" the voice concluded, leaving nothing but dead static.

To be absolutely sure that I'd transcribed it correctly, I scrolled the video and started all over again from the top. When I was finished I put my phone away and flipped my notebook around to show everyone the entire message written out.

FFAGFFEE FFAGFFEE FFFFEF FFFFEF
1447 35 75 2699 7675 4809 1124 3914 2490
1640 4570 8142 8289 2269 6270 9934 0104
0478 7512 2096 0023 5500 4472 0320 4135
6258 6335 5006 5451 9367 2052 8572 8175
0619 8532 9911 8672 7323

"Okay," I said, looking to Richard for the answers. "Now what?"

Richard pulled his chair forward and got ready to do some work. "First, send me a photo of the decoding key," he said. "And one of the messages written out as well."

I did as Richard instructed and soon he'd printed both of the pictures out in London and was examining them on the table in front of him.

"I think a better way to group the transmission letters and numbers is like this," Richard said, scribbling for a minute or two before holding up a page with both the coded text...

FFAGFFEE FFAGFFEE

FFFFEF FFFFEF

1447 35 75

2699 7675 4809 1124 3914 2490 1640

4570 8142 8289 2269 6270 9934 0104

0478 7512 2096 0023 5500 4472 0320

4135 6258 6335 5006 5451 9367 2052

8572 8175 0619 8532 9911 8672 7323

...and the decoding key to the camera.

```
2598 1447 7112 2526 6707 7471 5098 7190 9958 9585
3255 6815 5639 2660 2313 8533 3317 0766 0483 2073
3678 1824 0120 2677 7610 0579 3502 5833 0660 6311
4868 8353 4867 4157 3355 3709 4354 1223 7442 4388
1585 7879 1022 1423 9995 1779 1798 0918 1472 4317
2449 4266 1993 5285 5405 3894 8515 8111 6482 1391
3066 6537 5965 9366 7106 2496 3894 9792 8986 4806
4735 1519 4857 4067 5269 0523 4669 5465 6663 5317
1631 7286 0933 9887 5879 0651 5604 0303 3428 1475
7010 5151 0016 1066 6372 4561 2930 7955 4031 7437
```

"Okay, that looks good," I agreed, copying out the same structure on a new blank page of my notebook. "Although I'm not sure why that's a better organizational system for the information. What's so special about those three numbers—one, four, four, seven, thirty-five and seventy-five?"

The words had barely left my mouth when I suddenly realized what was special about them. Or at least what was special about the first two number groups.

"Richard! Look!" I cried. "One, four, four, seven! It's in the decoding key as well. Second number from the top left."

"Exactly," Richard replied.

By now, Charlie and the others had migrated onto the chairs and floor around me and were eagerly examining the complex grids of numbers that were laid out on the coffee table in front of us.

"So what does that mean?" Charlie asked. "What's the significance of the number being in both?"

I didn't have a clue what the answer to that might be.

"My guess is that it's a starting point indicator for the decoding key," Richard explained. "Don't forget that in these systems there are always two copies of the key—one with the sender and one with the receiver—and if I'm not mistaken, this number 'one, four, four, seven' is meant to tell the receiver to start decoding the message using numbers from that point forward in the key."

"But how do we even know to start on this first page of the key?" Charlie asked. "There's hundreds of pages in the little book."

Richard nodded slowly. "True," he admitted. "But I think we have to assume that the decoding key operates by working through the pages one at a time, tearing each off and burning it or eating it once it's used up."

"Eating it?" Vega asked, making a face.

"Certainly," Richard replied. "In fact, the whole book is probably designed so it can be crumpled up and quickly swallowed if need be. To destroy the evidence in an emergency."

"Okay, so what now?" Matteo asked, stifling a yawn as he tried to direct the conversation back on topic.

"The number thirty-five," I said proudly, pointing to my transcription of the message.

FFⵣGFFEE FFⵣGFFEE
FFFFEF FFFFEF
1447 35 75

2699 7675 4809 1124 3914 2490 1640
4570 8142 8289 2269 6270 9934 0104
0478 7512 2096 0023 5500 4472 0320
4135 6258 6335 5006 5451 9367 2052
8572 8175 0619 8532 9911 8672 7323

"Thirty-five?" Charlie asked, leaning closer and squinting at my handwriting. "I thought that was a four-digit group—three, five, seven, five. All the other groups are four digits. Why do you have those two numbers split in two?"

"Because I put spaces whenever the voice paused," I replied. "And the voice definitely paused between the three-five and the seven-five. I double-checked that specifically."

"Okay," Charlie nodded, not really understanding. "So what do those two numbers mean?"

I pointed to my notes again to explain. "I have no idea what the seventy-five means," I replied. "But thirty-five is the number of individual number groups in the coded message, each of them consisting of four digits. Seven columns across times five rows down equals thirty-five. You see?"

Charlie nodded and grinned at me. "Yes, I see," he replied, grinning more with every second. "But what about the number seventy-five? What does that mean?"

"I already said, I don't know," I replied, unsure why Charlie was grinning so much.

But then I noticed that it wasn't just Charlie who was smiling at me. Little by little I realized that *everyone* was staring at me with a crazy grin on their face, including Richard from all the way in England.

"Are you sure you don't know?" Matteo asked, barely able to contain himself from laughing out loud.

"What?!??" I asked, completely not understanding what was going on. "Why is everyone laughing at me?!?"

"Should we put her out of her misery and let her off the hook?" Charlie asked, turning to the others for confirmation.

"We probably should," Matteo replied. "I don't think she's ever going to figure it out."

"Figure *WHAT* out?!?" I asked.

But then I finally saw it. I'd just given them the answer myself in the first place. The main part of the coded message consisted of thirty-five groups of numbers, arranged by Richard and myself in a grid that was seven columns across and five down. Seven by five.

"Do you see why I arranged them like that, now?" Richard asked with a chuckle as he saw the expression on my face.

"Yes, I do," I replied, my face burning red hot in embarrassment. "Sorry for being so stupid."

"Don't be crazy," Charlie said, reaching over to give me a rough hug. "You're the one whose figured half of all this out so far while the rest of us have just been sitting along for the ride."

I smiled at Charlie appreciatively for a second and then turned back to the matter at hand in an attempt to put my embarrassing episode behind us.

"Okay, so that means we can start decoding now, right?" I asked, looking up at Richard.

"I think so," Richard replied as he held a modified version of the decoding key up to the video camera. "And if my guess is right then we're supposed to use *this* part of the key to decode the message."

Richard had taken his printout of the decoding key and crossed out all the numbers that he thought the coded message was telling us we should ignore. With that done, all that was left was a seven by five grid of number groups, starting after the group one, four, four, seven at the top left.

~~2598~~ ~~1447~~ 7112 2526 6707 7471 5098 7190 9958 ~~9585~~
~~3255~~ ~~6815~~ 5639 2660 2313 8533 3317 0766 0483 ~~2073~~
~~3678~~ ~~1824~~ 0120 2677 7610 0579 3502 5833 0660 ~~6311~~
~~4868~~ ~~8353~~ 4867 4157 3355 3709 4354 1223 7442 ~~4388~~
~~1585~~ ~~7879~~ 1022 1423 9995 1779 1798 0918 1472 ~~4317~~
~~2449~~ ~~4266~~ ~~1993~~ ~~5285~~ ~~5405~~ ~~3894~~ ~~8515~~ ~~8111~~ ~~6482~~ ~~1391~~
~~3066~~ ~~6537~~ ~~5965~~ ~~9366~~ ~~7106~~ ~~2496~~ ~~3894~~ ~~9792~~ ~~8986~~ ~~4806~~
~~4735~~ ~~1519~~ ~~4857~~ ~~4067~~ ~~5269~~ ~~0523~~ ~~4669~~ ~~5465~~ ~~6663~~ ~~5317~~
~~1631~~ ~~7286~~ ~~0933~~ ~~9887~~ ~~5879~~ ~~0651~~ ~~5604~~ ~~0303~~ ~~3428~~ ~~1475~~
~~7010~~ ~~5151~~ ~~0016~~ ~~1066~~ ~~6372~~ ~~4561~~ ~~2930~~ ~~7955~~ ~~4031~~ ~~7437~~

"Okay then," I replied, grinning broadly in excitement. "Here goes!"

At this point in the story I should probably remind you of what I said earlier–that decoding the message was actually an unbelievably, extraordinarily, ridiculously mind-bogglingly difficult thing to accomplish. I wasn't kidding when I said that because after all these numbers and math, I wish that I could tell you that I simply went ahead and successfully decoded the message.

I really wish I could tell you that. But unfortunately that isn't what happened.

CHAPTER NINETEEN
No More Math For Me For At Least A Week

"Don't be surprised if this doesn't work on the first try," Richard said to me as I flipped to a fresh blank page and began my calculations. "Or the second or third try either. These are some serious codes we're dealing with here and even though we have the key, there are still a thousand different simple ways to make things more complicated. In fact, there's no guarantee that we'll *ever* manage to solve it, to be honest."

Richard was more right than he knew at the time he said it. But the first step down that long road was to start with some basic calculations.

"Okay, the first number group of the coded message is two, six, nine, nine, so we'll start with that," I said aloud, giving everyone a running commentary of what I was doing. "That splits into two numbers—twenty-six and ninety-nine. And the first number group of the key grid is seven, one, one, two so that's seventy-one and twelve. Twenty-six minus seventy-one is forty-five, and ninety-nine minus twelve is eighty-seven."

"Both of those numbers are higher than the number of letters in the alphabet," Richard said. "So keep subtracting from each until you get a number less than that."

"Okay," I replied, and proceeded to subtract from each until I got the final numbers nineteen and nine—letters S and I respectively.

Yada yada yada, long story short, the resulting message I got when I'd finished all of these calculations was this:

    SIYWSBKUKFUZER
    KECRGXKJCANFCA
    CFWMDHEDTBNMCN
    GFUADTMCKCCRBJ
    WXOZOXPUDIYBGW

Complete nonsense, in other words.

"Okay, what do we try next?" I asked Richard cheerfully.

"Try this," Richard replied. "Try splitting the number groups into single digits and subtracting that way. So twenty-six becomes two and six, and seventy-one becomes seven and one."

"Got it," I replied, flipping to yet another fresh page in my notebook to start a new round of calculations. "Seven minus two is five. And one minus six is negative five, so that's actually five..."

And so on and so on, yada yada yada.

I'll spare you the pain and just skip to the end of that particular series of calculations as well and show you what we got:

```
CIYYUBKACFAZER
KWMVIXKJEONFCC
CFYMDHEDTBNOCN
GFUADTACKCCRBJ
WXUZOFTUDIENIY
```

More complete nonsense, unless you look at the top right of the two blocks of random text and think that "FUZER" and "FAZER" are actual words or that maybe their appearance in both separate decryptions might have some deeper meaning. Richard actually *did* think that they might be important and that led us down a very long road that ended up leading us absolutely nowhere.

"So much for that," I said more than half an hour later after we abandoned the whole FUZER/FAZER thing and decided to return to some more normal calculations. "Back to the drawing board."

Little did I know at the time how many more drawing boards were in store for us over the hours to follow, or how many notebook pages all of these calculations would fill.

As the hours continued to tick by, Richard and I kept plugging away at every possible permutation in calculating that he could come up with. Over in London Ellie finally said goodnight at some point and went home to sleep. Inspired by her example both Vega and Giulia went off to bed as well, leaving only Matteo and Charlie to keep us company.

Matteo made some fresh coffee and that managed to keep him awake for another forty-five minutes or so but eventually he crashed as well, falling asleep on the sofa over by the fireplace after he brought me some chocolates from the kitchen. That left only Charlie, but he wouldn't last much longer either. Slowly but surely the time between his yawns got shorter and shorter until even he fell asleep in the chair next to me.

Only Richard and I kept at it, fueled by adrenaline, chocolate and caffeine as we tried the seemingly endless number of different ways to manipulate the calculations.

We tried absolutely everything. Different parts of the decoding key, different pages, different numbers. We tried running the whole process backward and even tried some mathematical operations that I'd never even heard of. But nothing worked and it was getting more complicated with every new attempt.

"It can't be as complicated as all this!" Richard fumed in frustration. "This is a code system that someone in their house is supposed to be able to solve quite simply. We must be missing something!"

As the sky outside the living room windows started to get lighter with sunrise quickly approaching, I started to think about what Richard had said hours before. That maybe we might *never* be able to solve this.

But then we did it. We actually solved it.

Can you believe it?

And what was the secret? (You ask—although you might regret it.)

The secret was to apply an absolutely simple (but complicated) mathematical concept that Richard called *modular arithmetic*. It was something that the 9/11 hijackers had used in some of their communications, Richard explained, not to mention countless other instances throughout the history of cryptography. A simple way of creating a disguise for a series of numbers like a phone or credit card number.

The way it works is this. Take any number between one and nine and simply subtract ten from it. Then take the resulting negative number at its absolute value by dropping the negative from it.

Sounds complicated? It's not.

7 becomes 3
4 becomes 6
8 becomes 2.

Or a series of numbers like 2699 becomes 8411.

See what I mean?

And that, in a nutshell, was the answer we'd been looking for all night. All we had to do was take each individual digit from the coded message, flip its value using *modular arithmetic*, subtract the corresponding number from the decoding key, convert the results to letters and voila! Message decoded!

You think that's complicated? Tell me about it. Richard and I spent all night trying to figure that one out!

So there we were with the light of the sun starting to fill the sky and performing what would prove to be our last calculations of the entire night.

"M–I–S–S–E–D," I said, reading each letter aloud as I slowly worked my way through the number sequence. I could feel my heart rate quickening because even after just the first few letters, both Richard and I could see that we were on to something.

By the time we finished neither of us could believe our eyes. Instead of the nonsense that our previous calculations had been spitting out for the last few hours, there was instead an actual coherent message hiding in the series of letters we'd just deciphered:

      MISSEDYOUHOTEL
      SACHERCROWNJEW
      ELSUNDERTHREAT
      URGENTWEMEETPP
      OPOLOFRIDAYTWO

Clutching my pencil tightly in my hand, I re-wrote the entire message in a more readable format with spaces between the individual words:

```
MISSED YOU HOTEL SACHER
CROWN JEWELS UNDER THREAT
    URGENT WE MEET
   P POPOLO FRIDAY TWO
```

"We did it, Richard!" I cried out quietly, being careful not to wake Matteo and Charlie. "We actually did it!"

"I know!" Richard replied, his face beaming with excitement and happiness. "And just in time too because it's nearly sunrise."

"The sun's already up here in Rome," I replied, squinting my eyes at the bright light streaming in through the tall windows and stifling a yawn.

I was tired–completely exhausted, actually–but I was euphoric that Richard and I had been able to finally decipher the message.

No more math for me for at least a week, I thought (and by this point in the story I am sure you can agree with me). *Not even calculating the tip at a restaurant.*

"You'd better get some sleep, then," Richard suggested. "You have a busy day ahead of you."

"What do you mean?" I asked with a frown. As far as I knew I didn't have any plans that day at all.

"That sun you see outside your window means it's already tomorrow and that means it's Friday," Richard replied. "And from what this message says, it might be a good idea to be at the *Piazza del Popolo* at two o'clock to see who shows up there."

CHAPTER TWENTY
Urgent We Meet

Richard was absolutely right. It *was* Friday. And there was no denying that the last two lines of the decoded message seemed to indicate that at two o'clock that very day, right there in Rome, some person or persons unknown were planning to meet somewhere on the *Piazza del Popolo*.

"My God, Richard," I replied breathlessly. "That must be what it means. But what is this Hotel Sacher? Is that in Rome too?"

Richard shook his head. "It's in Vienna," he replied. "It's a hotel where the famous Sacher chocolate cake was invented."

Chocolate cake? My ears perked up at the sound of that, but I wasn't sure whether I was familiar with this particular type of cake. Not that it mattered anyway, since in my current condition I didn't even have the energy to be hungry, not even for chocolate cake.

"Okay, but wait a minute. What about the Crown Jewels?" I asked. "What is that supposed to mean?" Aren't the Crown Jewels in London?"

"The British Crown Jewels are in London, yes," Richard replied, nodding his head. "But there are Crown Jewels in Vienna as well. From back in the days of the Austrian Empire when they still had an Emperor."

"But do you think that's what the message is referring to?" I asked, my voice filled with doubt.

"For some reason, I don't think so," Richard agreed. "From the context it sounds more like it's code for something."

"It must be a codename," I mumbled to myself as I re-read the message over again for the hundredth time. "But a codename for what?"

"I'm afraid I have no idea," Richard said as he stifled a yawn.

"Oh, Richard, I am so sorry," I said. "You must be so tired."

Richard smiled. "I am," he replied. "But it was worth it."

I couldn't have agreed more but at that particular moment my ability to think about anything other than falling fast asleep was severely limited. I was completely and utterly exhausted and my brain was in the process of rapidly rebelling against the fact that I was still conscious.

"I think maybe I'd better call it a day," I said. "I'm getting so tired that I can't think straight. But I want you to know how much I appreciate all of your help. I never could have done this without you."

"You are most welcome, Ms. Hawk," Richard replied gallantly with an elaborate flourish of his palm. "I will head off to bed now as well, but I wish you luck in your quest."

"Thank you, Richard," I said.

"And please let me know what happens, all right?" he replied.

"Of course," I said. "You can count on it."

And with that we said goodnight and finally disconnected our video chat.

So what now? I asked myself as I rummaged around in my shoulder bag for a cable to charge my iPad. *I need to get some sleep, of course, otherwise I will be totally useless later today. But shouldn't I wake everyone up right away to tell them about the message? We'll have plans to make, after all, and will have to figure out what to do.*

I sat for a minute or two, my eyes drooping indecisively as I slowly thought this over. Unfortunately for me, thinking was a pretty difficult process since my head felt like it was swimming through a sea of molasses, but in the end I made the decision to at least wake Charlie up and tell him the news before I completely collapsed.

"Charlie..." I whispered quietly as I shook him by the shoulder. "Charlie... Wake up."

"I'm awake, I'm awake," he replied, rubbing his eyes sleepily as he pulled himself upright in his chair. "What is it? Is something wrong?"

I shook my head and grinned. "We did it, Charlie!" I whispered triumphantly. "It took us all night but we did it! We solved it!"

Charlie blinked hard a few times to wake himself up some more.

"That's unbelievable!" he whispered back. "Show me."

"Here, look," I said, handing him my notebook.

I watched as his eyes darted back and forth, reading the lines of text off the page.

"Missed you Hotel Sacher," he read aloud. "Crown Jewels under threat. Urgent we meet. P Popolo Friday two."

"I think that means today," I said. "It's already Friday."

Charlie thought this over quickly and nodded his head in agreement.

"We should be at the *Piazza del Popolo*," he replied, glancing down at his watch. "In a few hours."

"Exactly," I replied.

Charlie thought everything over a little bit more. "What's the Hotel Sacher?" he asked, finally.

"Richard says it's in Vienna," I replied. "It's famous for some kind of chocolate cake, or something."

"And the Crown Jewels?" he asked, echoing the same questions I'd asked just a few minutes earlier. "What does that mean?"

"Also in Vienna," I said. "But obviously it's code for something else."

Charlie nodded again and glanced up at me, catching me with my eyes half closed and trying to hold back a yawn.

"You need to sleep," Charlie said. "Matteo said that one of us could sleep in the guest room if we wanted to. So why don't you go there and catch a few hours of sleep?"

I wanted to protest and say that I would rather stay up and try to figure things out but before I could stop myself I was nodding tiredly instead.

"Okay," I replied simply as Charlie pulled me to my feet and helped me shuffle down the hall to one of the enormous apartment's many guest rooms.

The room was small but it had a nice soft-looking bed and at that particular moment that was all that mattered. I flopped down on the mattress while Charlie walked over to the window and pulled the heavy curtains closed, plunging the room into a respectable facsimile of darkness. Not that I would have trouble falling asleep, of course.

"I'll talk to the others when they wake up," Charlie said as he headed back for the door. "And explain about the message and everything that's happened."

"Okay," I nodded as I struggled to kick my boots off and curled my head up on the pillow.

Charlie chuckled and walked over to the foot of the bed to pull my shoes off my feet and set them on the floor.

"Sleep tight," Charlie said as he returned to the door and started to pull it shut behind him.

"Don't worry, I will," I replied sleepily, my eyes already closing involuntarily.

Missed you Hotel Sacher, I remember thinking as I heard the door click shut. *Crown Jewels under threat. Urgent we meet. P Popolo Friday two.*

But that was as far as I got because the next thing I knew I was already fast asleep.

CHAPTER TWENTY-ONE
The More Eyes, The Better

It's amazing how much better you feel even after just a few hours of sleep. Add to that a fresh cup of hot coffee and I felt as good as new as Charlie and I stepped out onto the wide open expanse of the *Piazza del Popolo* and headed for the base of the towering Egyptian obelisk at the center of the square.

The "square" was actually elliptical in shape with an imposing arched gateway at the northern end and two small fountains flanking the eastern and western sides of the plaza. Charlie and I had arrived from the south, walking straight up from the heart of Rome along the seemingly endless *Via del Corso*.

It was just after one thirty when we arrived, and as we approached the obelisk I craned my neck and shielded my eyes from the sun to try and make out some of the hieroglyphics that were etched on its sides. As I stared at the various symbols of animals and plants and something that looked kind of like a teepee, I couldn't help but think back to my adventures in London and Ireland a few weeks earlier when Katherine, one of the curators of the British Museum, had kindly given me a private tour and a basic introduction to Egyptian hieroglyphs. She hadn't been able to tell me much, of course—obviously it takes years of intense study to even scratch the surface of understanding the ancient Egyptian system of writing—but there was one symbol that was unmistakable. The ankh—the symbol for life.

"What are you grinning at?" Charlie asked me with a smile as we finally reached the steps at the foot of the obelisk.

"Just remembering something," I replied cryptically as we climbed up the steps.

Charlie looked at me suspiciously for a second and then nodded his head toward the end of the *piazza* that we'd just come from.

"There's Matteo and Giulia," he said.

I turned to look and saw the two of them pulling up to one of the buildings at the edge of the square on a bright red Vespa scooter. The two of them had driven over from their apartment while Charlie and I had gone on foot.

Giulia slid off the back and dusted herself off while Matteo parked the scooter along the side of a wall where a long row of other scooters were already standing. Charlie raised his hand and waved to them to get their attention. Giulia quickly saw and waved back as they headed across the *piazza* toward us.

From where we were standing behind one of the lion fountains at the base of the obelisk, we had a good view of nearly the entire open square. There weren't too many people around, which was a welcome relief from the otherwise crowded narrow streets of Rome, but there were still enough people milling about to make it difficult to keep an eye on everything.

"Hello again," Giulia said with a bright smile as she and Matteo climbed the steps and joined us.

"Vega is still at work," Matteo explained. "She's not sure if she can make it, but she said she'd do her best."

Charlie nodded. "The more eyes, the better," he said. "Especially since we have absolutely no idea what it is we're looking for."

Charlie was right. Even *if* our interpretation of the message was correct and there actually *was* someone on their way to the *piazza* for a kind of clandestine meeting, then there was still no way for us to know exactly who that was or how to recognize them. The best that we could do was to break up into two groups and linger around the square, chatting casually and taking pictures like tourists, while carefully keeping an eye out for anyone that looked like they were waiting for someone.

The only problem with that plan, I quickly realized, was that there were a *lot* of people loitering around the square who seemed to be waiting for someone.

The tourists were fairly simple to eliminate as possible suspects since they traveled together in small groups, stopping and laughing as they snapped pictures of each other from various angles. And even the solo travelers were pretty easy to spot, with their touristy backpacks and cameras slung around their necks. But the tricky ones were the people who looked more or less like locals and were standing by themselves, smoking a cigarette or just wandering around for no apparent reason. Those people were the ones that looked like they might be the source of the mysterious coded message, but there were far too many of them to possibly keep track of.

But, of course, we didn't have much choice. With the limited information that we had, we could only do so much.

"This is going to be challenging," I heard Charlie mumble as he pretended to take a picture of me standing in front of the obelisk.

"What else can we do?" I replied under my breath as I smiled and posed like a typical tourist.

Out of the corner of my eye, I could see Matteo and Giulia standing around on the opposite side of the fountains from us. They were pretending to have some kind of innocent conversation, with Matteo gesturing wildly toward the obelisk with his hands as he spoke quickly in Italian.

Just look at this beautiful obelisk! Matteo's body language seemed to be saying. *Isn't it beautiful? It's beautiful, isn't it? Just beautiful! Have I mentioned how beautiful it is?*

His flailing arms and over-the-top motions were so funny that I had to stop myself from laughing out loud as Charlie and I switched places so I could pretend to take a picture of him instead.

"Matteo doesn't seem to understand the concept of acting inconspicuous," Charlie said with a chuckle as he handed me the camera.

"No kidding," I replied with a grin. "He looks like a cartoon character."

But suddenly Matteo stopped his crazy hand gestures and slowly lowered his arms to his sides as he tilted his head and looked across the *piazza* to somewhere behind me.

What in the world is he looking at?!? I thought, my heart jumping into my throat. Clearly Matteo had spotted something.

Charlie and I both simultaneously turned our heads around to see what Matteo was looking at, but all I could see was a sparse crowd of random people going about their various business on the square.

I spun my head back toward Matteo and Giulia and saw that they were hurrying over toward us while they continued staring across the *piazza* at something behind me.

What is it?!? I thought, turning my head again to see what they might be looking at, but I still couldn't see anything out of the ordinary.

"Do you see that man there?" I heard Matteo whisper to me and Charlie as he rushed up next to us. "The one with the thin gray hair and the light brown jacket."

I scanned the crowd to see who he was referring to and after a second or two I finally saw whom he meant. About a hundred feet away from us, an ordinary-looking older man in his sixties was slowly making his way across the *piazza*, walking straight past the obelisk and heading for the exit to the street at the northern end of the square.

"Yes," I replied, confused. "I see him, but..."

"I've seen that man before," Matteo said. "I don't know where but I'm sure I've seen his face before. And if I'm not mistaken, he's some kind of acquaintance of our father's."

I glanced at Charlie's watch and saw that it was five minutes before two.

"I don't understand," I said. "Do you think that's who we're looking for? It's not even two o'clock yet and he just walked straight across the square without even taking a look around."

"I don't know," Matteo replied. "But I am positive that I've seen him before."

"Me too," Giulia added with a confident flick of her hair. "I've seen him before too. But many, many years ago, maybe with our father?"

Charlie and I turned back to watch the rather ordinary-looking man passing through one of the archways of the gate at the end of the plaza.

"Are we both talking about the same person?" I asked, quickly scanning the crowd again, suddenly unsure whether I'd been looking at the right guy.

"That one there," Matteo said, leaning over my shoulder and pointing across to the same man that I'd already been looking at. "The one who's disappearing out of sight just now through the *Porta del Popolo*."

"That's who I was looking at already," I replied, standing on my tiptoes to try and see if I could catch a glimpse of him again. But it was no use. He was already gone.

"It's still not two o'clock yet," I heard Matteo say, his voice sounding distant and far away because my thoughts were already racing off in a new direction. "Maybe he'll come back?"

"Wait a minute!" I cried suddenly, startling the others. "What did you just call that gateway over there across the square?"

Matteo looked completely confused. "What do you mean?" he asked. "The *Porta del Popolo*?"

As soon as he said it, Matteo's eyes instantly grew wide with realization. Giulia and Charlie looked confused for a moment but then they also figured it out and suddenly all four of us were staring across the plaza toward the ornate gateway that marked the spot where the northern entrance to the ancient city of Rome was once located.

We were waiting in the wrong place!

CHAPTER TWENTY-TWO
That Guy

It couldn't possibly be just a coincidence, could it? I asked myself as all four of us started walking briskly toward the gate through ancient Roman walls at the northern end of the square.

URGENT WE MEET P POPOLO FRIDAY TWO, the message had read. All of us had been assuming that the reference to *P POPOLO* meant the *Piazza del Popolo* but, of course, it could just as easily refer to the gateway we were now all rushing toward–the *Porta del Popolo*. And in light of the fact that some familiar acquaintance of Matteo and Giulia's father was heading to that same exact spot just minutes before the scheduled meeting time of two o'clock, I think it was probably a pretty good guess that this guy might actually be the person we were trying to find.

"The *Porta del Popolo!*" Matteo cursed to himself as we zigzagged across the plaza, weaving in and out of the various small groups of people who were milling around. "How could I be so stupid!?"

It didn't take long to reach the gate. Before we knew it we'd reached the entrance to the leftmost of its three archways where we'd seen the man pass through just seconds earlier. Just a few more steps and we emerged onto the sidewalk on the other side with a busy street full of cars right next to us.

Charlie was the first around the corner with me right behind him. I anxiously scanned the sea of faces in front of me for the man we were looking for, but he was nowhere to be seen.

"Did we lose him?" I asked, still desperately scanning the crowd.

I glanced up at Charlie to see if he could see anything but as I watched his eyes darting keenly from side to side, I could tell that he hadn't spotted him either.

"There!" Matteo whispered loudly in my ear as he pointed to a tour group of teenagers wearing matching track suits. The group was slowly making their way through the central arch of the gate and as they gradually all disappeared from sight, I finally saw what Matteo was referring to. It was the man with the thin gray hair and the light brown jacket that we were looking for. He had just leaned over to throw something in the nearby trash bin and that's why we hadn't immediately spotted him.

The man took a couple of steps away from the trash container and then leaned up against the wall of the gate underneath a statue of a bearded man pointing to some kind of book. On the outside he seemed perfectly calm as he casually looked around at the crowds but somehow I could also sense a bit of tension in him, as if he was also very nervous about something. He was clearly waiting for someone, but of course we knew that much already.

With the four of us simply standing there and gawking at him, I was about to suggest that we try to act a little more nonchalant, but it was already too late. The man's eyes locked with mine for an instant and an uneasy look flashed across his face.

I immediately looked away but seeing us there staring was apparently enough to scare him off. Without a moment's hesitation, he ducked through the archway nearest him and headed back toward the *Piazza del Popolo*.

"Don't let him double back on us and get away," Charlie said as he pointed for me to head after the man and follow him. "Kitty, you go after him and the rest of us will cover the other two archways."

I nodded and quickly hurried over to the passageway at the other end to make sure that the man didn't try to sneak back out again. With all three exits covered there was nowhere for him to go but back onto the *piazza*.

As I reached the corner of the arch, I was startled to find myself face-to-face with the mysterious man himself. He was hiding behind the wall of the archway and had just ducked his head quickly around the corner to see if we were still there. Charlie had been clever to stop us from just running back to the *piazza* blindly. This guy was clearly a sneaky customer and if we'd done that we would have ended up losing him completely.

The man looked up at me for a second and a look of panic flashed across his pale brown eyes for an instant before he turned around and headed through to the other side of the gate with me following close behind.

Keeping him constantly in my sights, I passed through the gate just three steps behind and headed out into the open space of the *Piazza del Popolo*. Charlie and the others were there too, emerging from their own passageways and quickly picking up the pace to fall in behind me.

The man tried to maintain his composure, but it was obviously quite difficult for him as he kept nervously looking back over his shoulder to find four complete strangers hot on his heels.

"*Mi scusi.*" Matteo called out to the man as he continued to try and make his escape. "*Le possiamo parlare per un momento?*"

"No Italiano," the man in the light brown jacket called back over his shoulder as he began to accelerate away from us. "*Kein Italienisch.*"

He's speaking German, I thought. *Or something, anyway. He clearly doesn't speak Italian.*

"*Per favore,*" Matteo said as he rushed ahead of the man and blocked his way so he was finally forced to stop. "*Le possiamo parlare per un momento? Credo che lei sia un amico di mio padre.*"

The man stood there, looking around as the four of us circled around him like some kind of strange pack of wolves.

"*Nein, nein,*" the man said as he tried to push past Matteo, only to be blocked again. "*Kein Italienisch!*"

The man continued to try and find a way out but Matteo kept blocking him at every turn.

"Please, sir," Matteo said, switching languages in the hope of somehow getting through to him. "Can we speak to you for a moment? We think you were a friend of our father's. He passed away recently and..."

"*Nein, nein!*" the man interrupted. "*Kein Italienisch, kein Englisch.*"

"It's no use, Matteo," Giulia said to her brother. "He doesn't understand and you're just frightening him."

Giulia was right. The man was pacing back and forth like a frightened animal, trying to find a way to escape from the odd group of strangers surrounding him.

"Please, we just want to talk to you..." I started to say when suddenly the odor of an overpoweringly strong tobacco filled my nostrils. It was a smell that I was already familiar with but it took me a moment to figure out where I knew it from.

"Perhaps I can be of assistance?" I heard a voice say from somewhere behind me.

I spun my head and my heart dropped into my stomach as I saw the enormous and broad-shouldered silhouette of a man in a black suit standing behind me.

It was Inspector Alighieri.

Or whatever his real name was. You know who I mean.

That guy.

CHAPTER TWENTY-THREE
Do You Really Not Know Me By Now?

The sudden appearance of fake police Inspector Alighieri left me completely stunned, not to mention the others as well. Before we could react he had turned his enormous frame sideways and squeezed through the gap between Charlie and me.

"*Guten Tag, mein Herr,*" Inspector Alighieri said, addressing the mysterious man in the light brown jacket.

"*Grüß Gott,*" the man stammered uncertainly in reply, looking quite frightened.

"*Ich bin Kommissar Alighieri von der Guardia di Finanza,*" Inspector Alighieri continued, completely ignoring the rest of us. "*Und mit wem habe ich die Ehre? Herr...?*"

"Weinberg," the man in the light brown jacket stuttered. "Herr Weinberg."

Inspector Alighieri looked at him with a wry smile and chuckled. "*Richtig, Weinberg,*" he replied. "*Natürlich.*"

"What's he doing here?!?" I hissed at Charlie.

Charlie looked over at me and shrugged his shoulders. "Beats me," he whispered back. "Maybe he followed us?"

Or maybe he followed Matteo and Giulia? I thought as I turned toward the two of them. For a moment we all stared blankly at each other with confused expressions on our faces, but it was clear that none of us had any idea what was going on.

All of this took only a matter of seconds but meanwhile the conversation between Inspector Alighieri and Herr Weinberg had quickly escalated into an intense and almost violent confrontation. Inspector Alighieri was leaning aggressively forward, his face just inches away from Herr Weinberg's as he bombarded the frightened man with one question after another in German. We couldn't understand anything that he was asking, but whatever it was, clearly Herr Weinberg didn't have any answers because with every vehement shake of his head he was finding himself slowly being backed into a corner near the fountains at the base of the Egyptian obelisk.

"*Das habe ich Ihnen doch schon gesagt!*" Herr Weinberg cried out, stumbling at the foot of the steps. "*Ich weiß es nicht!*"

"*Das glaube ich Ihnen nicht!*" Inspector Alighieri exploded in reply, his voice unexpectedly rising to a shout as he grabbed Herr Weinberg by the lapels of his jacket and smashed the helpless man's back against the faux Egyptian décor at the edge of the fountains.

"Charlie! Do something!" I cried, shocked at how quickly things had gotten out of hand. From the way that Inspector Alighieri was throwing the poor man around it was only a matter of seconds before someone was going to really get hurt.

Charlie didn't need me to tell him anything. Before I even finished my sentence, he was already moving forward to grab Inspector Alighieri by the arm and was trying to restrain him. Unfortunately, not even a big guy like Charlie was strong enough to handle the Inspector on his own, but by this time a crowd of people had started to gather around to watch the altercation and Matteo and two other bystanders also stepped up to help hold the enormous Inspector Alighieri back.

"Get your hands off me you fools!" Inspector Alighieri thundered as he violently twisted his incredibly wide shoulders like a caged animal to try and shake the four men off of him. "He's getting away!"

I spun my head around and saw that the Inspector was right. While everyone's attention was focused squarely on trying to contain his aggressor, Herr Weinberg had jumped across the low wall circling the fountain and had splashed across the shallow water to escape out the opposite side.

With Herr Weinberg dashing quickly across the *piazza* away from us, I looked to Charlie for help but he was still busy with Inspector Alighieri, slowly but surely gaining the upper hand and pinning him up against the wall. Unfortunately, his advantage over the enormous man was short-lived and with an enraged swing of his powerful arms, Inspector Alighieri knocked Charlie and the other men to the ground and wrestled himself free. Like a flash he was off, pushing through the crowd in close pursuit of Herr Weinberg.

"Come on, Charlie!" I cried as I ducked through the ring of onlookers and headed after them. Charlie didn't need any convincing and was on his feet in an instant, running after me just a few steps behind.

The bad news was that despite our quick responses both Herr Weinberg and Inspector Alighieri had a considerable lead on us. The Inspector was running much faster than I would have ever expected a man of his size to be able to and by shortcutting through the fountain Herr Weinberg had already had a considerable head start on all of us to begin with.

In a matter of seconds, Herr Weinberg had reached the edge of the *piazza* and was jumping on a motor scooter that he'd apparently left parked there, quickly cranking up the engine and peeling off down the nearest street. Inspector Alighieri missed grabbing him by the back of the jacket by just a second or two but without missing a beat he slid into the passenger seat of a black Maserati sedan that had suddenly appeared out of nowhere, squealing to a halt next to him and roaring off before he'd even closed his door.

"What now?!?" I yelled to Charlie as he and I reached the edge of the plaza and watched the two vehicles quickly disappearing out of sight in the traffic ahead of us.

"Take my Vespa!" I heard a voice say from behind us. I turned quickly and saw Matteo bolting past and crossing the street to where he'd left his scooter parked earlier.

Charlie and I were right behind him as he yanked his scooter out into the street and started the engine.

"Good luck," Matteo said as Charlie grabbed the handlebars and jumped onto the seat with me right behind him.

Charlie turned his head and looked at me for a quick moment, obviously not convinced that I should be riding shotgun with him on this one.

Seriously, Charlie? My expression said to him as he looked back at me over his shoulder. *Do you really not know me by now?*

For a second it looked like Charlie was going to say something but apparently he did know me well enough not to try and argue. "Hold on tight," he said simply, turning his head forward again and revving up the throttle.

With a sudden burst of speed, the powerful little scooter darted out into the traffic, narrowly missing a couple of cars as we zipped up the street in hot pursuit.

CHAPTER TWENTY-FOUR
I Told You It Was A Crazy Thing To Do

Weaving maniacally in and out of the crazy obstacle course of cars and people in front of us, we desperately tried to catch up to Inspector Alighieri and Herr Weinberg. The two of them already had a significant head start on us. They were so far ahead that I was worried that we might have lost them completely, but thanks to some seriously fancy (and somewhat dangerous) maneuvering by Charlie we were able to steadily close the distance until we could easily see them again.

Gripping Charlie tightly I peeked over his shoulder and saw Inspector Alighieri's black Maserati just a few hundred feet ahead of us. It was too far to make out how many other people were in the car, but there had to be at least one more person with him who was doing the driving. In fact, maybe the driver was the same unknown accomplice who'd broken into Matteo's father's apartment the other day and surprised us all by jumping out from behind the wall.

A couple hundred feet beyond them I was able to barely make out Herr Weinberg's thin gray hair over the tops of the cars, fluttering and flopping in the wind as he ducked in and out of traffic attempting to escape. He was still a long way off but suddenly we caught a break when Herr Weinberg was forced to pull on his brakes and skid sideways to a stop as a huge white truck appeared out of nowhere from his left and nearly flattened him.

"Oh my God," I cried in surprise as I watched Herr Weinberg nearly flip over sideways before regaining control and quickly circling around the back of the truck. It only took him a second or two to get back up to speed again, but in that precious time the distance between him and us had closed considerably.

Worried that the same thing might happen to us, I found myself glancing quickly left and right at every narrow intersection, terrified each time that I'd find the shiny chrome grille of a truck barreling toward us and that would be the last thing I'd ever see. But we were lucky and Charlie was too skilled to let anything like that happen. At every intersection he'd ease off the throttle and slow down, almost imperceptibly, to make sure we were safe to cross.

Up ahead, Herr Weinberg continued straight into a street that was closed to cars and Inspector Alighieri's black Maserati was forced up on the sidewalk for a moment to avoid a pair of concrete pylons in the pavement. Seconds behind them on our scooter, Charlie and I passed easily between the obstacles but now I found myself wondering why Herr Weinberg didn't use the fact that one set of his pursuers was in a big, bulky car.

Why doesn't he duck down one of these narrow side streets where a car can't fit? I wondered to myself as Charlie and I raced through another intersection and I caught a glimpse of the River Tiber off to the right.

Almost as though he'd read my mind, Herr Weinberg suddenly turned left and disappeared out of sight down a narrow pedestrian alleyway. The black Maserati up ahead squealed quickly to a halt and I saw the passenger door open just as Charlie and I zipped past them and around the corner. Glancing back over my shoulder, I saw Inspector Alighieri's enormous frame standing next to the car, pounding on the roof in frustration before climbing back inside again and roaring off.

So much for them, I thought with a grin, but somehow I had the suspicion that we'd be seeing them again pretty soon. I was just a mere tourist in the city of Rome and was easily confused with all of Herr Weinberg's twisting and turning, left and right, from one tiny street to the next, but something told me that Inspector Alighieri probably knew the city like the back of his hand and had a pretty good idea where we were headed.

Herr Weinberg turned another corner and then roared across an open square, sending pigeons and people scrambling for cover as he went.

"Sorry! Sorry!" I called out to the startled bystanders as Charlie and I raced past them. "So sorry! Out of the way! Sorry!"

Despite the seriousness of the situation, I couldn't help but laugh out loud as we dashed through another narrow street and up on the sidewalk across another open square with terrified tourists scattering to get out of our way.

Charlie glanced back at me for a second with a disbelieving grin on his face before suddenly turning forward again and hitting the brakes. Just ahead of us, Herr Weinberg had just dashed over a pedestrian zebra crossing across a familiar-looking busy street when the black Maserati abruptly appeared out of nowhere from our left and cut directly in front of us.

I told you so, I thought to myself as Charlie deftly maneuvered around the car and over the crosswalk to pick up the chase again. As we raced across the intersection, I spun my head around to look back at Inspector Alighieri and had just enough time to recognize what street we'd just crossed over. It was the *Via del Corso*—the same street Charlie and I had just walked up less than an hour earlier from Matteo's father's house. Off to the right in the distance I caught a glimpse of the bright white Vittorio Emanuele monument and straight up in the opposite direction to my left was the Egyptian obelisk at the *Piazza del Popolo*.

We were now back in a more touristy part of the city and one that I knew fairly well even after being in Rome for just a week.

But if that was the Via del Corso back there, I thought to myself as Herr Weinberg spun his scooter down another pedestrian street, *then we must almost be at the...*

My train of thought was broken as I watched Herr Weinberg disappear behind a horse-drawn carriage and into a sea of people around the next corner up ahead.

...the Trevi Fountain, I finished my thought as Charlie dodged the horse and slowed down to avoid smashing into the wall of hundreds of tourists crowding around the fountain.

Up ahead of us, Herr Weinberg was honking his horn and waving his arms as he slowly negotiated his way along the sidewalk. It didn't take long for his honking and frantic shouting to create a hole through the mass of people and soon he was clear and racing off again down yet another narrow alley.

"Sorry! Sorry!" I called out again as Charlie and I also tried to weave our way through the parted sea of bodies. I can only imagine what kind of lunatics we must have looked like, Charlie with his head down and his expression serious as he twisted left and right through the crowds while I sat on the scooter behind him, laughing and grinning at the heart-racing ridiculousness of the whole situation. It was like some crazy chase scene from a Hollywood action movie.

Still laughing hysterically as we passed close to the iron fence surrounding the area in front of the fountain, I found myself doing something absolutely crazy—something that to this day I cannot believe that I actually did, and as ridiculous as it's going to sound, I swear to God that it actually happened.

On the spur of the moment and before I could stop myself, I reached into my jacket pocket and pulled out a coin. Grabbing it in my right hand I sent it catapulting through the air with a quick snap of my arm. Whipping my head around, I watched it tumbling through a long, high arc toward the fountain's basin. The water was only about fifteen feet away when the coin left my hand but as it spun through the air, hanging there for what seemed like an eternity, Charlie poured on the gas again and as we raced away, I never got to see where it landed.

I hope it made it, I thought to myself as I remembered what my guidebook had told me about the legend of the Trevi Fountain. Apparently each visitor is supposed to throw three coins into the fountain. The first coin will ensure that someday you will return to the *Eternal City*. The second will bring you romance and the third will lead you to marriage.

I knew from the moment I arrived in Rome that I wanted to return there someday, so I'd already thrown my first coin into the fountain on my very first day in Rome. That meant that the coin I'd just thrown was my second one and since I hadn't seen where it landed, I had no idea whether or not I should expect to find romance or not.

Maybe that was a stupid thing to do, I thought to myself as I watched the fountain disappearing rapidly behind us as Charlie continued down the alley and turned the next corner. *Now I'll never know!*

"Not to mention that you might have beaned someone in the head with that flying coin and hurt them," the little voice in my head scolded me, sounding very much like my mother.

Yah, right, I thought. *That too.*

Well, what can I say? I told you it was a crazy thing to do.

CHAPTER TWENTY-FIVE
We're In A Bit Of A Situation Here

Unfortunately (or maybe fortunately), I didn't really have time to worry about things like coins or fountains or romance since Herr Weinberg was continuing to lead Charlie and I through a confusing labyrinth of tiny side streets as he desperately tried to shake us off his tail. We made turn after turn until my sense of direction was completely messed up and I had no idea where we were anymore.

Then, suddenly, we were out in the open again, back on a wider side street and racing up an incline as we dodged some oncoming cars.

We're going up a hill! I thought. *Now there's a clue to where we are!*

I knew from my guide book that the ancient city of Rome was built among seven small hills and it was a pretty good bet that we were now heading up one of those at that exact moment. But which one? I scoured my memory to try and remember the maps I'd seen.

The Quirinal Hill! I thought triumphantly as we scattered yet another group of tourists who were crossing the street. *That must be it! And that means we're now heading down toward the Colosseum and the Forum!*

Herr Weinberg made another turn onto a major street with lots of traffic that led down the other side of the hill. On that big, open street we could really go fast and as both scooters really cranked up their throttles, it felt like we were actually flying as we descended into the ancient heart of Rome.

As we gracefully swerved between one car and the next, staying as close as we could to Herr Weinberg, I suddenly heard the roar of a car engine behind us. I spun around and my heart dropped when I saw the familiar silhouette of the black Maserati closing in fast.

"Charlie! Watch out!" I yelled as the big car missed us by just inches as it roared past. Through the passenger window, I saw Inspector Alighieri flash by and give us a curt little wave as they cut quickly in front of us around the next corner and headed into a traffic circle.

As they cut us off, Charlie had to quickly slam on the brakes to avoid smashing straight into the side of the Maserati. As the scooter screeched to a halt, Charlie planted his feet down and skillfully steered us off to the side of the street, just barely managing to keep us upright. In seconds, he regained control but when he twisted the throttle open again I was aghast to hear the engine suddenly sputter and die.

"Oh dammit!" Charlie muttered angrily as he cranked the starter and tried to get the scooter running again. Off in the distance at the other end of the traffic circle, Herr Weinberg and Inspector Alighieri disappeared around a bend and out of sight.

"Come on you stupid piece of crap!" I swore as Charlie tried again and again to bring the scooter back to life.

Finally the engine caught and Charlie kicked off the curb with his legs to get us up to speed again.

"Hold on tight!" Charlie said as we reached the next corner and kept going straight instead of following the road further down the hill around the bend.

"What are you doing?!?" I cried as Charlie ramped up on the sidewalk on the other side of the street and headed for a gap between some buildings up ahead. "You're going the wrong way! They went down there, to the right!"

"I know! But we'll never catch up to them that way," Charlie yelled back. "And I think I know where they're headed. So if we're lucky we can head them off."

Okay, I thought to myself, not sure exactly what Charlie's plan was but clearly he knew what he was doing.

Or did he? As he gunned the engine and raced up to the end of the sidewalk, I started to question his judgment.

"Are you crazy?!?" I shouted at Charlie as he made a hard turn to the right and nosed the scooter toward a set of steps leading down toward the Vittorio Emanuele monument and the *Piazza Venezia* beyond.

"Just hold on!" Charlie shouted back as we hit the first step and began washboarding all the way down to the bottom, our teeth rattling inside our heads as we went.

To be honest, the ride down the stairs actually wasn't that bad, which probably shouldn't have been much of a surprise since I can vaguely remember doing such stupid things on my bike back when I was a kid and never getting seriously hurt. All I did was keep my arms wrapped tightly around Charlie's midsection and before I knew it we were safely at the bottom of the stairs and Charlie was hitting the gas again, making a run for the *Piazza Venezia* as fast as he could.

Well, that wasn't so bad, I thought as we sped across another side street, around a towering Roman column, and finally out to the edge of the famous *piazza* where Charlie hit the brakes and we skidded to a halt at the edge of the traffic.

"There!" Charlie cried, pointing to the opposite corner where Herr Weinberg and his scooter had just emerged from behind a tour bus with the black Maserati right behind.

"Go go!" I shouted, pounding Charlie on the back as he hit the gas one last time.

Unfortunately, that's where everything went completely and totally wrong. Just at the instant that we burst out from the side street and onto the plaza, a motorized Italian *gelato* cart appeared out of nowhere from behind a construction fence next to us. We swerved to the right and took a spill on the pavement while the *gelato* cart swerved left, falling over on its side and cutting in front of a taxi that was driving way too fast around the corner. The taxi swerved to avoid the *gelato* cart and from there the chain reaction accelerated. First the taxi, then a tour bus, another taxi, some kind of weird three-wheeled scooter followed by two more tour busses, and so on. By the time all the swerving was done, the traffic on the *Piazza Venezia* had snarled to a complete halt and it was a miracle that no one had smashed into anyone else.

Well, *almost* no one. I am not unhappy to say that at the tail end of the entire tangle of vehicles, the black Maserati did have a bit of a fender-bender with the last tour bus. But that was really their own fault since they were trying to fit through a gap between a pair of hop-on hop-off busses that was way too small for them. In their defense, however, they hardly had any other choice since Herr Weinberg expertly threaded his scooter through the narrow gap and was off like a shot.

Charlie tried to wrestle Matteo's scooter back on its wheels to pick up the chase again but this time the engine had apparently died for good and no matter how many times he cranked the starter, it simply wouldn't start. It was hopeless and all we could do was stand there as Herr Weinberg escaped down the tree-lined *Via dei Fori Imperiali*, driving fast under the umbrella pines toward the distant Colosseum.

As we stood there helplessly watching Herr Weinberg disappear, a crowd of angry Italians started to gather around us, waving their arms and shouting things that I didn't even want to know what they meant. In the distance, I could hear the whine of sirens converging on the *piazza*.

I glanced over at the black Maserati where Inspector Alighieri was standing and pounding on the roof of the car, yelling at the various drivers to move their busses out of the way so he could get past. The shouting match continued for a few seconds longer but then Inspector Alighieri apparently heard the sound of the approaching sirens as well and decided that discretion was the better part of valor and jumped back in his car.

"There they go too," Charlie muttered as the black Maserati pulled a quick U-turn and sped off down the street in the opposite direction from where Herr Weinberg had been headed. "So much for that."

Meanwhile, the crowd around us was growing larger by the second and I was reminded of those scenes in old black-and-white movies where angry villagers head out with torches and pitchforks to kill the local monster. The only difference was that in this case, the monsters in question were me and Charlie and apparently we'd committed some kind of unspeakable act of heresy by toppling over a *gelato* cart and causing a traffic jam. All around us it seemed like everyone was yelling and waving their arms around threateningly. Even the fat guy in the Roman Legionnaire's costume who always stood there at the corner taking pictures with tourists was yelling at us and waving his rubber short sword at Charlie.

I hope the real Roman soldiers were in better shape than you are, dude, I thought bitterly as I pulled my cell phone out of my pocket and quickly dialed Matteo's number.

As the phone began to ring at the other end, a couple of police cars finally pulled up to the chaotic scene around us.

"Matteo? Is that you?" I shouted into the phone, putting a finger over my ear and straining to hear the voice at the other end.

"Yes, yes, it's me!" I barely heard Matteo reply over the sound of the sirens and the angry crowd.

"Matteo, we're at the *Piazza Venezia*," I shouted into the receiver. "We're in a bit of a situation here and I think you'd better get over here as soon as you can."

CHAPTER TWENTY-SIX
Staring Me Right In The Face The Whole Time

It didn't take long for Matteo and Giulia to join us on the *Piazza Venezia*. Within minutes they had pulled up in a taxi and started trying to calm the situation. Their sister, Vega, wasn't far behind them and pulled up in her own taxi soon afterward.

As it turned out, Vega was the best possible person to have around under those particular circumstances because not only is she a lawyer, but she is a lawyer of the tough-as-nails-take-no-crap-from-anyone variety, which the angry mob and the police were soon learning, much to their dismay. In less than two minutes, Vega had easily out-shouted even the loudest of the irate bystanders and the crowd had begun to disperse while the police finally got traffic moving again. Even the fat guy dressed like a Roman Legionnaire went back to his spot across the street and resumed his trade of harassing tourists to take pictures with him.

Charlie and I did our best to stay invisible through all of this, standing off to one side while Vega and the others spoke with the policemen and the owner of the *gelato* cart.

"Okay, the good news is this," Vega said as she walked over toward us after several minutes of intense negotiations. "The police aren't going to be pressing any charges."

"Charges for what?" I asked defiantly. "Tipping over an ice-cream cart?"

"Probably for driving around the city like homicidal maniacs," Charlie suggested.

"Yes, exactly, that," Vega replied, pointing her finger at Charlie in agreement. "They had reports about you all the way across the city. However, fortunately for you *most* drivers in Rome drive like homicidal maniacs, so the police are not too bothered about it."

"What about the others?" I asked. "Inspector Alighieri and Herr Weinberg?"

Vega shook her head. "They suggest that we leave the police work to them," she replied. "But they have dutifully taken note of what we had to tell them about that and they'll file it along with the other reports that we made earlier in the week."

"In other words, they aren't going to do anything," I observed cynically.

Vega smiled a wry smile. "That's Rome for you," she said simply, as if that explained everything.

"What about the ice-cream guy?" Charlie asked, nodding his head toward the portly man who was standing nearby, bent over and inspecting the slightly twisted frame of his *gelato* cart.

"What about him?" Vega asked.

Charlie didn't answer but simply walked over to the man instead and began to help him turn his cart upright again. Matteo and I also quickly hurried over and somehow, between the four of us, we were able to get his cart back on its wheels again. Fortunately the *gelato* was well frozen and hadn't spilled anywhere. The only damage was some deep scratches along the sides and to the frame holding the colorful overhead awning.

"Can you please ask him how much he needs to fix it," Charlie said to Vega, pulling out his wallet, counting out all the cash he had inside.

"How is a hundred and twenty euros?" Charlie asked. "It's all I have."

I quickly reached into my pocket and pulled out all my cash as well.

"Plus forty more," I added, handing the money to Charlie.

Vega looked confused for a second and then did as Charlie asked. The portly man looked confused and shaken for a moment and then broke into a wide smile.

"Thank you, thank you," he said in broken English as Charlie handed him the money. He then turned to Vega and began speaking in Italian.

"He says that it's more than enough," Vega said, translating for him. "He's very grateful and is sorry that our scooter got damaged as well."

The man nodded with his head toward Matteo who was busy propping his Vespa up to inspect the damage.

"It's not so bad," Matteo said. "Just a few scratches."

Charlie opened his wallet again to look inside.

"Sorry," he said, his voice quite serious. "There's nothing left."

Somehow that made me really laugh, despite the fact that I was hardly in the mood for laughing. I was sweaty and tired, not to mention feeling quite depressed that Herr Weinberg had managed to escape before we could find out anything from him. He clearly had something to do with Giulia and Matteo's father and the strange radio messages he'd been receiving. Maybe he even knew something about the mysterious paintings we'd found hanging innocently in their father's living room. But since neither Giulia nor Matteo could remember who he was or how they knew him, unless their memories underwent some kind of miraculous recovery it was unlikely we'd ever be able to find him again.

All in all, it was a pretty crappy day once the adrenaline rush of the chase through Rome started to wear off. All I could think about was getting out of the sun, having a shower and taking a long nap. My hotel was close so after we made plans to meet up later that night, Charlie and I said goodbye to the others and he walked with me back to the front of my hotel before continuing along to his own.

Oh God, I look terrible, I thought as I examined my face in the bathroom mirror after my shower. *I look exhausted.*

Fortunately there was a sure-fire cure for that and seconds later I flopped into bed, pulling the covers up to my neck as I listened to the sound of traffic through my open window.

What are we going to do now? I asked myself after I sent off a quick email to Richard to tell him what happened and then closed my eyes and tried to think things through before I fell asleep. There was a solution to all of this somewhere. I could feel it. All I needed to do was figure it out.

But figuring it out was going to be more difficult than I could possibly have imagined at that point in time. Little did I know that there was still one more piece of the puzzle whose secret needed to be revealed. And it was staring me right in the face the whole time.

CHAPTER TWENTY-SEVEN
Sixteen Point Six Six Two Megahertz

"I won't even bother to ask if anyone wants to try my *nocino*," Matteo joked later that night after we'd finished an amazing home-cooked meal of pasta and chicken parmesan that he'd prepared for us. "You've all made it perfectly clear that you're not interested."

"Just coffee, please," I laughed in reply.

"For me too," Charlie said. "Sorry."

Matteo sighed theatrically and proceeded to efficiently whisk the dirty dishes away from the table, replacing them with tiny cups of espresso.

"Someday you'll appreciate my *nocino*," he said as he worked to clear the table.

"No they won't," Giulia said with a chuckle. "I've had your *nocino*, remember?"

"Me too," Vega added, making a horrified wincing face that made me laugh even harder.

It was nice to be able to laugh. I was amazed that everyone was feeling so cheerful after everything that had happened. All through dinner the mood had felt like a kind of celebration, even though there was nothing to celebrate other than the fact that we were all alive and well and in the company of our amazing new friends.

But what is more important than that? I asked myself as I looked over at Vega and Giulia and smiled. *Who cares about stupid coded messages and mysterious paintings?*

It was easy enough to tell myself that, but despite the light-hearted mood I *did* care about those things and it was killing me not to have figured it out.

Fortunately, however, I didn't have long to wait before the next piece of the puzzle fell neatly into place. It all started with my cell phone vibrating suddenly while we were all eating dessert. Matteo was in the middle of telling a story about how he'd accidentally fallen off a ferry when he was at university so I just silently glanced down at the screen to see who was calling.

It was Richard.

"So then this woman is screaming and screaming as I was flopping around in the water..." Matteo said, stopping suddenly and looking over at me as I raised my hand and interrupted his story.

"I'm sorry," I apologized. "But it's Richard calling me. I think I'd better get it."

"Of course," Matteo smiled graciously.

"Hello? Richard?" I said as soon as I'd pressed the button to connect the call.

"Kitty? Is that you?" I heard Richard say at the other end of the line.

"Yes, it's me, Richard," I replied.

"Are you anywhere near that apartment with the secret room?" Richard asked, his voice tense with excitement.

"We're all there now," I replied. "Having dinner."

There was a slight pause and then Richard dropped a bombshell. "I think you'd better turn on that radio," he said. "There's another message being transmitted."

I looked up from my phone at the others around the table, my eyes wide with disbelief. For a second no one moved, but then we all simultaneously pushed our chairs back and started to dash for the hallway.

"What kind of message?!?" I asked as Matteo rushed ahead of me and pulled open the wall panel for Charlie so he could switch on the radio.

"You'll see," Richard said cryptically. "Just go to the same frequency that the first message was broadcast at. Sixteen point six six two megahertz."

I leaned over Charlie's shoulder and watched as he flipped the power switch and spun the dial up to 16.662 MHz. It didn't take long before we heard the sound of that creepy woman's voice filling the room once again.

"*Zero–zero–zero–zero, zero–zero–zero–zero,*" the voice repeated over and over again. "*Zero–zero–zero–zero, zero–zero–zero–zero.*"

We all listened intently to the transmission for almost a minute but the voice was repeating nothing but zeros.

"What is this?" I asked Richard, pressing the button to put him on speaker and setting the phone down on the desk. "What do all these zeros mean?"

"Just wait," he replied.

"Wait for what?" I asked, but suddenly my question was answered and the message began to change.

"*Foxtrot–foxtrot–alpha–golf–foxtrot–foxtrot–echo–echo,*" the voice recited. "*Charlie–golf–alpha–echo–foxtrot–charlie–foxtrot–golf.*"

The voice then made a long pause.

"Is there anything more?" I whispered into the phone.

"Just wait," Richard said again and after another few seconds the voice started up again.

"*Uniform–romeo–golf–echo–november–tango,*" the voice droned on. "*Whiskey–echo–mike–echo–echo–tango.*"

The voice paused again for a second or two and then started repeating nothing but zeros again.

"*Zero–zero–zero–zero,*" the voice said over and over. "*Zero–zero–zero–zero, zero–zero–zero–zero.*"

"Isn't that remarkable?" Richard said, overflowing with excitement.

"I don't understand," I replied. "What does this mean? How did you know it was going to do that?!?"

Richard cleared his throat and quickly explained. "After our little codebreaking session last night," he said. "I sent an email to a friend of mine today who is interested in these kinds of things and I told him about this broadcast that you'd picked up. It was a completely new one to him so he was very interested and started monitoring the frequency right away. And he just called me a few minutes ago to tell me it was broadcasting again."

"Okay," I said. "But that still doesn't explain how you knew it was going to stop repeating zeros."

"The transmission is following a different format than before," Richard explained. "And it's been looping the same thing over and over again for the past ten minutes. About sixty seconds of nothing but zeros, then a short break followed by letter groups. No group count like before. No message precursor. Nothing like that at all. Just zeros and these same three letter groups, over and over."

"But what does it mean?!?" I asked, excited at this turn of events but dreading that I might lose another night of sleep deciphering this new message. "What is the message? And what are all these zeros?"

"The zeros, I believe, are a warning signal to everyone listening to destroy their current decoding pads," Richard said. "After what you told me in your email today, it must be clear to this Herr Weinberg that their codes have been compromised."

"I suppose that makes sense," I replied. "But then what about the rest of these letters?"

Even as these words were leaving my mouth, the creepy voice on the radio suddenly stopped transmitting zeros and started up again reciting the letter groups.

I should be writing this down! I suddenly realized and cursed myself for not thinking of it before. *What if the message hadn't repeated again?*

"*Foxtrot–foxtrot–alpha–golf–foxtrot–foxtrot–echo–echo,*" the voice began again, the same as before.

"Hand me one of those papers," I said to Charlie, pointing to the small stack of blank paper that was still sitting on the desk where we'd seen it the night before. Charlie understood immediately and quickly handed me the sheets of paper over his shoulder.

I grabbed the paper and was quickly fishing around in my pocket for a pencil when I saw something that made my heart stop.

"Do we have any other paper than this?" I asked distantly as I lifted the papers closer for a better look. "And maybe can someone also write down this message for me?"

"Don't worry, Kitty," I heard Richard say over the speaker phone. "I've already transcribed the message and double-checked it. In fact, I think I've already decoded it for you. Actually, it wasn't even encoded so it wasn't very difficult."

What Richard was saying was fantastic news, of course. No more math and sleepless nights required if he'd already decoded the message for us. But at that particular moment, my thoughts were about a million miles away as my eyes remained intently focused on the blank scrap of paper in my hands.

"What is it?" Charlie asked, narrowing his eyes as he looked at me in concern.

"Look at this," I said, my voice rising with excitement.

I handed the sheet of paper to Charlie. "I don't understand," he said, looking confused. "It's blank."

"Not *entirely* blank," I replied, turning the desk lamp so everyone could see it better.

In the glare of the lamp they finally saw what I was talking about. Imprinted on the top piece of paper was writing from the last time someone had used the stack of papers to write something down.

It was the text from some previously received message.

CHAPTER TWENTY-EIGHT
Urgent We Meet

No matter how long I stared at it, I simply couldn't believe my eyes. Apparently at some point in the past some unknown person (Matteo's father, most likely) had used the stack of papers to write out and decode an incoming message. The actual sheet of paper they'd used to write that message on was long gone, but the imprint of the writing was still left on the square of paper immediately underneath.

It was the oldest trick in the book, as they say—or more accurately, the oldest clue in the book. I mean, how many hundreds of detective novels have used this exact type of clue to help solve the mystery? It was so cliché that it was almost funny, especially since I knew *exactly* how to reveal the hidden message. It called for a technique that I'd already used twice before on my mystery-filled journey around the world and I couldn't believe that it was actually about to come in handy again. It was so funny that I could hardly keep myself from laughing as I was about to reveal my brilliant idea.

Unfortunately, Charlie had other plans.

"Can I borrow this?" Charlie asked, taking the pencil stub right out of my fingers, not to mention the wind completely out of my sails.

Charlie carefully placed the scrap of paper on the desk and began to rub the pencil lead back and forth across the surface of it until the message slowly began to appear.

"Hey! That was my idea!" I cried in mock irritation. "I was just about to do the exact same thing."

Charlie shrugged his shoulders and continued with the pencil rubbing.

"If it's any consolation," he said. "What made me think of it is the stories you told me the other day about how you'd done exactly this back in Ireland and Florida."

Well, that's at least something, I guess, I thought as Charlie finished and we all leaned in to read what the message said.

WILL MEET PACHELBEL
CATHEDRAL OF EIGHT TODAY
MEET ME HOTEL SACHER
SUNDAY TO DISCUSS

Will meet Pachelbel Cathedral of Eight today, meet me Hotel Sacher Sunday to discuss

"What in the world does *that* mean?" Matteo said, standing upright again after reading the message over a few times.

"What does *what* mean?" Richard asked from the other end of the telephone line. "What in the world is going on over there?"

"We found another message," I replied, picking up the scrap of paper from Charlie so I could read it aloud. "It says: *Will meet Pachelbel Cathedral of Eight today, meet me Hotel Sacher Sunday to discuss.*"

"That's remarkable!" Richard said. "What a stroke of luck!"

"But what does it mean?" I asked. "Who is Pachelbel and what is the Cathedral of Eight?"

"Johann Pachelbel was a 17th-century German composer," Matteo suggested. "He wrote the famous 'Canon in D Major'."

"Yes of course," Richard replied and started singing a familiar-sounding melody. "*Laaa, laaa, laaa, laaa, laaa, laaa, laaa, laaaa.* But presumably that's not who the message means."

"And the Cathedral of Eight?" I asked again.

I looked around at everyone but they all shook their heads.

"I have no idea," Matteo replied.

"Richard?" I asked.

"Maybe St Stephen's in Vienna?" Richard suggested. "This message mentions the Hotel Sacher again so maybe that's what it refers to? But, to be honest, I just Googled it and there wasn't really anything about a 'cathedral of eight' anywhere on the Internet."

"What about today's message, Richard?" I asked, suddenly remembering it when I heard the creepy voice on the radio switch from zeros to letter groups again. "You said you'd decoded it for us already."

"Well, I would hardly say that I decoded it," Richard laughed. "It wasn't even in code in the first place."

"What do you mean?" I asked.

"Copy it down the next time it repeats and you'll see what I mean," Richard laughed. "It will repeat again in about forty seconds."

I quickly rushed to grab my notebook from my bag in the living room and returned just in time to catch the next repetition of the message, just as Richard had predicted.

"*Foxtrot–foxtrot–alpha–golf–foxtrot–foxtrot–echo–echo,*" the voice recited before pausing for a moment. "*Charlie–golf–alpha–echo–foxtrot–charlie–foxtrot–golf.*"

Another pause.

"This is nonsense, Richard," I said, showing my notebook to the others. "It just looks like more of those letter groups from that list we saw before."

FFAGFFEE CGAEFCFG

"Just wait," Richard said dramatically. "Here it comes!"

"*Uniform–romeo–golf–echo–november–tango,*" the voice repeated the final letter group. "*Whiskey–echo–mike–echo–echo–tango.*"

Richard was right. The last letter group was a message. And it was definitely not encoded.

URGENTWEMEET

"Urgent we meet! I can't believe it!" I cried in excitement as the creepy voice went back to reciting zeros again. "So simple! But why isn't it encoded?"

"Like I was saying before," Richard replied. "I think it's not encoded because your Herr Weinberg knows that their codes have been compromised anyway and he's been forced to send a vague, uncoded emergency message instead. And I think that's what all these zeros are about. It's a warning for everyone else to destroy their decoding pads."

"Who is 'everyone'?" Charlie asked.

Through the phone line you could almost hear Richard shrugging noncommittally.

"I have no idea," he replied. "I guess it's everyone involved in whatever this whole radio thing is?"

"Including our father, apparently," Matteo said with a sad look on his face.

"Exactly," Richard said. "And based on this new message we've found, I think we have to consider the possibility that your father is the one who this Herr Weinberg was planning to meet at the Hotel Sacher."

"I don't understand," Matteo replied.

"Think about it," I interrupted, realizing what Richard was trying to say. "This message we just found is obviously an older message, right? Written down by someone in this very room, most probably your father."

"Okay," Matteo agreed reluctantly.

"And in that older message it says *meet me Hotel Sacher Sunday to discuss*," I said, picking up the paper to read the last half of the message.

"Okay," Matteo said again.

"And then we have the message that Richard and I decoded last night. A much more recent message from just a day ago," I continued, opening my notebook to the scribbled notes I'd made less than twenty-four hours before. "And in *that* message it says '*Missed you Hotel Sacher*'."

Finally Matteo and his sisters understood my meaning. Their father had been the one who was meant to meet the mysterious Herr Weinberg at the Hotel Sacher but he had died before that meeting could happen. And, in fact, until Matteo had mentioned it earlier that day on the *Piazza del Popolo*, Herr Weinberg hadn't been aware that their father had passed away.

For a few long moments all of us simply stood there, silently thinking our own sad thoughts.

"But if these previous messages were for our father," Matteo said, finally. "And Herr Weinberg now knows that he's no longer alive. Then who is this new message directed at? How many people are involved in this... whatever it is?"

"At least seventeen people, I think," Richard said. "Including your father and Herr Weinberg, of course."

CHAPTER TWENTY·NINE
I Know It's A Long Shot, But...

"Seventeen people?!?" I asked in surprise. "Why in the world do you think that?"

"Because that's how many letter groups were on that hand-written list that you showed me yesterday," Richard replied. "Clearly each of those groups of letters is a codename for someone involved in this thing."

Feeling rather lost and confused, I flipped to the page of my notebook where I'd left the hand-written list that Richard was referring to and quickly counted the letter groups.

```
FFAGFFEE
EFECDDDB
FFFFEF
FBFFBB
AGGFEDD
DEFGAFA
EDEBCBCG
FFACCCCAA
CGAEFCFG
FEFEFEGF
CBCDCDEE
GEGEBEG
DBCAAA
CFACDCACDE
FAAAGFC
GCDBCFFFE
CCEEGGE
```

"Seventeen, you're right," I said aloud as I finished counting.

"Now check the letter groups from the message we decoded yesterday and the one we just received today," Richard continued.

I flipped to the pages with my notes from the two messages and immediately saw what Richard was talking about. The first message was preceded by two distinct letter groups from the hand-written list:

>   FFAGFFEE FFFFEF
>   MISSED YOU HOTEL SACHER
>   CROWN JEWELS UNDER THREAT
>   URGENT WE MEET
>   P POPOLO FRIDAY TWO

And the shorter message we'd just received also had a similar pair of letter groups preceding it:

>   FFAGFFEE CGAEFCFG
>   URGENT WE MEET

"The first letter group is the same on both," I said in amazement. "They both start with FFAGFFEE."

"Exactly," Richard said. "You said yourself that maybe these letter groups were some kind of call sign. And because your mysterious Herr Weinberg seems to have sent both of these messages, I'm willing to bet that FFAGFFEE is his."

"And the other two?" Matteo asked, already anticipating the answer for the first one.

"FFFFEF was your father's call sign," I said, answering the question before Richard had a chance to.

"And the other one? CGAEFCFG?" Charlie asked, stumbling as he tried to repeat the long string of seemingly random letters.

I shrugged my shoulders. "I have no idea," I said.

"I don't think we know the answer to that," Richard agreed. "Not yet, anyway. But clearly Herr Weinberg is urgently planning to meet with this person."

"But meet them where?" I asked. "Somehow we have to figure that out!"

"I'm not sure that we *can* figure it out," Richard replied. "I don't think we have enough information. Maybe at the Hotel Sacher? Or the Cathedral of Eight, whatever that is? Other than that, we don't really have any idea."

While Richard and I were discussing this, Charlie quietly slid into the chair in front of the desk and began to inspect the pencil rubbing he'd just made.

"I think there's more on here than just that one message," Charlie said, sliding out of the chair again and handing the paper to me. "Take a closer look."

I took the paper from him and sat down in the chair to take a closer look under the light. Charlie was right. There *was* more writing on it than just the message text, but it was faded and overlapping with the other text.

"This must be from some earlier scrawled notes or something," I said.

"That's why it's so faint and jumbled all over the place."

"What does it say?" Vega asked.

"It's hard to make out," I replied, squinting and tilting the paper back and forth to try and read it. "There are different little bits and pieces of words and numbers here and there but nothing really coherent. Down here at the bottom it says something like *Karajanplatz*, I think. And over here it says *Judengasse*? Do these names mean anything? Are they street names?"

"It sounds like it," Charlie said, nodding his head as he leaned over next to me, so close that I could feel the warmth of his cheek against mine.

"What's this number here?" Charlie asked, pointing at the top of the pencil rubbing. "*Four, four, four, seven, three, four*?"

"I think so," I replied.

"And what's this over here?" Charlie asked again, pointing to a different spot on the paper. "*Three, seven, three, four, two*?!?"

"Maybe," I replied. "But I think that all of this is just scribbled notes, just like I was writing in my notebook yesterday when Richard and I were decoding the message."

"That's probably what it is," Charlie had to agree.

"So that doesn't tell us much of anything," I said, disappointed.

"Maybe it does," Richard replied. "I just checked Google Maps for those street names. The *Judengasse* doesn't really help since there's a street with that name in half the cities in Germany, but you'll never guess what's across the street from *Karajanplatz* in Vienna."

"What?" I asked, holding my breath as I awaited the answer.

"The Hotel Sacher," Richard said.

My head was absolutely spinning from all this new information—all these codes and messages and call signs. It was getting to be too much. But there was one thing that was perfectly clear to me at that moment.

"We have to go to Vienna!" I cried.

"Vienna?!??" the others replied in surprised unison.

"What for?" Matteo asked, confused.

But Charlie understood. "To see if Herr Weinberg shows up there to meet someone," he said, nodding his head.

"Shows up *where*?" Vega asked. "The Hotel Sacher?"

"Maybe," I nodded. "Or this cathedral that Richard mentioned. What was it? St Stephen's? Maybe that's the Cathedral of Eight?"

"But we don't know where or when," Matteo protested. "We don't know anything."

"I know, it's a long shot," I agreed. "But there's five of us. Between us we should be able to cover a few different possible locations. And besides, it's all we have to go on. If these people do change their codes or go into hiding or something, then this will be the last chance we'll ever have to figure this whole thing out."

"Kitty's right," Vega agreed, nodding her head resolutely. "We might not know very much but we do know that this Herr Weinberg is planning to meet with someone, somewhere, probably within the next day or two. If we don't try to find him now, we'll lose our last chance to know what it was that father was up to."

"But Vega..." Giulia began to say.

"No! We have to try," Vega replied decisively. "I always thought that father and I were very close and yet in the past few days we've discovered a side of him that *none* of us even knew existed and suddenly I feel like I didn't even know him at all. I feel like I've lost more than just our father. I feel like maybe we never even knew who he was in the first place."

"That's ridiculous," Giulia interrupted. "Of course we knew him."

"Did we?" Vega replied. "Did we know about these priceless paintings hanging on the wall of his living room? Did we know about this secret room hidden right under all of our noses behind the walls of the house we grew up in? Do we know what he was doing in here with these crazy radio messages and secret codes? We didn't know *any* of these things!"

Vega's eyes began to well up with tears as she finished what she had to say, and Giulia and Matteo put their arms around her as they slowly nodded their heads in agreement.

"My sister is right, and so are you, Kitty," Matteo said finally. "We have to go to Vienna. We at least have to try."

CHAPTER THIRTY
The Cathedral Of Fight?!?

Early the next morning, the five of us found ourselves at Leonardo da Vinci Airport checking in for our flight to Vienna. The night before Vega had called a friend who worked for Alitalia and managed to get us all on the first direct flight of the day.

Obviously it would have been better to leave the night before but by the time we made the decision to go, it was already too late to catch the last flight out. Charlie suggested driving there but after checking on Google Maps, we realized that the distance is so far that there was no point since a morning flight would arrive around the same time anyway. Matteo also tried to find some train connections that would get us there earlier but unfortunately those schedules didn't work in our favor either. The only option was to fly.

I know what you're thinking. Why didn't I just fly there myself? I have my own plane, after all.

Unfortunately (as you might recall from my adventures in London and Ireland), things are not always that easy. For one thing, my plane was moored at a marina almost an hour away on the ocean so there was no way to make it there before complete darkness set in and I was grounded for the night. Not to mention that the crowded airspace of Europe is a far cry from the relatively open skies of western Canada (or Alaska, the Florida Keys and Iceland for that matter) and you can't just jump into your plane on the spur of the moment and fly wherever you want to. Things need to be planned a bit ahead of time and because of this, as much as I was enjoying Europe from ground-level, I was looking forward to putting Europe behind me and getting back into some clear open skies where I could fly free again. We could have flown in my plane in the morning, of course, but as much as I love my trusty little De Havilland Beaver, when it comes to sheer speed, a big fat commercial jet wins hands-down every time. The fastest way for us all to get to Vienna was to fly there on the earliest commercial flight possible and that's how we found ourselves in the airport boarding lounge, drinking coffee from paper cups and yawning as we waited for the gate to open.

Yet again I hadn't slept much the night before. Not just because there wasn't much time, but I'd also stayed up late surfing the Internet trying to figure out some kind of plan for our stakeout in Vienna the next day.

Keeping an eye on the Hotel Sacher was fairly straight-forward—one person in the lobby, perhaps, another outside in front to watch the *Karajanplatz,* and another in the café where the hotel's famous chocolate cakes were served. (Trust me when I say that I was looking forward to volunteering for that last one.)

The Cathedral of Eight was a different story, however. I checked out Richard's suggestion that this name might refer to the prominent St Stephen's Cathedral in the heart of Vienna, but I actually couldn't find anything anywhere to confirm this. The closest I could find was a reference on the Wikipedia page for St Stephen's that the cathedral had once been surrounded by eight separate cemeteries. That little tidbit of information seemed promising but since those cemeteries were closed all the way back in 1735 after an outbreak of bubonic plague, I wasn't feeling all that confident about it.

The Cathedral of Eight could be anywhere, after all. Who says that it had to be in Vienna? But since I couldn't find anything on the entire Internet that referred to any cathedral *anywhere* as the Cathedral of Eight, St Stephen's was still the best lead that we had. What other choice was there? And at three in the morning when I had to be awake again in just a couple of hours, I had decided to leave it at that.

But something about it kept bugging me and once we were at the airport and I had a fresh coffee in my hand, I decided to take advantage of the airport WiFi and continue my research.

This time I decided to try a new tactic. *Will meet Pachelbel Cathedral of Eight*, the earlier message we'd found had said. That particular planned meeting had already been and gone long ago but the truth was that we had absolutely no idea who Herr Weinberg was planning to meet on this particular day, other than the fact that their call sign was apparently CGAEFCFG. For all we knew that could be this Pachelbel again, right? So I decided to find out whatever I could about the famous German composer with the same name.

Johann Pachelbel: born 1653 in Nuremberg, Germany, died 1706 in Nuremberg, Germany. A famous German Baroque composer famous for his organ music. Educated in Altdorf and Regensburg, he later moved to Vienna to start his career and found work as an organist at St Stephen's Cathedral.

Well, that just about ties it up, doesn't it? I thought as soon as I read that last part. And yet, somehow I was still not convinced. Something about it simply didn't feel right.

"Are you ready to go?" I heard Matteo call to me as he headed for the line of people waiting to board the plane. "They're calling for our flight now. We have to catch a bus out to the plane."

"I'm ready," I replied, putting my iPad into airplane mode so I could put it away in my carry-on bag. "I'll catch up in one second."

But then something strange happened, something that seems almost mystical when I look back upon it. As I lifted my notebook to put it into my shoulder bag, a scrap of paper fell out and tumbled down onto the floor by my feet. It was the pencil rubbing that Charlie had made the night before.

"Doh!" I cried as I reached down to pick the small square of paper up from the ugly airport carpet. But as I grabbed it and was about to slide it back between the pages of my notebook for safekeeping, I noticed something about it that I hadn't noticed before.

Did it *really* say "Cathedral of Eight"? Or was it something else? Because now that I saw it again in the bright sunlight that was streaming through the windows, it seemed like there were lots of these older scribbles overlapping the letter E in "Eight", including the crossbar of the letter J from the word *Judengasse* that had obviously been written sometime separately from the coded message.

Frowning, I leaned closer and squinted my eyes.

Is that actually "Eight"? I asked myself, suddenly unsure. *But if not, then what is it? What other five-letter words end in "IGHT"?*

Across the room Charlie was looking at me strangely. He could tell from the expression on my face that something was up.

Just start at the beginning of the alphabet and work through it one letter at a time, I told myself.

AIGHT? No.
BIGHT? Is that even a word?
CIGHT? No.
DIGHT? No.
EIGHT? Already have that one.
FIGHT? Maybe, yes. The Cathedral of Fight? That sounds weird but maybe.
GIGHT? HIGHT? No and no.
IIGHT? Definitely not a word.
JIGHT? KIGHT? No. No.
LIGHT?

My heart skipped a beat.

The Cathedral of Light?

I don't know why but something about that sounded promising.

"What's the matter, Kit?" Charlie asked me as he walked toward me with a look of concern on his face. "Is something wrong?"

"Just give me a second," I said as I pulled out my iPad again and waited impatiently for it to connect to the Internet again.

"The flight is finished boarding," Charlie said, pointing to where Matteo and his sisters were waiting for us.

"Just one second," I said again as the WiFi finally connected and I typed something into Google and hit search.

"Umm, guys? The bus is waiting," Matteo called out to us from across the room. But I didn't hear what he was saying because I was too stunned at what had just come up on my iPad screen.

"Tell them to go without us," I said to Charlie, looking up at him with a look of absolute seriousness on my face.

"What?!?" Charlie replied in astonishment.

"What's going on?" Matteo asked as he and Vega joined us at the other end of the lounge. "We have to go. The gate is going to close."

"You have to go without us," I said to Matteo, rising to my feet and talking quickly. "You guys go to Vienna and stake out the Hotel Sacher just as we planned."

"And what about us?" Charlie asked in confusion. "What are we doing?"

"We're going to Nuremberg," I said simply.

CHAPTER THIRTY-ONE
Exciting Modern Miracles

"Nuremberg?!?" Charlie asked in disbelief. "Why Nuremberg?!?"

Charlie couldn't believe what he was hearing but of course I had an answer for him—thanks to Google.

Google has the power to turn anyone into Sherlock Holmes, doesn't it? In fact, I have to say that if it was me that had lived back in 1880s London instead of him, then I would definitely have been a far less effective mystery-solver than I am able to be in the modern world. All thanks to Google and that great repository of knowledge and wisdom (not to mention a lot of other totally crazy and unbelievably weird things) that we call the Internet.

"It's simple," I said as I rushed over to show Charlie the pencil rubbing that was still in my hands.

"Matteo, we have to go!" Giulia called from over by the gate where she was standing with Vega and two irate-looking airline employees.

"Just one more second," Matteo called back as he rushed over to hear my explanation as well.

"Okay, look at this," I said, talking fast so Matteo wouldn't miss the plane. "We thought the message said '*Will meet Pachelbel today Cathedral of Eight*' but what I think it *actually* says is the '*Cathedral of Light*'. See how the different scribbles overlapping the letter E might be from something else?"

Charlie took the paper and looked closely while Matteo leaned in past his elbow.

"Okay," Charlie replied in agreement, glancing up at me to hear the next bit.

"So I was checking on the Internet about this Pachelbel guy," I continued. "Maybe it's this guy's nickname or something, I don't know. But when you look up the composer with the same name here is what it says: Johann Pachelbel, born 1653 in Nuremberg, Germany, died 1706 also in Nuremberg. Famous German composer... yada yada yada."

I looked up at Charlie and Matteo to see if they were following me so far.

"Okay," Charlie said again slowly. "Nuremberg."

"And now the clincher," I said, flipping my iPad around so they could see my Google search. "The Cathedral of Light. Look what the very first thing that comes up is. In fact, not just the first thing, but basically the *only* thing."

Cathedral of light - Wikipedia, the free encyclopedia
en.wikipedia.org/wiki/**Cathedral_of_light** ▾
The **cathedral of light** was a main aesthetic feature of the Nuremberg Rallies that consisted of 130 anti-aircraft searchlights, at intervals of 12 metres, aimed ...

Charlie frowned and took my iPad from me so he could read the text off the screen.

"*The Cathedral of Light was a main aesthetic feature of the Nuremberg Rallies that consisted of 130 anti-aircraft searchlights, at intervals of 12 meters, aimed skyward to create a series of vertical bars surrounding the audience,*" Charlie read aloud.

"See? Nuremberg again," I said, looking at him hopefully. "I think the two of us need to go to Nuremberg."

Slowly but surely Charlie began to nod in agreement as he stared down at the iPad screen.

"Matteo!" Giulia called again from over by the gate where the two airline employees were looking extremely impatient. "Are we getting on this flight or not? Because it's about to leave without us."

I glanced up at Matteo who looked back and forth uncertainly between us and his sisters waiting at the gate.

"I'm coming," he finally said, taking a few quick steps toward the gate.

"Matteo! Call us when you get to the Hotel Sacher!" I called after him as he broke into a run.

"We will!" Matteo yelled back over his shoulder. "And by the way, there won't be a direct flight to Nuremberg from here. You're better off catching that flight to Munich at the gate across from us and then taking the train from there."

I turned to look at the gate that Matteo was talking about and saw that there was a Lufthansa flight to Munich leaving in less than forty-five minutes. Just enough time for me and Charlie to be on it, if we were lucky.

"Good luck!" I called to Matteo and his sisters as they disappeared through the doors and headed for their plane. I'm not sure whether or not they heard me, but Charlie and I didn't have any time to lose.

Weaving through the airport crowds, we ran over to the gate for the flight to Munich.

"Excuse me, can you tell me whether or not this flight is full?" Charlie asked the woman behind the desk.

"No, no, it shouldn't be," the woman replied after a moment.

"Fantastic," Charlie said with a sigh of relief. "Now what's the fastest way for us to get a ticket to be on it?"

"You don't have a ticket?" the woman asked in confusion. "How did you get past security without a ticket?"

"Sorry, we had a little unexpected change of plan," Charlie explained. "We were supposed to fly to Vienna but now we need to go to Nuremberg instead."

"This is a flight to Munich, not Nuremberg," the woman replied.

I couldn't tell whether the woman was being intentionally difficult or not but I could sense Charlie's patience with her quickly coming to an end so I reached out my hand and slid it into his, giving it a warm, friendly squeeze to remind him to stay cool.

"Yes, we are aware of that," Charlie said, his voice and posture relaxing slightly as I held his hand. "But we'll take the train from Munich. Now can you please tell me what the fastest way is for us to get a ticket for this flight?"

The woman smiled thinly and then pointed down the concourse with one bony finger. "There's a Lufthansa service desk just down there," she said. "They will be able to help you. But you'll have to hurry. This flight is almost ready for boarding."

"Thank you," Charlie replied and turned to hand me his carry-on bag.

"What's this for?" I asked.

"You wait here and I'll run for the tickets," he said.

"Okay," I replied, taking his small duffel bag from him.

"And whatever happens," he said, glancing up at the woman behind the desk. "Do NOT let this flight leave without us."

"Got it," I replied with a grin, and as Charlie dashed off and disappeared into the crowd, I imagined all sorts of scenarios where I would have to make a terribly dramatic scene in front of the flight gate in order to delay the flight. But fortunately it didn't come to that and after less than ten minutes of nervously watching the clock and scanning the crowd to see if he was coming back, Charlie appeared with a pair of airline tickets in his hand.

"That was fast," I said, handing his duffel bag back to him as we joined the line to board the plane. "The flight only just started boarding."

"The people at the service desk were a little more helpful," Charlie whispered to me as he handed our boarding passes to the woman at the gate and we headed down the jetway to the plane.

From that point on it was just the normal steps you go through whenever any of us fly on a commercial airline. You wait in line, shuffle forward, wait in line some more, show your boarding pass to the flight attendants, find your seat, and so on. We've all gone through this before, right? It's the price we pay to see the world. Of course, it's always a bit of an exciting modern miracle that we can be in one place at one moment and somewhere completely different only an hour or two later.

The only difference for me and Charlie was that we were about to end up somewhere completely different than we'd expected to when we'd woken up that morning. But I guess the fact that we can do things like that is also a bit of an exciting modern miracle as well, isn't it?

CHAPTER THIRTY-TWO
Die Reichsparteitagsgeländetennisspielmauer

Just a few hours later, thanks to the miracles of modern transportation, Charlie and I found ourselves standing at the edge of a small platform in the middle of a massive stone and concrete grandstand. It was a beautiful day outside with hardly a cloud in the sky and the sun warming our faces, but as I stood there staring uneasily across the enormous field stretched out in front of me, I couldn't help but feel an icy cold chill run down my spine.

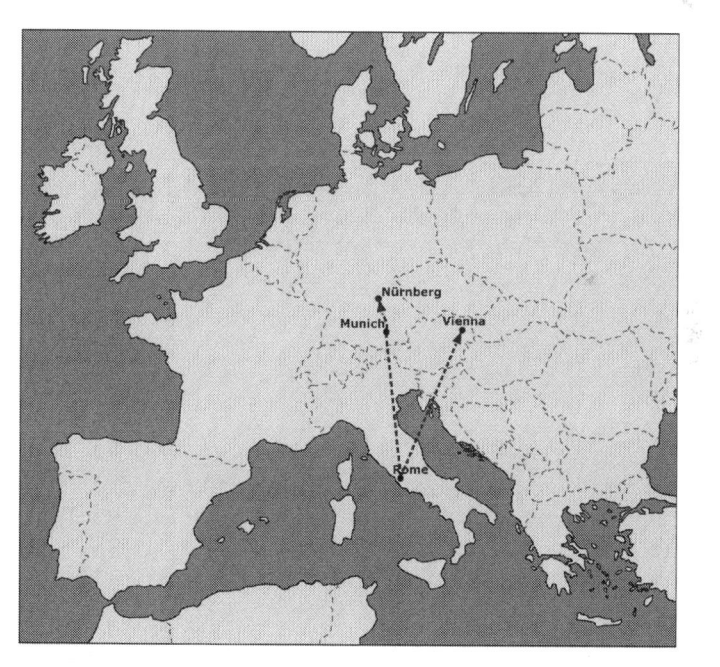

The reason for my discomfort was as obvious as it was simple. I was standing at the exact spot where Adolf Hitler had once stood and addressed adoring crowds numbering in the hundreds of thousands.

"*The Cathedral of Light was a main aesthetic feature of the Nuremberg Rallies,*" the Google search I'd made back in Rome had read. But what I hadn't realized at the time was that the Nuremberg Rallies referred to an annual series of Nazi Rallies that had taken place in Nuremberg before the outbreak of the Second World War. The so-called Cathedral of Light wasn't a cathedral at all. It was a temple to the horrors of mass spectacle and delusion of one of the most destructive and evil regimes in the history of the world. And I was standing right there in the middle of it—at the place that was once the spiritual heart of Nazi Germany.

As we stood there in stunned silence, Charlie pulled out the guidebook he'd bought back at the train station when we'd arrived on the train from Munich. He'd bought the book to show the taxi driver where we wanted to go but the driver actually didn't need it. Where we were standing was a place he knew very well since it is visited by thousands of tourists every year.

According to Charlie's guidebook, the grandstand where we were standing is called the *Zeppelintribune*—a colossal white stone structure more than a thousand feet wide. But this immense structure merely forms a single side of a four-sided area of spectators' stands enclosing a gigantic outdoor field built to accommodate one hundred thousand goose-stepping soldiers and more than three hundred thousand onlookers.

"Charlie, this is unbelievable," I said, stumbling and faltering over my words as I unsuccessfully tried to come to terms with what I was seeing.

Charlie nodded and stared out into the distance through the trees off to our right where another massive structure that resembled the Roman Colosseum rose up at the far side of a small lake.

"And yet, this is just one small part of the larger Nazi Party Rally Grounds that cover this entire area," he said, lifting his guidebook to show me a map of all the structures that the Nazi's had either built or planned to build. "In fact, you can see the remains of the *Kongresshalle* just over there through the trees."

Compared to all of that massive architecture, any individual human beings are dwarfed into insignificance and lost in a sea of faces. And yet, at the center of the massive *Zeppelintribune* where Charlie and I were standing is the *Führer Platform* where a single man once stood and commanded the attention of almost half a million people, captivating and mesmerizing them with his twisted dreams of a *Thousand-Year Reich*.

Of course, as we all know, that *Thousand-Year Reich* didn't last much longer than just twelve short years before collapsing destructively in on itself. But as I was quickly learning, many remnants of that dark chapter in history could still be found all around me like painful scars on the landscape, crumbled and overgrown with weeds, but still clearly visible. It seems that the imposing structures of those tortured and violent Nazi dreams were built to stand the onslaught of time and even after the armies of a thousand more years of decay march over them, they will still be standing for all to see.

And perhaps that's exactly how it should be. Those events should be remembered. They *demand* to be remembered. But that didn't help my feelings of uneasiness as I stood there looking out across that open field where hundreds of thousands of fanatical supporters once stood.

"And you're sure this is where the Cathedral of Light was?" I asked Charlie, nodding to his guidebook.

"Absolutely sure," he replied, flipping to show me a photograph.

"One hundred and thirty anti-aircraft searchlights were spaced out around this entire field and pointed at the sky," Charlie read. "The beams of light towered above the crowds, reaching as high as twenty thousand feet in the air, and the combined effect was of a shimmering and towering wall of light surrounding the entire audience. A Cathedral of Light. Or, as the British Ambassador Sir Neville Henderson, who was in attendance at the time, also described it, a Cathedral of Ice."

"A Cathedral of Ice," I whispered to myself as I tried to imagine the scene. And maybe that was an even better description of it since I could almost hear the deafening chants of *Heil Hitler* in my ears and my heart felt cold from just the thought of it.

Suppressing an involuntary shudder, I forced my thoughts to return to the present and our search for the elusive Herr Weinberg. If nothing else, at least the view from the top of the *Zeppelintribune* gave us a clear view of the entire surrounding area. We had a lot of ground to keep an eye on but if Herr Weinberg did plan to show up there, then Charlie and I would hopefully be able to spot him. Until then, however, there was very little for us to do but sit and wait.

Charlie and I took turns alternating between sitting to watch the area in front of the *Zeppelintribune* and pacing back and forth along the rear of the structure. It was mind-numbing work but unfortunately there was no other way to keep an eye on everything at once.

Matteo called several times to check in with us from their stakeout many miles away in Vienna at the Hotel Sacher. The three of them were doing things in much the same way that Charlie and I were, with one of them sitting in the lobby pretending to read a newspaper, another in the café drinking a coffee and the third one patrolling the area out in front. I joked that their operation sounded a lot more fun than ours because at least they had coffee and newspapers, but in reality their setup was just as tedious as ours.

"At least you have the sun there," Matteo told me when we spoke for the fifth time that afternoon. "It's started to rain here and I'm feeling pretty miserable standing outside here in Vienna."

"True," I conceded. "But even in the sunshine it still feels dark here somehow, like there's some sinister shadow hanging over this place."

"I can imagine," Matteo replied with a cynical chuckle.

"I can't wait to get back to Rome and away from all this horrible dark history," I said.

Matteo laughed again. "I think there's some pretty dark shadows over Rome as well," he said. "The Germans aren't the ones who invented fascism, after all."

"What do you mean?" I asked. "Who did, then?"

"The Italians, of course," Matteo replied. "Long before anyone had ever heard of Adolf Hitler and the Nazi party there was already a fascist state in Italy under Mussolini. Hitler was an admirer of the Italian fascists."

"That sounds vaguely familiar," I said as I struggled to remember what we'd learned about it back in social studies class.

"After the war our grandfather was accused of being a fascist, in fact," Matteo continued. "Not that this is anything unusual, of course. In Italy, lots of people's grandfathers were once supporters of Mussolini."

Matteo and I talked a while longer to pass the time until Vega came to switch places with him. Once she was in position, he returned to warm up with some hot coffee at the café inside the hotel.

After we said goodbye, I put my phone away and continued to scan the area as the time continued to pass painfully slowly. Down below on the paved area in front of me a group of adults were racing radio-controlled cars around while a never-ending stream of curious visitors climbed the grandstand and took in the view from Hitler's *Führer Platform*. Most of the tourists were quiet and respectful but occasionally one might make some inappropriate joke or click their heels together and execute a stiff-armed Nazi salute.

"I wonder what Hitler would think of everyone using his beloved *Zeppelintribune* for tennis practice?" Charlie joked as he climbed back up the grandstand to switch with me.

I laughed through my nose at this. I knew exactly what he was talking about. All along the back of the structure there were countless tennis players practicing by hitting balls against the enormous rear wall. I didn't know whether to laugh at the absurdity of such a thing and whether it was appropriate or not, but the sight of such a mundane activity taking place in such a surreal place was so strange that I couldn't help but be amused.

"Do you think we missed him?" I asked as I started down the steps to take over the watch of the back of the building. "Herr Weinberg, I mean?"

Charlie took a deep breath. "Maybe," he replied honestly. "We didn't get here until past noon, after all. If he was coming here at all he could easily have already been and gone by that time."

I nodded tiredly. "What if it gets dark and he still hasn't shown up?" I asked.

Charlie shrugged and gave me a reassuring smile. "Then I guess we find a place to sleep for the night and come back here tomorrow," he said.

CHAPTER THIRTY-THREE
Why Don't We Take The Train?

I am afraid to say that Herr Weinberg didn't show up that day—at least not when Charlie and I were there. And after the sun had set and night started to set in, we caught another taxi back into the center of the city and found a couple of rooms at a cozy little hotel just inside the old city walls.

We hadn't eaten all day so after we checked in we wandered around the charming streets of the old town until we found a McDonald's and had a little indulgent feast of cheeseburgers and fries before saying good night and heading off to our rooms to crash.

The next morning we were up early and headed back out to the *Zeppelintribune* where we repeated the boring cycle of surveillance that we'd settled into the day before. Hundreds of miles away in Vienna, Matteo and his sisters returned to the Hotel Sacher for another long day as well, and every time my phone would ring I would desperately wish that they were calling to say that they'd spotted Herr Weinberg. But they never did. The hours dragged on and on and still no sign of him at either location.

By the time the sun began to set on our second full day of the *Big Exciting Stakeout* (as I had started calling it), Charlie and I were discussing with Matteo about what our plans should be for the next day. Vega and Giulia had to return to work but he was committed to staying on one more day to try and keep an eye on things by himself, if that's what we decided to do too.

I couldn't bear the thought of spending yet *another* incredibly long and boring day sitting on the steps of the *Zeppelintribune* but with Herr Weinberg nowhere to be seen and no other hope of ever finding him, I forced myself to say yes when Matteo asked us if we would be willing to give it just one more day.

"Okay, Matteo," I said. "We'll do it."

"*Fantastico!*" Matteo replied with a surprising degree of enthusiasm, and we agreed to call each other again the next morning.

With the sun long gone and the night setting in again, Charlie and I took yet another taxi back into the city center and had yet another mini feast of cheeseburgers and fries at the same McDonald's as the night before. The repetitiveness of our whole routine was slowly becoming a tiny bit comforting and I was feeling a lot better by the time we set out the next morning for the *Zeppelintribune* with our cups of McDonald's coffee in hand. It felt like we were going into work, somehow. Like our job in life was to go to the Nazi Rally Grounds every day and simply hang out there watching people from dawn to dusk.

"Today's the day!" I said cheerfully to Charlie as he headed for his first shift patrolling the back wall of the grandstand. "That's what Mel Fisher used to tell his treasure-hunting scuba teams as they set out each day to find the long-lost ships of the Spanish 1622 treasure fleets off the coasts of Florida."

Charlie laughed. He knew all about my treasure-hunting adventures down in the Florida Keys.

"And they eventually found the treasure, right?" he asked with a grin.

"That's right," I replied cockily.

"And, remind me... How long did it take them?" Charlie called back to me from the foot of the stairs.

I smiled sheepishly. "Fifteen years, I think?" I said.

Charlie shook his head sadly. "I'll see you in fifteen *minutes*," he replied. "And then we'll switch off."

I waved goodbye and watched Charlie disappear around the corner. It was early but over the sound of the breeze and the cars passing on the road behind me, I could hear the sound of tennis balls thwopping against the back wall over and over again. Some people were out early for tennis practice, apparently.

As I drank my coffee and scanned the area, I tried to keep my spirits up but with my butt aching from sitting so much and the horribly mind-numbing monotony of it all, I found myself growing increasingly depressed.

I was happy to change with Charlie and give my butt a rest for a while, but after a few hours of switching back and forth over and over again, my feet had also begun to ache and I found myself spending most of my sitting shifts rubbing my feet. It was tiring and boring and it seemed like it would never end.

Even the normally chipper Matteo was feeling the pain of the whole dreary exercise and every couple of hours when he would call, he sounded a little bit less enthusiastic each time.

"I think we have to accept that we either missed him or he was meeting up somewhere else," I told Matteo as the sun began to get low in the sky again for the third day in a row. "Plus the weather report says it's going to rain here tomorrow and I can't imagine sitting out here all day in the rain. There's no shelter anywhere."

"I could lend you my umbrella," Matteo joked. "I had to buy one on Saturday when it started to rain here as well."

"Oh, sorry!" I replied, laughing and blushing in embarrassment at the same time. "I feel so rude for daring to complain about the weather when we've had nothing but sunshine here the whole time."

"Don't worry, don't worry," Matteo laughed in reply. "But I think you're right. I think the time has come to admit that we're never going to find him this way."

Part of me was ecstatic to hear him say this. My butt and feet were particularly happy, but of course another part of me was also very sad that we were forced to give up. But to keep trying also didn't make any sense either. We couldn't just sit around in Vienna and Nuremberg waiting for something that might never happen, after all.

"So what do we do now?" I asked sadly as I spotted Charlie heading up the stairs toward me. He was visibly tired, dragging his feet with every step but still trying to keep a smile on his face.

"I'll fly back to Rome tomorrow," Matteo said. "What about you and Charlie? What will the two of you do?"

I actually had no idea how we were going to get back to Rome. I had assumed we would fly but as Charlie slumped down on the cold, hard stone next to me, I suddenly had an interesting idea.

"Why don't we take the train back to Rome?" I asked Charlie.

Charlie grinned that wonderful Charlie grin of his and that told me everything that I needed to know.

CHAPTER THIRTY-FOUR
Are You Sure You Want To Do This?

"Are you sure you want to do this?" Charlie asked the next day as we stepped off a bus and he popped an umbrella open over my head to protect me from the cold rain that had been falling all morning.

"I'm sure," I nodded. "I think I need to see this."

Charlie looked at me for a moment, examining my face carefully. He looked like he was very tired and I could only assume that I probably looked a hundred times worse.

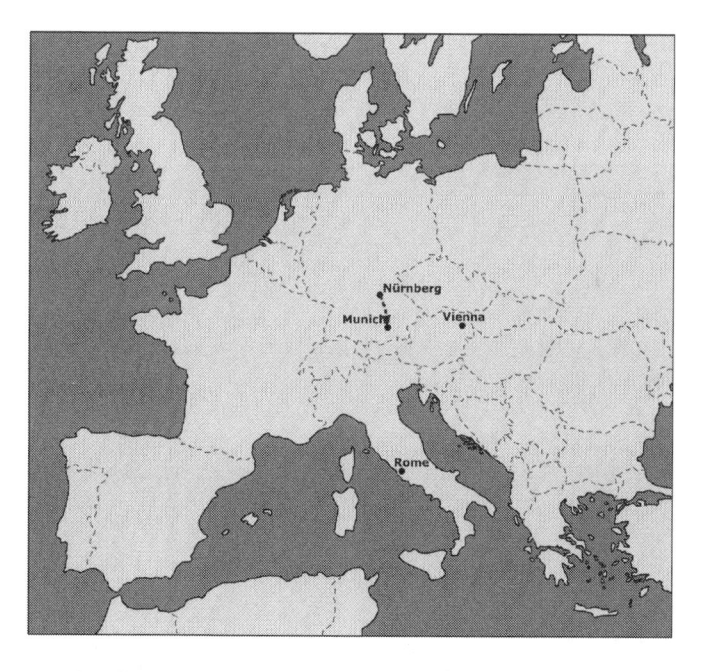

The two of us had woken up early and caught the first train to Munich. Our original plan was to continue on from there another nine or ten hours to Rome but on the way I was reading Charlie's guidebook and decided that there was a place just outside of Munich that I really wanted to see—or what I actually should say is that it was a place that I felt I *had* to see, even if it might be extremely unpleasant.

"Okay, Kit," Charlie said after a few more moments of studying my facial expression as we walked along a charming tree-lined path toward a white stone gatehouse with a passageway running through it to an elaborate metal gate beyond. "I just wanted to be sure because obviously this isn't going to be a lot of fun."

It's not meant to be fun, I thought to myself as I stopped in front of the gate to read the simple message that was fashioned into it in cold, lifeless black iron.

Arbeit Macht Frei, the gate read. *Work Makes You Free.*

Those few simple words mark the entrance to one of the most notorious places on Earth—the site of the former Nazi Concentration Camp of Dachau.

You're probably asking yourself why in the world I would want to visit such a vile and sinister place and the only answer I can really give you is that after spending so many hours sitting there on the *Zeppelintribune* in Nuremberg, alone with my thoughts and surrounded by the ghosts of thousands who made horrific places like this a reality, something inside me simply had to see it.

Pushing open the wrought-iron gate, Charlie and I stepped inside the walls of the camp and tried to take in the enormity of it. Off to our left, barbed-wire fences and ominous guard towers stretched off into the distance, running parallel to the foundations of the former barracks where tens of thousands of prisoners were forced to live in deplorable and crowded conditions. In front of us was the open area of the camp's parade ground where the prisoners were forced to stand for hours, no matter the weather conditions, during twice-daily camp roll calls. Finally, off to our right where Charlie and I were slowly heading was the camp's enormous maintenance building where the permanent exhibition and museum for the memorial site is located.

First established shortly after the Nazis came to power in 1933, Dachau was designed as a camp for political prisoners and other persons deemed undesirable by the regime. Although not an official death camp like other notorious places such as Auschwitz, Dachau was the model for these later camps that spread all across Europe. As the grip of the Nazis tightened all across Germany and occupied Europe, Jews, homosexuals and even priests were sent to the camps, millions of them never to return. Businesses and homes were seized and all private property and possessions confiscated or stolen by the Nazis as their dark and ugly shadow seeped throughout the continent.

The horrors of Dachau and Nazi Germany only finally came to an end in the spring of 1945 when the camp was liberated and the regime finally fell. American soldiers who first discovered the camp were so horrified and disgusted that they forcefully marched German citizens from nearby towns to clean the camp up and to witness the horrors and depravity for themselves. These regular citizens appeared shocked by the conditions there and claimed to have had no knowledge of what had been going on there.

I thought about this as Charlie and I walked through the museum and down the center of the camp past row upon row of foundations from the original prisoners' barracks.

How could they possibly NOT have known? I thought. It's not like the camp is in some isolated location out in the middle of nowhere. The camp is just outside of what was, and still is, one of Germany's largest cities and mere minutes from the regular houses and businesses of the town of Dachau itself. *They had to have known.*

Charlie and I continued to the far end of the camp where some religious memorials had been constructed, including a secluded Carmelite convent hidden behind the north wall of the camp. Turning left Charlie and I passed through a barbed-wire fence and across a short bridge where a perfect little mountain stream with cold, crystal clear water babbled happily beneath us.

Such beautiful natural surroundings made the place seem peaceful and idyllic and perfect. And yet the pouring rain from the gloomy skies above reminded us that this was all just an illusion, and as we turned a final corner we arrived at some small buildings where the camp's gas chamber and crematorium are located.

If there is one thing that I've learned throughout my travels around the world it is that there are some places which absolutely defy any attempt to describe them. Fortunately for all of us, most of these places are of a beauty that is too far beyond belief to convey in words but some of them are also simply too awful, and this small corner of Dachau was most certainly one of those.

Charlie and I walked in stunned and wordless silence through the surprisingly small building. According to his guidebook, there is some debate as to the extent to which the gas chambers at Dachau were used. Certainly they were never used to the extent that those in the so-called death camps like Auschwitz were utilized, but none of that really makes any difference as you move slowly through these frightfully sinister constructions. The uneasy chills that I'd experienced back in Nuremberg when we'd first stepped out onto the *Führer Platform* of the

Zeppelintribune were amplified to a deep and agonizing fever that ran as cold as ice. Suddenly the British Ambassador's description of the Nazi Rally's *Cathedral of Light* as a *Cathedral of Ice* seemed far too fitting.

As I stood there silent in those terrifyingly real rooms, I also realized that Charlie and I had somehow come full circle. We'd traveled from the spiritual heart and origins of Hitler's *Third Reich* in Nuremberg to these dim and dismal spaces in Dachau and somehow spanned one of the darkest periods of human history. And yet, it occurred to me that this camp at Dachau had been constructed years before the ambitious architecture glorifying the Nazi regime had been built in Nuremberg. The Nazis had literally constructed darkness before building their own version of what they called light. And maybe in that simple fact is revealed the great and horrible lie that was Nazi Germany itself?

All of these thoughts weighed heavily on my mind as Charlie and I made our way back toward the forbidding main gate of the camp to head back to the train station.

Never again! a memorial near the exit optimistically proclaimed in five separate languages. I laughed a cynical laugh as Charlie and I passed by the equally cynical inscription on the main gate–*Arbeit Macht Frei.*

Such things will always happen again when even the people living in the same town turn a blind eye to them, I thought, wondering what I myself would have done had I found myself in such circumstances. I wanted to believe that I would have been courageous and strong in the face of such horrors but the truth was that I actually had no idea how I might have acted, and as Charlie and I rode the train back into Munich in silence, I found myself pondering this question like in a deranged and endless loop.

In Charlie's guidebook there was a quote that I kept reading over and over and over again as the train rattled through the gray and misty day. It was a quote from a German novelist I'd never heard of called Alfred Döblin who, in 1946, made an observation about the responsibilities of the citizens of Germany in the face of the horrors that had been inflicted during the course of the Nazi era:

"*There are two types of guilt,*" he wrote. "*Systematically committing a crime, and making it possible and permitting it. We didn't want this and didn't know that. But it was up to us to have wanted and to have known.*"

This quote has stuck with me ever since because it describes the kind of citizen that I would want to be if I ever found myself in similar circumstances. One who not only wanted to know, but one who was also brave enough to know.

CHAPTER THIRTY·FIVE
I'll Bet Your Jaw Hits The Floor

Not long after leaving the dismal surroundings of Dachau behind us, Charlie and I found ourselves on a train heading south toward Italy. The morning rain had finally begun to clear and up ahead of us the sun was starting to poke dramatically through the clouds as the peaks of the Alps slowly rose up from under the horizon.

It had been a long day, or at least that's what it felt like. The day wasn't even half over yet. There was still a long way to go before we would get to sleep that night but at least from there on out I would have to do nothing more than sit and stare out of the window as the world rattled and rolled past me. And so far, from what I could see with all those beautiful mountains in the distance reminding me of home, the ride was going to be nothing short of wonderful, which was a welcome change from the depressing morning that we'd just had.

The train was pretty crowded but Charlie and I had found a spot in the dining car of the train where a young man graciously welcomed us to sit at his table with him. With nowhere else to sit we gratefully accepted his offer and sat down on the bench next to him. He was apparently some kind of orchestra conductor because he had stacks and stacks of musical scores laid out on the table in front of him and I watched in admiration as he carefully worked his way through each of them, his head bent down in concentration as he waved an invisible baton through the air as he closed his eyes and silently listened to each of the pieces of music as they played inside his head.

Charlie ordered lunch for us and I was surprised at how good the food was, considering the fact that we were on a train. I had a delicious potato soup and an amazing salad while Charlie decided to try some authentic *Nürnberger Rostbratwürstchen*–Nuremberg sausages–with an amazing kind of Bavarian potato salad made with vinegar and oil. (I know it was amazing because I tried some of it–or maybe a little more than just *some* of it, to be perfectly accurate.)

After lunch we ordered something more to drink and a small piece of chocolate cake to split between us as we watched the Alps grow ever closer, majestically filling the view outside of our window. Charlie slowly nursed a tall glass of beer and gazed out of the window while I aimlessly stirred my cappuccino with a wooden stir stick and tried to get my head around everything that we'd experienced over the course of the last week.

Despite the fact that Herr Weinberg had managed to slip through our fingers, it was difficult to dismiss the expeditions to Vienna and Nuremberg as complete wastes of time. I didn't know about Matteo and the others but despite the painfully long days that Charlie and I had spent sitting on the *Zeppelintribune*, I still felt like we had seen and experienced something special. Nuremberg itself was a charming little town with its city walls and lovely medieval squares, complete with tiny castle peering down from a rocky crag overhead. And that's just what we'd managed to see on the way to and from our hotel and the nearby McDonald's.

As the train clattered on, I flipped through Charlie's guidebook and read more about Nuremberg and Munich and the surrounding areas, seriously considering taking some time to go back there before I continued on my around-the-world flight.

Too bad Wasabi Willy's doesn't open a restaurant in Munich, I thought. I would definitely be interested in seeing some more of that city as well.

But before I could do any of that, Charlie and I would be returning to Rome where he would have to finish off his work for the World Food Program and I would have to start getting my plane ready for the next leg of my journey around the world.

It felt sad, somehow. Like the train we were on was somehow hurtling me inevitably toward the close of the current chapter of my life when I wasn't yet ready to move on. The mystery of Herr Weinberg and the radio transmissions and paintings was still unsolved, after all, and I found myself having a hard time accepting that the solution might never be found.

As I continued sipping my coffee, I pulled my notebook from my bag and flipped slowly through the various pages of notes and comments, trying desperately to find some clue or piece of information that maybe we'd missed somehow.

Unfortunately, the problem wasn't that we'd somehow missed a clue somewhere, but rather it was the fact that the clues we had were so cryptic that we probably would *never* be able to figure them out.

These coded call signs, for example. Those had been bugging me ever since the first day we'd found that creepy hidden room behind the walls of Matteo's father's apartment. What did they mean? As far as I was concerned, they must be call signs for the different people involved in this whole mysterious operation with the strange radio messages, but why these letters? And what was it about them that had been nagging at my brain ever since the first day we'd found them.

I took the piece of paper with the list of letter groups on it out of the notebook and sat and stared at them for a while, trying to see something in them that maybe I'd missed before.

"What are you looking at?" Charlie asked me.

I looked up and saw him smiling gently at me across the table. Sitting beside him, our table mate the orchestra conductor continued to sit with his eyes closed, conducting the imaginary symphonies in his head.

```
FFAGFFEE
EEECDDDB
FFFFEF
FBFFBB
AGGFEDD
DEFGAFA
EDEBCBCG
FFACCCCAA
CGAEFCFG
FEFEFEGF
CBCDCDEE
GEGEBEG
DBCAAA
CFACDCACDE
FAAAGFC
GCDBCFFFE
CCEEGGE
```

"Nothing, really," I replied. "Just thinking."

Charlie nodded understandingly and went back to his beer to leave me to my thoughts.

I looked down and stared at the letter groups again for a while, but it was no use. There was nothing there. No pattern. No meaning. Not as far as I could see, anyway.

I slid the paper back into my notebook at the page where I'd written down the final broadcasted message just a few days earlier.

Was it really just a few days? I thought. It felt like a lifetime since Richard had read out the uncoded message for me to write down.

"*Foxtrot–foxtrot–alpha–golf–foxtrot–foxtrot–echo–echo,*" Richard had read out. "*Charlie–golf–alpha–echo–foxtrot–charlie–foxtrot–golf.*"

FFAGFFEE CGAEFCFG

Two of the groups from the list of letter groups that I had just been looking at.

"*Uniform–romeo–golf–echo–november–tango,*" Richard had continued. "*Whiskey–echo–mike–echo–echo–tango.*"

URGENT WE MEET

The three words that had sent all of us off on wild goose chases across Germany and Austria.

Uniform–romeo–golf–echo–november–tango–whiskey–echo–mike–echo–echo–tango, I thought to myself, echoing the last letters of the message in my head. *There was something different about those last ones, wasn't there?*

I frowned and pulled out the list of letter groups again to stare at it, lost in thought.

There IS something different about them! I thought suddenly, my heart starting to beat faster in excitement as I stared at the seemingly random letter groups.

But they actually weren't random at all and I felt stupid that I hadn't seen it before. On the entire list of letter groups—seventeen groups and hundreds of individual letters—there was not a *single* letter that was higher than the letter G. Every letter was either A, B, C, D, E, F or G—the first seven letters of the alphabet.

"And what is the significance of that?" the little voice inside my head seemed to be asking me. But of course it's the voice in *my* head, right? And that means that it must have already known.

As far as I was aware, the only system in the world that used only the first seven letters of the alphabet were the notes on a musical scale. I'd only had a couple of years of piano lessons when I was a kid plus music class in grade school, but that much I could remember perfectly.

"Okay, but what does that mean?" the little voice in my head asked stubbornly.

I was already way ahead of that, excitedly reaching into my bag to pull my iPad out. I was so excited, in fact, that I didn't even notice that Charlie was carefully watching me, fully aware that I was on to something but not wanting to disturb my train of thought.

Where is it, where is it? I thought as I flipped through pages of apps on my iPad. *Stupid Apple has some kind of music app on here somewhere, don't they?*

They did. Garage Band. I finally found it under an app group I'd created called *Useless Crap I Don't Need.*

I tapped on the app and quickly scrolled through it to the keyboard option. A screen with a piano keyboard soon appeared and I tried to find an option to have it show the letters for each note on the keyboard for me.

Stupid Apple, I cursed in frustration. *Why don't they have this option?*

In the end I had to give up and just try it from memory. I was too impatient. I just had to know what those letter groups meant.

I put in my headphones and started with the first one on the list, tapping each note on the keyboard in sequence—FFAGFFEE. I was expecting some jaw-dropping revelation but instead my frown of concentration deepened as I listened to each note in confusion.

What in the world? I thought to myself, starting to feel rather disappointed.

But I wasn't disappointed for very long because the jaw-dropping moment came just a few more seconds later when I tried out the second group of letters on the list. I swear to God that my mouth must have fallen straight open and hit the floor when I heard that one.

But I'm getting ahead of myself, aren't I? In fact, maybe right now would be a good time for you guys to try this little experiment for yourselves at home? I'm sure you have a piano (virtual or real) somewhere where you can access it. I'll even include a little picture of a piano keyboard below with letters to help you out.

Just give it a try and I'll bet your jaw hits the floor too.

FFAGFFEE
EEECDDDB
FFFFEF
FBFFBB
AGGFEDD
DEFGAFA
EDEBCBCG
FFACCCCAA
CGAEFCFG
FEFEFEGF
CBCDCDEE
GEGEBEG
DBCAAA
CFACDCACDE
FAAAGFC
GCDBCFFFE
CCEEGGE

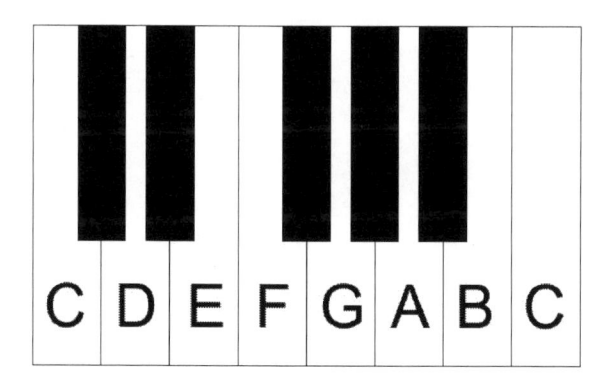

CHAPTER THIRTY·SIX
Da Da Da Duh, Da Da Da Duh

What in the world is that? I thought to myself after trying to play the first sequence of letters on the piano keyboard. It sounded familiar somehow, but I couldn't really be sure. Maybe something like a little bit of a song?

Moving on to the second group, I tried that sequence of letters instead and was absolutely stunned when I heard it. It *was* a song.

Da da da duh, da da da duh.

Everyone knows that one! I thought. *Beethoven!*

My heart was racing as I worked my way through the rest of the letter groups, one after the other. Most of them sounded a bit like what might be songs, others sounded kind of totally random, but a few of them were absolutely definitely melodies that I'd heard before. DEFGAFA, FFACCCCAA, FAAAGFC, CCEEGGE. Even FEFEFEGF sounded a bit familiar.

Of course, I was getting the timings completely wrong and I had no idea where any of these little snippets of songs were from but two things were absolutely certain: they were definitely from songs and I had definitely heard them somewhere before.

"You've figured something out," I heard Charlie say.

I looked up and saw Charlie watching me in fascination, a gigantic grin on his face.

"Oh my God, Charlie, yes!" I replied with a grin that was just as big on my face as well. "Listen to this!"

I pulled the headphones out of my ears and handed them to Charlie. He put them on and listened while I played a few of the more recognizable letter groups for him. This time I tried to play them in proper rhythm and watched as the smile on his face widened with every passing note.

He pulled the headphones off after I'd finished and looked at me in disbelief. "They're songs," he said in amazement. "I can't believe it!"

"Me neither," I replied, blushing bright red in pride at my discovery.

"What about the other ones?" Charlie asked, pointing to the other letter groups that I hadn't played for him. "Are they songs too?"

"Probably," I replied. "But they don't really sound familiar to me. Plus, other than this Beethoven one, I don't even know what songs these ones I just played are either. I just know that I've heard them before."

"This one was 'Blue Danube'," Charlie said, pointing to FFACCCCAA on the hand-written list. "Johann Strauss."

"And the others?" I asked.

Charlie shrugged. "I have no idea, but why don't you ask him?" he suggested, nodding to the man sitting next to him who was still lost in his own little world, conducting orchestras that no one but him could hear. "I'll bet he knows."

Charlie was right. What a stroke of luck! If anyone would know, it would be this guy.

"Excuse me, sir," I said, reaching across the table to catch the man's attention. "I'm sorry to bother you but we couldn't help but notice that you have some kind of musical training and were wondering if you could help us identify some pieces of music?"

The man smiled kindly and carefully folded up the musical score in front of him to give us his full attention.

"Of course," he replied. "I mean, I'll do my best."

"I'm Charlie, by the way," Charlie said, reaching out to shake the man's hand. "And this is Kitty."

"Hi," I said, blushing. "Sorry, that was rude."

"No, no, don't worry. I'm Linus," the man said in reply, shaking each of our hands in turn. "Now, what kind of music is it that you need help with? I'm afraid that I'm not very up to date with modern music. Anything newer than the Beatles I won't be much help with."

"Don't worry, I'm pretty sure that all of these are much older than that," I replied, laughing as I unplugged my headphones from the iPad and turned up the volume on the external speaker.

I picked up the hand-written list of letter groups and placed it on the table beside me. As we already knew, there were seventeen different call sign groups on the list, but in actual fact three of them in particular were of interest to us since those were the ones that had appeared on the two coded messages we'd received.

From what we could tell, the first message we'd received appeared to be sent by call sign FFAGFFEE and directed to FFFFEF:

FFAGFFEE FFFFEF
MISSED YOU HOTEL SACHER
CROWN JEWELS UNDER THREAT
URGENT WE MEET
P POPOLO FRIDAY TWO

The second message seemed to have the same sender as the first, FFAGFFEE, but was addressed to CGAEFCFG instead:

FFAGFFEE CGAEFCFG
URGENT WE MEET

After everything that had happened, we could only assume that the sender of both messages was Herr Weinberg and since his assumed call sign FFAGFFEE was at the top of the list, that was the one I played first for Linus.

"That's Mozart," Linus said with a quick nod immediately after I'd finished playing. "Definitely Mozart."

Mozart! I thought to myself. *Of course! I knew that I recognized that song!*

"It's '*Eine Kleine Nachtmusik*'," Linus continued. "Although you're not playing it quite right."

"I know, I'm terrible," I admitted with a delighted grin.

Linus reached across the table and tapped the keys of my iPad piano to play a proper rendition of the instantly recognizable melody.

"Da da, da da da da, da da," Linus sang while he played like some kind of incredible iPad piano virtuoso. "Da da duh da, da duh. But that one was too easy. Do you have any others?"

"We do," I replied, skipping over the second group on the list that we already knew was Beethoven. "That one we already know, but how about this one?"

I leaned over my iPad and played the third letter group for him—FFFFEF. This was the call sign that the first coded message seemed to be directed to, presumably Matteo's father.

Linus frowned deeply and scratched his head uncertainly for a few moments after I'd finished. "That's a tough one," he said. "There's not a lot to work from there."

"Sorry," I replied sheepishly, as both Charlie and I looked at Linus hopefully.

"No, I'm sorry," Linus replied after humming the simple melody to himself a few more times. "I can't say that I know that one."

Dammit, I thought. *That was an important one.*

"How about this one, then?" I asked, moving on to the next one on the list—FBFFBB.

"Saint-Saëns, I think," Linus replied. "'Danse Macabre'."

Okay, that's good, I thought. *That's three out of four.*

"And this?" I said, moving along to the next one.

Linus closed his eyes as he listened intently.

"Bizet, perhaps?" he said. " 'Carmen'?"

"That's amazing," I said in genuine admiration. I couldn't believe that he could recognize all of these from my poorly played renditions.

"May I see this list you are reading from?" Linus asked, pointing to the hand-written list of letter groups that was lying on the table next to me.

"Of course," I replied, handing the piece of paper to him.

Linus looked the list over, nodding occasionally while he hummed the various melodies to himself.

"None of these are in their original key," he explained as he continued scanning down the list. "They've all been transposed into C."

"Okay," I replied, not really sure what he was talking about, although something about it sounded vaguely familiar.

As I watched Linus continue to scan down the list, I was utterly astonished by his level of skill and knowledge. I couldn't imagine being able to simply read letters off a page and instantly recognize what composers and pieces of music they represented.

"Edvard Grieg," he said as he continued scanning. "Dvořák. Strauss, of course, that's easy. Pachelbel..."

"Pachelbel?!?" both Charlie and I cried at the same time.

CHAPTER THIRTY-SEVEN
And While We're On The Topic...

"Which one is Pachelbel?!?" I asked, leaning suddenly over the table and startling Linus with my unexpected outburst.

"This one," he replied, pointing at an entry about halfway down the list—CGAEFCFG. It was the call sign that the second message had been addressed to.

You were right, Charlie's expression said to me as he looked up with a grin on his face. *About Pachelbel and Nuremberg.*

But how did we miss the meeting with Herr Weinberg, then? I wondered. *Maybe we just arrived in Nuremberg too late.*

"What about the rest of these?" Charlie asked Linus as he leaned eagerly forward.

Linus nodded and continued reading down the list.

"Tchaikovsky," he said. "The next is Bartók, I think. Then maybe Holst, although that one I'm not sure of. Then Chopin, Prokofiev, Vivaldi, Bach, Haydn. The last ones are pretty obvious."

"Obvious to *you*, maybe," I said, grinning widely as I made notes of each of these composers that Linus was mentioning. "It's absolutely amazing that you can recognize these."

"They are all quite famous pieces," Linus replied with a humble shrug. "In fact, most of them are the absolute signature pieces for most of these composers. Which is why this one here bothers me so much. I really cannot figure it out."

Linus held the list up and pointed to the third entry that we'd skipped over earlier—FFFFEF.

"Maybe some kind of Italian composer?" I suggested, thinking that if it really *was* the call sign for Matteo's father, as we suspected, then perhaps he would have selected someone Italian. "From Rome?"

Linus thought about this for a moment then his face suddenly lit up.

"Of course!" he cried. "From Rome! The 'Miserere'!"

"The 'Miserere'?" I asked, confused.

"Allegri!" Linus continued, smiling widely like an excited schoolboy. "Gregori Allegri! He was born in Rome."

"And that's what this piece is?" Charlie asked. "This F–F–E–whatever?"

"Yes, yes, definitely," Linus replied. "I hadn't recognized it before because this is simply one of several melodies in the piece's main harmonies. But it's definitely what it is."

"Unbelievable," I said, leaning back in my chair with a huge smile on my face.

"It's quite a famous piece, actually," Linus continued. "With quite an interesting history. It was originally composed to be performed only in the Vatican's Sistine Chapel during two special masses at Easter. An order issued by the Pope himself decreed that it should neither be written down nor performed anywhere else on threat of excommunication from the Catholic Church."

"Seriously?" I asked, chuckling.

"Absolutely serious," Linus replied. "In fact, if it wasn't for Mozart maybe no one outside of the Sistine Chapel would *ever* have heard it because when young Mozart was a teenager, his father took him to the Mass there on Holy Wednesday and afterwards he wrote down the entire thing from memory, all nine singing parts, and then returned again for the Good Friday Mass two days later to make sure he'd got it right."

Absolutely amazing, I thought to myself. I could hardly imagine the kind of raw talent and musical training that would have been required for Mozart to memorize an entire choir arrangement from memory, not to mention how much talent Linus had to be able to recognize all of the composers and their music for us.

"Thank you so much for all of this, Linus," I said sincerely. "I can't tell you how much I appreciate it."

"Of course, of course, any time," Linus replied with a wave of his hand and a wide smile on his face. "But may I ask what all of this is for? Is it some kind of game or scavenger hunt?"

Charlie laughed and nodded. "Something like that," he said.

At that moment the crackly, distorted sound of the conductor's voice came over the public address system to announce the train's next stop. As he was speaking, I tried to think through everything we'd just learned to see if any of this new information actually helped us. I wasn't sure whether it did or not. I mean, we already knew that the letter groups were some kind of call signs for the various people involved in this whole secret organization. The only thing we knew more than that now was that each call sign seemed to correspond to a different piece of music and a different composer.

But each of those composers comes from somewhere different, right? I thought to myself. *This Pachelbel person, whoever they were, seems to live in Nuremberg just like their namesake. And Matteo's father, codename Allegri, of course was from Rome. And we already knew that Mozart was from Vienna because that's where the Hotel Sacher is. So have we really learned anything new from all of this?*

Outside the windows, the countryside flashing past gradually began to slow down and was replaced by quaint rows of houses and city streets. The train began to rumble and shake as it screeched through various railway switches on its way into the center of a city.

"Are we still in Austria?" I asked.

"No, not anymore," Linus replied, shaking his head. "We're already in Italy. The next station is Bolzano."

"Why do you ask?" Charlie said, looking confused.

I turned to Charlie and just stared at him blankly for a second.

"I'm just thinking that maybe we should go to Vienna after all?" I replied, my mind still racing to make sense of what we'd just learned.

"To Vienna?" Charlie asked. "What for?"

"Because that's where Mozart is from," I replied. "So that means it's also where Herr Weinberg is from."

Charlie looked at me funny. "Didn't we already know that?" he asked. "And what are we supposed to do there to find him? Just sit around the Hotel Sacher every day hoping that maybe he'll eventually show up?"

Something like that, I thought to myself as the train began to pull into the station. But Charlie was right. Sitting around waiting and hoping for something to happen was hardly a convincing plan. So, despite all the excitement of the past twenty minutes, we hadn't really learned anything that we hadn't known already. Or should I say, until a few seconds later when Linus happened to mention a couple of juicy tidbits of information that we'd hitherto been unaware of.

"You're right that Mozart is famous for having lived and died in Vienna," Linus said. "But he was actually born in Salzburg."

"Salzburg?!?" I asked in surprise.

Linus nodded. "Absolutely," he said. "And while we're on the topic, there are actually *two* Hotel Sachers–the original and famous one in Vienna plus one in Salzburg as well."

I was completely stunned and all I could do was stare at Linus for a second or two in utter disbelief before quickly turning to face Charlie.

"We have to go to Salzburg!" we both cried at exactly the same time.

CHAPTER THIRTY-EIGHT
There's A Fine Line...

After bidding a hurried farewell to Linus, Charlie and I had quickly grabbed our bags and jumped off the train in Bolzano. From there we began a long journey north again toward Salzburg, first backtracking to Innsbruck along the way we'd just come and then switching trains to head east to Salzburg. We had some bad luck with connections and unfortunately didn't get to our destination until quite late, by which point we were both completely exhausted.

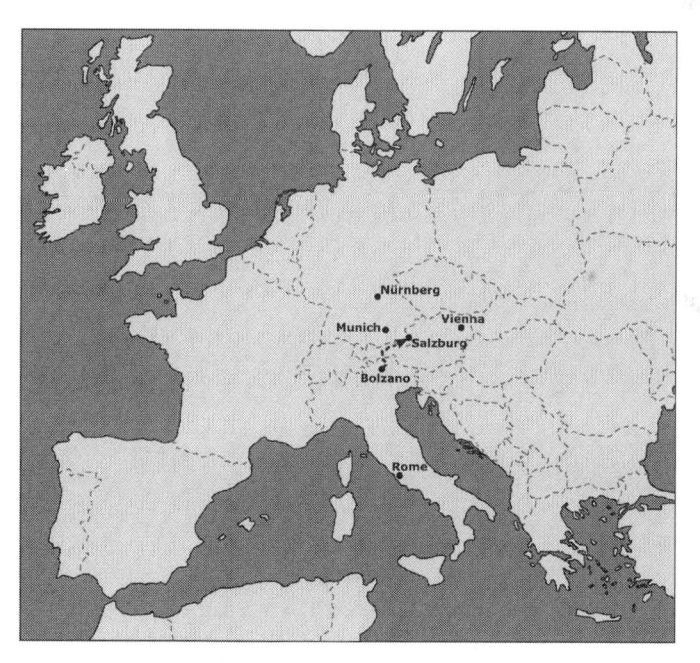

Once we arrived, I suggested that maybe we could stay at the Hotel Sacher, but one look at their room rates on the Internet quickly killed that idea. Charlie did manage to find a room for me in a small hotel in the old part of the city but they didn't have anything for him so instead he booked himself into a nearby hostel for the night.

We met up the next morning in the breakfast room of my hotel where I was already discovering that I have a love for crispy *Kaiser Brötchen* with various types of fruit jam. The secret, I discovered, is to cut them in half and then scoop out the soft bread inside so you're left with basically all crust.

"Good morning," I smiled at Charlie as he slid into the seat across from me. "How did you sleep?"

Charlie laughed. The only room the hostel had available for him was a dorm-style room where he had to share with ten other people.

"It was... interesting," he replied with a grin. "No problem sleeping with a bunch of strangers, of course. But sometime around three in the morning, a guy came in to bed and was trying so hard to not disturb everyone else..."

Charlie started laughing again.

"What?!? What is it?" I asked. "What's so funny?"

"It's not even *that* funny," Charlie admitted. "But he climbed into bed and it was all dark and quiet and I guess he was hungry because he had this big bag of chips and..."

"And...?" I asked, still wondering what Charlie thought was so hilarious.

"Well, let's just say that you can't eat a bag of chips quietly in the middle of the night," Charlie said, continuing to chuckle to himself.

Somehow I found myself laughing along with him, although more in amusement about how funny he thought this story was than from the actual story itself.

"I guess you had to be there," I suggested.

"Something like that," Charlie replied. "And then, this morning in the shared shower room, I took a picture to show you."

"You did what?!?" I replied, nearly choking on my *Kaiser Brötchen*.

Charlie gave me a *get serious* look.

"Not pictures like *that*," he said, shaking his head and laughing.

Charlie pulled out his crappy old Samsung Galaxy phone to show me.

"You really need a new phone," I said as he flipped through his pictures to find what he was looking for.

"I like my phone," he said simply in his defense and turned the screen toward me. "Look at this one. This is kind of funny."

I looked and saw a picture of some graffiti that someone had scribbled on the shower room wall with a pen.

> *Since writing on bathroom walls is*
> *done neither for critical acclaim nor*
> *financial rewards, it is therefore the*
> *purest form of art. Discuss.*

"I'm not sure that 'funny' is the right word for it," I replied, laughing at Charlie's strange sense of humor that morning.

"How about this one?" he asked, flipping to the next photo.

> *Roses are red. Violets are blue.*
> *You think this is going to rhyme*
> *but it's not gonna.*

I have to admit that I smiled a bit at that one. "Okay, that's a *bit* funny," I replied.

"It's actually this next one that I *really* wanted to show you," Charlie continued, flipping to yet another similar photo.

> *Why is it that whenever I come down to*
> *have a shower in the morning that I have*
> *to read all this hating on each other?*
> *We are all human beings, after all.*
> *Signed, a Canadian girl without a*
> *Canadian flag sewn on her backpack.*

I wrinkled my forehead and read the message over and over again a few times, convinced that I must be missing something.

"What does that mean?" I asked, looking up at Charlie and wondering if his sense of humor had gone somehow completely haywire since the last time I saw him.

"All over the shower room walls there was all sorts of stupid graffiti," Charlie explained, leaning back in his chair. "And most of it was just stupid, of course, with a few slightly funny ones. But the hostel had a lot of backpackers and other people from all sorts of different countries so there was also a lot of messages like 'Americans suck' or 'Australians suck' or whatever, depending on the nationality of whoever was writing it."

"And?" I asked, still unsure where Charlie was going with all of this.

Charlie shrugged and gave me a bit of a wry smile. "I don't know," he said. "I just thought that what this girl wrote was kind of interesting."

I thought this over for a second. "Show me again," I said, leaning across the table to read the message off his phone one more time.

"I was thinking a lot about this on the walk over here this morning," Charlie said. "About how Canadian backpackers and tourists all over the world always wear these little Canadian flags on their backpacks, or how we Americans love our flag so much. And then I was thinking about everything we saw in Nuremberg and Dachau. And I was wondering, is there really any difference between sewing a flag on your backpack and wearing a swastika on your arm?"

I was totally shocked. "Are you crazy, Charlie?!?" I cried, incredulous. "They are *COMPLETELY* different things!"

Charlie looked at me with a serious expression on his face. "I know that what they *represent* is completely different," he replied. "But what I'm talking about is this desire that people have to wear a badge of nationalistic pride on their backpack like that."

"It just means that they're proud of their country," I said. "What's wrong with that?"

"Maybe there's nothing wrong with it," Charlie mused. "But I'll bet those hundreds of thousands of people at the Nazi Party Rallies in Nuremberg were proud of their country too."

"But they were all evil Nazis," I replied.

Charlie looked at me and raised his eyebrows. "All of them?" he asked. "The whole country was evil? All of those tens of millions of normal German citizens were all evil?"

I was about to say yes, but then I stopped myself. I was starting to understand his point. They couldn't possibly have all been evil, no more than all Canadians could possibly be good.

"I'm not sure that I agree with you," I said. "But I think I am beginning to understand what you mean."

Charlie nodded slowly and continued staring off into the distance. "You asked me what I thought this graffiti meant," he said, speaking slowly as he thought things through. "And I think it means that maybe there's a fine line between being proud of your country and something more sinister. Because once you stop seeing yourself and the people around you as fellow human beings and start seeing them as something else—Canadians or Americans or whatever—then where does it stop?"

CHAPTER THIRTY-NINE
There's More After The Wedding?!?

After my strangely philosophical breakfast with Charlie, we were both ready to get out into the city and see if we could find Herr Weinberg.

"So what's the plan?" Charlie asked. "How do you expect to find him in a city where tens of thousands of people live?"

It was a good question and one that I admit I didn't really have an answer for yet.

"We should start at the Hotel Sacher, of course," I replied. "We can get ourselves a coffee and just scope things out there for a while. Maybe we get lucky?"

Charlie raised his eyebrows skeptically. "Do you seriously think so?" Charlie asked with a grin.

"No," I admitted with a laugh. "But at least we'll have some good coffee while we figure out what else to do."

So we finished breakfast and headed outside into the daylight, walking through the narrow streets of Salzburg's old town. I had Googled the city a bit the night before and had seen some amazing pictures but nothing could have possibly prepared me for how breathtakingly beautiful and charming it was in real life. It was like stepping into an absolute fairy tale of quaint shopping streets, churches, plazas and fountains. And watching over all of this, with the majestic mountains of the Alps as a backdrop in the distance, a magnificent white fortress is perched at the top of the rocky heights overlooking the city.

"Charlie, this is absolutely unbelievable!" I cried as we slowly wandered through the narrow streets. "I've never seen anything so beautiful!"

Charlie smiled and nodded his head in agreement. "It's really amazing, isn't it?" he said over the pealing of church bells that seemed to echo from all across the city.

As we continued to meander through the city, it seemed that we had completely forgotten our plan of heading across the river to the Hotel Sacher for a coffee. But who could blame us for getting distracted? Everywhere we looked, a postcard-perfect view was waiting for us and every time we tried to steer ourselves back toward our destination, we'd turn another corner where some new and wonderful enchantment was waiting for us. With so many new things to experience, we couldn't help but be excited to try and see it all. And besides, Herr Weinberg could wait, right?

Of all the amazing discoveries we made that first day in Salzburg, there was one in particular that ended up sidetracking us from our plans for most of the day. It wasn't the cute little shop selling nothing but thousands of hand-painted Christmas tree ornaments made from hollow egg-shells (although that ended up consuming at least forty-five minutes of our time while I worked my way through the entire store, intent on looking at each and every different design). The thing that single-handedly diverted us the most from our plans that day was my realization that the movie *The Sound of Music* was filmed in Salzburg.

Actually, let me correct myself a bit there. It's not really accurate to say that I suddenly came to this realization because no visitor to Salzburg could ever possibly escape the city without being acutely aware of this fact. There are constant reminders of it everywhere you look. But as I flipped through the small booklet that Charlie had bought outlining the various filming locations around the city, I was completely hooked and immediately decided that we had to embark on an extensive Sound of Music walking tour.

"What is this here?" I asked, pointing to an entry in Charlie's booklet for something called the *Petersfriedhof*. "It says that this is the cemetery where the Von Trapp family was hiding in the scene at the end of the movie."

Charlie looked over my shoulder at the photo of the cemetery with its various headstones and arched funeral vaults. "Yes, that definitely looks like it," he said, nodding. "Don't you think?"

I looked up at Charlie, wrinkling my nose as I tried to remember which part of the movie he was talking about. Little did I know that I was about to experience a startling and embarrassing string of personal revelations.

"I haven't seen the movie since I was a kid but I really don't remember any cemetery scene," I replied. "Is this after Maria and the captain guy get married?"

"*Way* after they get married," Charlie said. "It's at the end of the movie, right before the family runs away and escapes over the mountains into Switzerland."

Escapes over the mountains into Switzerland?!? I thought. *When did THAT happen?!?*

"Are we talking about the same movie, Charlie?" I asked. "I don't remember any of this."

Charlie looked at me funny. "You're kidding, right?" he asked.

"I'm totally serious!" I replied. "I have no idea what you're talking about. Why would they run away over the mountains?!?"

Charlie looked at me even funnier, like he thought I was crazy. "To get away from the Nazis, of course," he said. "Why else?"

"The Nazis?!?" I replied in utter confusion. "Since when are there Nazis in *The Sound of Music*?!?"

Charlie stopped in his tracks and stared at me for a few long seconds.

"The Nazis are there for almost the entire second half of the movie," Charlie said. "Right after Maria and the captain get married until the end."

It felt like my head was spinning. "Right after they get married?!??" I replied. "But the wedding *IS* the end of the movie!"

Charlie stared at me with a look of disbelief on his face. "When was the last time you saw this movie?" he asked me.

"When I was a kid," I replied. "My parents and I would watch it on TV. I would always beg them to let me stay up until the end."

"Do you mean the wedding scene?" Charlie asked. "Is that what your parents told you was the end of the movie?"

Suddenly it all made sense. My parents had been sending me to bed right after Maria and the captain got married and the innocent little younger version of me had always happily accepted this as the end of the movie. But from what Charlie was now telling me, it seemed like there was a lot more that came after that. It was like having some childhood dream shattered in the blink of an eye—like learning that Santa Claus or the Easter Bunny aren't real.

"I'm gonna have to call my parents later to discuss this," I said angrily as Charlie and I continued walking. "I can't believe they didn't tell me there was more after the wedding!"

Charlie laughed. "Don't worry," he said. "We'll figure out a way for you to see the rest of the movie before we leave Salzburg."

I couldn't believe that I'd been missing out on half of the movie for all those years. That fairy-tale wedding scene seemed like such an obvious ending that I couldn't imagine what could possibly happen afterward.

"So what happens after the wedding?" I asked. "Do Liesl and Rolf end up together?"

Charlie laughed again, even more loudly this time. "Sorry, Kit," he said to me with a grin. "Rolf becomes a Nazi too."

CHAPTER FORTY
What Do You Think The Odds Are?

Following my rude awakening to the fact that I've lived my entire life in ignorance about the true ending of *The Sound of Music*, Charlie and I proceeded on an extensive walking tour of the film's shooting locations.

Despite only having ever seen the first half of the movie, I was still familiar with the scenes of Maria and the children frolicking around the city of Salzburg. I could remember most of them quite well, which came in handy over the next couple of hours as Charlie and I made our way around the city singing and skipping our way through various gardens and around fountains. I did most of the singing and skipping, of course, while Charlie filmed me re-enacting various scenes from the movie. But I am proud to say that I did manage to convince Charlie to pose next to one of the many dwarf statues in the tiny park that you see in the movie known as the *Zwerglgarten*–the Dwarf Garden.

I also tried to convince Charlie to sing "Do-Re-Mi" with me nearby on the famous steps from the scene in the movie where the Von Trapp children do the same. Fortunately for him, another group of tourists came along who needed an extra person to re-enact the song with them, so Charlie was off the hook. Instead, he just stood back, laughing with us and filming the spectacle of us jumping around on the steps, singing and shouting like lunatics.

"You should have joined us, Charlie!" I said to him after saying goodbye to my newfound Von Trapp brothers and sisters.

"Someday you'll thank me for standing back and making a video record of all this," Charlie replied, still laughing at my craziness. "Although you might never want to share it with anyone."

As we walked back through the garden in the direction of the Hotel Sacher, Charlie handed me my phone so I could watch all the movies he'd made that day. He was absolutely right on both counts. I was definitely glad to have them, but it was so completely ridiculous and silly that, other than showing it to my parents, I doubted I would ever want it to see the light of day.

Cutting around in front of the Opera House, we waited at some traffic lights before crossing the street and finally arriving at the infamous Hotel Sacher. It was a strange feeling to walk down the sidewalk next to that proud old hotel with its commanding view across the river to the old town of Salzburg. After everything we'd been through, all these strange coded messages and hints of clandestine meetings, it felt like we were suddenly closer than ever before. And as we walked in the front doors and down through the lobby to the elegantly decorated café, I was somehow half expecting to see Herr Weinberg sitting waiting for us.

He wasn't, of course, but somehow I couldn't shake the feeling as we made our way through the long, narrow café and past the black-and-white photos of all sorts of famous people I'd never seen before. In truth, the café was almost empty. Aside from a couple of older gentlemen dressed in quaint traditional Tyrolean clothes and reading newspapers, Charlie and I were the only people there.

We found a nice table by the window and sat down to order. A slice of the famous cake–*Sachertorte*–for both of us plus coffee. Charlie decided to go with what he knew and got a normal coffee with milk and cream but I was feeling a little more adventurous and ordered something called an *Anna Sacher Kaffee*, which was coffee, milk and eggnog mixed together.

"Are you sure about that?" Charlie joked as the waitress finished taking our order and was walking away.

I shrugged my shoulders. "You only live once," I grinned.

And to be honest, the *Anna Sacher Kaffee* turned out to be pretty good, amazingly good, in fact, with the various familiar flavors and textures swirling together into a delicious earthy sweet union. I was less impressed with the world-famous *Sachertorte*, however, despite its fame and long history.

According to the wooden-framed menus of the Café Sacher, the cake was first invented in 1832 when one of the Austrian Empire's most important statesmen, Prince Metternich, was hosting a dinner party. Obviously wanting to impress his many high-ranking and powerful guests, the Prince informed his kitchen staff that he wanted something extra special for dessert. Unfortunately, his master chef was ill that day and instead the task fell to his promising young apprentice named Franz Sacher. The result was a rich chocolate cake topped with apricot jam and sealed within a thin but dense layer of chocolate icing served with unsweetened whipped cream. The Prince's guests loved it and a legendary dessert was born, one that would later become the centerpiece confection of the Viennese hotel opened by Franz Sacher's son.

There's a lot of history there and believe me when I say that even though I'd never heard of this Sacher cake before, it is definitely quite famous. Although, to be honest, I'm not sure why. It's okay, I guess, but I'd personally rather have some frozen McCain's chocolate cake from the freezer section of 7-11. But what do I know? Charlie liked his piece of *Sachertorte* very much, after all, so maybe I'm just an uncultured slob. At any rate, an authentic *Sachertorte* seemed like a pretty good gift for my parents back in Canada so after sitting for a while I left Charlie behind and went to stretch my legs, dropping into the hotel cake shop on my way to order a cake to be shipped home to them. Maybe they would have a better appreciation for it than I did.

Charlie and I sat around the café for quite a while, talking and lingering over our coffee and desserts as we watched people come and go, vainly hoping that we'd see Herr Weinberg magically appear.

Outside the window, the evening began to set in over the streets of Salzburg so Charlie and I left the Hotel Sacher behind and took a leisurely stroll across a small footbridge to the opposite side of the river and the narrow streets of the old town. As we walked, we talked about the amazing day that we'd had. We hadn't found Herr Weinberg, of course, but maybe he was just a convenient excuse for the two of us to explore a few more little corners of Europe before we had to return to what we were actually supposed to be doing in life—Both of us back to Rome where Charlie would finish his work with the World Food Program before heading back home to Alaska while I continued my flight around the world.

"Look at this, Charlie," I cried as we passed through an arched passage and out onto one of the old city's main squares where some horse-drawn carriages were lined up and waiting for customers. "We should totally take a carriage ride, Charlie! It would be so romantic... I mean..."

I stopped myself abruptly in mid-sentence, blushing bright red in embarrassment. I actually wasn't sure *what* I meant. But it didn't matter anyway because Charlie hadn't even heard me. As I spun around to face him, I saw that he had stopped short five or ten feet behind me and was staring intently at the doors of a ticket office that had long since closed up for the night.

"Look at this!" Charlie said.

"What?!?" I asked as I hurried over toward him. "What is it?"

Charlie pointed to one of the posters hanging on the green wooden shutter-doors of the ticket office.

Festungskonzerte

Tomorrow evening for ONE NIGHT ONLY enjoy a delightful dinner and evening concert at the Hohensalzburg Fortress featuring the sublime music of Wolfgang Amadeus Mozart and the extraordinary talents of the world renowned guest violinist Julia Fischer.

"Herr Weinberg is a fan of Mozart, right?" Charlie asked, a wide smile spreading across his face as he turned to face me. "What do you think the odds are that he'll be at this concert?"

I looked at Charlie and grinned. I had no idea what the odds were, and maybe it was just wishful thinking for an excuse to spend just one more day in the delightful city of Salzburg, but at that moment it seemed to me that if we were going to find Herr Weinberg anywhere, that concert was going to be the place to actually do it.

CHAPTER FORTY-ONE
Like The Plot Of A Bad Movie

"Oh my God, Charlie, look at the view," I cried as Charlie and I stepped out onto a terrace at the foot of the walls of the *Hohensalzburg* Fortress. Spread out in front of us was an absolutely stunningly beautiful panorama of green fields and trees stretching out into the distance where the formidable barrier of the Alps rose up into the sky like some great wall in a land of giants.

"Unbelievable," Charlie agreed, which probably says a lot since both he and I come from a part of the world where breathtaking views and mountains are almost commonplace. But somehow this was different. This wasn't a view across rugged mountains and wilderness that we would have had back at home. There was a different human history here, as was evident by the fact that we were standing at the foot of a medieval castle that construction had started on more than one thousand years before.

And what a castle it was. Built by the powerful Prince-Archbishops of Salzburg to protect their dominance over the valuable gold, silver and salt mines in the area, the fortress has a commanding view over the entire city and river below it. With sheer, high walls and daunting battlements, it was a virtually impregnable fortress that no enemy in their right minds would even have dared to try and make an assault on. It was difficult enough to find your way around the labyrinth of courtyards and passages on the inside as a modern-day tourist, much less if you had to somehow fight your way through it.

But Charlie and I weren't just there for sightseeing, of course, so after familiarizing ourselves with the confusing layout of the place and the interior rooms where the concert would take place later in the evening, we staked ourselves out on an outdoor terrace of one of the fortress's modern restaurants.

"So, we now know that there's only two ways in and out of this place," Charlie said after we'd ordered some cold drinks and found a nice spot in the shade with a clear view of all the comings and goings. "There's the huge, long road on the opposite side of the fortress which winds all the way around the whole thing and eventually leads you back into the old city. Or there's the vastly more popular funicular trains that can bring you all the way up here in just under a minute or so."

Charlie nodded his head toward the steep railway tracks nearby that plunged down the steep sides of the fortress's tiny mountain and down into the old city below us. All day long, a pair of train cars called the *Festungsbahn* had been going up and down carrying visitors to and from the fortress high above the city. It was actually quite fascinating to watch them because the two little trains shared the same track for most of the way, each running in opposite directions. Just as one would leave the bottom station, the other car would simultaneously depart from the top, emerging from inside a tunnel in the fortress walls and out into the sunshine. From there, the two cars would then run directly toward each other until they both reached the halfway point where the single track briefly separated into two so the trains could pass each other. It was quite a clever little system, although I was sure it was something fairly commonplace in this part of the world where ways of getting up and down the sides of mountains were probably in high demand.

"Which way do you think Herr Weinberg will go?" I asked Charlie after taking a sip of sparkling water.

Charlie grinned. "I think it's a pretty safe bet that he'll be taking the funicular," he replied. "That looks like an awfully long walk to go all the way down on foot. Besides, the fortress closes for tourists at six and the concert doesn't start until eight thirty, so I suspect that late in the evening the trains are the *only* way to get from the city to here."

"Makes sense," I agreed with a nod of my head.

"So, since the concert was sold out tonight and we don't have any tickets," Charlie continued. "The best place for us to watch for Herr Weinberg isn't going to be up here, but down at the lower train station instead. It's like a maze up here in the fortress. But down there he'll have nowhere to hide."

Charlie looked at me with a slightly mischievous grin on his face.

"And once we find him?" I asked. "Then what?"

Charlie apparently hadn't thought that far ahead and for a moment he looked confused. "We follow him, I suppose," Charlie said.

"Shouldn't we talk to him?" I asked. "And try to get some answers?"

Charlie shook his head. "Don't forget how that turned out last time," he said. "No, this time we're going to keep a low profile and simply find out where he lives. Once we know that we can report back to Matteo and the others and they can decide what they want to do."

Charlie seemed to have everything figured out. Everything, that is, except what we were going to do for the next few hours until Herr Weinberg was likely to show up for the concert—assuming he would even show up at all.

"Should we head back down into the old town and get something quick to eat before it's time to start our stakeout?" I asked.

"Maybe at that place we ate at last night," Charlie suggested as he left some money to pay our bill and we headed over to the *Festungsbahn* to line up for the next train. "I think that was the best Wiener schnitzel I've had in my entire life."

All this talk of food was starting to make my stomach rumble. Or maybe that was just the rumbling of the funicular train as we started down the side of the little mountain.

Watching the amazing view out of the train car's huge windows, we emerged from the fortress walls and rattled our way toward the oncoming train that was headed right for us from the lower station. As the two cars drew closer and closer, they each split off to opposite sides right on cue.

I couldn't help but smile as I watched this in fascination. It's stupid, I know, but I just felt like a little kid watching those two train cars veer off at the last second and safely sweep past each other.

I looked back at Charlie and noticed that he wasn't smiling at all. Just the opposite, in fact. His expression was one of intense concentration as he slowly turned his head to watch the other funicular train slide past us.

I spun my head around to see what he was looking at, but in the pit of my stomach I somehow already knew what I was going to see. It was cliché, totally predictable—like the plot of a bad movie. But there it was all the same.

Through the windows of the little train cars, I saw Herr Weinberg moving smoothly past us, riding up to the top of the fortress while Charlie and I were already on our way down.

CHAPTER FORTY·TWO
Wait A Minute... Do You Smell That?

"Oh my God, Charlie," I whispered as the other funicular train swept past. "Do you think he saw us?"

Charlie shook his head. "No, definitely not," he replied as he watched the train continue its way up the steep side of the mountain. "He looked like he was completely lost in his own little world."

The two of us watched the other train car for a moment longer and then turned toward each other, smiling triumphantly.

"We were right!" I whispered excitedly. "Herr Weinberg is from Salzburg! It was him! It was really him!"

"It sure was," Charlie agreed, beginning to smile a bit himself.

"But what should we do, Charlie?" I asked as the other train car disappeared into the walls of the fortress high above us. "Should we go back up there again and keep an eye on him?"

Charlie wrinkled his forehead as he thought this over. Our own train car slowly came to a stop at the bottom station and when the doors opened everyone began to spill out.

"Excuse me," Charlie said to one of the *Festungsbahn* operators as we made our way toward the exit. "Can you please tell me what time the fortress museum closes today?"

"Of course!" the man replied in heavily accented English as he pulled back his sleeve and checked his watch. "It closes in about twenty minutes. At six o'clock."

"And these people we've just seen go up in the other car?" Charlie asked. "Are they going for the concert tonight?"

The man nodded his head in reply. "Most likely, yes," he said. "The museum wouldn't be letting anyone else in so late."

"But isn't the concert at eight thirty?" Charlie asked. "Why would anyone for the concert go up as early as this?"

The man laughed and smiled. "For dinner," he said. "Many of the concert tickets include dinner at the restaurant as well."

Charlie and I both nodded. That made perfect sense.

After thanking the man for his time, Charlie followed me out toward the exit and onto the street.

So what do we do now? I asked myself as Charlie and I stared at the exit of the building that we'd just walked out of—the same exit that Herr

Weinberg would eventually have to use sometime in the next few hours.

"Maybe we should skip dinner," Charlie said apologetically. "And just stay here and keep an eye on things."

I nodded my head emphatically. I couldn't have agreed more. Even though Herr Weinberg probably wouldn't be leaving the fortress until after the concert, in truth we didn't really know for certain so now that we'd actually found him again, there was no way we were going to let him slip through our fingers. Not even if we had to stay there all night waiting for him to come out.

Unfortunately, that was basically what we would have to do—wait there all night. It was like Nuremberg all over again. All this detective work involved a lot of waiting around, but at least this time we weren't waiting and wondering whether or not Herr Weinberg would even show up. This time, no matter what happened, he would have to come out of those doors eventually.

We found a spot on some steps across the street where we had a good view of both the entrance and exit of the *Festungsbahn* building and since we could hear when one of the funicular trains arrived at the bottom station, we could always predict when the small crowd of people would begin to come out of the exit and head down the narrow cobblestone street toward the old town.

"Are you hungry?" Charlie asked me after my stomach had grumbled several times in protest about our skipping dinner.

"A little bit," I replied, blushing.

"Wait here and keep an eye on this," Charlie said. "And I'll go get us something to eat."

"Okay," I replied as Charlie sprung to his feet and headed down the street.

"Call me if anything happens," he said, grinning back at me over his shoulder as he disappeared around the corner.

Charlie wasn't gone for long. The old town of Salzburg isn't that big so it was only a few minutes before he returned with bottles of water and a couple of small packages wrapped in paper.

"What are these?" I asked, taking one of the warm packages from him.

"Something typically Austrian," Charlie replied. "Or at least that's what the guy at the stand told me. It's called a Bosna."

"It looks like just a normal sausage to me," I said, unwrapping mine to reveal a white bread roll with an ordinary-looking sausage inside.

"It's the curry powder that makes it special, apparently," Charlie replied as he handed me some napkins and took a bite.

"How is it?" I asked, uncertainly.

Charlie shrugged. "It's okay, I guess," he said. "Not as good as those ones you got at the market stall yesterday. What were those called? The ones with the sweet mustard on the side?"

"*Weisswurst*," I replied. "Those were so good!"

"And remember those sausages we had when we switched trains at Munich train station?" Charlie asked.

"Oh my God, yes," I replied with a grin. "I think those were the best sausages I had in my entire life."

All this talk of sausages was making me even more hungry so I finally decided to try the one that Charlie had just given me.

"And...?" Charlie asked as I bit into it. He'd been right about the curry powder. The sausage was swimming in some kind of curry flavored mustard.

I shrugged in reply. It was okay, I guess. But unless we could figure out a way to magically transport ourselves to Munich train station, it was the best we were going to get.

As we ate, another funicular train arrived at the lower station and a group of tourists slowly began to trickle out onto the street across from us. We watched carefully as we struggled to keep from dripping curry mustard all over ourselves but Herr Weinberg wasn't with them. It was still far too early.

We finished eating and Charlie collected our trash, disappearing around the corner for a moment to get rid of it. After that there was nothing left to do but kill time and wait. As late in the evening as it was, the *Festungsbahn* apparently went into some kind of reduced service schedule because the trains were now arriving with far less frequency, leaving long periods of quiet between each one.

"You're freezing," Charlie said, putting his arm around me as the sun disappeared below the horizon and a brisk wind began to whip through the nearly deserted streets. "I wish I had a jacket to offer you, but why don't you just go grab a jacket while I wait here? The concert shouldn't end for at least another twenty minutes and your hotel is only a couple of minutes from here."

I hesitated for a moment but Charlie was right. A trainload of passengers had just disembarked at the lower station a few minutes earlier and I could easily grab a jacket from my room and be back long before the next one arrived.

"Good idea," I replied, scrambling to my feet and hurrying down the street in the direction of my hotel. "Call me if anything happens."

"I will," Charlie assured me as I disappeared around the corner.

It was a strange experience walking through the streets of old Salzburg so late at night. Not a scary experience but somehow incredibly surreal.

In the distance I could hear the singing of some unknown drunken revelers. They sounded like the normal stumbling and inebriated party-goers that you find in every city of the world, but in this charming city of classical music, the drunken songs they sang were operatic choruses executed in perfect five-part harmonies that echoed off the buildings and cobblestones and filled the dark and vacant streets with glorious music.

Smiling to myself at this beautiful music swirling around me from the unseen singers nearby, I pulled open the front door of my hotel and vaulted up the steps to my room on the top floor. I grabbed a windbreaker for myself as well as my oversized Canada hoodie for Charlie to wear. I wasn't sure it would fit him but with the mountain air turning cold and him in nothing but shirtsleeves, it was better than nothing.

Locking my room behind me, I hurried down the steps so I could get back to Charlie as soon as possible.

"Good night!" I called out to the friendly old man who ran the hotel as I headed for the front door. He gave me a smile and a wave as I rushed past him at the reception desk.

Pulling open the door, I stepped back out onto the dark streets of Salzburg's old city and was about to head up the street back to where Charlie was waiting but then something happened that made me stop dead in my tracks.

Wait a minute, I thought to myself as I instinctually backtracked into the shadows of the arch of a nearby door. *Do you smell that?!?*

I *did* smell something. And it was a fragrance that I knew quite well by that point in time–a faint odor of some very strong and pungent tobacco smoke.

There was only one person in the world that I knew of who smoked such horrible stinky cigarettes.

Inspector Alighieri.

CHAPTER FORTY·THREE
Were All These Things Connected Somehow?

Oh my God, oh my God, oh my God, I thought as I shrunk further into the shadow of the doorway, spinning my head around every which way in a panic as I tried to see where Inspector Alighieri was.

At first I couldn't see him and nearly screamed when my jacket brushed up against the side of the doorway and I thought it was him waiting for me there in the shadows.

Don't panic, I thought as I tried to get a hold of myself. *You don't even know if it's really him or not. He can't be the only person in the world who smokes such stinky cigarettes.*

But it *was* him. I just knew it was. And my thoughts were confirmed just a few seconds later when I finally spotted his wide-shouldered silhouette all the way down at the end of the street, slowly walking away from me and out onto the open square beyond.

What is he doing?!? I asked myself. I'd been expecting him to jump out of the darkness and try to grab me but instead he was just casually walking away as if he didn't even know I was there.

"Maybe he *doesn't* know that I'm here," I whispered quietly to myself as I peered around the corner of the doorway to keep a close eye on him. My heart was pounding in my chest as I waited for him to suddenly spin around and start running back toward me, but he just kept on walking, relaxed and slow across the square before crossing in front of the church at the end of it.

Where in the world is he going? I thought to myself, but then my heart suddenly dropped into the pit of my stomach when I realized where he was headed. He was heading straight for the lower station of the *Festungsbahn* where Charlie was waiting obliviously.

He can't possibly know that Charlie is there, can he? I asked myself as I quickly pulled out my phone to call Charlie and warn him.

"Hello?" Charlie said as he picked up his phone at the other end.

"Charlie, listen, it's me, Kitty," I said, whispering as loud as I dared as I quickly tiptoed down the street to keep Inspector Alighieri in my sights.

"I know, Kit," Charlie replied. "But why are you whispering? Is something wrong?"

"It's Inspector Alighieri, Charlie!" I replied. "He's here and he's on his way toward you."

The line went silent for a moment as Charlie registered this new information. "How long?" Charlie asked, his voice suddenly serious.

"A minute or two?" I guesstimated.

"Okay. I'll text you back in a second," Charlie replied curtly and quickly ended the call.

The next few seconds were like a terrible agony as I waited for Charlie to text me back.

You'd better put your phone on silent, I reminded myself as I continued to sneak through the streets of the old city, keeping Inspector Alighieri in sight. I was trying to stay back as far as possible to avoid the risk of being noticed, but if my phone suddenly made a noise that would completely ruin those plans in a hurry.

I ducked into another dark doorway and fumbled with my phone to set it to silent mode. And just in time, as it turned out, because seconds later I received a message from Charlie.

Ok. Don't worry. Found a place to hide just up the street.
Charlie wrote.

Are you sure he won't be able to find you????
I quickly wrote back.

Not likely he's looking for me. Probably he's here for the same reason we are. Herr Weinberg.
Charlie wrote back.

I hope you're right about that, Charlie, I thought as I poked my head around the corner of the doorway and continued up the street after Inspector Alighieri. By this time, the Inspector was almost at the corner where the *Festungsbahn* station was located and the narrow street curved abruptly to the left.

Suddenly Inspector Alighieri stopped in the middle of the street and for a moment I thought he'd somehow spotted me. In near panic, I ducked into the shadows next to a statue of a hideously faceless hooded figure sitting on top of a square marble base. Safely out of sight, I waited a moment before taking a deep breath and carefully peeking over the edge to see what the Inspector was doing.

I breathed a sigh of relief when I saw that he hadn't noticed me at all and had simply stopped to light another cigarette. Once he had done that, he sidled over into the shadows of the wall of a nearby souvenir store and simply stared up the street toward the exit of the *Festungsbahn* station.

Charlie was right, I thought. *He IS here for the same reason we are. And from where he's standing, Charlie can almost certainly see him as well.*

Ducking down behind the base of the statue, I quickly pulled out my phone to write to Charlie.

You were right.
I wrote simply.

It makes sense that we're not the only clever ones.
Charlie wrote back.

Sorry. I mean you are still clever, of course.
Charlie wrote again.

I mean. You know what I mean.
Charlie wrote yet again.

I almost laughed aloud and decided to let Charlie squirm uncomfortably for just a few seconds longer before letting him off the hook.

Don't worry. I know what you mean. But what do we do now?
I texted back.

We just stay out of sight for now and wait to see what the two of them are up to.
Charlie wrote back.

Of course Charlie was right. That was exactly what we had to do.

For some reason it suddenly felt as though he and I were nothing but spectators to some larger dramatic performance being played out right in front of our eyes. And like the audience in any fast-paced psychological thriller, we were just being swept along by the action and mystery without even having the faintest clue about what was really going on.

Who was this Inspector Alighieri? And why was he here in Salzburg? To find Herr Weinberg, obviously, but why? Who was Herr Weinberg and why was he of such interest? And what did either of them have to do with Matteo's father and the secret radio room hidden in the hallway of their house? Or with the mysterious paintings we'd found hanging on the living room walls? Were all these things connected somehow? They had to be, didn't they?

I hoped that soon we would find out at least some of the answers to these questions because at that exact moment, out of the corner of my eye, I caught a glimpse of one of the funicular cars emerging from inside the fortress walls on its way down to the foot of the mountain. I glanced at my iPhone clock. The concert in the fortress had just ended a few minutes earlier and with any luck Herr Weinberg was on his way down to us at that very second.

CHAPTER FORTY-FOUR
The Real Surprise Was Yet To Come

I quickly reached for my phone to warn Charlie about the train full of people heading his way.

Heads up Charlie. There's a train on the way down.
I wrote quickly and hit send.

Ok. Got it.
Charlie wrote back.

I held my breath as the one car descended while the other made its way up toward the fortress. At the middle point the two cars split to pass each other and then both continued on their way, each disappearing from my sight at opposite ends of the track. In my imagination, I could see the train car slowly coming to a halt and the doors opening to let everyone out. They would make their way toward the exits and out onto the street.

Right on cue, the first of the passengers began to emerge from the building. I was too far away to make out any individual faces, much less recognize whether Herr Weinberg was among them, but fortunately Charlie had a much better vantage point than me.

Target acquired. He's on his way toward you right now.
Charlie wrote.

Looking up from my iPhone screen, I tried to spot Herr Weinberg in the scattered group of people who were slowly making their way down the street and out onto the plaza in front of me. I scanned the crowd but it was dark and they were still too far away for me to see properly.

As the groups of people reached the open space of the plaza, they began to spread out more, moving at different speeds and in different directions until there were finally enough gaps that I could spot what I was looking for. It was Herr Weinberg walking briskly by himself across the square.

Now, what about Inspector Alighieri? I thought, scanning the back of the quickly thinning crowd to see if he was there too.

"Bingo!" I muttered under my breath when I spotted the silhouette of the Inspector's unmistakably broad shoulders in the distance. He was moving slowly and carefully, keeping Herr Weinberg in sight as he followed him across the plaza.

Now for the next question, I thought. *Where is Charlie?*

I didn't have to wait long to find out the answer to that one. Within seconds I saw Charlie quickly peek his head around the corner at the end of the street to check if the coast was clear before continuing down in pursuit of the other two men.

It was actually almost comical to watch the three of them make their way across my field of view, each successive one oblivious that he was being followed by the others in some kind of weird human convoy.

But if that's the case, I thought. *Then who is following Charlie?*

The answer to that was simple. It was supposed to be me. And as they all disappeared around the corner of the church to my right, I pulled myself out of the shadows and fell in behind them. I quickly caught up to Charlie and he held a finger to his lips as we ducked from one dark doorway to the next.

Fortunately there were plenty of shadows and doorways around for us to hide in and up ahead of us Inspector Alighieri was doing the same as we were, slipping in and out of the shadows as he stayed close on the trail of Herr Weinberg.

After making our way like this along several narrow streets, we heard the sound of keys jingling and saw Herr Weinberg stop in front of a doorway at the end of the street. Unlocking the door, he disappeared inside the building and started up a set of stairs inside.

Frozen in place, we watched breathlessly as Inspector Alighieri dashed silently out of the nearby shadows and caught the door with the palm of his hand before it locked shut. For a long moment he simply stood there, his fingers in the door as he waited and listened until we saw the lights of a second-floor apartment suddenly switch on. Inspector Alighieri saw it too and quickly ducked inside the building as well, hurrying up the stairs in pursuit of Herr Weinberg.

For the briefest of moments, I simply stared at the Inspector's feet disappearing up the steps as the outer door closed rapidly behind him. Without even thinking, I suddenly darted out of the shadows and sprinted down the length of the street, my eyes intently focused on that door as I desperately tried to reach it before it clicked shut.

Come on, come on! I thought as I dove for the door, fingers outstretched.

I didn't think I was going to make it, but at the last possible second before the door had swung completely closed, my hand slipped through the gap and stopped it from locking us out.

"Nice one," Charlie whispered as he caught up with me and pushed the door open again with his palm.

As the door swung open, we could hear the sound of violent shouting echoing down the stairs from up above. We couldn't make out what was being said, and it wouldn't have mattered anyway since they were speaking in German, but the voice that was doing all the shouting clearly belonged to Inspector Alighieri and we could only assume that the target of his anger was Herr Weinberg.

"Oh my God," I whispered as both Charlie and I tiptoed cautiously toward the stairs and tried to look up to see what was going on. "What is he bellowing about?"

"I don't know," Charlie replied with an expression of concern on his face as he sidled over next to me to peer up the stairwell as well.

As we stood there listening, Inspector Alighieri's voice continued rising higher and higher in intensity. In-between his furious tirades we could hear timid and muffled responses of Herr Weinberg that seemed to only make the Inspector angrier.

"Charlie, we need to do something," I said as Inspector Alighieri's rage continued to get more and more out of control. "He might do something to hurt him!"

"Or worse," Charlie nodded as he started up the stairs toward the source of the yelling.

As we climbed the steps to the second floor, it wasn't difficult to figure out which door led to Herr Weinberg's apartment. The door was half ajar and the sounds of shouting were clearly emanating from inside.

By this time, the Inspector sounded like he was about to completely lose it and I looked to Charlie to see what he was going to do. I had no advice to offer him, unfortunately, but I knew that we couldn't just stand by and let this continue.

But I needn't have worried because Charlie was in complete control. He pushed open the apartment door, revealing a modest living room beyond. It looked exactly like the Austrian equivalent of the type of room that a kindly old retired man might live in, with some dusty-looking outdated old furniture and various knickknacks and small animal heads hanging from the walls.

At the right side of the room near the fireplace we immediately saw the broad-shouldered Inspector towering over a frightened and cowering Herr Weinberg, gripping him tightly by the arms as he violently shook him back and forth.

"Hey! Get your hands off him!" Charlie hollered as he thrust the door open the rest of the way and took a few steps toward the two fighting men.

"This is none of your concern!" Inspector Alighieri snapped as he turned to see Charlie striding toward him. For the briefest of moments he looked surprised to see the two of us but then his face turned serious and business-like once again.

"Oh, please help me, please help me!" Herr Weinberg cried out in perfect English. "This insane man just burst into my apartment and is trying to kill me!"

Something about what Herr Weinberg had just said should have set off warning bells ringing in my head, but from that moment everything just happened so fast that there was no time to stop and think.

Inspector Alighieri spun his head around to face Herr Weinberg. As he turned, it almost looked like he was rolling his eyes in disbelief, but whatever his facial expression might have been, Charlie took advantage of the momentary distraction and moved in fast.

Grabbing the receiver of the telephone that was sitting on the side table next to him, Charlie pushed the Inspector away from Herr Weinberg and up against the wall. He then pulled the coiled telephone wire like a rope and in a flash of lightning-fast movements, he somehow managed to tie the Inspector's hands behind his back before pushing him down onto the sofa where his heavy body bounced around for a moment like a stiff doll before settling down. It was like watching one of those rodeo guys hogtie a calf, except in this case the calf wasn't some helpless little animal, but a very large and dangerous man in a black suit.

And yet, lying there on the sofa with his hands behind his back, the Inspector didn't actually look all that dangerous and threatening after all. In fact, he was chuckling to himself and smiling at Charlie as if he appreciated the skill it had taken to so quickly immobilize him like that.

"Nicely done," the Inspector said with a smile of genuine admiration. "I wish we had more men like you. But I'm afraid you tied up the wrong man."

The wrong man? I thought.

"Oh thank God you saved me," Herr Weinberg said, interrupting my chain of thought.

Wait a minute... I thought suddenly.

"You speak English!" I said in surprise as I turned toward Herr Weinberg. But the *real* surprise was yet to come. As I spun my head around, I caught a flash of motion out of the corner of my eye and was completely astonished to see that Herr Weinberg had picked up a large chunk of wood from next to the fireplace and was suddenly swinging it toward Charlie's head.

Before I could do anything to stop him, Herr Weinberg had walloped Charlie over the head and was turning to do the same to me as well. As Charlie crashed to the floor next to me, I was paralyzed as the huge hunk of wood arced toward the side of my head. God only knows what would have happened if it had actually hit me. But as I stood there frozen in disbelief, Inspector Alighieri quickly kicked the coffee table with his foot so that it struck Herr Weinberg in the shins and tripped him up. As Herr Weinberg stumbled, I finally snapped out of my paralysis and managed to pull my head back out of harm's way, throwing myself off balance in the process. As I tumbled to the floor, the chunk of wood swished past my face with a burst of wind and missed me by mere inches.

"See what I mean?" Inspector Alighieri said as Charlie and I lay crumpled at his feet and Herr Weinberg bolted out the front door of the apartment. "You tied up the wrong guy."

CHAPTER FORTY-FIVE
That's Good Enough For Me

"What the hell is going on?" Charlie said in angry frustration as he lifted himself uneasily to his knees and rubbed the back of his head.

"There's no time to explain," Inspector Alighieri said as we listened to the sound of Herr Weinberg's heavy footsteps fading down the stairwell. "You need to untie me. Now!"

Charlie braced himself on the coffee table and pulled himself to his feet.

"No way," Charlie said with a cynical smile as he helped me to my feet as well. "Not until someone explains to us what's going on. And since Herr Weinberg just left, I guess that leaves you to do all the talking."

Inspector Alighieri clenched his jaw angrily and stared out the open door where Herr Weinberg had just disappeared out of.

"You have no idea what you have gotten yourself into," the Inspector observed coldly.

"You're right, we don't," Charlie replied, equally coolly. "And that's precisely why you're about to explain it all to us."

Inspector Alighieri stared at Charlie for a moment and then glanced over at the doorway again in frustration as he yanked and twisted his arms, trying to wiggle his hands free. But it was no use. Charlie had tied him securely.

"Please listen to me," Inspector Alighieri said, his voice calm and even as he tried to reason with us. "It is very important that you let me go after this man. If I don't, he'll disappear forever and we'll never find him again."

"He's probably already long gone by now," Charlie said. "You'll never figure out where he went so you might as well..."

"He's not gone yet," Inspector Alighieri interrupted. "He's just down the street, walking quickly in the direction of the *Mozartplatz*."

I frowned and wrinkled my forehead in confusion. "How in the world could you possibly know that?" I asked.

But then I saw it. Snaking out from underneath the shoulder of the Inspector's neatly tailored suit jacket, a thin wire ran to an earpiece that he was wearing in his right ear. Obviously the Inspector wasn't working alone and whoever was at the other end of that radio could clearly see exactly where Herr Weinberg was and where he was going.

"Charlie, look," I said, pointing to the nearly invisible earpiece.

Charlie tilted his head to the side for a better look and then nodded curtly.

"It seems like you already have things completely under control," Charlie observed.

"Maybe we were wrong about him," I said, turning toward Charlie. "Maybe he *is* a policeman after all."

"Do you think that if he really *was* a policeman that he would just let us leave him tied up on the sofa like that without saying something?" Charlie replied, shaking his head. "Isn't that right, Inspector–or whoever it is that you are?"

The Inspector sighed deeply and stared down at his chest for a moment before answering. "You're quite right," the Inspector replied. "I'm not really an Italian police Inspector."

Charlie and the Inspector simply stared silently at each other for a moment, playing a tense waiting game as Charlie patiently waited for him to volunteer some more information.

"Maybe we should just let him go," I said to Charlie as I glanced nervously at the open door leading to the stairs. It suddenly occurred to me that if the Inspector was getting all this information about Herr Weinberg's whereabouts from over that radio, then whoever was at the other end could probably hear every word that we were saying as well. And who knew who might come bursting through that door at any moment.

"Don't worry," Charlie said, reading the worried expression on my face perfectly. "No one's going to come to the Inspector's rescue."

"How do you know?" I asked.

"Because there's only two of them," Charlie answered. "And the Inspector's partner is too busy staying on Herr Weinberg's trail to come back here and save him."

"Are you sure, Charlie?" I asked.

"I'm positive," Charlie replied. "If there were more than just two of them, the Inspector here wouldn't be so worried about whether or not we're going to let him go. He'd just wait for the cavalry to show up and save him."

"I suppose that's true," I replied, still feeling a bit nervous.

"In fact," Charlie continued. "I think we can be quite sure that the Inspector's partner in all of this is the same guy who jumped at us out of the wall of Matteo's apartment a few days ago and made off with the digital recorder and God knows what else."

The Inspector chuckled for a moment. "Your clever friend is quite right," the Inspector said, turning to face me and giving me a smile. "About most of it, anyway."

"I know I am," Charlie said simply. "But that still doesn't explain what all of this is about or who you are and why it's so important to you that we cut you loose when your partner clearly has everything under control without you."

The Inspector bowed his head in resignation and sighed deeply again. "My name is Avner," the Inspector said. "Avner Rifkind."

"And...?" Charlie said, waiting for him to continue.

"And you're quite right that everything is under control without me," Avner said. "But I need you to let me go because capturing this Herr Weinberg of yours is something that is very important to me. And to my partner."

"Why?" Charlie demanded. "What is all of this about?"

Avner tilted his head slightly to the side for a moment as though he was listening to something coming through on his radio earpiece. "Herr Weinberg just entered a private parking garage not far from here," he told us. "I can only assume that means that he's there to pick up a car. But it's not too late. There's still time for us to catch up to him as long as you untie me right now."

"*Us*?" I asked, raising my eyebrows. "There's still time for *us* to catch up to him?"

Avner looked over at me and smiled warmly. "Yes," he said. "If you untie me right now then you can come with me and I'll explain everything to you on the way."

I glanced over at Charlie uncertainly.

"What do you think?" Charlie asked with a grin. "Do we trust him?"

I thought about this for a moment. I wasn't sure whether I really *did* trust this man we'd known only as the enigmatic Inspector Alighieri or whether I simply just wanted to finally know what all of this craziness was about, but before I even knew what I was doing I started to nod.

"I trust him," I said.

"That's good enough for me," Charlie replied and he reached down to release the wide-shouldered Avner from his makeshift bonds.

CHAPTER FORTY·SIX
What Do You Mean By 'Our People'?

"Thank you," Avner said as Charlie finally untied the last of the telephone wire that was wrapped around his wrists. "Follow me."

In a flash, he sprung to his feet and dashed for the door, heading for the stairs beyond while Charlie and I struggled to keep up with him.

Oh God, I hope this wasn't a mistake, I thought as the three of us pounded down the stairs. *Maybe this was all a trick and he's just planning to leave us in the dust and disappear.*

If that was Avner's plan, he was certainly doing a pretty good job of it. Bursting out of the door at the foot of the stairs, he broke into a full-on sprint down the narrow cobblestone street, leaving Charlie and I in his dust.

"Come on, come on!" Avner bellowed at us from far ahead. "You have to keep up!"

That was enough for me. Obviously he wasn't *trying* to get away from us but that didn't mean that he wasn't going to leave us behind if we couldn't run any faster.

Charlie responded by putting his head down and running full tilt after Avner, looking back over his shoulder to make sure I was still with him. It was reassuring to know that Charlie wasn't going to leave me behind but I knew that I was going to have to step up, bring my A-game and run like never before in my entire life.

"I'm with you," I cried breathlessly to Charlie as Avner ducked through various alleys and passageways until we emerged onto the main road that ran parallel to the river.

Just upstream from us on the opposite bank I could see the well-lit outline of Hotel Sacher, and out of the corner of my eye I caught the flash of a dark gray sedan roaring across the bridge toward us.

Avner stopped short at the curb and watched as the sedan disappeared around a corner and behind some of the buildings on the other side of the river. Charlie and I quickly caught up and for a moment I thought that we were too late but then, out of nowhere, a familiar black Maserati peeled out of a side street and screeched to a halt right in front of us.

"Get in!" a stunningly beautiful woman in the driver's seat yelled at us.

Avner didn't have to be told twice. He already had the front passenger door open and was twisting his massive frame inside. Charlie quickly followed suit and yanked open the back door, pushing me inside before clambering in behind me.

Before the doors were even closed, the dark-haired woman driving the car hit the gas and we squealed off across the bridge in pursuit of the gray sedan. Hitting the corners like a professional stunt driver, the woman skillfully maneuvered the streets of Salzburg, steering with one hand as she reached into the glove box with the other.

"Hello again," the woman said to me and Charlie as she glanced into the back seat where we were struggling to stay in our seats as she whipped the car around one turn after another.

"Hello," I said, confused. "I'm sorry, have we met before?"

"Not formally," the woman said, grinning mysteriously as she pulled a notepad from the glove box and tossed it in Avner's lap.

"What's this?" Avner asked as he flipped open the notebook.

"His name is Rudolf Feiersinger," the woman said as she changed gears and accelerated down a long straight stretch of empty road, glancing quickly down every side street as we raced past.

"Feiersinger," Avner replied thoughtfully as he stroked his chin and read through the hand-written notes on the first few pages of the notepad.

The woman said something in reply to this that I didn't understand and for the next minute or so, she and Avner had some kind of intense conversation in a language I couldn't recognize.

"Do you know what language they're speaking?" I whispered loudly to Charlie over the noise of the car's engine.

"I have no idea," Charlie replied, shaking his head.

"There!" the woman cried as our car emerged from behind a long row of buildings and the dark gray sedan appeared up ahead in the distance, turning onto a busy street.

Gearing down to a much slower speed, the woman merged with the other cars on the street and kept her distance as she continued to follow the other car. Keeping the sedan always in sight up ahead of us, she reached into her jacket and pulled out a serious-looking device with some kind of map display on the screen. I couldn't really tell what it was but I'd seen enough movies to guess that it was some kind of tracking system. Apparently Avner's partner had managed to plant some kind of tracking device on Herr Weinberg's car.

Who are these people?!? I thought suddenly. *If that's what I think it is, then this is some serious James Bond kind of stuff.*

Avner took the device and studied it carefully, glancing up occasionally at the gray sedan in the distance ahead of us. While he was doing this, the woman turned around to face Charlie and me.

"I'm Ayelet," she said, sticking out her hand in greeting.

"You're the one who broke into Matteo's father's apartment back in Rome," I said as I shook her hand hesitantly. "And pushed us all down when you were trying to escape."

"Sorry about that," Ayelet shrugged.

"We didn't know you were a girl," I said as Charlie reached over to shake her hand as well. "You were all in black and everything happened so fast and..."

My voice trailed off as I tried to make sense of all this new information.

"You certainly don't fight like a girl," Charlie commented, subconsciously reaching for the spot on his back where the black-clothed figure had hit him.

Ayelet shrugged again. "That depends on what you think fighting like a girl means," she said. "Where I'm from, there are plenty of girls who are pretty tough. Even around handsome men like you."

Is she flirting with Charlie?!? I thought to myself with a chuckle as I watched Ayelet smile and flutter her eyelashes in the rear-view mirror.

"Touché," Charlie replied apologetically. "You're right, of course. But since your partner hasn't been very helpful so far, maybe you could explain exactly where it is that you and him are from, and what you're doing breaking into apartments and chasing after people all over Europe?"

"I could ask the two of you the exact same thing," Ayelet replied.

"We're just trying to get some answers for our friends back in Rome," I said, frowning. "Because in the last week they've learned that there's a lot of things about their father that they didn't have the slightest idea about."

"Exactly," Charlie agreed. "And we came to Salzburg to try and find out some of those answers from Herr Weinberg—or whatever his name is—but you and your partner clearly know just as much about all of this as he does so we're just as happy for either of you to tell us."

"Feiersinger," Avner said, speaking to us for the first time since we got in the car.

"Pardon?" I asked.

"His name isn't Weinberg," Avner said. "It's Feiersinger. Rudolf Feiersinger."

"And how do you know that?" I asked.

"Ayelet here called our people and they ran the address after I followed him back to his apartment," Avner explained, holding up the notepad with the hand-written notes. "That apartment is owned by a man named Rudolf Feiersinger."

APT 5, JUDENGASSE 3, SALZBURG RUDOLF FEIERSINGER

Judengasse?!? I thought. *That was one of the street names from the pencil rubbing.*

"What do you mean by '*our people*' ran the address?" Charlie asked with a suspicious frown.

"Our people back in Tel Aviv," Ayelet said offhandedly as though that explained everything.

CHAPTER FORTY-SEVEN
Maybe Even Thousands

"Tel Aviv?!?" I replied in surprise. "As in Tel Aviv in Israel?!??"

"Of course," Ayelet replied.

"You're from Israel?" I asked, still not sure I understood.

"Yes, of course," Ayelet replied. "We work for the Israeli government."

Suddenly the tracking devices and James Bond stuff made a lot of sense.

"Like spies?" I asked.

Ayelet laughed loudly. "Not quite," she said. "Although Avner here likes to think he is sometimes."

"Then what?" I asked, getting angrier and frustrated at the lack of information. "What exactly do you do for the Israeli government?"

"Our job is to track down various antiquities and art works that might be of interest to the government of Israel," Ayelet replied. "Strictly speaking, we work for the Ministry of Culture, but..."

Ayelet stopped short in mid-sentence.

"But what?" I asked, prompting her to finish.

"What my partner is trying to say," Avner explained as he turned around in his seat to face me. "Is that even though we both officially work for the Israeli Ministry of Culture, the work we do is not always the kind that our government likes to see splashed across the front pages of newspapers."

"You mean it's illegal," I said.

Avner shrugged. "It depends what you consider illegal," he replied.

"Things that are against the law," I said. "That's what I consider to be illegal."

"Perhaps," Avner said.

"Like breaking into people's apartments, for example," I continued. "Or impersonating police officers."

"Yes," Avner replied coolly. "Things like that, for example."

I frowned and sat back in my seat to think this over for a minute. There were still so many questions.

"But what does this have to do with our friend's father?" I asked. "And what does *he* have to do with this Herr Weinberg or Feiersinger or whatever his name is? And why was there that secret room in their house? And what's with all these weird coded radio messages?"

"One question at a time, please," Avner said, holding up his hands.

"Our friends in Rome," I repeated. "What does all of this have to do with their father?"

"Their father was part of a network of art dealers," Avner explained. "He and Feiersinger and many others. They were all part of a secret network of dealers who specialize in buying and selling stolen works of art."

"Art works stolen from who?" I asked.

"From various people, some of it from more recent years," Avner explained. "But the majority of it from Jewish owners and art dealers before and during the Second World War."

"By the Nazis?!?" I asked.

"Exactly," Avner replied. "The Nazis were the greatest art thieves in the history of the world and plundered hundreds of thousands of works of art from one end of Europe to the other.

"Even before the war began, the Nazis had already begun to confiscate thousands of works of art from within the museums in Germany itself," Avner continued. "Art that was deemed to be subversive in nature, which basically meant anything modern, was removed from the museum walls and seized by the state. The Nazis banned the exhibition of these works and gathered them together for a final series of cynical art shows designed to show the people of Germany just how degenerate the art world had become and how the Nazis were putting things right again by eliminating works of such debauchery.

"Not long after these so-called degenerate art shows had finished touring Germany, a decision had to be made about what to do with all this art. At the time, Hitler was deep into his plans for building the greatest art museum in the world in the town of Linz in his native Austria so it was decided to sell off these useless works of degenerate art and use the proceeds to acquire more suitable works by the old masters to line the walls of that museum. As a result of this program, thousands of priceless works of art were bought for next to nothing by various unscrupulous art collectors and dealers, including some high-ranking members of the Nazi party itself, who had already spent years quietly buying up invaluable works of art from Jews and others who were fleeing Nazi Germany and desperately needed money to do so.

"It was a very profitable time for art collectors and dealers who had no moral difficulty doing business with the Nazis. But the worst of it was still to come because with the start of the war, the real treasure hunt was on. As the countries of Europe fell like dominoes before the Nazi onslaught, their museums and private collections were seized and systematically looted for shipment back to Germany. Year after year the carefully packed crates full of priceless artworks filled hundreds of boxcars on trains bound for Germany. Some of the art was earmarked for Hitler's museum in Linz while other works were hand-picked by members of the Nazi leadership for their private collections. It is estimated that more than half a million individual works of art were plundered by the Nazis–

enough to fill entire warehouses. Many of those works were eventually recovered when the Allied troops finally liberated Europe, but some items simply disappeared secretly into the hands of the less scrupulous, never to be seen again."

Avner's voice trailed off as he reached the end of his explanation. His eyes were focused straight ahead, staring through the cars in front of us to the innocent-looking gray sedan driven by the man we now knew was Rudolf Feiersinger.

"And that's what you think this guy Feiersinger is involved with?" I asked after a few moments of silence. "Not to mention our friend's father back in Rome?"

"Correct," Avner replied with a curt nod.

I thought about that for a second. "Aren't they too young for that?" I asked. "The war was so long ago that neither of them could possibly have been alive at the time."

"Of course they're too young," Avner agreed. "But their fathers and grandfathers would have been alive at the time."

"You think this has been going on for that long?!?" I asked, surprised.

"We *know* it has been," Avner replied. "Our intelligence services have been tracking the radio transmissions of this group for decades. But all they had were the indecipherable coded messages to work from. With no other information available, our people just assumed that the transmissions were related to some kind of governmental intelligence operation or something. Our own government uses similar means of communicating with our operatives, after all."

"In fact, we think that's how this whole network of clandestine art dealers came about in the first place," Ayelet said, interrupting Avner's explanation.

"Precisely," Avner agreed, nodding his head. "After the war, so many members of Nazi intelligence flipped sides and went to work for the British or Americans or Russians instead so we suspect that this particular group may have been using these stolen Nazi paintings to finance their official operations for years. But once the Cold War ended and the operation fell into disuse, it seems that the whole network was picked up again by the same individuals for a completely different purpose. They already had the contacts and means of secret communication in place, after all. All they had to do was put their skills and expertise to work at filling their own pockets. And for years it worked perfectly but then last week all of that changed when an article appeared in the newspapers about the surprising discovery of some mysterious paintings of unknown origin hanging on the walls of an apartment in Rome. That's when Ayelet and I were instructed to investigate what was going on."

So THAT'S how it happened! I thought to myself. *When Matteo hears about this, he's going to be even more mad at Giulia for breaking the story in the news.*

But that got me thinking. "Wait a minute," I said. "That Van Gogh painting we found wasn't stolen by the Nazis. It was stolen from a museum in Amsterdam only something like ten or fifteen years ago."

"True," Avner agreed. "But obviously this network of dealers is trafficking all sorts of different kinds of stolen art, both those from more modern thefts and those from the plundered artworks from the Second World War."

"Are there even any of those paintings left?" I asked. "The war was so long ago."

Avner nodded emphatically. "Absolutely," he replied. "There are still many works of art unaccounted for—two of which were found on the walls of your friend's apartment in Rome."

"The Monet?" I asked. "And the... what was it? Picasso?"

"Pissarro," Avner replied, correcting me. "Yes, exactly. Those two paintings appear to have originated from the collection of a well-known Jewish art dealer in Paris during the Second World War. We don't know yet how they came to be in the possession of your friend's father. It's possible that they were acquired legally by your friend's family before the seizure of that collection by the Nazis, but it seems unlikely. It appears that your friend's father was very much a part of this whole illegal operation and simply held onto those paintings you found because he had a personal fondness for them."

My heart sank to think of what effect this news would have on Matteo and his sisters. They would be devastated.

"So what now?" I asked, nodding to the gray sedan far ahead of us on the road. "It seems you already know everything you need to about this whole situation. Why are we still following this Feiersinger guy?"

Avner turned around in his seat to look back at Charlie and me. "There's far more to this than just the three paintings you found back in Rome," he said, frowning in confusion. "There are more than a dozen other operatives in this network of stolen art dealers and we believe that Feiersinger is one of their ringleaders."

"So what does that mean?" I asked.

"We're pretty sure it means that there are more paintings out there still to be found," Avner explained. "And we need Feiersinger to help us find them."

"How many more paintings do you think they have?" I asked.

Avner thought this over for a moment. "Hundreds," he said. "Maybe even thousands."

CHAPTER FORTY-EIGHT
Right Into The Heart Of Darkness

"Thousands?!??" I asked in disbelief. "You think there are still thousands more paintings to be found? How is that possible?!?"

"The Nazi plunder of Europe's greatest art treasures was executed on an absolutely massive scale," Avner explained. "It's possible that there are even tens of thousands of works still out there waiting to be found. But no one really knows for sure because in many cases no one even knows what is missing in the first place."

"But thousands?" I asked. "After so many years, how could Feiersinger and his partners still be hiding away so many paintings?!? Why wouldn't they have sold them all and gone off into hiding on some South American beach somewhere?"

Avner thought about this for a moment before answering. "These are men who love art," he explained. "To them, it's not about the money or retiring on some sunny beach with a cocktail in their hands. They love the art itself and want to surround themselves with it. Just take that Van Gogh you found back in Rome as an example."

"What about it?" I asked.

"That painting plus another of Van Gogh's earlier works was stolen in the dead of night right off the walls of the Van Gogh Museum in Amsterdam," Avner explained. "The thieves walked into an open space where such well-known masterpieces as *Sunflowers* and *Wheatfield With Crows* were hanging no more than twenty feet away, and yet they ignored those and took two incredibly obscure paintings instead. The thieves were later arrested and put on trial but the paintings themselves were never recovered and the police believed that they had been sold to an unknown third party."

"So they were hired by someone else to steal the paintings?" I asked.

"If you ask me, yes, I think that's exactly what happened," Avner replied. "They knew exactly what they were after and stole exactly the paintings that the people who hired them wanted. And I guess now we know where at least one of those paintings ended up–hiding in plain sight on the wall of an apartment in Rome where the man who wanted it so badly could look at it every single day and admire it."

Once again, I felt a pang of sadness for Matteo and his sisters. These revelations about the secret life their father had been living were going to be painful for them. I was still thinking about this when suddenly on the road up ahead of us I saw the signal lights of Feiersinger's gray sedan blink briefly as he slowed down and pulled off the main road. Seconds later, as we continued following him from far behind, we passed a sign announcing the name of the next town that we were just entering.

Berchtesgaden

"Big surprise," Avner muttered to himself derisively, frowning as he shook his head. "Right into the heart of darkness."

I was about to ask him what he meant but I was surprised when we didn't slow down and just continued driving straight on down the road past the turn.

"What are we doing?" I asked, spinning around to watch Feiersinger's car disappearing down a side road and behind some trees. "Aren't we still following him?!?"

"Don't worry," Ayelet said, checking carefully in her rear-view mirror. Confident that Feiersinger was definitely out of sight, she hit the brakes and pulled a quick U-turn in the middle of the road, the car behind us honking angrily as it passed by.

"He's not going anywhere," Avner said, pointing to the display on their tracking device as Ayelet finished her skillful turn and we roared back toward the turn-off. "But it's critical that he doesn't know we're following him."

Of course, I thought, nodding to myself as we made the turn and headed down the same road into a charming alpine village.

In the minutes that followed, we played a clever game of cat and mouse, following Feiersinger through the deserted streets of the little town and out into a confusing maze of winding mountain roads beyond. Using their high-tech tracking device and Ayelet's expert driving skills, we managed to stay close on his tail without ever actually seeing him (or him seeing us in return, naturally). It was actually all very impressive and I was about to say something about it to Ayelet when she suddenly hit the brakes, sending all of us in the car jostling violently around as she quickly pulled off to the side of the road.

"What is it?!?" Charlie asked as Ayelet switched off the headlights and killed the engine.

In the sudden darkness I squinted to see up the road ahead but there was nothing there–just darkness and trees as the road continued up around yet another winding bend.

"He stopped," Ayelet said simply, pointing to the display on the tracking device where the signal from Feiersinger's car had indeed stopped moving.

Without a word we stared at the display for the next few minutes, breathlessly waiting. But nothing happened. The circle marking the location of Feiersinger's car on the digital map stayed in the same spot.

"Maybe you'd better go check things out," Avner finally said, looking up at Ayelet. "I'll stay here with the car."

Ayelet nodded smartly and quickly pulled open the car door. In a flash, she had jumped out and quietly closed the door behind her before making her way up the side of the road, quickly disappearing into the darkness.

None of us said a word as we sat and waited. I strained my eyes to try and spot Ayelet in the inky blackness, but she was as stealthy and silent as a panther stalking its prey and I couldn't see a thing.

The minutes passed one after another, dragging out like hours as we waited wordlessly for something to happen. Then suddenly the driver's door was yanked open again and Ayelet slid quickly inside, her sudden reappearance seemingly out of nowhere nearly giving me a heart attack.

Oh my God, I didn't even see her coming back, I thought to myself as I took a deep breath and tried to slow my heart rate down again. Sensing how startled I'd been, Charlie reached over and patted me on the shoulder as Ayelet updated us on the situation.

"There's a house up ahead," Ayelet reported, slightly out of breath. "Probably belonging to Feiersinger. His car is the only one in the driveway and he seems to be the only person there."

Avner thought about this for a few moments and then nodded curtly and reached for the handle of his car door to open it.

"What are you doing?" I asked him as he swung open his door and began to stick one foot out the door.

Avner looked back in surprise. "I'm going to pay Mister Feiersinger a little visit," he replied. "What else?"

"Have you ever considered having a little patience?" I asked. "Like maybe watching and waiting for a while to see what he's going to do instead of always busting in like a bull in a china shop and scaring the crap out of people?"

Next to me in the dim light I heard Charlie chuckling under his breath and I glanced over to see him grinning at me.

Avner seemed taken aback by my sudden audacity and simply stared at me wordlessly for a few long moments. I continued staring right back at him, stubbornly refusing to lower my eyes.

"Okay," Avner finally said, slowly starting to nod his head. "We'll try it your way."

He turned to Ayelet.

"I'll grab the remote camera," Ayelet said, slipping out the driver's door and hurrying around the back of the car where I could hear her rummaging around in the trunk. Meanwhile, Avner pushed open his door and began to step outside again.

"Aren't you coming?" he asked with a strange grin as he turned back for a second toward Charlie and me.

"Of course," I replied, pulling open my own door and slipping out into the darkness with Charlie right behind me.

It was an amazing night outside. The mountain air was fresh and cool on my face and with the smell of the trees filling my nostrils, I could tilt my head back and see a beautiful sky full of stars watching us from high above.

Ayelet finished whatever it was she was doing in the back of the car and quietly closed the trunk before leading the way up the side of the road toward Feiersinger's house. We walked in silence, carefully feeling our way through the grass as we tried to keep up with the far more agile Ayelet.

I was surprised at how long a walk it was. It seemed like we'd been walking forever before the road finally curved around one final bend and a building up ahead of us slowly came into view. It was a cute little Bavarian mountain chalet style house with whitewashed walls crisscrossed with heavy wooden beams and a long wrap-around wooden terrace running the entire length of each side. The house was located just off the road, on an open plot of land down a short gravel driveway where Feiersinger's gray sedan was parked. Inside the house, the interior lights were shining brightly but I couldn't detect any signs of movement.

"We wait here," I heard Avner say in a nearly silent whisper. He pointed over to the tree line where the darkness would protect us from being spotted.

Charlie nodded in reply for both of us and we followed Avner while Ayelet continued on toward the house, quickly disappearing into the shadows and out of sight.

Once we reached the cover of the trees, Avner knelt down and carefully pulled out a small, flat device from a black zipper case that Ayelet had handed to him. As Charlie and I gathered around him, I saw that it was some kind of small tablet computer that was apparently connected remotely to a camera that Ayelet was carrying with her. On the dim screen I could see a close-up view of the outside of Feiersinger's house as Ayelet slowly made her way up the side of it.

I glanced up to see if I could spot where Ayelet was but she was just too stealthy and I couldn't see a thing. From the image on the screen I could tell that she was somewhere in the murky darkness at the left side of the building, but as hard as I tried, I simply couldn't see her.

The image on the screen flipped around chaotically for a second and it took me a moment to realize that Ayelet must be climbing up the side of the house to the wooden terrace. I glanced up again and was finally able to spot her, slowly emerging from the gloom and making her way along the wall of the upper floor like a cat burglar until she reached a set of large glass doors that led from inside the house out onto the balcony. She stopped at the edge of the doors and knelt down before carefully aiming the tiny pocket camera around the corner.

As she did this, I looked down at the computer screen again and saw the brightly lit living room of the house slowly come into view. The room looked exactly like something you'd expect to see in pictures in a brochure for some luxury alpine ski lodge or something. At one end a beautiful stone fireplace stood surrounded by tiny animal heads mounted all over the wall. A pair of crystal chandeliers hung from the wood-beamed ceiling over the variety of soft chairs filling the room below.

At the center of the room sat Feiersinger, sunk deep into one of the comfy chairs, looking slightly nervous as he slowly sipped what appeared to be a cup of tea. I nearly gasped when I saw him but what was even more amazing was what I saw lying on the floor and tables and chairs all around him.

Paintings. Everywhere there were paintings stacked and leaning at strange angles on nearly every surface available. Some were in elaborate frames, others were just simple canvases stretched across bare frames, while others still were rolled up and tied with loose bits of string. There were dozens of them—maybe even hundreds—and for a moment I almost couldn't believe my eyes. If Avner was right and there were still thousands of missing paintings left unaccounted for, then it didn't take much to guess that we were probably looking at quite a lot of them there in Feiersinger's living room at that very moment. These were clearly the "*crown jewels*" that the cryptic message we'd decoded earlier had referred to.

"So what do we do now?" I whispered, glancing over at Avner, his face thinly illuminated by the dim light of the computer screen.

Avner looked at me with an uncharacteristic hint of a smile at the edges of his normally serious facial expression. "We do exactly as you suggested," he replied as he sat down on a comfortable-looking log nearby. "We watch... and wait."

CHAPTER FORTY·NINE
Where In The World Does He Think He's Going?

A couple of hours later I was starting to regret suggesting that we wait to see what Feiersinger was going to do. The answer to that question, apparently, was nothing. He was doing nothing.

Well, not exactly *nothing* but certainly nothing interesting. At first he just sat there, staring blankly into the distance as he sipped his tea. Then he spent some time looking around at the collection of paintings surrounding him, his eyes lingering briefly on each one and his face getting sadder with every passing minute. He did this until he finally dozed off in his chair, slumping slightly off to the side at an odd angle with his head tilted back and mouth hanging wide open. And that's how he stayed. Minute after minute, hour after hour, until I had dozed off a few times as well, startling myself awake again to discover that nothing had changed.

Avner was keeping an eye on things through all of this, sitting on top of a fallen tree and staring at the camera display screen in his hands while Charlie and I had found a spot on the ground and leaned up against the log next to him.

How much longer are we going to sit here? I wondered after waking up suddenly from another short snooze to discover that the sky to the east was starting to brighten, washing the stars from the sky as the curtain of black sky slowly faded into blue. *Maybe Avner should just bust in there and rough Feiersinger up a little.*

That would be cruel, of course. But sitting propped up against a fallen tree all night with the cold and the insects wasn't much fun either, although of course it didn't bother Charlie all that much. He was used to this kind of thing from his outdoorsy kind of life back in Alaska. Every time I woke up from another short, unplanned nap, I found him sitting there, awake and alert, watching the boring non-happenings on the video screen right next to Avner.

"He's moving," Avner whispered suddenly, startling me instantly awake just as I was about to nod off again.

I quickly pulled myself up onto the log to watch the video screen over Charlie's shoulder. Feiersinger was slowly pulling himself out of his chair, collecting his teacup as he went, and carefully making his way into another room, which looked like some kind of kitchen.

As Feiersinger walked across the room, the camera panned along with him and I suddenly remembered that Ayelet was still up at the house, sitting there and waiting the same as the rest of us had been.

Poor Ayelet, I thought as Feiersinger disappeared from view into the other room for a few moments before returning again to the living room. He paused for a moment at the center of the room, rubbing his eyes tiredly as he surveyed the stacks of paintings scattered all around him. He then began to slowly collect them together, stacking them neatly into various different piles.

"What in the world is he doing?" Charlie muttered under his breath as we watched Feiersinger gathering his paintings together.

"He's organizing them," I whispered back.

"Yes, but why?" Avner asked with a concerned frown.

It didn't take long to find out the answer to that question. After painstakingly arranging the collection of paintings, Feiersinger scooped up an armful and disappeared down a set of stairs at the back of the room. Seconds later, a bright light switched on at the side of the house and he emerged from a door leading out onto the driveway.

Avner quickly switched off the video screen so its glow wouldn't give away our position and ducking our heads low and out of sight, we watched anxiously as Feiersinger trundled out to his car and loaded the paintings into the trunk. Once he was finished, he turned around and headed back to the house again, disappearing out of sight through the door before re-emerging again with another armful of paintings.

On and on this went, back and forth over and over again until the trunk was completely full and Feiersinger started to load up the back seat of the car with dozens and dozens of rolled-up canvases as well—maybe even hundreds of them.

"It looks like someone's planning to take a trip somewhere," Avner muttered under his breath after Feiersinger disappeared into the house again after yet another trip out to his car.

Both Charlie and I nodded silently in agreement as Feiersinger emerged from the house again with another load of paintings. He carefully packed those onto the stacks of other canvases in the back seat of the car and then turned around and headed back for more.

I hope Ayelet is okay over there, I thought. By this time the sky above us had grown quite bright as sunrise was quickly approaching. Charlie, Avner and I were safely tucked out of sight behind some logs and bushes but over at the house there were increasingly fewer shadows for Ayelet to hide in and I was worried that Feiersinger might be able to see her. But Ayelet was a real professional and had somehow found a corner or something to hide in because no matter how hard I tried to figure out where she was, I simply couldn't spot her anywhere.

"How many more of these things does he have?!?" Charlie whispered after Feiersinger finished loading the back seat of his car almost completely to the roof and began to fill the empty front passenger seat with paintings as well.

"Hundreds," Avner muttered. "He'll never be able to take them all."

"I don't think he's trying to take *all* of them," I whispered. "I think he's just trying to take his favorite ones."

Avner glanced over at me and nodded slowly. From what we could see, that appeared to be exactly what he was doing–carefully filling every available bit of space in his car with his favorite works of art.

Feiersinger made one final trip out to his car with several canvases tucked under his arm and then closed the doors for the last time and simply stood there for a moment, looking sad as he stared blankly off into space before slowly turning around again and heading back in the direction of the house.

"I'm going to need the two of you to wait here, please," Avner said after we watched Feiersinger disappear into the house again.

"Of course," Charlie replied, putting his hand on my arm just as I was about to say something in protest.

Avner nodded gravely and pulled himself to his feet, carefully picking his way through the bushes and out onto the open field between us and Feiersinger's house. He ducked low and hurried across the open space until he reached the corner of the house and headed for the same doorway that Feiersinger had just used. As he did this, we suddenly saw Ayelet appear from the shadows up on the balcony and spring into action, climbing down from the upper floor and taking cover up against the building's outer wall as Avner disappeared inside.

"We should have gone with them," I whispered, turning to Charlie for a second. "What if Avner hurts him or something?"

"He won't," Charlie replied confidently.

"How can you be so sure," I asked.

"Because Feiersinger's not inside the house," Charlie responded simply.

I shook my head in confusion. "What do you mean?" I asked. "Where is he, then?"

"Right there," Charlie said, pointing way over across the open field to our far left where a familiar-looking figure was hurrying along the tree line with a bunch of rolled-up paintings tucked precariously under each of his arms.

I couldn't believe my eyes.

"How did he get all the way over there?!?" I asked aloud as we watched Feiersinger vanish into the dense trees and underbrush at the far opposite end of the field. "And where in the world does he think he's going??!?"

CHAPTER FIFTY
Startling And Dizzying Beauty

"Come on," Charlie said, reaching out his hand so he could quickly and quietly pull me to my feet. In seconds we emerged from our hiding place in the bushes and were hurrying as quietly as we could toward the spot in the trees where we'd just seen Feiersinger disappear.

He must have seen Avner coming and ducked out another door to try and escape, I thought to myself as we raced across the grassy field.

As we ran, I glanced over in the direction of the house and saw Ayelet watching us in bewilderment. She took a few steps toward us and then stopped for a moment in hesitation.

I waved my hands at her in a brisk "*hurry up and follow us*" gesture and she took another couple of tentative steps before stopping again and shrugging her shoulders in incomprehension.

Come ON! I gestured at her, pointing wildly ahead of us toward the dense forest. *It's Feiersinger! He's getting away!*

Finally Ayelet got my meaning and broke into a silent run, sprinting along the far side of the field parallel to us.

Charlie and I reached the tree line first and Charlie quickly examined the brush and ground for traces in the dim light of the early morning.

"What is it?!? Is it Feiersinger?!?" Ayelet whispered breathlessly after she finally reached our position.

I nodded my head.

"He went this way," Charlie said, pointing into the deep forest leading up the sides of the towering wall of mountains looming above us.

"I should probably go get Avner," Ayelet whispered indecisively.

"There's no time," Charlie replied, already starting into the forest, hot on Feiersinger's trail. "If we don't go right now, we'll lose him."

Ayelet glanced back toward the house for a second and then turned back to peer into the dark forest.

"Okay," she finally agreed. "Are you able to track him?"

Charlie nodded his head and led the way into the trees, quietly picking his way through the brush along the side of the field and into the earthy smelling darkness beyond. I followed him through, staying right on his heels, while Ayelet brought up the rear.

The forest was dark and grim. Seconds earlier, out in the open air, the glow of early morning had been enough to see the world around us but now that we were under the cover of the trees, it was much darker. I had to be extremely careful where I was placing each and every footstep to make sure I didn't fall down or make any unnecessary noise. That made things pretty slow going, of course, but up ahead of me Charlie was expertly picking his way through the trees and brush as silent as a mountain cat while Ayelet and I stumbled along far behind him.

The déjà vu was almost overwhelming. With Charlie skillfully clambering over the fallen trees and rocks up ahead, I was taken back in time to when he and I first met. Our first meeting had been frightening and awkward, for sure, but the backbreaking climb to the summit of the Chilkoot Pass with him and his brothers that previous summer had also been something incredibly special that I could never possibly forget. And here we were again, almost a year later, making our way through another sweet-smelling forest on the opposite side of the world and heading out into the wilderness again.

Let's just hope we don't meet a bear this time around, I thought, smiling to myself as I continued to struggle to keep up the pace with Charlie. It was a difficult balance between trying to move quickly and not making so much noise that Feiersinger would hear us coming a mile away. At least it was getting lighter in the forest now that sunrise was rapidly approaching. That helped a lot but it still wasn't easygoing.

Glancing behind me I saw that Ayelet wasn't doing much better than I was. Apparently she also wasn't much of an outdoorsy type and despite her impressive nimbleness and dexterity back on city streets, she was still just as out of breath and struggling up there in the woods as me. Charlie was doing fine, however, moving quickly through the trees and increasingly pulling further and further ahead of us.

Come on, Charlie, slow down, I thought to myself. But I knew that he couldn't. Who knows where Feiersinger was heading to up there in all that wilderness, but unless we could somehow keep up we might risk losing him forever.

Then suddenly, almost as though he'd read my thoughts, Charlie reached the top of an incline up ahead of us and stopped dead in his tracks, leaning up against a tree and peering off into the distance. Ayelet and I stopped suddenly as well, our muscles tense as we watched and waited to see what Charlie would do.

I tried to see what Charlie was looking at but it was out of sight down the opposite side of the ridge ahead. For a second, I thought I heard something over the sound of the wind in the trees and tilted my head to the side to hear better. It was the faint sound of rushing water coming from somewhere up ahead. Obviously, whatever was down on the other side of that ridge involved a lot of water.

Charlie turned toward us and motioned for Ayelet and me to come up and join him. We carefully climbed the rest of the way up, still being careful to make as little noise as possible, but by the time we reached the top the roar of water from down below was almost deafening.

Crouching down next to a fallen log, Charlie waved us over and pointed down into the gorge that I could only now see opening up below us. I reached for the trunk of a nearby tree to balance myself and approached the edge with caution because just in front of where we were standing, the ground suddenly plunged a hundred feet straight down into a rocky abyss where thin ribbons of water as white as bridal veils streamed down the steep sides and into the boiling wild maelstrom of water coursing along the bottom.

"Oh my God," I breathed in awe at the startling and dizzying beauty of it.

"Do you see him?" Charlie asked, leaning over to whisper loudly in my ear over the sound of the rushing water as it plummeted at a forty-five degree angle down through the side of the mountain.

See who?!? Feiersinger?!? I wondered, frowning as I scanned the dark shadows along the sides and bottom of the narrow canyon.

"There!" Ayelet cried, pointing down to a precarious footpath running along the side of the wild ravine.

I turned my head and saw the outline of a man propped up against a large boulder with various rolled-up paintings piled on the ground at his feet. At first I panicked thinking that somehow Feiersinger had fallen down and was now lying there unconscious and seriously injured, but then he suddenly moved, lifting his arm to look at his watch for a moment.

"What's he doing?" I asked, glancing over at Charlie.

"I think he's just resting," Charlie replied.

I nodded and turned back to look down into the canyon again. That made sense. I was quite out of breath myself from having climbed all the way up through the forest like we'd just done and Feiersinger had done exactly the same plus a bit farther down into the gorge to where he was now sitting.

Which reminds me, I thought suddenly. *Exactly how DID he get all the way down there to the bottom of the gorge?!??*

I looked around but couldn't see any possible safe route from where we were standing down to where Feiersinger was. You'd have to be crazy to try and climb down the sheer rock faces that were lining the sides of that rocky chasm.

"Come on," Charlie said, climbing to his feet and gesturing for Ayelet and me to follow him.

"Where are we going?!?" I asked.

But, of course, I unfortunately already knew what the answer to that question was going to be.

CHAPTER FIFTY-ONE
Why Don't You Put The Gun Away?

"Are you crazy?!?" I whispered loudly, reaching up to grab Charlie by the arm. "Climb down there?!?? We'll break our necks!"

Charlie looked at me strangely for a second and then knelt down next to me again.

"Feiersinger managed to do it somehow," he explained calmly. "His trail leads from here up along the ridge to the left so my guess is that there must be a spot somewhere upriver where there's a path or something that leads down into the gorge."

I looked up to where Charlie was pointing. The ridge continued up alongside the gorge, following the course of the river below as it curved off around to the right and out of sight.

"Okay," I replied simply. What else could I say? Charlie was right, of course. Somehow Feiersinger made it down there without plunging to his death. And he was old. If he could do it, then surely the three of us, young and agile as we were, could do it too.

"Ummmm, I'm not sure if you're as agile as Ayelet and Charlie," the little voice in my head commented unhelpfully.

Shut up, I snapped to myself as I pushed myself to my feet and scrambled to catch up with Charlie as he followed Feiersinger's trail along the ridge.

As we walked, we kept our heads down and stayed out of sight just below the top of the ridge so Feiersinger couldn't see us. Occasionally I would pop my head up for a second to see where we were going and quickly saw that Charlie had been right. Just around the corner of the next bend in the river, the steep sides of the canyon began to flatten out and a reasonably easy hiking trail led down from the top of the ridge to a rickety wooden bridge leading to the footpath on the other side.

"You see?" Charlie said, grinning smugly.

"Yah, yah," I mumbled in reply. "You were right, you win."

Charlie led the way, scrambling down the trail like a mountain goat and heading across the wooden bridge, stopping for a second in the middle to peer down into the swirling chaos of water below as he waited for Ayelet and me to catch up.

"It's not quite the Zambezi River," he said to me with a grin when I finally caught up with him. "But it's still beautiful."

I wasn't really sure what he meant about that but I didn't really have time to ask him because before we knew what was happening, Ayelet had dashed past us and was sprinting down the footpath on the opposite side toward the spot where we'd last seen Feiersinger.

What the hell?!? I thought, standing there like a deer in headlights as I watched her disappear around the corner of the next bend with Charlie already racing to catch up.

I quickly pulled myself together and headed down the path after them, cursing myself for being so slow. But even though I was only a few seconds behind, as I came around the corner of the bend I saw that they were both already far below me. Ayelet was almost on top of Feiersinger, in fact, and as I ran I watched him slowly rising to his feet, a worried expression on his face and his hands over his head.

What in the world is he doing? I laughed to myself. *Why is he putting his hands up like that?*

It's funny how your mind thinks of such strange things at times like these. As I continued running toward him, I was laughing and thinking to myself of how we used to play cops and robbers on the playground at school when we were kids and for some crazy reason I actually glanced over at Ayelet to see if she was maybe clasping her fingers together in the shape of a make-believe gun. Of course she wasn't doing that but when I did look over, I gasped in shock when I saw the sinister black outline of a *real* gun in her hands that she was pointing directly at Feiersinger.

Seeing that gun gave me a sudden uncomfortably cold feeling deep in the pit of my stomach and in the blink of an eye, I was brusquely reminded that this wasn't some childish game of cops and robbers. This was a serious business that Charlie and I had found ourselves caught up in.

"Whoa, whoa, whoa, just keep cool," Charlie said to Ayelet as he positioned himself protectively between me and her. "Why don't you put the gun away? I don't think we really need that."

Ayelet ignored Charlie and took a few steps closer to Feiersinger.

"Just leave the paintings where they are," she said, gesturing with her pistol for Feiersinger to back away from the spot where the rolled-up canvases were piled on the ground.

With his hands still held high in the air, Feiersinger glanced at his watch again and took a few careful steps back. The expression on his face was one of such deep pain and sorrow that I actually found myself feeling sorry for him for a moment.

"Why don't you put the gun away?" Charlie suggested calmly.

Ayelet glanced over at him and then back at Feiersinger again before lowering the pistol and returning it to the shoulder holster inside her jacket.

"Please just let me go and take these few paintings here with me," Feiersinger begged pitifully after Ayelet had put her weapon away.

"The paintings don't belong to you," Ayelet replied sternly.

"They do!" Feiersinger protested. "All of them! My father left them to me when he died. They are all from his own private collection!"

"And exactly how did your father acquire so many paintings?" Ayelet snapped back. "Did he steal them?"

"Of course not!" Feiersinger replied. "He legally bought and paid for every one of them!"

Ayelet laughed cynically. "The collection of art that we just saw back at your house must be worth half a billion dollars or more," she scoffed. "Do you really think your father acquired all of that legally?"

"He did," Feiersinger mumbled in protest, sounding less convincing than he had a few seconds earlier.

"How is that possible?" Ayelet asked. "Did he buy them at bargain sale prices from innocent families in desperate need of money to flee the horrors of Nazi Germany? Or worse yet, did he buy them from the Nazis themselves who'd just seized them as they sent their rightful owners to the gas chambers? Do you really consider such transactions to be legal?"

Feiersinger apparently had no response to this and simply stared at the ground in front of him, shifting nervously from one foot to another.

"I think you've made your point," Charlie said quietly as he held up his hands and continued to try and calm the situation.

Ayelet slowly turned her head toward him and was about to say something when we all heard a sudden sound like the loud crack of a breaking tree branch coming from somewhere behind us.

Spinning my head around, I immediately began searching for the source of the noise, scanning the rugged wall of rock and waterfalls behind me. It wasn't difficult to pinpoint the source of the noise, however, and I almost immediately spotted the familiar broad-shouldered form of Avner perched precariously at the top of the ridge above us. He had apparently slipped while trying to find a way down the steep rock face and was now clawing at the branches off a nearby tree as he tried to regain his balance.

"Avner! No!!" Ayelet cried as she took a few steps past me toward the edge of the river. "There's no way to climb down here! There's a path and a bridge further upstream!"

Avner grunted something in reply and continued to try and climb back up to safety, his fancy designer shoes slipping on the smooth stone.

It looked like he was going to make it okay but Charlie wasn't taking any chances and took off in a full sprint toward the bridge upstream so he could cross back over to the other side and help Avner.

"I'll take care of him, don't worry!" Charlie yelled back to us over his shoulder as he ran full tilt up the narrow footpath. "Just take care of Feiersinger!"

"Don't worry about that," I scoffed in reply, looking over at Ayelet as I turned my head back around. "Feiersinger's not going anywhere."

As it turned out, this actually was a rather unfortunate thing for me to say since Ayelet and I soon realized that while all of us had been watching Avner's antics up at the top of the ridge, Feiersinger had taken advantage of the fact that we were distracted and had completely vanished.

CHAPTER FIFTY-TWO
Into Thin Air

"Oh my God, how can I be so stupid?" I cried as Ayelet and I frantically tried to figure out where Feiersinger had disappeared to. With the steep canyon walls towering above us on either side, the answer was obvious. There was only one place that he *could* have gone—down the footpath.

Ayelet reacted more quickly than me and was already ten steps ahead, racing down the path that ran alongside the raging and foaming narrow whitewater river beside us. I started running too and did my best to keep up with her, moving fast and staying close to the wall of rock on my left-hand side so I could balance myself against it with my hands.

The path was treacherous in places with slippery wet moss and rocks underfoot forcing me to slow down occasionally, but somehow I managed to stay reasonably close to Ayelet as she continued her pursuit. Up ahead around the next bend, I saw that the canyon gradually opened up into a lush green forest beyond and through the dense trees and branches I caught glimpses of color and motion as Feiersinger continued to make his escape. He had a pretty good head start but Ayelet was too quick and I could easily see that in a few minutes she was going to catch up with him.

I, on the other hand, was never going to catch up. It took everything I had just to keep the distance between Ayelet and me from increasing too much and as I descended into the dark cover of the forest, things became even slower going as I carefully watched where I was putting my feet, making sure I didn't fall down or something. The path we were on was clearly some kind of day-use hiking trail, cutting fairly cleanly through the trees, but it was still uneven with tree roots and various other natural obstacles that needed to be avoided unless you wanted to trip and break your neck.

In the thick of the trees, I lost sight of both Feiersinger and Ayelet but I could still hear them pounding and pushing their way through the brush up ahead of me. But then I heard some other unexpected sounds, like the slamming of a car door and the gunning of an engine with tires spinning on gravel followed by the familiar chirp of rubber on pavement.

Oh God, what now? I asked myself as I broke through the last of the trees and emerged onto a small makeshift parking area at the side of a road. Feiersinger was nowhere to be seen but Ayelet was close by, angrily kicking a tree in frustration as she cursed in some foreign language.

Suddenly it made sense why Feiersinger had been looking at his watch so much. He'd been waiting for someone to come and pick him up here.

"Did you...?" I asked, bent over and hopelessly out of breath as I clutched the painful stitch in my sides that had formed from running so much. "Did you see which way he went?"

"No," Ayelet replied, breathing heavily as she leaned over with her hands on her knees to catch her breath.

"Did you at least see what kind of car it was?" I asked. "Or a license plate?"

Ayelet shook her head. "Nothing," she replied, lowering herself down onto the grass at the side of the road and pulling her knees up to her chest as she rested. "I was too late."

I glanced up and down the deserted road for a second and tried to think of something comforting to say, but in the end I just sat down next to her and stared into the distance. We sat silently for a few minutes before we heard the sound of heavy footfalls echoing through the forest behind us. As the sound grew closer, we looked over to see Charlie and Avner emerge from the nearby trees and step out onto the gravel. For a moment they both looked surprised to see us just sitting there but quickly realized what had happened.

"So Feiersinger had yet another accomplice," Avner said, nodding grimly as he stared up the road and lit one of his stinky cigarettes. "I wonder who it was this time. Beethoven, maybe? Bach? Haydn?"

"Probably none of those," I muttered in reply. "Those radio call signs were part of some network of secret long-distance communications, right? Whoever just picked him up was obviously someone who lived fairly close by."

Avner looked at me and frowned. "How do you figure?" he asked. "He was waiting all night for them. They could have driven here from just about anywhere. Venice, Vienna, wherever."

I shook my head stubbornly. "I don't know what he was waiting for all night," I replied. "Maybe he was just tired, I don't know, but I'm sure that whoever just picked him up probably got a message from him this morning while he was making his escape through the woods. Otherwise why would he load up his own car with paintings if he was waiting for someone to just come and get him?"

"His car!" Ayelet cried suddenly, springing to her feet and reaching inside her jacket pocket to pull out the tracking device she'd been using the night before. "If he goes back to get his car and the rest of the paintings, we'll be able to track him!"

All of us gathered around Ayelet as she powered up the device and waited for it initialize and pick up the signal.

"There!" I said excitedly as the maps spun around for a second, trying to figure out where we were, and the tracking icon finally appeared on the screen.

Ayelet shook her head. "It's still parked in the same place," she said. "It hasn't moved."

"Maybe they just haven't got there yet," I suggested. "How far away is it?"

Ayelet kept shaking her head in disappointment. "They would have been and gone from there by now if that's where they were going," she replied. "It's only a few kilometers from here."

Avner grunted thoughtfully and stood up straight. Pitching his cigarette butt into the grass, he lit up another and started walking briskly up the side of the road.

"We'd better get going then," he called back over his shoulder. "We have a bit of a walk ahead of us."

Ayelet and I hurried after him and as I walked, I glanced back to see Charlie picking up Avner's cigarette butt from the ground and extinguishing it on the pavement. He grinned at me and slipped it into his pocket before jogging to catch up.

"The last thing we need around here is a forest fire," he said, blushing sheepishly.

"You don't have to explain to me," I replied, grinning back at him as he fell into step next to me.

With Avner leading the way, we walked most of the way in silence, enjoying the fresh, cool air and the beautiful mountains and trees surrounding us. It was quiet but as the sun began to peek over the tops of the horizon to the east, the world all around us slowly started to wake up. We turned off the road we were on and onto another one that was slightly busier, with the occasional car zipping past our strange little wandering band. After a while we started to come across a few houses along the way, each of them looking remarkably similar to Feiersinger's and prompting false hope in me that we were finally at our destination.

"There it is," Avner finally said, breaking the silence and pointing up ahead to where the roof and upper floor balcony of another house had come into view. I have to admit that I was pretty glad to see it because "*a few kilometers*" going up and down and back and forth along the winding mountain roads like we were definitely felt like a lot more.

Ayelet and Avner began walking more quickly as we approached the house but Charlie and I just let them pull ahead of us. We weren't in any hurry, after all.

"No! No, no, no!" we heard Avner suddenly start to cry out from up ahead of us. He broke into a run as he reached the corner of the house and disappeared from view with Ayelet close behind him.

Charlie and I glanced at each other in confusion for a second and then hurried after them. As we rounded the corner of the building, it wasn't difficult to see what had upset Avner so much. Feiersinger's gray sedan— and all the paintings he'd crammed inside—was nowhere to be seen. All that was left was Avner standing in the middle of the empty driveway, clenching his fists and bellowing some of the same foreign curse words that I'd heard Ayelet use earlier that morning.

"I don't understand," Charlie said as we approached where Ayelet was standing. "Can't you track him?"

Ayelet smiled thinly. "Feiersinger must have figured out how we managed to track him all the way up here," she said wryly as she held up a tiny black device with a thin wire antennae attached to it. "Because they took the car and left the tracking device behind."

"That's the tracking device?!?" I asked in amazement.

Ayelet nodded and handed me the tiny device so I could take a closer look. I was impressed. Whenever my dad and I would go to Vancouver, we would always stop in at the Spy Store and check out all their various high-tech spy equipment, including the different types of tracking devices. I'd always been amazed at how small the ones in the store were but the tracking device that Ayelet had been using was so tiny that it absolutely blew my mind. In fact, it was so small that it started to give me a bit of an uneasy feeling as well. Just like that sinister-looking black pistol that Ayelet had pulled out of her jacket, this tiny little piece of unbelievable technology reminded me in no uncertain terms that whatever organization the two of them were working for, they were definitely not messing around. As reasonable and normal as Ayelet (and even the temperamental Avner) seemed to be, there was still something about all of this James Bond stuff that made me a bit nervous.

"He left a note with it too," Ayelet said, breaking my train of thought. She reached into her pocket, pulled out a small sheet of folded paper and handed it over so I could read it. As I unfolded the small scrap of paper, Charlie moved closer so he could lean over my shoulder to read it too.

Sorry.

"*Sorry,*" the note said simply.

"You're kidding, right?" I said, glancing up and almost laughing at the ridiculousness of it.

Ayelet simply shrugged her shoulders while a short distance away from us Avner paced back and forth nervously as he smoked another one of his foul cigarettes.

But that was it. He was gone. Vanished into thin air.

You're probably expecting me to tell you how I went back to my hotel room that night and lay in bed thinking about the whole confusing string of events until I somehow found another clue that put us right back on Feiersinger's trail again. Of course I did those things—went back to my hotel and lay in bed thinking for hours—but it was no use. No matter how hard I tried, I simply couldn't think of anything and that morning up there in the mountains was the last we ever heard or saw of Rudolf Feiersinger.

CHAPTER FIFTY-THREE
Not All Puzzles Have Solutions

A few days later, Charlie and I were on the train again, rattling through the mountains of the Alps, heading south through Italy on our way back to Rome. After Feiersinger had slipped through our fingers, there wasn't much else to do except for Ayelet to drive us back to Salzburg, leaving Avner behind to stand guard at the mountain house to make sure no one came back to get the rest of the paintings that were scattered everywhere.

Amazingly enough, it turned out that in addition to the stash of paintings up in the mountains, there were even more of them hidden away in Feiersinger's apartment in Salzburg. And as if that wasn't enough, he even had yet another apartment in Munich where even *more* works of art were later found once the police and Interpol became involved in the case and conducted some intensive searches of the three locations. All told, they found more than a thousand works of art squirreled away. Most were paintings by such well-known names as Picasso, Matisse, Renoir and dozens of other artists. Nearly all of the paintings were thought to have gone missing during the time of the Second World War, but like the Van Gogh that we'd found hanging innocently on the wall of Matteo's family apartment in Rome, some of the works that were found had been stolen from collectors and museums in more recent times and had somehow found their way into the hands of this odd network of black market art dealers.

The last that I heard of it, the authorities were painstakingly working their way through the scores of paintings and other artworks, trying to unlock their history and ascertain who their rightful owners might be. Attempts were also made to figure out the identities of the various other members of the strange radio network of musical call signs, but as far as I know no progress was ever made. As Ayelet pointed out to me the last time I saw her, the network of art dealers appeared to be based on a much older network of intelligence agents left over from the Cold War. A network of spies, in other words. And one that was passed down from father to son reaching as far back as the Second World War. These people were professionals who had remained hidden for generations and more likely than not, they were going to stay that way.

But all of these things happened long after Charlie and I had already left. With Feiersinger having disappeared and Ayelet and Avner calling in the proper authorities to investigate the case, there really wasn't any reason for Charlie and me to be there anymore.

But we didn't leave Salzburg right away. We stuck around for another few days eating *Mozartkugeln* and watching *The Sound of Music* in the common room of Charlie's hostel. On the last evening we went for dinner in the fortress restaurant followed by a classical music concert, and of course we went for coffee one last time at the Hotel Sacher on the morning that we left.

A few hours later, our train pulled out of the station and crossed a bridge over the river, giving us a final view of the church towers of the old city in the distance and the imposing white fortress looming high beyond. It was a beautiful and magical view and the instant it disappeared beyond the trees and houses I knew that I had found yet another city in the world where I simply had to return to someday.

With all these places I want to come back and visit, I'll have to fly around the world all over again once I finish this first flight, I thought.

My mind wandered as I stared at the endless stream of villages and countryside flashing past my window. I wondered what we were going to tell Matteo and his sisters once we arrived back in Rome. They'd expected us to find out some answers about exactly what it was that their father had been involved in, but with Feiersinger gone it was clear that no such answers were going to be forthcoming.

Had their father been some kind of criminal? Or a spy? All we had were guesses and assumptions and the more I thought about it, the more I realized that not all puzzles have solutions. This one most definitely did not and I was dreading telling Matteo, Vega and Giulia that as far as we could figure out, it seemed that their father might have been one of the *bad guys*.

As it turned out, I needn't have worried about all of that. By the time Charlie and I stepped off the train in Rome, Matteo and his two beautiful sisters were there waiting for us, with flowers and emotion-filled hugs all around as though we were dear old friends who hadn't seen each other in years.

It was such a festive occasion that I was loathe to ruin it by giving them the bad news, but I forced myself to be strong and as we all stood there on the train station platform, I told them about everything that had happened.

As I spoke, I watched their eyes and waited anxiously to see what their reactions would be, but they simply listened quietly and waited for me to finish.

"So, that's unfortunately all we know," I said nervously as I brought the story to an end. "It seems that we don't really know for sure who the good guys and the bad guys are. And we can only guess at what your father may or may not have had to do with all of it."

Matteo glanced over at his sisters for a moment and then turned to me and grinned. "Well, I don't know about my sisters," he said. "But as far as I'm concerned, all of this actually sounds pretty cool."

I blinked in confusion. "What do you mean?" I asked, not sure if Matteo had understood correctly.

"I mean, it seems pretty cool to me to think of our father as some kind of spy," Matteo said.

"But what about all the stolen paintings?" I replied. "Especially the ones that might have been stolen by the Nazis?"

"True," Matteo replied sheepishly, looking embarrassed.

"I think what my brother is trying to say," Vega interjected, putting her arm around Matteo. "Is that we have no idea what our father's role in all of this might have been, but to us he's still our father. He took care of us and raised us well, so no matter what this secret life of his might have involved, we will still always love him."

"I understand," I said quietly as I slowly nodded my head.

For a moment there was a long silence and then Matteo grabbed Charlie and me by the arms in a burst of energy and began to lead us down the platform to the main hall of the train station.

"Enough of this gloominess!" he said. "My sisters and I have planned a special dinner for the two of you to welcome you home!"

As Matteo maneuvered us through the busy crowd to the front of the station and stuffed all of us into an oversized taxi, I thought about what he'd just said about welcoming us home. Somehow he was absolutely right about that, and as the taxi raced through a confusing warren of unfamiliar backstreets, I really did feel like I was returning home somehow.

As the taxi abruptly pulled to a stop in front of the same little *trattoria* where Matteo had taken us the week before, the same two handsome brothers who ran the place were waiting outside to open the doors and usher us inside to our corner table near the back. In the kitchen beyond, the same older woman we'd seen before was hard at work preparing the food but she took the time to raise her hand to us in greeting as we each took our seats.

Matteo had arranged everything in advance for us. All we needed to do was sit and talk and laugh as a seemingly endless parade of foods passed in front of us. Cold meats, cheeses, olives, pasta dishes and fish. It was almost too much–I could hardly eat everything as it was and yet Matteo kept reminding us to save room for dessert. The *dolce*, he said, was a special surprise that he'd baked himself.

I was surprised at how fast the hours and the meal passed us by. It was almost as though we were on a speeding train, hurtling toward the moment when I would have to say goodbye to these newfound friends of mine and the home-away-from-home that they'd created for me. I couldn't help but feel a pang of sadness as the waiters cleared away the remains of the meal and placed sparkling clean dessert plates in front of all of us. It was all a bit too much and I found myself getting a little emotional.

"No time for wet eyes, my dear," Matteo whispered to me as the waiters distributed steaming cups of coffee all around and placed a beautiful multi-layered chocolate cake on the table in front of us. With a few skilled cuts of a long knife, they deftly cut off slices for each of us and slid them onto our plates with a dollop of cream to top them off.

"This cake looks amazing," I said, distracting myself as I wiped an almost-tear from the corner of my eye.

"Matteo is actually an amazing chef," Vega said as she cut away a small piece of cake with her fork.

"Would anyone care for a *digestivo*?" one of the waiters asked as he finished serving us. "An after-dinner drink?"

"Some of my homemade *nocino*, perhaps?" Matteo asked with a sly grin.

"Oh God, no thank you!" Giulia laughed as she cut off a mouthful of cake for herself as well.

Matteo sat quietly and watched as everyone tried his cake. "Little do they know that they're trying my *nocino* after all," Matteo said, leaning over to whisper conspiratorially in my ear. "I baked this cake using it. A special chocolate *nocino* cake."

Somehow this made me laugh and I had to stop for a moment with my fork in midair before taking my first bite. And a good thing I did too, because almost immediately Vega made a disgusted sound and quickly held her palm up to her mouth.

"*Oh mio Dio*, what is this vile thing?" Vega asked as she attempted to politely extract the cake from her mouth with a napkin. Next to her Giulia was trying to do the same, turning red with embarrassment in the process, and even Charlie was choking and coughing as he struggled to wash the awful taste from his mouth with some water.

I stared down for a second at the forkful of lovely looking cake in front of me and then quickly decided to put it back without tasting it.

"What do you mean?!?" Matteo asked, surprised by everyone's dramatic reactions.

"It's horrible!" Giulia cried, reaching for a glass of water.

"How is that possible?" Matteo asked, leaning down to cautiously sniff his own piece of cake.

"I don't know, but it's really terrible!" Vega replied. "What in the world did you put in it to make it so revolting?"

Matteo glanced over at me with wide, fearful eyes but I didn't know what to say to him. All I could do was shrug my shoulders and laugh.

The others probably had no idea why I was laughing so much but they all laughed along with me anyway. And as I looked around the table and wiped another bittersweet tear from the corner of my eye, I knew that this would probably be our last meal all together like this. Matteo, Vega and Giulia all had jobs and lives that they had to return to and Charlie had a few more things to take care of at the World Food Program before returning to Alaska as well.

I had responsibilities of my own as well, of course. I couldn't forget that I had a flight around the world to get on with and that meant spending the following several days preparing my trusty De Havilland

Beaver seaplane for the next leg of the journey. And as sad as I was to say goodbye to this beautiful city and my new friends, I was also yearning to get back to flying again. It was something I'd been missing after spending so much time in Europe with my feet planted firmly on the ground.

    I looked forward to being back in the cockpit again soon—flying high up in the clouds, as free as a bird. But there was still one more thing that I had to do first.

CHAPTER FIFTY·FOUR
All Part Of The Adventure

"What do you think?" the man in the immaculately tailored Armani suit standing next to me asked. His name (believe it or not) was Paolo Panini, which I suppose is a great name if you own a sandwich shop but less great if you're in the sushi business, which he was. He was the senior vice-president in charge of marketing for the Wasabi Willy Family Sushi Restaurant chain's Italian division.

"I look like a superhero!" I replied in amazement as I stared at myself in the full-length mirror in front of me. I was dressed in a costume that the Wasabi Willy company had provided for me—a pair of knee-high red boots with a skirt and a snug-fitting long-sleeved shirt that had a stylized crest of a hawk emblazoned on the front. And as if that wasn't superheroish enough, I was also wearing a mask and a cape and was poised ready to fight with my hair flying wildly behind me.

"Yes! That's exactly the point!" Paolo replied with a broad smile. "We've been doing some market research since your appearances at the other restaurants in Europe and we've discovered that the customers are a bit confused as to why you and the Wasabi Willy character are fighting."

For those who don't already know, I should probably mention that the Wasabi Willy company had been funding my little flight around the world and in exchange I had made a few special appearances at restaurants across Europe, where part of the show involved me wearing a giant inflatable sumo wrestler suit and squaring off against an even more giant and inflatable Wasabi Willy character. Needless to say, I always lost and the company's mascot always won, but of course I didn't mind. They were the ones paying all my bills, after all.

"I always wondered about that too," I replied, still staring at myself in the mirror (just between you and me, I couldn't stop myself—I have to admit that I looked pretty cool as a superhero). "About what I was fighting Willy for, I mean."

Paolo shrugged his shoulders for a second. "To get at the sushis?" he suggested. "I don't know. But anyway, people thought it was confusing. They didn't know who was the good guy or the bad guy. Not to mention that the Wasabi Willy character's costume was so big that it actually frightened a lot of children."

"I can understand that," I laughed. "I was a bit scared of him myself."

"So because of that," Paolo continued. "Many people actually thought that *Willy* was the villain and you were the hero. But in that case it didn't make sense that you were always losing the wrestling matches instead of winning."

"Makes sense," I replied.

"Anyway, long story short, we've made some changes to the concept and now you're the hero," Paolo said as he pulled the cloth cover off a nearby easel with a dramatic flourish. "Voila!"

I gasped in disbelief when I saw what was mounted onto the easel. It was an enormous poster showing a comic book superhero version of myself with a little Wasabi Willy floating next to me as a sidekick.

"Oh my God, that is so cool!!!" I cried, stepping closer for a better look.

"And that's just the cover art," Paolo explained. "We're actually developing an entire comic book series dedicated to you and Willy and your amazing adventures."

"I... just can't believe it," I stuttered, covering my mouth with my hands in disbelief as I continued to stare at the poster. It was the coolest thing that I'd ever seen.

Paolo smiled and stood patiently off to one side waiting for me until there was suddenly a soft knock at the door and a young woman stuck her head into the room.

"Mr. Panini, we're ready for you," the woman said.

The woman was Paolo's assistant, Mia, whom I'd met just a few minutes earlier when she'd shown me up to his office. Her sudden reappearance snapped me out of my spellbound state and reminded me that my actual purpose of being there that day was to take part in a grand opening ceremony for one of Wasabi Willy's new restaurants in Rome. It was a gig that I was familiar with, of course, but since I'd been expecting to put on the same old sumo wrestler costume again and go fight Wasabi Willy, all of this new superhero stuff was a complete surprise and it would take a bit of getting used to.

"Please, please, bring Willy in so Kitty can see the changes we've made," Paolo said with a wave of his hand.

Mia nodded and pushed the door all the way open before stepping out of the way to let the person in the Wasabi Willy costume behind her waddle in through the door.

"Kitty, this is Aria," Paolo said, gesturing toward Willy. "She'll be your partner today for the meet and greet."

"Hello," I said and giggled when Willy/Aria gave me a silly wave in return.

"As you can see, we've made Willy much smaller and less scary-looking," Paolo explained as he gently ushered the two of us toward a set of doors at the opposite end of the room. "We've even manufactured some small plush toys of his character that we'll be giving away today at the event."

"Oh! Can I have one of those?!?" I asked excitedly.

"Of course, of course! I'm sure that Mia will be happy to save one for you," Paolo replied, nodding at the woman who was hurrying ahead of us to open a set of large double doors.

As the doors swung open, they revealed a large open atrium from a modern shopping mall with bright summer sunshine streaming in from above and glinting brightly off the walls of glass and steel. At the far end there was a short stage set up with a podium and a microphone with hundreds of assembled guests milling around in front, sampling free sushi that was served to them by uniformed waiters carrying silver trays.

For the next couple of hours my job was to mingle with everyone at the party, having fun taking pictures with the children and talking with their parents. The whole scene seemed completely bizarre and surreal and as we paused by the door for a moment, I found myself thinking back on everything that had happened to me over the past year—wondering how in the world it was that I now found myself standing there, about to spend my last night in Rome dressed in a superhero costume and eating sushi. Never in my wildest dreams could I have imagined I would ever be doing this. But then again, I never would have imagined I would have been doing *any* of the amazing things that I'd done during the course of my epic flight around the world. And the next morning that flight would continue, with me scheduled to be airborne and flying east to where I knew that a whole new set of surprises and adventures were already waiting for me.

I took a deep breath and looked up at Paolo for a moment. He gave me a kind smile as he continued to wait patiently.

"I'm ready," I said and he gave me a simple nod in return.

This is all part of the adventure, I told myself with a grin as Paolo led Willy and me out into the crowd of people.

And it was. Because every breath of precious life that we take during our time here on this beautiful planet—no matter how strange or exotic or ordinary—is all part of the adventure that we call our own lives.

EPILOGUE

Three Coins In A Fountain

At the end of it all—after all the sushi had been eaten and guests had gone home, and after all the speeches had been made and photographs taken—Charlie and I found ourselves wandering together through the streets of Rome for the very last time.

Charlie had dropped by the sushi party to see me so we could spend a bit more time together on my last evening before I headed off again on my around-the-world flight. But he wasn't the only one who dropped by. Matteo, Vega and Giulia had each stopped in as well—not only to cheer me on but also to say goodbye and thank you. With me flying out so early the next morning, this would be the last time that the three of them would be able to see me.

Now, I know that superheroes aren't supposed to cry, but I am sure you can understand that saying goodbye to each of them was pretty emotional and despite my best efforts to keep my eyes dry, I have to admit that I failed miserably.

Saying goodbye to Matteo was the worst. His sisters were tough and strong as we hugged and promised to stay in touch. But by the time it was Matteo's turn, his eyes were already welling up with tears and of course that just set me off crying as well.

"Don't forget to write," Matteo sniffled. "I know you'll be busy flying and everything, but just write whenever you can, okay?"

"I will, I will," I replied as I lifted my mask to wipe away the tears. "And you don't forget to write to me. Especially if you find out anything new about this whole situation with your father's paintings and stuff."

"Of course I will!" Matteo replied, hugging me again and setting off a fresh round of tears.

Eventually we managed to pull ourselves together and said our final goodbye before I returned to the floor of the sushi party to continue mingling and posing for photographs with my partner Willy.

Charlie arrived just as Matteo and the others were leaving and out of the corner of my eye, I could see them going through another series of emotional farewells with him as well before they finally made it out of the building. After he was done with that, Charlie spotted me from across the room and gave me a wave as he grabbed a couple of tuna *maki* off a passing tray and found a place to sit and wait for the party to finish.

Part of me felt a little bad that Charlie had to wait but I do have to admit that I was actually having the time of my life walking around and meeting with everyone at the party and hamming it up with Willy in various dramatic poses so they could take pictures. It was like being a kid again, playing superhero without a care in the world. But eventually the carefree evening had to end and after I changed back into normal clothes I made some final arrangements with Mr. Panini and his assistant before picking up Charlie by the door and heading out into a perfectly warm summer evening in the Eternal City.

We found a gelato stand and strolled along the river eating ice cream until we reached the brightly illuminated walls of the *Castel Sant'Angelo* and its statue of the archangel Michael standing at the summit with his wings outstretched.

Seeing those wings made me long to be airborne again, flying free high above the Earth in my trusty De Havilland Beaver, with nothing but the clouds and my own thoughts to keep me company. After so many weeks in Europe—as incredible as they might have been—I was looking forward to getting back on the road again, so to speak, and back up into the sky where I belong.

I glanced over at Charlie and I could tell that he knew exactly what I was thinking. He gave me a smile and without a word we continued our walk along the river for a while then turned back into the narrow streets of the city.

"It seems like just yesterday that we went flying through here on that scooter," Charlie said, breaking our comfortable silence as we reached some familiar-looking twists and turns in the maze of streets. Up ahead, the murmur of what sounded like a loud cocktail party echoed off the corners of buildings and it took me a moment to realize where we were.

Somehow, on our roundabout route back to our hotels, we found ourselves back at the Trevi Fountain, although this time we were on foot and under such circumstances that we could actually stop and relax on the steps as we finished our ice cream.

"Have you thrown a coin in the fountain yet?" Charlie asked, nodding toward the white-lit statues and pale green waters of the fountain.

"At least one," I laughed, realizing that I hadn't even told Charlie yet about the crazy thing I'd done the last time we'd passed by there. "Maybe two, but I'm not sure."

"What do you mean?" Charlie asked, wrinkling his forehead.

Feeling slightly stupid, I told him the story of how I'd thrown my first coin into the fountain on one of the days just after I'd arrived in Rome, and then tried to throw a second one from the back of our speeding motor scooter during the high-speed chase through the streets.

"Pretty dumb, huh?" I asked, finishing my story and turning red with embarrassment.

Charlie just shook his head and laughed. "Too bad you didn't see whether you made it or not," he said. "Although I'm willing to bet that you did."

Charlie reached into his pocket and pulled out a shiny new one euro coin. He held it up between his fingers and offered it to me.

"What's this for?" I asked, taking the coin from him.

"Aren't you supposed to throw three coins in?" he replied.

Now it was my turn to laugh. "I think the legend is that throwing the first coin means you'll come back to visit Rome someday," I said. "The second means that you will find a new romance."

Charlie looked surprised. "And the third?" he asked.

"I think the third means that you'll soon get married," I explained.

Charlie looked down and stared at the coin in the palm of my hand. "There's a lot riding on that one coin, then," he said with a chuckle.

I looked down and stared at the coin for a while as well, wondering what I should do. "Have *you* thrown a coin in the fountain yet?" I asked, looking up at Charlie again and straight into his hazel-green eyes.

Charlie shook his head. "Not yet," he said.

"Then you'd better take this," I replied, folding the Euro coin back into the palm of his strong hands.

Charlie looked at me and smiled a warm and beautiful smile as he held the coin up between his fingers again. On the back of the coin I could see the familiar outline of Da Vinci's *Vitruvian Man* imprinted on it and glinting in the bright lights that were reflected off the waters of the nearby fountain.

"Okay," Charlie said simply as he reached out and flicked the coin into the air with his thumb.

Tilting our heads back, we watched the coin sail almost magically through the air, sparkling and flashing as it tumbled end over end until it hit the surface of the water with a satisfying splash and slowly sank.

"I guess that means that we'll both eventually come back to Rome again someday," I said after the coin finally settled on the bottom.

"I guess it does," Charlie replied as he looked over at me with one of his infectious Charlie-like grins. "Both of us together."

Some Further Reading (Spoiler Alert)

The Circus Maximus: Like nearly all places in any Kitty Hawk book, the Circus Maximus is a real place. It's located just slightly off the beaten path, just up the street from the Colosseum and on the opposite side of the Palatine Hill from the Roman Forum. There's not much to see there since most of it has been overgrown with grass, but the enormity of the structure and the mark it has left on the landscape is still obvious. Standing at the edge of that huge oval-shaped depression in the ground (more than 2000 feet long) it is quite humbling to think that more than two millennia ago crowds of a quarter-million people surrounded the inner chariot racing track to watch and cheer on their favourite competitors. Nowadays you can cheer on your favourite joggers, if you like. Try searching for the Circus Maximus on Google Maps and you'll see how enormous it really is.

Primo and Secondo: The structure of a traditional Italian meal is something that is beyond the realm of my understanding of the world (and consists of far more than just the primo and secondo courses). However, I always found it interesting (as Charlie notes this in the course of the book) that pasta is not really considered a main course in Italy like it often is in North America. "*Pasta is never secondo*" my Italian friends tell me. For more information about the various stages of the traditional Italian meal check out the following Wikipedia page which explains it far better than I am capable of doing:

en.wikipedia.org/wiki/Italian_meal_structure#Dinner_.28Cena.29

Nocino: Poor Matteo and his nocino, right? I probably don't have to explain at this point that nocino is a traditional Italian liqueur made from walnuts.

Van Gogh's View of the Sea at Scheveningen: As detailed in this book, this is a real painting that once hung on the walls of the Van Gogh Museum in Amsterdam but was unfortunately stolen in December of 2002 and has not been seen since. This painting has always been a favourite of mine, not only for its historical value as one of the very first paintings that Vincent van Gogh ever made, but also because the sand dunes from where he painted the scene are not far from the apartment where I used to live in Holland. The painting is also interesting because of the amount of paint that Vincent piled onto it. His classmates during his very brief stint studying art in Antwerp would complain about what a mess he made when he was working, with paint flying everywhere as he applied gobs of it to the canvas. This aspect of his style was evident throughout his working life, even in such early works as this view of the sea where the waves seem almost sculpted in gobs of dried paint. But, of course, no one can see any of this anymore. The Van Gogh Museum website once had further information about the theft of this painting in a press release, however the site has been completely redone since the writing of this book and it is no longer there. Try Googling "view of the sea at scheveningen" for more information about the robbery from various other websites. (And if you're in the mood, try Googling the proper pronunciation of both Van Gogh's name and the town of Scheveningen.)

The Van Gogh Museum: Even though this museum plays only a very small role in the book I wanted to make a special mention of it. Everything that Kitty Hawk learns about the museum and the life of Vincent van Gogh (from the very helpful Petra) is true and I hope in the book that I have captured a bit of what it's like to visit this wonderful museum. Last of all, if you're ever lucky enough to be walking around in Amsterdam, keep an eye out for tourists carrying distinctive long triangular poster boxes from the Van Gogh Museum. Vincent was always very keen on having his art be available to the masses for everyone to enjoy and I think he would have been very pleased to know that so many people were doing exactly this and taking his works home with them. Check out the official Van Gogh Museum website for further information about the life and work of Vincent van Gogh himself:

www.vangoghmuseum.nl

Other Paintings - Monet and Pissaro: In addition to Van Gogh's View of the Beach at Scheveningen there are two other paintings which feature prominently in this book. The first is of the interior of the Gare Saint-Lazare train station in Paris by Claude Monet and the second is a view over Boulevard Montmartre at night by Camille Pissarro. Unlike the Van Gogh painting, neither of these stolen works of art from the book are real. Or are they? I chose to use these two on purpose because both Monet and Pissarro painted more than one version of each of these subjects. It was therefore not entirely impossible that there might exist some additional versions of these paintings that might exist. Try Googling "boulevard montmartre pissarro" and "saint lazare monet" to see the many different existing versions of both of these paintings.

Impressionism: One of the reasons I chose in this book to feature an early Van Gogh painting and two others by Impressionistic painters was because I find it very interesting to see how drastically Van Gogh's style changed between his early years of painting in Holland and his later years in Paris and France. Vincent was an avid letter writer and would regularly correspond throughout his life with many people, including his brother Theo, with whom he was very close. During the time that Vincent was trying to find his own painting style back home in Holland his brother was working at an art gallery in Paris and the two would discuss the immense impact that Impressionism was having on the world of art. Theo, being in Paris, was situated at the very heart of the movement, whereas Vincent, back home in Holland, had barely the tiniest idea of what Impressionism even meant. In reading the letters between him and his brother one almost feels sorry for poor Vincent for his rather backward and provincial ideas of what the Impressionistic movement was even about.

Impressionism was born following the invention of paint being sold in sealed tin tubes just a few decades earlier. Renoir always said that without tubes of paint the Impressionist movement would never have come into being. Prior to that ground-breaking innovation painters had to mix their own colours by hand using ground pigments and oil–a process that took a lot of time and resources to complete. But once they had access to a plentiful supply of pre-mixed paint everything began to change. The artists were now able to complete a painting in a much shorter period of time, thus allowing them to quickly capture an "impression" of a short moment in time, such as Monet did in his famous work "Impression Sunrise", from which the Impressionist movement got its name.

While this revolution in art was going on, however, Vincent was still back in Holland surrounded by the heavy influence of Rembrandt and other Dutch and Flemish masters and this explains why Vincent's early works are so dark and drab. But all that changed once he picked up and moved to Paris. Only then was he able to truly experience the works of the Impressionists for the first time and the familiar Van Gogh style of bright and outlandish colours was born.

Check out the excellent website www.vangoghletters.org which has an amazing collection of Vincent's letters to his brother and other contemporaries in which he discusses his work and life.

<u>The Sistine Chapel</u>: I am sure that anyone who's been to Rome would agree that the experience of visiting the Sistine Chapel is usually very much as described in this book–disappointing, in other words. The paintings are astounding, particularly Michelangelo's Last Judgement, but the atmosphere certainly leaves a lot to be desired.

<u>Numbers Stations (aka Conet Transmissions)</u>: I have to credit Cameron Crowe and the director's commentary track of Vanilla Sky for introducing me to the strange and enigmatic world of the so-called Numbers Stations. The explanations given in this book regarding the source of these radio transmissions (that they are coded messages used by government intelligence agencies to communicate with agents in the field) is probably as good a guess as anyone's. If you ask me, spy transmissions are almost certainly what they are, but in truth no one really knows. That's what makes them so fascinating. And who knows? Maybe there really ARE some former intelligence agents out there running a stolen art ring using transmissions just like described in this book? Anything is possible and the only thing we know for sure is that anyone who wants to buy a shortwave receiver and dial around the radio bands at any given time of the day can stumble across these strange and enigmatic transmissions.

Check out this website for some slightly out of date, but good introductory information about these Numbers Stations (aka Conet Transmissions): www.irdial.com/conet.htm

Also visit this website to listen to some audio files of these transmissions:

www.archive.org/details/ird059

For another good site also check:

www.numbers-stations.com

Yet another good site with recordings and profiles of the various transmissions:

www.numbersoddities.nl

But if you only check one site of all of these then this last one is the one to go to. It has an up-to-date list of all active and inactive stations, profiles, archive logs, recordings AND (most important) a schedule of where and when you can hear some of these transmissions for yourself: www.priyom.org

Make sure to visit www.priyom.org and see that the various real life Numbers Stations usually have a set message format that their transmissions always follow. The Numbers Station and messaging format used in this book is entirely made up, of course, but I have tried to create a compilation of various real life formats that I find interesting and the result is generally true to form, including a group count, repeater, and end signal.

One final note: In recent years the stations using human-sounding voices appear to have gone into decline and for me this is unfortunate since these transmissions are far more interesting to listen to than the digital or morse-code based stations. There are still a few voice-based stations around, however, using different languages and formats.

The One Time Pad: This cipher system is, of course, based on real life principles. Hopefully the explanation within the book of how these one-time-pad encoding systems work is sufficient, but let me just also add a short apology for all the math contained in the book. I tried to keep it as short as possible for both our sakes.

The Piazza del Popolo and the Porta del Popolo: Needless to say these are two real places at the northern edge of the Roman city walls. Check them out on Google Maps. And perhaps one small (and hopefully interesting) detail I can add about the plaza is that the obelisk standing at the centre of it was brought to Rome from Egypt more than 2000 years ago and was originally erected at the Circus Maximus (Kitty Hawk's favourite spot in Rome, remember?) before being moved to the Piazza del Popolo in 1589.

The Cathedral of Light: Just as described in this book the so-called Cathedral of Light of the Nazi Rallies in Nürnberg during the 1930s was a real effect created with rows of searchlights lining the edges of the enormous outdoor Zeppelin Field. Try Googling "cathedral of light" just like Kitty Hawk did and check out some of the images of this chilling lighting effect and the equally chilling mass rallies they were featured in. Also check the following website for more information on the Zeppelin Field itself:

www.reichsparteitagsgelaende.de/englisch/zeppelinfeld.htm

The Nazi Party Rally Grounds: Try searching for "Nuremberg" on Google Maps and it's not difficult to spot the enormous area of land and lakes to the south-east of the city centre that make up the former grounds of the annual Nazi Party Rallies. Today this area is used for various recreational purposes but is also home to an extensive documentation centre and museum about Germany under the Nazi regime. Check out these websites for more information about the grounds and documentation centre:

www.museums.nuremberg.de/documentation-centre/index.html

and

www.reichsparteitagsgelaende.de

The Zeppelin Tribune (aka *Die Reichsparteitagsgeländetennisspielmauer*): This gigantic stone structure on which Kitty Hawk and Charlie spend most of their time in Nürnberg is a real place where hundreds of thousands once gathered to hear Adolf Hitler speak. Many features of the structure were destroyed following the end of the Second World War, but it was impossible to demolish it all. It's simply too big. And just like described in this book, on good weather days there are almost always people hitting tennis balls off the back of it, hence my silly nickname for it. Check out some of the history of this structure at the following website:

www.reichsparteitagsgelaende.de/englisch/zeppelintribuene.htm

The City of Nürnberg: Despite its very dark past, the city of Nürnberg is actually very charming and beautiful. Only an hour and a half from Munich it is home to one of Germany's best Christmas Markets in the winter and with its picturesque side streets and castle overlooking the old town it is equally wonderful in the summer as well. It is also home to the courtroom where the infamous Nuremberg war crimes trials were held for leading Nazis after the end of the Second World War. This courtroom (#600) is still in use today and is accessible to the public on weekends. Check out this website for more details:

www.memorium-nuremberg.de

Dachau: Yes, I know that this is a pretty dark place to be included in a Kitty Hawk novel, but I like how it helps to illustrate the way in which Kitty herself is coming to terms with the world around her—both good and bad. Bottom line: Germany has a dark past and I suppose it's useless to pretend that it doesn't. But I tried to limit the negative stuff as much as possible. For more information about memorial and museum at the former concentration camp of Dachau you can check out the centre's website:

www.kz-gedenkstaette-dachau.de

Famous Musical Masterpieces: Believe it or not I once sat in the dining cart of a train directly across from a character almost exactly like Linus (the conductor and musical prodigy that Kitty Hawk and Charlie meet). He was obviously a big help for them, but in truth they would have been able to eventually figure it out on their own since (as Linus says) the pieces of music are all well-known signature pieces for each of the composers. Just in case anyone is interested I include here a list of each composer and their corresponding signature piece (but just in case anyone who's not read the book yet is reading this I will not put all this into a nice neat table that might ruin the surprise for you). In order of their appearance in the book the composers are as follows: Mozart (Eine Kleine Nachtmusik); Beethoven (5th Symphony); Gregorio Allegri (Miserere); Camille Saint-Saëns (Danse Macabre); Georges Bizet (Carmen Fantasy); Edvard Grieg (Hall Of The Mountain King); Antonin Dvořák (New World Symphony); Johann Strauss (Blue Danube); Johann Pachelbel (Canon); Pyotr Ilyich Tchaikovsky (Nutcracker Reed Flutes); Béla Bartók (Romanian Folk Dance); Gustav Holst (Neptune The Mystic); Frédéric Chopin (Prelude Opus 28 #7); Sergei Prokofiev (Peter's Theme); Antonio Vivaldi (Four Seasons Spring); Bach (Aria Bist Du Bei Mir); Haydn (String Quartet, Op. 1).

The Sound Of Music: Have I mentioned that the Sound of Music was filmed in Salzburg? Even if I had somehow failed to mention this I can guarantee that any visitor to the city will never be allowed to forget it anyway. The city is famously known as not only the place where the real-life Von Trapp family lived, but also where the classic movie adaptation of their life was filmed. Check out this website for a pretty good list and details of most of these filming locations:

www.bigboytravel.com/europe/austria/salzburg/soundofmusicfilmlocations

The Sound Of Music Do-Re-Mi Stairs: Google this phrase to see endless pictures of countless tourists re-enacting the famous scene in the movie (just as Kitty Hawk does in the book) where the Von Trapp children and Maria sing Do-Re-Mi while jumping around on a set of stairs. It occurs to me that there is a certain convenient symmetry in these stairs being included in this book and the fact that musical notes play such an important part in deciphering some of the codes. (Shhhh. Enough said. Who knows what people who haven't read the book are reading this right now!)

The City Of Salzburg: Salzburg is one of my absolute favourite cities in the entire world. I have long dreamed of taking a couple of months off and renting an apartment there so I can go and write a book. Unfortunately, as usually happens to all of us, life always seems to get in the way and I have never been able to actually do this, not even for this book (ironically enough).

The Hotel Sacher: As detailed in this book, the Hotel(s) Sacher are real hotels located not only (famously) in the city of Vienna, but also in the city of Salzburg as well. And of course it goes without saying that the world-famous Sacher Torte is also a real dessert served in these same hotels and was invented in very much the same way as detailed in this book. For more information about the hotels, the cake, or anything else Sacher-related, check out the following website: www.sacher.com

Salzburg Festungskonzerte: Musical performances in the Hohensalzburg Fortress overlooking the city of Salzburg are more or less a nightly occurrence, but the one featured in this book includes a special appearance by the real-life virtuoso Julia Fischer. Check out www.juliafischer.com for more information on Julia and check out www.salzburghighlights.at/en/CONCERTS/ for more information and a performance schedule of the concerts themselves.

Weißwurst: I probably could have written an entire book about my favourite sausages in Germany and Austria, but suffice it to say that if you ever visit Salzburg or Munich you absolutely must try Weisswurst–literally white sausage. It is a kind of minced meat sausage made from veal and parsley, traditionally eaten before noon with sweet mustard (*Süßer Senf*) and the skin removed. Check out en.wikipedia.org/wiki/Weisswurst for more information on this second-favourite sausage of mine.

My First Favourite Sausage (you might ask)?: If Weisswurst is my second-favourite sausage, then what (pray tell) is my absolute first favourite? Well, I have no idea what they are called, but if you're ever in the Munich train station, go to the part where the train platforms begin and head to the north side where there is a kiosk selling various types of sausage. One of those available is a thin grilled sausage that is served in pairs linked together. It comes with bread and mustard, of course, and is the best sausage you will ever have in your entire life. Seriously. No really. Seriously.

Cornelius Gurlitt–The Real-Life Rudolf Feiersinger?: While I was thinking about this book and also during the actual writing of it there was some strangely similar events happening in the real world involving the aftermath of the discovery of an enormous cache of stolen paintings in the Munich apartment of Cornelius Gurlitt, the son of an infamous art dealer who had some questionable dealings with stolen Nazi artworks during the Second World War. Even as I write this the story is continuing to unfold, but I'll spare you my poor re-telling of it and direct you to the Wikipedia page instead:

en.wikipedia.org/wiki/2012_Munich_artworks_discovery

While I was putting together this book in my head some of these real-life events inspired me, such as this article from 05 March 2014 from theartnewspaper.com which helped convince me to use Pissarro's Boulevard Montmartre as one of the stolen paintings in this book:

www.theartnewspaper.com/articles/Israel-steps-up-hunt-for-Nazilooted-art/31991

Other real-life events came as a complete surprise to me, such as the discovery of an *additional* cache of paintings in Cornelius Gurlitt's Salzburg home. This seemed to be an incredible coincidence since I'd already decided back at the start of my planning to include Salzburg in the plot of my story. It was a bit like life imitating art somehow.

Check out www.lostart.de for more information about this topic in general, as well as more specifically the so-called Munich Art Trove. There are links on this website to a detailed inventory of all the works of art found in the various seizures relating to Cornelius Gurlitt. (I wish they'd had this complete database online a few months ago when I was still writing the book!) Just flip through the hundreds of works of art and you can get a sense of the scene that faced Kitty Hawk, Charlie and the Inspector Alighieri when they burst into Feiersinger's apartment.

Berchtesgaden: I didn't want to go too much into Nazi history in the book but there's a reason Avner makes the comment that they're driving "right into the heart of darkness" when they pass the sign at the outskirts of the tiny Bavarian village of Berchtesgaden. This was where Hitler built his infamous *Berghof* mountain lodge and where other members of the high-ranking Nazi leadership also had houses. (It is also where Hitler's sister Paula is buried.) Near the overgrown site of Hitler's former mountain chalet is an excellent museum and documentation center. Check out the website:

www.obersalzberg.de/obersalzberg-home.html?&L=1

But perhaps the most famous (or infamous) construction in the Berchtesgaden area is the so-called *Kehlsteinhaus* (the Eagle's Nest) which is a small mountaintop retreat built as a present for Hitler's 50th birthday. Perched dizzyingly high atop one of the mountain peaks of the *Obersalzburg*, the Eagle's Nest is now a tourist attraction and restaurant with an amazing view. A special bus takes you up a precarious mountain road where you enter the mountain through a pedestrian tunnel and ride a polished brass elevator up through the rock and directly into the restaurant.

But despite it's incredibly dark past this part of the world is still breathtakingly beautiful and definitely worth a visit if you're ever in the area.

Wimbachklamm: The word "Klamm" in German refers to a kind of narrow mountain gorge carved into the rock by a small river or stream. Although not mentioned specifically by name, this is the kind of place where Kitty Hawk and the others find themselves near the very end of this book. Try Googling "klamm" to see some amazing pictures of these beautiful gorges. You can also Google "wimbachklamm" which is the specific gorge that inspired the location of the final chase in this book.

Cypress and Sky: Buried underneath the text of the pencil-rubbing of the decoded message in this book there are some scribbles of past notes. They are faint and difficult to read but Kitty Hawk and Charlie are able to make a few of them out. *Karajanplatz*, for example. And *Judengasse*, as well as some other numbers. But they fail to notice what is perhaps the most enticingly interesting one of all. Is it just my imagination or at the top right of the pencil-rubbing does it not appear to say "*Cypress and Sky*"?

"*Cypress, Sky and Field*" is the name of a painting by Vincent van Gogh that was recently discovered in a safety deposit box in Spain during a seizure of assets by the tax authorities. The painting appeared to be genuine and had apparently last been seen in the Museum of Art History in Vienna during the early 1970s. Check out this news article:

www.huffingtonpost.com/2014/05/12/lost-vincent-van-gogh-painting-spain-deposit-box_n_5301169.html

Hmmmmmmmmmm. Interesting.

Just in case you enjoyed this book, please allow me to try and entice you into reading another one by providing a sample of a new book series that I am working on and have already finished the first book of:

the dragon of the month club

chapter two
the book

Following their most unlikely of beginnings, the friendship of Ayana and Tyler grew quickly, and before they knew it, they were the best of friends, meeting up with each other almost every day. Sometimes they met up with Ayana's mother after school at the downtown Dairy Queen for ice cream. Other times they climbed the edges of the coulee behind Ayana's school and went to Tyler's house where they did their homework together in his room. But most of the time, they just agreed to meet up at the place where they'd both accidentally bumped into each other on that very first day—amongst the dusty old bookshelves of the old library at the row between the history of the anatomy of earthworms and the illustrated guide to the indigenous mosses of Iceland.

It was on just such a day like this that Ayana and Tyler first discovered THE BOOK—a name that would be forever capitalised in their minds whenever either of them dared to utter the phrase aloud.

It was a magical book. That much was clear almost from the outset, so perhaps the manner in which these two unlikely friends happened to come across it was magical as well.

It all started on a typical Friday afternoon. Ayana and Tyler had agreed to meet at the library right after school. Tyler had a dentist appointment and would either be a few minutes late or a few minutes early, depending on how long that took. Not surprisingly Tyler was a few minutes late. This could have been expected since Tyler took dentist appointments *very* seriously. For weeks ahead of time he would be sure to brush his teeth five times every single day—once when waking up, once after breakfast, once after lunch, once after dinner, and once again before bed—which was two more times a day than he usually did. (He normally deemed the wake-up and after dinner steps unnecessary.) All of this was in addition to flossing, rinsing, and otherwise generally trying to keep his teeth in the best possible shape for the check-up.

To Tyler, going to the dentist was like studying for a test in school. Failure was not an option. So it shouldn't be much of a surprise that once he was actually in the dental chair, he expected the dentist to be every bit as thorough as he was, a process that required a bit more time than it normally would with less fastidious patients.

So Tyler was late.

And so, when he finally arrived, he hurried down the stairs and quickly navigated through the maze of shelves at the back of the library and found Ayana sitting there, crouched on the floor, sobbing her eyes out.

Tyler sighed heavily. He could already guess what must have happened: Heather van der Sloot... again.

He took off his backpack and set it on the floor. Folding his legs under him, he lowered himself down until he was sitting next to Ayana, not too close, of course, but as close as he dared to.

"What happened this time?" Tyler asked.

Ayana sobbed and buried her face even deeper in her hands. After a moment her left arm shot out, pointing an accusing finger toward a stack of soiled and dishevelled papers lying in a heap on an empty space on the shelf opposite them.

"That," Ayana cried, her voice thin and cracking.

Tyler stared at the papers, and it took him a moment to realise what they were.

"Your poems," he gasped.

Tyler had to take a breath and swallow. Ayana's poems were a work of art, neatly written in careful flowing script, one to a page. Ayana carried them with her sometimes in a stiff green cardboard folder with trees on it that had little strings that you used to tie it shut.

Ayana nodded, still sobbing.

"She threw them all over the playground," she said, her voice raspy. "She grabbed my tree folder away from me and threw them everywhere. I... I...."

Ayana stuttered and couldn't speak for a second.

"I don't know if I got them all back," she finally said, finishing her thought. "I think I lost some."

Tyler nodded and crawled over on one knee to pick up the chaotic stack of papers. He sorted through them, one by one, trying to put them back into some kind of order. They were smeared and scratched and crumpled. One even had a dirty footprint stamped squarely on it.

Normally Ayana wouldn't even let Tyler glance at one of her poems, so he was surprised that she wasn't bothered by his looking through all of them now. She clearly wasn't thinking straight, so he tried to make as neat a stack out of them as possible and set it down on the carpet in the middle of the row of shelves.

"There are a lot there," he said, sitting close to her again. "Maybe you *did* get them all."

Ayana shrugged her shoulders hopelessly.

"It doesn't matter," she said, staring blankly at the pile of papers. "I don't care."

Tyler felt a sudden squeeze around his heart. He had no idea what he was supposed to do to make Ayana feel better.

But as his mind was racing, trying to think of something, the universe intervened.

"I hate her, Tyler," Ayana said. "I HATE her!"

On this second last syllable, Ayana kicked at the opposite shelves with the heel of her shoe, making the wooden frame shudder and some of the books rattle around. One particular book—a small, thin one high up on the very top shelf—tipped forward as if in slow motion until it was hanging precariously at an impossible angle, almost as if it was levitating, before tumbling end over end to the floor.

Tyler tried to catch it but he was too slow, and instead it crashed into the stack of papers, scattering them slightly, before it fell flat on its back, right side up right in front of them.

how to conjure your very own dragon in six easy steps

...read the front cover of the book in bright yellow letters against a wavy blue background.

Tyler frowned and Ayana stopped crying for a moment. They both stared at the book with wide-open eyes, neither of them quite able to believe what they were seeing.

"How to conjure a dragon?" Ayana asked, kneeling forward to grab the book.

Tyler crawled next to her as she opened the front cover.

The book was very thin—more like a pamphlet, really— with no table of contents, no copyright page, no dedication page. There wasn't even an indication of who the author might be. It just went straight into the first chapter, which was entitled:

the water dragon

"A water dragon?" Tyler read over Ayana's warm shoulder.

Underneath the chapter title was a brief list of the various characteristics of the water dragon.

category: lesser dragon
difficulty: medium
classification: common

Below that was a basic introduction and explanation of the dragon followed by some advice to those who might want to conjure one:

> this spell is a relatively simple one, but be forewarned that the water dragon is a somewhat damp and clumsy creature, prone to making messes and causing trouble. It is recommended to have plenty of towels at hand when undertaking this conjuring.

Underneath this brief introduction was a list of materials needed to actually conjure the dragon.

required material(s): water, towels (optional)

And last but not least came the instructions, six simple steps to conjuring your very own dragon. Tyler could hardly believe what he was reading. The steps were so simple. Just a series of strangely specific hand gestures performed by two people simultaneously. The instructions had little helpful sketches to help you understand.

It reminded Tyler of IKEA assembly instructions when his parents bought new furniture and let him put it together for them. But that was furniture made of wood and fabric and those little IKEA screws that needed a special tool to screw them in. This was supposed to be a dragon, whatever that meant. How could such simplistic instructions possibly result in assembling *anything*, much less an actual dragon?

"We *have* to try this!" Ayana said excitedly.

Tyler was sceptical. *How can this possibly be real?* He took the book from Ayana and scanned the pages of introduction and instruction for a second time.

"I don't know," he said hesitantly. But that's when Tyler looked at Ayana and saw her staring back at him. Gone were the tears of pain that had been streaming down her face just a minute earlier. Gone was the anger and frustration that had led to their discovery of the book in the first place. All that was left written on her beautiful face was the wide-eyed thrill of discovery and excitement and belief that something as crazy as this dragon book might actually work.

What have we got to lose? Tyler thought, smiling at Ayana's newfound enthusiasm. *Besides, at least Ayana is happy again and not thinking about Heather van der Sloot.*

"Okay," Tyler said. "Let's do it!"

Ayana smiled broadly and grabbed the book from Tyler, pulling herself to her feet as she did so.

"Come on," she said, gesturing for him to follow her to the checkout desk so they could sign the book out.

"What about your poems?" Tyler asked, glancing at the rumpled pages stacked loosely in the middle of the aisle.

Ayana winced.

"Just leave them," she said angrily and walked off, leaving Tyler standing there all by himself.

Frowning, Tyler reached down, carefully gathering the poems together and sliding them into his backpack.

"Wait up!" he called after Ayana, hurrying to catch up. But Ayana was already at the checkout desk where grumpy Ms. Bergstrom was busy at the end of the day sorting through a mound of recently returned library books.

"Excuse me," he heard Ayana say, her voice thin and distant. "I'd like to sign this book out please."

"Come back tomorrow," Ms. Bergstrom replied coldly, without looking up from her book sorting. "The library is closing. No sign-outs after five thirty."

"But I'd really like to sign this book out today," Ayana replied, smiling sweetly as she pulled herself onto her tiptoes to peer over the edge of the counter. "Do you think you could maybe make an exception just this one time?"

Ms. Bergstrom continued sorting, obliviously unsympathetic.

"No sign-outs after five thirty," she repeated, pausing only long enough to point one stubby finger at the sign on the wall behind her head.

No sign-outs after five thirty, the sign read.

"Okay, sorry," Ayana said, lowering herself again before taking a step backward. "I'll come back again for it tomorrow."

As Tyler approached, Ayana took another step back and appeared to nonchalantly turn as if she were heading back toward the shelves to replace the book. But as she did so, she was making a series of frantic hand gestures to Tyler behind the cover of the counter where Ms. Bergstrom couldn't see.

Tyler frowned. What in the world was she doing? He watched her free hand flailing at him crazily while she waved with her other hand, the one with the book in it. *Does she want me to do something with the book?*

Tyler stopped cold when he realised what she wanted. She wanted him to grab the book from her without Ms. Bergstrom seeing.

And then what? Tyler already knew the answer. She wanted him to take the book and sneak it out of the library. She wanted him to steal it.

It's not stealing, he could almost hear Ayana's voice saying to him inside his head. *We're just borrowing it, like we would have done properly if stupid Ms. Bergstrom would have let us.*

Tyler started to sweat nervously. Ayana was silently waving him over more frantically than ever.

Just do it! a voice in Tyler's head told him. *Ms. Bergstrom is going to get suspicious if you keep standing in the middle of the library looking like an idiot.*

But Tyler was frightened. He'd never stolen anything before. Okay, if you consider stealing change from his mother's purse to go to the store and buy candy, then I guess that might count, technically. But he never took more than a dollar in total, so it wasn't *really* stealing, was it? Plus, that was his mother. This was the public library.

What if I get caught? Tyler worried, but it was too late. His feet were already walking forward, and Ayana was already sidestepping toward him.

"Meet me at your house," she whispered as she brushed past him, close enough that he could smell the apple shampoo her mother always bought for her. In one quick fluid motion, she slipped the thin book into his jacket as she passed by then on toward the back of the library once again. Tyler kept going, tense and nervous as he continued toward the exit with the book crammed underneath his hot, sweating armpit.

Ms. Bergstrom glanced at him as he walked past the checkout desk.

"Have a good night, Tyler," she said, friendly but still unsmiling. Tyler had been a regular at the library for years.

"Thank you, Ms. B... Bookstrom," Tyler stuttered in reply. "I mean, Ms. Bergstrom."

Tyler blushed conspicuously, but Ms. Bergstrom didn't seem to notice, and Tyler continued out the doors and up the stairs without her saying another word.

As he stepped out into the cool outside air, Tyler felt a sudden rush of relief wash over him. But he knew he wasn't home free just yet. He continued glancing over his shoulder as he headed across the parking lot, half-expecting to see Ms. Bergstrom rushing up behind him with her thick arms outstretched, ready to grab him. By the time he reached the crosswalk at the intersection and the light turned green, he was already running. He didn't stop until he ran all the way home, in through the front door, past his mother in the kitchen, and all the way up the stairs to his bedroom where he closed the door behind him and looked around desperately for a place to hide the book.

Tyler lifted his mattress and quickly slipped the book underneath, carefully replacing the bedspread afterward. He took a step back, worrying that it looked too suspicious. Shaking his head, he ironed the quilt flat with the palm of his hand until it looked perfect.

Now it looks TOO perfect, he thought, panicking. His room was kind of a mess, with books lying around all over the place, including several strewn across his bed. The perfectly flattened corner of the quilt stuck out like a sore thumb, so Tyler repeated the entire process for a second time, rumpling the blankets and flattening them out again more naturally.

He took another step back to examine his handiwork. He still wasn't satisfied. What if his mother came in and saw that one corner of his bed was so perfectly made up? She would be suspicious.

But by then it was too late. Downstairs he heard the ring of the doorbell and the sound of someone answering it.

Tyler panicked.

It's Ms. Bergstrom and the police! he thought, looking around his room for a place to hide.

But of course it wasn't.

"Tyler! Ayana's here!" his mother called out. A second later, he heard the sound of Ayana's footsteps pounding up the stairs and down the hall toward him.

"Hey," Ayana said, breathless from running as she burst in through the bedroom door. "Do you have the book?"

Tyler shushed her.

"Not so loud!" he whispered. "My mother might hear you!"

Ayana rolled her eyes as she slipped off her jacket and threw it over the chair at Tyler's desk.

"Do you have it or not?" she asked.

"Of course I do," he replied. "I hid it."

Ayana looked at him, her eyes flashing.

"Well, get it out," she said, grinning. "We're going to conjure a water dragon."

A MESSAGE FROM THE AUTHOR

As always, first things first, thank you so very much for buying this book. The fact that there are people out there in the world sharing the adventures of Kitty Hawk with me seems quite unbelievable and it is extremely humbling. So thank you from the bottom of my heart.

So here we are at the end of yet another book. It's been a while, hasn't it? But you'll be glad to know that even while life went on a few twists and turns these past months I still managed to find time to do some writing. In addition to this fifth adventure in the Kitty Hawk series I also completed two other books.

The first of these is about a girl named Samira with some very special and magical gifts who lost her parents during the war in Yugoslavia when she was still a child. As she struggles to come to terms with her new-found abilities she decides to travel back to Srebrenica to find out more about her past. The book turned out to be rather dark and nasty in the end so unfortunately I'm not sure it will ever see the light of day. (But if you're interested in reading it, send me an email. We'll talk.)

The second book is one that I am really really excited about and can't wait for people to read it. It's called The Dragon Of The Month Club (check out the sample chapter just a few pages before this) and it will be released within a week or two of this very book you now hold in your hands. You can even join the club by conjuring your very own dragon and entering it to win a one-of-a-kind personalised hardcover version of the book. Check out www.dragonofthemonthclub.com for more details.

Other than that I just wanted to mention a couple of final things that I think are pretty cool.

First, if you haven't already seen it, check out this video of a De Havilland Beaver seaplane (just like Kitty Hawk's!) narrowly avoiding a surfacing whale as it comes in for a landing: edition.cnn.com/2014/07/16/us/alaska-plane-on-whale/

Second, please check out #LikeAGirl. I think this concept speaks entirely for itself so I will say no more. But please check it out because it's really cool and really important.

Thank you so much again everyone. I can never thank you enough for sharing all of these adventures with me.

Next up... The Wizards of Waterfire book #2!

Printed in Poland
by Amazon Fulfillment
Poland Sp. z o.o., Wrocław